Hear My Whisper

B.L. THOMA

Paperback ISBN: 978-1-958783-43-6
Hardback ISBN: 978-1-958783-44-3
EBook ISBN: 978-1-958783-42-9
Cover Design by Emma Unger
@Unger.Creative
Behance: https://www.behance.net/emmaalyssa
Published by Ozark Hollow Press
PO Box 4573
Joplin, Missouri 64803
Lia Wu, Publisher
Ozark Hollow Press Edition 2025
Printed in the USA

Contents

Chapter One

AUTUMN, 1904

SAVANNAH, GEORGIA

THE SCENE in the lobby resembled a train station at mid-day. *Where have all you people come from?* Julia hated mingling with strangers. Why couldn't they find something better to do than congregate here like pigeons in a barn loft? It was impossible to tell those coming from those going, for they were all dressed as though they were coming from a late dinner or going to an early supper at the hotel or elsewhere. Every whisper—every ripple of laughter—deepened the flush in Julia's cheeks. She knew what they were thinking, what they were talking about. They were talking about her, though they might not know it directly. They were talking about the scandal, about the brazen hussy caught with the senator just a few hours ago. Julia looked at her hands. She willed them to stop shaking, but they refused to obey.

Voices hummed all around. She dreaded what she might hear and what she might not.

How could this be happening? Only a few hours ago, she'd stood in a quiet room, all alone and dreading the predictable, boring days that lay ahead. She dreaded them still, but not because she faced boredom. She faced something far worse now —scandal. Not one prone to self-pity, Julia wallowed in it now, longing to re-wind the clock and stand in that room again. Though she hated to relive it, Julia retraced her every step toward disaster in her mind and, with each one, her inner voice moaned, *If only...*

Just a while ago, she'd been in her room unpacking. The blue silk of her dress slipped over her arm with a softness that seemed to whisper Julia's name. She smoothed the sheer fabric at the neckline and hung it in the wardrobe. Stroking the rich, moiré taffeta of the skirt, she sighed, doubting she'd wear it while in Savannah. Mother had gone overboard this time. Deep down, she knew she wasn't one to put herself forward to make new friends. Without an invitation, what parties or home gatherings would she attend? Turning to the trunk, she pulled out her much more practical tweed skirt and jacket. With the pleasant weather, this would be nice for outings on cooler days.

A sudden outburst in the corridor made Julia's heart pound. A deep voice uttered something, its words garbled by shrieking and the opening and closing of several doors. Tossing the clothes aside, Julia took a deep breath, forcing herself to approach the door and jiggle the knob. Relieved to find it was still locked, she placed her ear against it. Voices faded away and

Julia could hear more doors opening and closing. Preferring to keep to her own business and stay out of things that didn't concern her, Julia hesitated. As she eyed the key that lay on the dresser, her courage began to rise. Snatching it up, she unlocked the door and leaned into the hall. All was quiet, except for the clicking of other locks, indicating that other occupants hadn't been as reluctant to satisfy their curiosity as she'd been.

Julia closed the door, whispering into the room, "Where are you, Mother?" She paced, agitated at the thought that perhaps Mother might have become involved in the unpleasantness, whatever it was. She reasoned with herself that the Wentworth Hotel, having a reputation for being the finest in Savannah, likely had competent staff handling disruptions such as this. After giving the doorknob one last jiggle for safety's sake, Julia decided she may as well get on with the unpacking.

The noise of Savannah's bustling streets drew Julia to the open window. She stood drinking in the loveliness of the grand, old city and feeling appreciative that General Sherman had spared it on his infamous march to the sea. Tops of colorful parasols jiggled along silently below like runaway blossoms scattered by the clattering carriages and occasional chugging automobiles. "Oh, I want to explore every inch of you, you wonderful, old town!" she whispered as the sun warmed her cheeks. Then, the question returned to her mind, *Where on earth is Mother?* The answer came with a turn of the doorknob, the rustle of skirts, and a cheery greeting.

"Hello, my Lovely One! Oh, but won't it feel marvelous to stretch out for a bit? Train rides are interesting, and you meet so many wonderful people, but they do go on and on." Beatrice Lansing placed her handbag on the bed, pulled off her gloves, and looked in the mirror. "First things first—and the first thing to go is *this*!" She pulled out the pin, removing her smart traveling hat. Mother studied her reflection, as if asking herself what one could expect of one's curls after being smashed all the way from Missouri to Georgia. She sank into a chair and began taking off her shoes.

Julia smiled at her mother's term of endearment, grateful, as always, that it was reserved for when they were alone. At times, it indicated that Mother was troubled on her behalf and about to start consoling her, but, in most cases, it signaled a state of happiness. All outward signs at the moment seemed to indicate elation, which came as a bit of a surprise considering how exhausted they were. However, Mother was often pulled aside by something or someone and Julia listened, curious as to what, or who, it had been this time.

"I was beginning to wonder what happened to you, Mother. There was the loudest commotion in the hall just a bit ago. I was beginning to worry that you'd gotten into the middle of all that—uproar."

"I was just going to ask you what happened! I heard it all the way down in the lobby. Goodness! I thought a fight must have broken out or something. I didn't see a thing on my way up to the room." Mother closed her eyes for a moment. "Oh, my!" she whispered, the sigh betraying her exhaustion. "I'm sorry I kept you waiting. You must have thought I'd gotten lost on my way to get a newspaper and let the desk clerk know when to wake us in the morning, but there was already a message waiting for me from Mrs. Thomas Grayson. Well, when the young lady standing next to me heard the clerk, she asked me if I was a friend of Mrs. Grayson's. As it turns out, she, a Miss Abigail Hadley, is the daughter of Jeremiah Hadley, the prominent jeweler. You remember seeing some pieces he designed for Mrs. Grayson, don't you, Dear? I must say that man is a true artist."

Julia gave a dreamy nod. "Yes," she recalled, "I remember that amethyst pin."

She sat down on the bed. This story might end in Miss Abigail Hadley admiring Mother's traveling suit, or it could just as well conclude with Mother being invited to meet the Queen of England. Mother rambled. Sometimes her ramblings were enjoyable chronicles of daily life, but this one sounded like it might be leading up to something promising.

"So, as we chatted, I found that the Hadleys are here at the Wentworth, enjoying an extended stay while her father meets with some of the best families to show his designs. I explained, of course, that although your father isn't with us, we are here meeting with some of the same people in my capacity as dressmaker. Her mother and brother joined us and I was introduced to them. I *do* wish you'd been with me. Anyway, we're breakfasting with them in the Oglethorpe Room tomorrow morning."

"Oh, that's nice," Julia offered up half-heartedly as Mother paused for breath and reached down to massage her aching feet before continuing.

"I adore Abigail's mother. Her name is Rose. All people named Rose should rightly be pleasant and peaceful after all, shouldn't they? James, their son, seems... like a highly intelligent young man, and well-mannered."

But not captivating, or handsome, or sweet-natured, or interesting—some of the other adjectives Julia would have preferred. As much as Julia's interest in young men had grown, she found herself put off by many of them. None seemed to have what she was looking for, but she had to admit she wasn't sure what that something was. However, at twenty-two years of age, she'd had some amount of time to form strong opinions of what she *wasn't* looking for in men. Braggarts topped the list, along with those who seemed to turn their affections from female to female like butterflies flitting from bloom to bloom. She'd often seen a man pursue a girl, acting as though she were the first and only one to capture his heart. Then, following the girl's disinterest, he'd appear at the very next social event with a new girl on his arm, acting as though there had never been another. Julia found this spectacle nauseating. She put these men on her mental list under the "No" column. One or two had made it into the "Maybe" column, but after some time conversing with them and finding little to keep the exchange of ideas alive, they, too, had ended up in the discards. The clean, white "Yes" column remained, with nothing penciled in and no erasures, waiting for an entry. From time to time, she asked God to fill in the blank, reminding Him that she'd prefer only one name be written and remain. Heartbreak was no more a part of Julia's plans for the future than for any other member of the human race.

Shifting her weight on the bed, Julia flinched. She slipped a hand under her thigh, carefully removing Mother's handbag. Surprised for an instant by its weight, she remembered with a shudder that it had every reason to be heavy, considering its contents. Holding it aloft between her thumb and forefinger, she crossed the room and placed it on the dresser.

Mother wrinkled her nose. "You act as though that thing has a terrific stench. That's exactly the way I've felt carrying it ever since we left home."

"Oh, Mother, I know Papa's only trying to look out for us, but having the Protector with us makes me squeamish. We don't have to go around armed to the teeth back home. I'm not used to it."

"Well, you know how he feels about having his womenfolk travel without him. I suppose that makes him feel every bit as squeamish as we do toting that thing around. I'm trying to make peace with the idea that it's not going to go off all by itself in my bag. It's like carrying a loaded pocket watch!"

Mother began unbuttoning her jacket, returning to the subject of the Hadleys. Julia acknowledged the breakfast arrangements and went back to unpacking the trunk. Abigail Hadley might prove to be likeable, but Julia found herself full of reservations. Staying in the same hotel put her in close quarters with other guests, and if this Abigail turned out to be boring, snobbish, or downright silly, it would require elaborate schemes to avoid spending too much time with her. On the other hand, if Abigail turned out to be enjoyable and interesting, it could make all the difference. With Mother going over fabrics, patterns, and measurements with clients, Julia would have plenty of hours every day to fill with what she hoped would be fun, but dreaded would be boredom. She loved to explore and make the most of her surroundings and didn't relish the thought of spending hours upon hours listening to people who liked nothing better than the sound of their own voices.

Julia didn't quite know what her feelings were about these Hadleys and didn't know why all these reservations had sprung to mind. Nevertheless, she'd find out at breakfast.

She glanced at Mother, who had slipped off her dress and stretched out on the bed in her petticoats to rest before supper, her long, lean body nearly reaching to the foot rail and her great mass of curls spread over the pillow. Their highlights, along with the green eyes beneath her closed lids, made Julia aware of her Irish ancestry, though she hadn't received such a dominant expression of it herself. A glance toward the mirror reminded her once again that she'd taken after her paternal grandmother. Though almost as tall as Mother and with skin nearly as milky, pale pink, Julia's curls were light, her eyes a sky blue, and her jaw a little sturdier.

Julia intended to follow Mother's example and rest, but nothing seemed more appealing—or more necessary—after the trip across country than a warm, soapy bath. Gathering soap, hairbrush, and her cream-colored dressing gown, she made her way down the hall. Just as she reached her destination, a bellboy appeared at the end of the corridor, followed by a young couple, both of whom had eyes full of a secret, shared happiness and cheeks flushed with embarrassment.

"Yes, indeed," said the bellboy a little too loudly. "You couldn't have picked a finer place for your honeymoon trip than the Wentworth. You'll enjoy your time in Savannah. You just ask me anything and I'll fix ya right up. My name's Marty. Ask me where anything is in the city and I'll get ya there. That is, if you two lovebirds ever get around to leaving your room."

The new bride's flushed face deepened in color.

Poor thing. Julia hoped her question might redirect the flow of conversation. "Pardon me, sir, but when you have a moment, could you please see that there are fresh towels in the bath?"

"Oh, yes, miss. Right away, miss. Just as soon as I get this young couple settled in, miss." Marty led the newlyweds away, acquainting them with the extent of his knowledge concerning the cleanliness and abundance of linens provided by the Wentworth Hotel. The new bride smiled at Julia. She seemed sweet, but Julia didn't hold out much hope of getting to know her. It would never do to take a wife's attentions away from her new husband.

Julia tapped on the door of the water closet. There was no answer. Still, she hesitated. Surely one wasn't expected to reserve a trip to the water closet in a hotel such as this. Leaning her ear to the crack, she listened for a bit, but jerked herself upright as she heard footsteps approach. Marty came smiling along the corridor, looking as though the tip he'd just received had been satisfactory.

"You don't suppose there's anyone in here, do you, Marty? I've knocked, but no one answered."

"Likely not, miss." Marty rapped on the door and cleared his throat. "Pardon me. Is there anyone in there?"

When no answer came, Marty smiled and gestured for her to enter.

"Thank you, Marty," Julia smiled. "I'm Julia Lansing."

"Any time, Miss Lansing. I'll be right back with those towels." Marty disappeared at the end of the hall and Julia fumbled with the knob, shifting the soap and hairbrush into one hand to open the door with the other. As it opened, the soap slipped from Julia's fingers. She closed the door and stooped to catch it as it clattered along, coming to rest against the opposite wall. Julia scrambled after it, trying to capture the elusive little chunk.

"Ah! You can't get away from *me!*" she exclaimed, grasping it and holding it aloft with a satisfied sigh.

A sudden, loud snort caused Julia to stiffen. The sound, something like a horse might make, came again. Lifting her eyes and focusing them beyond the soap, Julia was aghast. The shock couldn't have been greater if there had been a horse in the bathtub—but it was no horse. A portly gentleman, all whiskers and eyebrows, began to rouse from sleep and splash about as though he feared going under. Julia could think of only one thing—escape without notice. The only thing worse than this man observing her presence would be the prospect of having him stand to his feet naked. Scurrying along on her hands and knees, she tried to be silent as she crept toward the door. If he heard nothing else, surely he must hear the pounding of her heart! Sliding her hand up the door frame, she groped for the knob. Giving it a slow turn, she opened the door a bit to scan the corridor. To Julia's horror, Marty, true to his word, rounded the corner with the promised towels.

"I say there, madam, what business do you have in my bath? What was that? Resuscitate? Eradicate?" bellowed the deep voice behind her.

Julia scrambled into the hall, closed the door, and sprang to her feet.

Marty responded to the sudden appearance of Julia's face over his tall stack of towels as though he'd been struck by a thunderbolt. His startled yelp made Julia want to clasp her hand over his mouth. It was too late. Doors flew open up and down the corridor and heads began popping out to see what sort of commotion had occurred. Julia heard their murmurs of speculation. One of the heads belonged to her mother, who appeared in a lavender dressing gown. She held a brush in her hand and had several hairpins in her mouth. Marty, darting after the towels which lay strewn in all directions, began apologizing profusely. It may have appeared to the onlookers that Julia had been exiting the bath and collided with the bellboy, had it not been for the explosion that went off next.

Julia spun around as the door behind her opened wide.

"What the devil is going on here?" Whiskers and Eyebrows stood dripping in the doorway. The vast amount of yardage in the maroon dressing gown he had applied to himself only made him appear larger and more formidable. His booming voice carried through what Julia felt must be the entire hotel. "I demand to know, woman, what you were doing crawling around in my bath! What is the meaning of this outrage?"

Julia, summoning all the willpower at her disposal in order not to burst into tears and run screaming to her room, felt her cheeks flame. Nothing could be worse than this. She altered this opinion immediately as Marty's jaw dropped several inches and he exclaimed in a voice that Julia would have sworn she hadn't heard since last Fourth of July, when the mayor of Morgan's Landing announced the opening of the festivities over a megaphone.

"Senator Thornhill!"

Chapter Two

Though it frustrated her at times, Julia had never known her mother to be put off by anybody. Truly, it had always seemed as though she had never met anyone who remained a stranger for long. Now, as she stood in the wake of this disaster, followed by the collective response of the hotel guests that would later be recorded in her diary as "the gasp heard round the world", Julia needed Mother's self-assuredness. She met her questioning eyes with a silent plea and felt relief as she watched Mother shove hairpins in at random intervals, smooth her hair, and glide to the rescue with a smile warm enough to melt the frosty stares of the gaping onlookers. In her frantic desire to flee, Julia took a step back, glad to pass the responsibility on to someone who had some inkling as to what to do. Still, she found herself holding her breath. A lifetime of experience told her that Mother's tactics sometimes leaned toward the unorthodox.

"Gracious me! Senator Thornhill! You simply can't know how thrilled we are to meet you. I'm Mrs. Roderick Lansing. I understand my husband has corresponded with you concerning his inventions."

"That's what I want to know. What *were* her intentions?" blustered the senator.

"Well now, that's obvious," Mother explained. "This nice bellboy bumped into the poor girl and you must not have had the door latched properly. Naturally, when the door came open, they took a tumble."

"Exactly! That's all they've *done* is mumble!" the senator fumed. "Now will somebody speak up and explain this intrusion on my privacy?"

Julia watched her mother take a deep breath, as if to summon all her best efforts at diplomacy as she smiled at the gawking hotel guests, waving them away with apparent nonchalance.

"Well now, shall we all be getting back to our rooms? It's almost dinnertime and I'm sure this helpful, intelligent bellboy and I can explain things to the good senator."

The guests, with a commendable display of good manners, retreated behind their doors.

Mother smiled at Marty. "Dear boy, would you please deliver those towels to their destination and bring the senator some refreshment to his room before dinner?"

"Yes, ma'am. Right away!" Marty deposited the towels on a

table by the bathtub and hurried away, disappearing around the corner in a manner that left Julia to assume that he'd be taking his own sweet time. Mother would have to make sense of this whole mess long before he ever got back.

"Mother," Julia whispered, "I knocked and so did Marty. He was asleep in there!"

"I see. Oh, I *see*! I'll see what I can do." Mother turned to the senator. "Senator, tell me, have you finished with your soak?"

"I certainly *could* use a smoke!" Senator Thornhill patted his hands over his dressing gown, checking the pockets.

Julia didn't blame her mother for the ill-mannered sigh that escaped her. After all, he hadn't heard it. The sigh seemed to give her the strength to broaden her smile as she screamed at the top of her voice, "Senator Thornhill, has anyone ever told you that you are hard of hearing?"

"What's that?"

"You don't hear well! You're nearly deaf!"

"You are? Me, too! My wife says it's enough to drive her mad. I've got one of those confounded horn things, but I didn't take it to the bathtub. Wasn't planning on anyone being in there with me to start up a conversation." He cast a suspicious eye toward Julia.

"You took a nap in the bath!" Mother yelled.

"Yes, of course, there's a tap in the bath. Fine hotel. Fine hotel."

Mother's patience seemed to wane a little. Then, taking a deep breath, she leaned in to the senator's ear and bellowed,

"You were sound asleep! My poor, dear daughter knocked. So did the bellboy, but you were *asleep*! Can you imagine the shock it gives a young lady to find a gentleman bathing in a room she felt certain was unoccupied?"

Pulling Julia close, Mother patted her, waiting for Senator Thornhill to gain full comprehension.

The Senator stared at both ladies for a moment, his eyes growing wider.

"Why, my goodness! This is *dreadful*! My dear girl, you must have been... How can I ever apologize for my foolish assumptions and awkward behavior. You must forgive me. I was just so startled, you see. Oh, dear! Wait till Mrs. Thornhill hears about this! I'd better go and tell her before she hears it from some other source. Would you do Mrs. Thornhill and myself the honor, Mrs... Ah, I'm sorry. As you probably know, I didn't get your name earlier."

"Lansing," Mother screamed. "Mrs. Roderick Lansing. This is my daughter, Julia."

"Lansing... Lansing... Say, I've been giving some thought to some interesting inventions by a fellow named Lansing."

"My *husband*," Mother roared.

"Well, well, well!" exclaimed the Senator. "Then you will certainly do my wife and me the honor of dining with us downstairs this evening."

Though her eyes pleaded again with her mother's, Julia heard her give Senator Thornhill a loud and beaming acceptance, agreeing to dinner at seven-thirty.

"Marvelous!" boomed the senator. "And too bad about

your hearing problem. I know it must be as vexing to your husband as it is to my wife!" He turned and scampered down the hall at a speed Julia wouldn't have thought possible for a man of his girth.

A calming silence descended on the corridor. As her mother turned to her, Julia saw her expression shift into compassion mixed with a determination to seek refuge as she clutched her elbow and pulled her into the bath and shut the door. She realized she must look as though she'd just survived a natural disaster of biblical proportions. After a moment, Julia was able to voice her newest fear.

"Mother, I'm so glad you smoothed that over, but what I want to know is *why on earth* you accepted a dinner invitation from a man I've just discovered completely undressed! I never want to see him again as long as I live!"

"Well, what I'd like to know is *exactly* how on earth my daughter ended up in a prominent senator's bath! But, I'm afraid the details of both these stories will have to wait to be told until you've bathed. I'll bathe, too, but I think I'll be waiting outside this door for you to come out before I go in! We can swap stories while you fix my hair."

Julia watched the corners of Mother's mouth begin to turn up a bit. Though a stickler for propriety, past experience had taught Julia that once a situation had passed out of her control, Mother had the ability to relinquish it into the hands of God and let her natural sense of humor take over. Julia had yet to find any humor in the ordeal, though she had to admit, as the expression back home went, this bull was out of the chute. It wasn't as if she could undo any of the events that led up to the dinner invitation. Her dread of the evening ahead had already begun to settle in, leaving her feeling numb.

"Remember, Lovely One," Mother reassured her, "if the choice is laughter or tears, you may as well laugh. Besides, we've likely solved the mystery about what all that ruckus was about earlier! You might not have been the senator's first victim."

Julia nodded as Mother's arm slipped around her shoulders but stiffened as she felt her squeeze her to her side.

"Mother, you *didn't*!"

After a moment of puzzlement, Mother reached into the recesses of her dressing gown and pulled out the Chicago Pocket Protector.

"I did. Well, that's what we brought it along for, isn't it?"

"Ugh! Put that thing away, Mother!"

Mother looked at the tiny firearm nestled in the palm of her hand.

"You have to admit, it's really rather pretty if you take a good, long look at it. All this floral engraving on the barrel and these imitation pearl panels on the sides—if I didn't live in constant fear of accidentally squeezing this firing lever, I might think it quite nice. I have the safety on... I think."

Julia shuddered. "Take it back to the room and put it in the dresser drawer."

"Here." Mother thrust the gun forward. "Keep it with you."

"Me?" Julia shrank back. "Why should I keep it with me?"

"It's already proven that you're more likely to run into trouble in the bath than I am back in the room."

"If we did have to shoot the thing, I'd never remember how Papa showed us to reload it. We'd have to take the whole gun apart and put it back together again!"

"Heavens, Julia! If we use up all seven of those bullets while we're in Savannah, we'll end up in jail!"

Julia slipped the pistol into the pocket of her dressing gown and hung it on one of the pegs on the wall near the door. As soon as the door closed behind Mother, she clicked the lock on the underside of the doorknob into place and hastily washed. Once again clothed in her dressing gown, she sighed with relief when she cracked open the door and found the hallway empty. The hotel room felt like a refuge once she returned and began to dress for dinner, leaving Mother to brave the dreaded water closet. She found herself fumbling with every button and fastener as she envisioned having to leave the room and face the dining room filled with staring eyes.

Having donned the last petticoat, Julia sat before the mirror, putting the finishing touches on her hair. Having swept her blonde curls up at the back, she twirled the escaping ringlets around her fingers. They softened her hairline and framed her cheeks and eyes, which still showed a distinct redness from having shed a tear or two and a rosiness from embarrassment. Though she dreaded the impending scene in the dining room, she resolved to be cheerful and smiled at the reflection over her shoulder as she heard the door open.

"I see you've arrived unharmed, Mother. I didn't hear any cries for help."

"Well, no matter how hard I tried, I couldn't have outdone your earlier performance," Mother teased. "Come fix my hair—if it hasn't passed beyond all hope." Stepping to the wardrobe, she reached for the plum-colored dress that hung on the door. "You're going to turn more than a few heads in this, if I do say so myself. All it needs is a little pressing."

Holding the dress against herself, she swayed before the mirror, admiring her work for a moment before spreading it over the open trunk.

"I don't relish the thought of any more heads turning in my direction, but that dress does make me feel nice," Julia admitted.

Its simple lines were just right for tonight. It was more than a day dress, but definitely not for a party or ball. Worn with understated jewelry, Mother's work would speak for itself. Julia smiled at the dress and rose from the dressing table to allow Mother to take her place. As she stepped aside, she felt her stocking feet begin to slide and realized she'd stepped on the silk hem of the skirt. Her hand shot out, fighting to grasp the chair, but Julia still found herself falling. As her feet continued to slide, she twisted away, reaching for the bedpost, but fell backward and felt the trunk lid give way under her weight. She pushed herself away from it with a gasp and landed on the floor. She turned around, facing it. Other than Mother's shriek, the only other sound in the room was the thud of the heavy trunk lid, muffled by layers of plum-colored silk.

Julia sat on the floor, her eyes darting back and forth between Mother's shocked face and the victim trapped in the trunk's jaws. She stared in disbelief as Mother lifted the lid to survey the damage. About a foot above the hemline, glaring at her, a two-inch, crimped area encircled a small hole where the trunk latch had been. She ran her finger across the damage.

"It might not have been so bad if I hadn't sat on it."

Like a warm breath against a cold pane of glass, Julia's ability to look on the bright side evaporated. Pent-up sobs of exhaustion, humiliation, and now guilt had their way.

Beatrice buttoned Julia up the back.

"It's nearly seven-thirty."

"I can't do it! I just can't do it!"

Beatrice took Julia's face in her hands and looked into her eyes.

"You can do it, Lovely One. You can do *anything*!"

She could see that Julia's nap, while easing some of her exhaustion from the trip and guilt over ruining the dress, hadn't done a thing to reduce her apprehension over dining with the Thornhills. Beatrice explained that, although her reluctance was understandable, it must be done. Avoiding them in public after what happened would only fuel gossips. Being seen enjoying pleasant company with the Thornhills would assure everyone that the afternoon's events were a mere misunderstanding—nothing improper. Then, there was the fact that Roderick had been trying to interest

Senator Thornhill in one of his inventions. It hurt to see Julia so disturbed. Beatrice longed to let her stay in the room and make excuses for her. It was a relief to see Julia's affirming nod.

"Oh, why did we have to come here, Mother? I suppose I can take some comfort in the fact that if all goes well, we won't be in the immediate proximity of the Thornhills for more than a few days. I wish we'd never gotten that telegram."

The telegram had awaited them at the train station with news from her friend, Ruby Allen, with whom they'd planned to stay while in Savannah. Ruby, her daughters, and most of the help had been unexpectedly called away to Charleston due to an illness in the family. Since Ruby's husband was already away on business, there would be no one at their home to host them. Arrangements had been made for the Lansings at the Wentworth and Ruby would send for them upon her return, hopefully within the week. Beatrice had telegraphed Roderick immediately, informing him of the change in plans.

"As I tell your father, contrary to his insistence, telegrams are just as capable of bringing good news as they are bad. Ruby went to great expense to put us up in such a lovely hotel, even though she's the one inconvenienced with family illness. Until she gets back, we'll make the best of it. Why, for all we know, Providence may have placed us here to meet the Thornhills on behalf of your papa. We're bound to encounter all sorts of people while we're here and some of them may even be interested in my designs."

"I've met enough new people this afternoon to last me a

lifetime!" Julia sighed. "I'm so nervous. I hope I don't trip over my own feet or, Heaven forbid, anyone else's. Let's get this over with, Mother."

Gathering gloves and bags, they checked the mirror one last time. In answer to a knock at the door, Julia opened it to find Marty holding an envelope.

"Telegram for Mrs. Lansing."

Beatrice stared at the envelope until the door clicked shut and Marty's footsteps faded in the corridor. "I can't imagine your father spending money on a telegram that wasn't a matter of life and death." Though never one to expect anything but good news, she wondered what this could be other than something urgent from home.

"I suppose it could be more news from Mrs. Allen," said Julia. "I hope no one else has taken ill."

"Well, I suppose the news is on the inside." Beatrice's fingers tore open the flap.

They read it together.

PAPERS SAY THORNHILL IN SAVANNAH **STOP**
ARRANGE PERSONAL INSPECTION **STOP**
EXPLOSION MINOR **STOP**
DAMAGE MINIMAL **STOP**
PURCHASE CURTAIN MATERIAL **STOP**
WAIT 30 DAYS **STOP**
REMAIN YOURS UNHARMED **STOP**
RODERICK **STOP**

"My goodness, this certainly leaves much to the imagination!" Beatrice looked at Julia, whose face reflected her own curiosity and concern. "It'll take some sorting out. What on earth are we to inspect, do you suppose?"

"I hope it's not Senator Thornhill. I've inspected him as closely as I care to already," said Julia.

"I wonder what type of explosion there's been in Morgan's Landing."

"I would imagine it happened with one of Papa's experiments, Mother. Remember about three years ago when Papa's... well, whatever that thing was supposed to become... exploded in the workshop and the blast knocked out all our kitchen windows on the south side?"

"Hmm... that could be why he wants me to buy curtain material, though I can't imagine why I'd need to wait thirty days to do it."

Beatrice paused, re-reading the telegram with a knitted brow before looking up at Julia. "You don't think it'll take that long to clean up the damage, do you? I'm guessing there isn't a dish left unbroken in the whole house! See now, why I keep Grandma's soup tureen packed away under the bed?"

Julia took the telegram and read it again. After murmuring the words aloud to herself, she looked up with a sigh. "You'd think if Papa was sacrificing money for telegrams, he'd at least say what he meant."

"You know, Julia, we'll have to use caution at dinner tonight. We don't know which invention your Papa was corresponding with the senator about. If he starts asking us questions about something that's been blown sky high, it wouldn't be good for your papa, to say the least. That is, unless it was *supposed* to blow up. That would mean he's had a success, but just got a little carried away with a steam valve or dynamite or something."

"Probably steam. He was working on that tiny, little engine the other day when I took some doughnuts and milk out to the shop for him. I think we've no choice but to act like helpless females. We'll say Papa's work is a mystery to us and we don't know a thing about what's going on out in that workshop."

"Well," said Beatrice, waving the telegram, "do we? I'm determined to look on the bright side, though. If it was tiny as you say, maybe we still have windows. Oh! My heavens! Look at the time!"

Julia pointed at the top dresser drawer. "What are we going to do with *that* during dinner?"

"Hm?"

"The Chicago Pocket Protector."

"For Heaven's sake, leave it there!"

JULIA RETURNED her mother's smile as they descended the grand staircase and lifted her chin a little higher. She wished her outlook could be as positive as Mother's. Oh, to be tucked away at the Allens', away from prying eyes! Her thoughts raced alongside her pulse, as if the contest were to see which one could overtake her before she reached the Oglethorpe Room. One threatened to induce flight. The other seemed intent on making her faint. A moment from the past flitted through Julia's mind and she saw herself, as a small child, forcing her feet to step forward on the platform at her first school program to recite a poem. She lifted her skirts with more than usual care. *Whatever you do, don't trip on the stairs.*

The green dress, a miracle worked by Mother, had been low in the neckline. It would have shown off more of her shoulders and arms than would have seemed appropriate at dinner. The girls Julia knew who insisted on revealing as much as possible when the occasion didn't call for it only succeeded in getting themselves talked about. She had reservations about appearing at a quiet dinner in something that ought to be reserved for a dance or party, but Julia had awakened from her nap to find it transformed.

After searching through the trunk, Mother had found cream-colored lace and ribbon. Gathering the lace into narrow pleats, she'd attached it to the underside of the neckline. Gathered again into puffed scallops, it raised the neckline a couple of inches. More lace, added to the bottom of each sleeve and gathered at the outside edge, extended them further over Julia's arms. Cream-colored, satin ribbon, passed around the waist and formed into a rosette with the ends hanging down, made the lace appear as if it had been part of the original design.

Inwardly, Julia counseled herself to keep smiling. Though her insides churned, she had, thanks to Mother, cleaned up well on the outside. Showing off Mother's work while in Savannah was vital. When potential clients met Mother and discovered she would be outfitting Mrs. Grayson, their wardrobes would be scrutinized from head to toe.

Nodding cordially to a few people she met on the stairs, Julia struggled to look them in the eye. *Have they heard?* Oh, to run back upstairs, jump into bed, and continue the peaceful dream she'd been having earlier! She'd been curled up inside one of the many trunks in the train's baggage car. The rhythmic rocking of the locomotive on the rails had kept her swaying to and fro, comforting her. It had felt nice, being hidden away rather than being with other passengers who might notice her torn dress. She would be delivered to the hotel with the rest of the baggage and Mother would take care of everything.

But alas, Mother had wakened her and now Julia paused at the bottom of the stairs, shrinking back at the thought of being recognized and pointed out. If only the path would clear at the bottom of the staircase—she would at least be able to step onto the floor and mix into the throng. Another minute of being elevated for display on the staircase and Julia's racing heart might leap from her chest.

The frantic pace in the hotel lobby began to slow and form into two disorganized lanes. In response to a nod from her mother, Julia followed her and they moved to the edge of a group that looked as though it might be collecting near the Oglethorpe Room. The other group, to Julia's relief, seemed to be migrating toward the hotel entrance. Looking ahead, she caught the gaze of three women near the dining room doorway. They averted their eyes, exchanging looks that made Julia feel sick and clammy. She counseled herself that, being an adult, she should keep her chin up and look these people right in the eye.

The child within her won out. Her gloved hand instinctively reached for Mother's.

It was just like Mother to be so preoccupied with crowd-watching and exchanging pleasantries with total strangers that she didn't even notice the gesture. *Goodness, Mother!* Julia squeezed, but received only a slight flinch in response. After a pause, Julia felt her hand being enveloped in a firm but gentle embrace. A tender memory flashed through her mind of walking hand-in-hand with Papa.

Papa?

Julia froze. She dropped her eyes. Mother's left hand held her bag. Her right one moved in concert with her words as she greeted others near her. The hand clasping her own belonged to someone else entirely.

It's a man! And I'm holding his hand!

Chapter Three

Julia's spasm prompted an instant release. She pulled her hand to her throat, scanning the faces in the crowd, wondering just how much of a fool she'd made of herself. Everyone seemed oblivious to anything out of the ordinary—either that or they were too well-bred to show it.

One person, however, possessed a keen awareness of her blunder. Julia turned to face him.

They had not been introduced. Awkwardness held them silent. Something had to be said. Julia opened her mouth. His face, as red as her own, made her pause. She looked up into the stranger's clear, blue eyes. Her hand moved slightly toward the kindest face she'd ever seen. She jerked it back. *I almost touched him—touched his face!* The instinct had been there—an involuntary urge to place her hand against his flushed face and reassure him that it wasn't his fault.

"Forgive me, sir."

He extended his hand. Julia tore her eyes away from his face and gave it a brief shake. It trembled as much as her own. His flush deepened at her quick withdrawal.

"I'm sorry. I... I suppose we've already done that. Please don't think..."

"No, no!" Julia whispered. "It's my mistake! I thought you were my mother."

He opened his mouth and closed it again. Julia saw the corners of his mouth twitch.

He must think I'm an idiot! It felt strange, this awkwardness that should have made her want to flee. Yet, she had no desire to turn away.

"Up until this point, I've rejected the idea of a mustache. Perhaps I should reconsider if this type of misunderstanding becomes commonplace."

"Well, you see, I..." Her voice trailed off as her mind failed at finding any explanation that wouldn't make her appear ridiculous.

He inclined his head toward Julia.

"Anyway, all is well?"

"All is well," she repeated after him, reasoning that it was the safest response.

The crowd shuffled. Julia moved along behind Mother toward the dining room. She stole a glance over her shoulder, only to find the face she'd nearly touched replaced by another. Searching the crowd, she caught sight of him again and watched as he made his way toward a young lady and offered his arm.

Once inside the Oglethorpe Room, Julia felt relief at finding the Thornhills seated in a secluded spot; but it did little to cause them to go unnoticed, for as soon as Senator Thornhill caught sight of Mother, he leaped to his feet and came toward them, bellowing.

"Mrs. Lansing, there you are, and Miss Julia! Come! Come! You must meet my dear wife, Dahlia! Dahlia, this is Mrs. Lansing, wife of that inventor fellow I was telling you about. And this young lady is their daughter, Julia." He seated them at the table and leaned toward Mrs. Thornhill. "Mrs. Lansing's nearly deaf, Dahlia. Try and speak up. Ah! There's the hotel manager. I've been wanting a word with him. Excuse me, ladies."

Though grateful for her own reprieve, Julia hadn't an ounce of envy for the poor hotel manager, who was in for quite a trial.

Mrs. Thornhill, a petite lady who appeared to be in her early sixties, had sweet, girlish features. Julia liked her face.

Leaning toward Mother, Mrs. Thornhill raised her voice.

"It's so nice to meet you, Mrs. Lansing. I'm sure we'll enjoy each other immensely. Won't you call me Dahlia?"

Julia caught the quick glance her mother gave her. It let her know that Beatrice Lansing had no intention of spending her entire stay in Savannah being yelled at by the entire populace. She wasn't likely to let this sort of thing get out of hand and spend what might amount to a month or more of her time trying to explain to customers that she could hear perfectly well. Leaning toward Dahlia, she kept her voice low.

"I'm happy to meet you, Dahlia. Please call me Beatrice. I want you to know that my hearing is excellent. Earlier today, your husband came to the erroneous conclusion that I had a condition similar to his. You'll be relieved, I'm sure, to know we can speak unhindered. You can save your vocal cords for your husband. I know he must require your assistance often."

"Praise be!" Dahlia sighed. "I thought I was going to endure dinner with *two* foghorns!" She looked around before leaning in and speaking in a hushed tone, "I'm rather glad he stepped away. Perhaps we can get better acquainted before Percy gets back. I've been wanting to speak to you, Miss Lansing," she said, turning her attention toward Julia, "concerning that unfortunate incident which occurred this afternoon."

Scrumptious smells wafted to their nostrils from trays carried by passing waiters, but Julia felt cold and clammy. Nausea rose from deep inside. She forced a weak reply.

"Oh, yes?"

"Yes, indeed!" said Dahlia. "Don't think for one minute that I would allow my Percy to embarrass a sweet, young lady such as yourself and not offer my sincerest apologies. Percy told me all about it the moment he returned to our room and I was simply... Well, I should have expected something appalling like this sooner or later."

Julia felt her shoulders relax as Mrs. Thornhill graciously lifted the blame from them and continued.

"You see, my husband is such a busy man and many times succumbs to exhaustion. He probably wasn't in the bath five minutes before falling asleep. And, mercy's sake, you've already had a sample of what his hearing, or rather, lack of it, is like! I suppose it was an unfortunate set of circumstances, but you must have been humiliated beyond description. We'll do our best to squash the inevitable talk. You know," she whispered, "it may even polish his manly pride a bit to be the talk of the smoking room because pretty young girls rush into his bath, but I'm sure it won't do you a bit of good amongst Savannah's young men, who are, no doubt, already wondering if they may be just the sort of suitor you had in mind."

The three ladies were having a wonderful time when Senator Thornhill returned. They worked through the rest of the dinner conversation as well as could be expected. The ear trumpet proved to be of some help. Formed into a shape that seemed a combination of a bugle and a smoking pipe, the outer portion of this brass invention appeared to have been given a black lacquer finish, perhaps in an attempt to make it more masculine and less flashy. Julia doubted anything could make the man in front of her less flashy and wondered where that "confounded horn thing" had been this afternoon when it was needed most. She considered it a blessing for Papa to be making his attempts to promote his invention by correspondence. She shuddered to think what sort of agreement might be struck verbally with a man as deaf as Senator Thornhill.

Dahlia Thornhill's graciousness went a long way in restoring Julia's appetite and the Wentworth made quite an impression with its bill of fare. Savoring every morsel, she stole a glance at every tray being delivered to nearby tables, tempted to order one of everything on the menu. Though the Lansings and Thornhills dined heartily and professed their inability to hold another bite, their resolve crumbled when the waiter brought around the spectacular array of sweets.

Julia only hoped the friendliness displayed at their table was adequate to dispel any rumors floating about the dining room. However, she felt her spine stiffen from time to time as patrons passed nearby, speaking in whispers. She'd felt as though all eyes were boring into her back from the moment she entered the room. Talk was to be expected, but it made her want to fidget. Over and over, she reminded herself that when Mother had handed the dress to her with a smile, it came with a warning to be careful, as the embellishments were merely attached with a line of basting stitches. Fiddling with her neckline or sleeves might break the thread. Though it hadn't been a habit up until now, Julia found herself struggling to resist the urge.

During dessert, two ladies passed behind Julia and Mother.

"See that girl in the green dress?" one whispered.

Julia blushed. She felt Mother give her hand a squeeze under the table.

"Who do you suppose she is?" replied the other.

"I don't know, but I'm going to find out. I want a dress *exactly* like that!"

Julia returned a second squeeze. Things weren't always as bad as they seemed.

She ventured a glance around the room, relieved to see diners engrossed in their own meals and conversations. A few, however, cast a haughty sneer her way. Certain that they'd heard the rumors, she returned a steady, pleasant gaze until they looked away, hoping this outer display of assurance concealed how she felt on the inside. *Remember who you are,* she reminded herself. Mother's favorite exhortation, often issued to her over the years when she needed courage, kept her from making an excuse to go to their room several times during dinner. She knew the full meaning of it for her family. The Lansings weren't any better than anyone else, but they certainly weren't any worse. Chin up and shoulders back, they held their place.

Another pair of eyes drew her attention as she surveyed the room. They belonged to the young man whose hand she'd held in the lobby. Seated across the room in a party of six, he seemed to be ignoring the conversation at his table for the moment as he looked at Julia. He acknowledged her with a guarded smile before rejoining the conversation. She made a quick assessment while their eyes met and for a moment afterward. He was hand-some, but not to the degree that caused automatic conceit in men. His hair lay in dark brown waves. His blue eyes seemed as kind and gentle as when they'd been so close to hers in the lobby. It struck Julia as odd that, somehow, she sensed that it would be impossible for him to be boring.

She couldn't help but steal another glance as his party rose to leave. She watched his tall, muscular frame as he held the chair for the lady seated next to him. Julia silently willed him to look at her once more and, as if words had traveled by some invisible telegraph, he did. His eyes sent a message and, before she could restrain herself, she felt her own eyes return it before she forced herself to look away.

Julia hoped the others at her table didn't notice the flush

she felt sweep over her. She liked the way he looked at her and, unlike the others, he didn't seem to be judging her. *But,* she sighed, *he probably just hasn't heard the rumors yet.*

THE LANSINGS and Thornhills strolled across the lobby and began their ascent up the curving stairway to their rooms. Senator Thornhill turned to Mother.

"So, tell me about this invention your husband's been so confounded determined to show me, Mrs. Lansing. Does he really think it's going to make that much of a difference in how things are done?"

Things? What things? Julia looked at her mother, detecting a slight wince at the introduction of the subject. Now, Mother's pleading eyes seemed to be begging her for help. She felt sorry for Mother, but her mind seemed void of anything helpful. As she watched Mother take a deep breath and plunge in, Julia felt an immense relief that she wasn't the one doing the explaining.

"Why, Senator, perhaps I shouldn't be saying this, but this very day, moments before we came down to dinner, I received a telegram—a *telegram*, mind you! My husband informs me that the latest developments in his work have made our whole town sit up and take notice!"

True, Julia conceded. *Oh, help her, Lord!*

"My word! That *is* exciting!" boomed the senator. "I'm interested in anything that is a boon to the economic welfare of the country, revolutionizes industry, strengthens the military!"

"Shh!" When Mother placed her hand on his forearm, the senator paused on the stairs. She spoke into his ear trumpet. "I couldn't agree more. That's why my husband only releases to the public the most elementary stages of his work. He conceals sensitive details, even from Julia and myself. Who knows? Vital information could *explode* through the press and jeopardize his future plans! We must exercise extreme caution. It may be prudent, Senator, to confine our conversations to superficial matters. Dahlia and I have enough to discuss, just getting to know one another. After all, Senator Thornhill, our national security could be at stake!"

"Oh, yes! *Yes!* Yes, indeed. You're absolutely right, Mrs. Lansing. Complete confidentiality is the key. Mr. Lansing is fortunate to have a wife who understands."

"Well, I certainly *do* understand. Why, if one of his inventions were to... well, be spread far and wide before its time, there'd be no telling what disastrous consequences might result. A messy situation—chaotic!"

"We'll speak no more of it."

Good! Julia had dreaded being drawn into the discussion as she followed them up the stairs, but as they paused in the corridor leading to their rooms, she realized Mother wasn't quite finished yet.

"My husband feels further written correspondence is risky. You and he must meet privately as soon as possible. Of course, it would require a trip to Morgan's Landing. We'll do our best to make your stay as pleasant as possible."

Julia's eyes widened. *It's just like you, Mother! Once things are going along in the right vein, you reach for the stars!*

"Yes, I do see the merits of conferencing in private. I'll try to rearrange my schedule."

"Yes, of course. Well, it's late and a good night's sleep will help you do just that."

After exchanging goodnights and wishes for sound sleep at the end of the corridor, Julia and Mother strolled toward their room.

When even Mrs. Thornhill was out of earshot, Julia whispered, "Mother, you were smooth as cream. I was praying you'd be able to answer his questions."

"Good! I needed it, because I hadn't the faintest idea what was going to come out of my mouth."

"I'm sorry I was no help at all, Mother. I've been so...well, rattled... ever since we've arrived. I've hardly been able to think since I came out of that water closet and realized I'd brought scandal and disgrace on us both." Julia sniffed and fought back tears as the day's events replayed in her mind. "Everything else seems nothing in comparison, but even so, I did ruin the dress. I had to face all those people at dinner. I'm just exhausted from it all. I don't recall ever getting two telegrams in one day—Mrs. Allen sending us here, Papa telling us something's exploded and that he wants to see the senator—*that* senator—and then that confusing business about waiting thirty days. Here we are at last!" she sighed as they approached the door to their room. "I want nothing more than to get on the other side of this door, lock it and never come out!"

Mother unlocked the door, dropping the key as she removed it from the lock when Julia shrieked. "*Thirty days!*"

"Thirty days?" Mother stared blankly.

Julia ran into the room, snatching the telegram from the dressing table.

"Papa doesn't want you to wait thirty days to buy curtain material. I think he wants you to delay the senator's visit for a month, so he can rebuild his invention!"

"Oh," Mother stood for a moment with her lips parted and her eyes seemingly unfocused. "*Oh!* And I made it sound so urgent! Now I won't get a wink of sleep all night for trying to figure out how I'm going to get the senator to Morgan's Landing, but not *now*. Oh, I wish your father had been a little more clear in his meaning."

"Well, I'm going to bed. Don't stay up all night worrying, Mother. Tomorrow is bound to be a better day."

Mother sat before the mirror to begin the task of feeling for hairpins. Julia slipped into her nightgown, put her toes under the covers, and propped her chin on her knees. Her eyes closed for a few moments before opening again. She looked at the night table where she had placed two volumes earlier while unpacking. She contemplated picking up where she'd left off in *Thomas Wingfold*—a captivating story—but realized she was far too sleepy. She wouldn't remember what she'd read in the morning and would have to re-read the whole chapter. A Bible verse or two would have to suffice. Pulling the ribbon that marked the place where she left off reading on the train, she found that the poetry and strength of the psalms seemed to make the events of the day fall into place.

"It's been a long journey, Mother, and a long day. All our steps," she said, tapping the open page with her finger, "are already known by Him."

Julia saw her mother's shoulders relax as she turned from the mirror and gave a nod. "All will be well."

Mother slipped her nightgown over her head and climbed into bed. "I believe there's a passage about our steps being ordered and how we delight in it," she said, pulling the blanket over her knees. "Well, your father needed us to make an impression on Senator Thornhill, and your steps were ordered right into his bath!"

"Yes, but I *didn't* delight in it. Not one bit!"

Mother shook with laughter. "It makes you wonder what tomorrow will bring," she pondered with a shake of her head. "But, as you said, tomorrow is bound to be better—if you can manage to stay out of trouble."

"I think the best way for me to stay out of trouble tomorrow is to avoid taking chances."

"That might prove difficult, Lovely One, considering the only thing you were attempting to do today was take a bath. Are you going to give up bathing while we're in Savannah?"

"No," Julia chuckled. "I just don't want to go begging for trouble. I think *you* should be the one to carry the Protector— either that or leave it in the room. If I can't manage a bath without disaster, who knows what'll happened if I'm armed!"

"Oh, that reminds me!" Mother hopped out of bed and ran to the dresser.

"What are you doing?" Julia gasped as she saw her mother pull the Protector from the top drawer.

"I promised your papa I'd sleep with it."

"What!"

"Well, he wanted me to sleep with it under my pillow, but the closest I can bring myself to keeping that promise is to have it under the mattress," Mother explained with a grunt as she heaved the corner of the mattress up and shoved the small, round pistol underneath.

Julia shuddered. "If we have to have it there now, let's leave it there tomorrow."

"You know what your papa said. If you're out exploring, it's either the Protector or a trusted male companion. At this point the only one who fits the latter description is Percival Thornhill. Shall we ask him if he'd mind?"

A few seconds of giggling like schoolgirls felt like medicine. Sleep came, deep and dreamless.

Chapter Four

Breakfasting with the Hadleys didn't seem quite so formidable after a good night's sleep, though the idea of these new acquaintances Mother had only met at the front desk yesterday still played upon Julia's nerves as they crossed the lobby together. She'd been attempting to soothe herself as she dressed with the notion that perhaps, at this early hour, they might possibly be the only people in the hotel who hadn't heard about her encounter with Senator Thornhill. The breakfast room beckoned them, its windows allowing the morning sun to lay a patchwork across carpets, dining tables, and potted plants. Mr. Hadley and James stood as they approached and graciously seated Mother and Julia amid introductions. Their appearances struck Julia much as the Allens' did. Their refined taste and discreet manners tempered their obvious wealth which, by necessity, had to be on display if one wanted to attract the best of clients in the fine jewelry business. Julia reminded herself not to stare at the jeweled pieces before her. They shone beautifully against fine fabrics and calm colors.

As the waiter departed from taking their orders, the conversation turned to the reasons for both families' trips to Savannah, how far they'd traveled, and the places they called home. Mr. and Mrs. Hadley didn't seem to bat an eye when told of a town in the middle of Missouri called Morgan's Landing. Based on their reaction, one would have thought they found it every bit as interesting as their own Atlanta, Georgia.

Ravenous, and comforted by the thought that perhaps not everyone was repeating scandalous rumors behind her back, Julia enjoyed the meal. Abigail Hadley proved to be a delight. Her light blonde, fluffy curls, though pulled back from her face, refused to be contained. Curly wisps escaped, making a pleasant halo around her face, accenting her pale green eyes and the freckles across her cheeks. Julia studied her face and thought of peaches and cream with a sprinkle of cinnamon.

She and her mother had made a game of studying faces ever since Julia had been old enough to refrain from making public observations. They made it a pleasant and non-judgmental pastime. Julia remembered Mother's assessment once of a bank president's chiseled features and long, regal nose—"a face like an eagle's", she'd said—noting that the attribute ought to make people confident in his ability to keep a sharp eye on the money. Mother had confessed to being resolved years ago in getting to know a total stranger due to her kitten-like features, assuming they must surely accompany a playful nature. They had become the best of friends.

Julia often entertained these private little amusements, but struggled at times to separate the true person from the mental image that sprang to mind. No unnerving distractions arose with the Hadleys. Jeremiah and Rose Hadley seemed as pleasant as their daughter, Abigail, though Mr. Hadley spoke few words and had an air about him as though he carried the world upon his shoulders. He moved with precision, as though sipping coffee required great expertise. The slightest sound or movement drew his attention. Julia thought this befitting for a jeweler, assuming it to be the result of traveling about with velvet-lined cases full of diamonds, emeralds, and rubies at risk of being stolen.

His son, though more slight of build, seemed the mirror image of his father. The demeanor that so suited Mr. Hadley made James appear far too serious for his age. Mother had been right in her assessment that he was well-mannered, intelligent, and pleasant, but Julia wondered what his face would look like if he relaxed.

With each forkful of peach-filled pastry, Julia turned from the study of her companions and began to inspect each bite of the sweet delight, savoring it and trying to memorize the flavor. She questioned whether an ordinary cook such as herself could accomplish such a feat.

Abigail sipped her orange juice.

"Mother's lunching with friends today and Father's with

clients until evening. Since your mother's lunching with Mrs. Grayson, it would be great fun if you and I strolled about the squares today. Won't you come, Julia?"

Julia looked at her mother, who smiled in approval. "You two go right ahead. All I ask, Julia, is that you wait a bit. I'd like you to send a telegram for me before you leave. I'll go up to the room and get it ready."

"Of course." *Telegram? Why is Mother sending telegrams?* Julia hadn't detected an ounce of worry or concern. Mother had been chatting with Rose Hadley as though she'd found a long-lost friend and hadn't a care in the world. Julia chaffed at the thought that, unless it somehow slipped her mind, Mother would likely be handing her more than a telegram. If she and Abigail were to be out and about without a male companion, the Chicago Pocket Protector would likely be considered the next best thing.

When they'd finished, Abigail led the way across the lobby. "We'll get started right away—as soon as you send your telegram. There are quite a few beautiful squares. Let's stroll through a few of them—all the way to Forsyth Park and back. Then, there's a lovely dresser set in the window on Congress Street. It has mother-of-pearl and... you *have* to see it."

"That sounds perfect, Abigail, but I was just this minute thinking of a stop I need to make."

"Of course. I didn't mean to take charge. Where would you like to go?"

Julia's eyes twinkled. "The kitchen!"

With Abigail following, Julia re-entered the dining room

and crossed to the kitchen door. Abigail's curls brushed her cheek as she joined her in peering through the small pane of glass.

"Do you really think we should be doing this?"

"No, I don't. You can wait here, Abigail, if you want to. I'm sure you've never done anything like this. I've done it back home and a few other places, but those were much smaller establishments. I've never done this in a hotel of this size before."

"But what *are* we doing?" Abigail fidgeted, looking as though tempted to run from the scene of the crime.

Julia shot a determined look over her shoulder. "I'm going to get that pastry recipe. The filling was perfect, but if they won't part with both, I'll settle for the crust recipe. It was beyond compare. Mr. and Mrs. Schmidt will be thrilled."

"Who are Mr. and Mrs. Schmidt?"

Julia opened her mouth to answer, then thought better of it. The answer would have to wait until she found the time and the nerve to explain fully. She ignored Abigail's puzzled expression and turned her attention back to the kitchen. The staff, overhearing their whispers, began looking toward the door. Julia smiled, entering the kitchen with the hope that she appeared confident and friendly.

"May I help you, miss?" asked a thin, young man with a large knife in one hand and a wedge of cheese in the other.

A mouse! Julia issued herself a mental reprimand, refusing to be distracted by his small, dark eyes and pointy nose. Refocusing her thoughts, she attempted to pave the way for good relations.

"I'm sorry to take you away from your work. I *so* wanted to compliment the chef on the exquisite meal I had last evening and the superb breakfast this morning. I don't know when I've tasted such delightful dishes."

The man's guardedness evaporated. "Very good, miss. I'll be sure to tell Chef Plouff that you are pleased."

A voice bearing a French accent called from an unknown location, "Please, allow me to meet this lady who speaks so passionately of my life's work!" A small man emerged from behind tall shelves of serving ware, pots, and pans.

Julia extended her hand toward Chef Plouff as she stepped forward to give her compliments and was delighted to hear him offer to show her around his domain. She cast a quick glance over her shoulder and caught Abigail's eye, trying to convey a mixture of apology and a request for patience as she followed him on this unexpected adventure. Though Abigail seemed agog with interest, she raised a hand, seeming to indicate that if this was intended as an invitation, she'd rather not join whatever might be happening.

Julia and the little Frenchman seemed to bond in an instant. His eyes sparkled. His hands gestured and his eyebrows rose as he spoke of delights he'd created and hoped to create.

"Ah!" Chef Plouff exclaimed when Julia asked how to acquire the proper texture or prevent an oozy filling.

"Oh!" Julia marveled as he opened canisters of flours,

sugars, powders, and starches, placing a pinch in her palm and explaining his expertise in the use of each.

Julia had spent her life in the kitchen, learning to cook from her mother and Mrs. Schmidt, but this experience felt like a dream. She felt this must be what it had been like for people who received direct revelations from one of the major prophets.

As Julia jotted down final notes on some paper the chef had provided, she brushed the flour from her nose and promised him she'd return early in the morning for her first lesson. Then, realizing that she'd lost track of time entirely, hurried out of the kitchen and offered Abigail her apologies as she glanced across the lobby at the clock on the wall.

"Forgive me, Abigail! I've delayed us by at least half an hour."

"You're a fascinating person, Julia Lansing!" Abigail remarked as they went to get their hats and bags.

"Why so?"

"I've never seen anyone so excited over flour, butter, and salt! You certainly had that Chef Pluff right in your hip pocket."

"Plouff," said Julia, putting her tongue to the roof of her mouth. "Like this. *Plouff*."

"*Pleeoooouf*... I think your Missouri tongue manages French a little bit better than my Georgia one," laughed Abigail. "I didn't suppose you had interests along those lines. Oh, I don't mean any offense. It's just that I suppose I thought you were like me." Abigail paused with a sigh and continued in a tone that carried a mixture of resignation and apology. "I'm afraid I'm a lady of leisure—what they call 'accomplished'. I'm well-educated, I play the piano extremely well, and my embroidery is decent. But, Father's business places us in a segment of society that pretty well excludes me from places like the kitchen."

Julia stopped in the middle of the corridor.

"Abigail, if you've no objection to being seen all about Savannah with someone whose place in society is… somewhat different, I'll tell you the whole story."

"Oh, I've no objection—you're turning out to be lots of fun!"

"Then let's get our things and Mother's telegram and be on our way." Julia hurried ahead as they picked up their pace along the main corridor. "And…" she called over her shoulder, "wait till you hear about *my* father's business!"

"I think I'm becoming giddy with anticipation. I may have to hear all about that before I can give another thought to that dresser set!"

"I can't wait to see it!"

The subject turned to sightseeing and then back to toiletries as they reached Abigail's room. Pausing, they agreed that Abigail would return to the lobby in a quarter of an hour and await Julia's return with the telegram.

As Julia entered her room, she found the room tidied and her mother in her dressing gown, her head bowed over paper and ink. Mother looked up from the dressing table, her face relaxing into a smile.

"You and Abigail seemed to be enjoying one another."

"Oh, yes! She's nice, Mother. Abigail's genuine. I think

she's just as interested in getting to know me as I am in finding out about her. My, you've accomplished much since breakfast!"

"Well, when I saw you and Abigail heading in the opposite direction of the staircase, looking as though you were on some mission of high priority, I thought, surely, I had time to wash my hair so it could dry while I figured out how to word this. I've been taking great pains with this telegram."

Mother's long, wet ringlets hung down her back. She hardly looked as though she were ready to meet with an important client such as Mrs. Grayson to discuss dressmaking, but Julia knew her mother would save her hair for last. Once she finished the telegram, dressed, and gathered everything she needed for her appointment, she would put it up into a soft chignon under her lace brimmed hat.

Julia leaned over her shoulder. "Is there an emergency?"

"Well, of sorts. I am simply *demanding*, as much as I can without hurting your dear father's feelings, that he write again immediately—a detailed letter—explaining exactly what he's working on and what he wants us to do with Senator Thornhill! I don't mind telling you, it's all I can do not to be in a dither over this. We must know everything, so we'll know what to do, and especially so we can know what *not* to say. This is quite a pickle we're in, I must say."

Mother handed Julia the telegram, which read:

SEND LETTER IMMEDIATELY **STOP**
INSIST SPARE NO DETAILS **STOP**
MUST KNOW HOW TO HANDLE PROSPECT **STOP**

ONE TOPIC PER PARAGRAPH **STOP**
NEED NAME OF IT **STOP**
DO I HAVE DISHES? **STOP**
LACK OF INFORMATION WILL CAUSE SECOND
EXPENSIVE TELEGRAM **STOP**
LOVINGLY, BEATRICE **STOP**

"That last line ought to get a ten-page letter out of Papa!" said Julia.

Mother raised an eyebrow. "That's the idea. Here—take this."

Julia shrank back, but saw her mother tilt her head and raise both eyebrows as though any attempt at refusal was out of the question. She shoved the Pocket Protector toward Julia.

"Now, you know your papa would insist."

With a heavy sigh, Julia opened her bag and held it forward.

THE TWO GIRLS started out along Abercorn Street, breathing in the sweet smell of moss and old bricks that had enjoyed a quick shower just before dawn. Crossing to Bull Street, they made their way toward Forsyth Park, admiring the fine homes and peaceful gardens along the way. When Abigail began to tell how General Sherman burned his way through Georgia during the War Between the States, Julia listened with a rekindled interest to the story she'd learned in school. Hearing how he'd left a wide path of utter destruction seemed somehow more horrifying coming from someone who was raised in the South. Abigail's tone softened a bit as she told how the streets they now strolled affected even that single-minded military leader and how, when he found Savannah too beautiful to burn, he chose to make it his headquarters during the war.

"Now here we are, Julia, two generations later. When I think of how the citizens of Savannah and, in fact, all of Georgia still bear the ugly scars of war, it makes me want to cry. If we could peek behind the doors of these graceful homes, we'd find many who lost a handsome bridegroom, one or more beloved brothers, cousins, and childhood playmates. And how many are there, behind these doors, raising families of their own now, having lost fathers and uncles and grandfathers they could only come to know through the portrait on the mantlepiece or the treasured lock of hair kept in a locket and worn close to the heart?"

Julia's eyes darted up and down the street. The lovely homes, standing regal and proud, took on a sense of loneliness as she listened to Abigail. She nodded, but only managed to whisper, "I know."

They walked in silence for a moment. Julia pondered how she'd judged Abigail prematurely on her wealth and her excitement over such a frivolous item as the dresser set. Certainly, there was more to Abigail than being a spoiled rich girl.

"Do you visit here often?"

"Oh, yes," Abigail nodded. "My father's business is in Atlanta, but it's brought us here several times. War memories were especially bitter back home. From time to time, he'll talk about his memories of Atlanta, engulfed in flames, and how his family struggled to rebuild their lives after the war, and it hurts my heart to hear it. So many have clung to all that pain and bitterness, but," Abigail paused to give Julia a sweet smile, "my father's pains were purged from his heart by the hand of Providence."

"Oh?" Julia dared not appear nosy by asking details, but hoped Abigail would share more.

"After the loss of his father, they were forced to flee north and take refuge with their only remaining relatives. Concealing their southern connections, they made a great many Yankee friends, and my father was able to enter an apprenticeship with a watchmaker. That's where he met and married Mother. Her love extinguished the last of his prejudice toward northerners. They came back to Atlanta when its restoration and economy were at a peak and that enabled him to build a fine business, despite the fact he'd married a Yankee."

Julia chuckled at the way Abigail referred to her mother as a Yankee with a flare of her nostrils and feigned aversion to the idea. She pulled her features back into a sober expression as she met the gaze of a woman just in front of her. Unless she was mistaken, the woman, having overheard Abigail, displayed this aversion to marrying Yankees in all sincerity. Abigail seemed to have noticed it too, for she turned her eyes toward Julia and raised her brows to indicate as much. Though she found Abigail's stories fascinating, foot traffic around them soon increased to the point where they ceased conversing altogether and gave their full attention to returning the nods and smiles of other pedestrians.

Julia had been to Savannah only once before. She remembered well the day, just over a year ago, that Mother got the letter. She and Ruby Allen had known each other all their lives and correspondence between them should have been nothing unusual. The letter that arrived that day had been different. As Julia made way for the other pedestrians, her mind replayed the day that had changed everything and she still felt a pang of guilt for unwittingly becoming an eavesdropper.

Chapter Five

AUTUMN, 1903

MORGAN'S LANDING, MISSOURI

Entering through the front door of the workshop, Julia looked around, surprised that she hadn't heard the greeting from Papa that usually came just after the hinges creaked. She looked around for him, for as he'd finished his lunch he'd said he planned to be busy here for the rest of the day. Finding only the mare, Molly, stamping and munching oats in her stall in the southeast corner, Julia assumed he must have gone out the back way on some errand and continued on her mission. Climbing the ladder steps to the loft, she began her search for some old baskets she could fill with baked goods for families in need. Rummaging through some old crates, she managed to find three that were passable in appearance. As she nested them together, something red inside a crate caught her eye and Julia soon found herself nestled against a few bales of hay, sorting through a collection of her childhood things. She didn't mind most of them being stored in the loft, but the red book deserved better treatment lest the mice use its pages to make a nest. She opened it and held her face close to the pages, inhaling the smell. Yes, it was just as she remembered—one of those books that smelled like books ought to smell. Julia settled back and lost herself in the sweet, familiar story. After all, the bread dough she'd just kneaded and left in a pan on the shelf above the kitchen stove had almost a full hour left to rise.

As Julia became aware of a scraping, tapping sound, she forced her heavy eyelids open. She lifted the book from her chest and sat up. Over the edge of the loft, she could see Papa's profile as he sat at the workbench with a clock in his hands, performing some meticulous task. She thought of the bread and wondered how long she'd been asleep, but hated to jump up and startle Papa while he adjusted some small mechanism. Though various inventions awaited him, Papa, being adept at taking things apart and putting them back together again, often repaired clocks and machinery for people in and around Morgan's Landing. It provided a source of income he couldn't afford to overlook.

The front door hinges squawked and Mother bustled in with a letter in her hand. She began reading a portion aloud, all the while giving Papa her most expectant smile.

Julia opened her mouth to announce her presence, but, despite a pang of guilt, found herself listening. What could be in this letter that couldn't wait till Papa came in for supper?

Mother had known Ruby all her life. Best friends throughout school, they'd kept up a constant correspondence ever since Ruby's husband, Clifford, inherited his uncle's lumber exportation business in Savannah. The postman rarely delivered a letter to Ruby's address without picking up another the next day addressed to Beatrice Lansing. Mother read most portions aloud to Julia and Papa, but the girlhood chums confided matters of the heart that they shared with no one else. Stories of lost dogs, snipped obituaries, and other news items filled the stream of correspondence exiting the post office in Morgan's Landing, Missouri. Mother included fabric swatches and rough sketches of dresses she made for her customers. Just as when they were schoolgirls, Mother and Ruby discussed hemlines and colors, laces and bodices—only now, they made do with letters. Though almost a thousand miles separated Savannah and Morgan's Landing, it seemed a million. A journey by train would be expensive and cause work to be neglected back home. Yet, as Julia listened, she clearly heard Ruby Allen's invitation for them to come.

Julia looked from Mother, who now stood waiting expectantly, to Papa, who appeared to be aware of nothing but the clock.

"Hm?" he finally muttered. "Uh, say that again, Beatrice. I was just... well... tarnation!" he exclaimed as one of the hands rattled down into the clock's casing. "I almost had that." Pushing back his chair, he looked up at Mother, his eyes softening in response to the excitement on her face.

"I say," she sighed, "that Ruby and Clifford have invited us for an extended visit. We haven't seen each other in *years*. We've always talked of going, and they've been here only once, but... she says she has all sorts of things planned for us. Clifford is able to leave his business in capable hands for most of our stay and plans to take you fishing on the islands... The weather should be wonderful next month... Julia's never been to Savannah... Oh, Roderick! She's simply *pleading* for us to come!"

"Hmmm... it's an awful expense. Quite a distance. I've got all this *work.*"

Mother's head turned as her gaze followed his gesturing arm. The workbenches lining the walls were loaded down with things neither Julia nor Mother could identify, not that either of them cared to try. Larger contraptions occupied the center of the room, and what any one of them might someday become was anybody's guess. Papa didn't keep his inventions secret from them. He spoke freely about them each night at the supper table when asked how they were coming along. Most of the time, however, as Julia and her mother listened, they struggled to make sense of the parts and procedures he described. Likely, being preoccupied with details, he also often forgot what he'd told them about and what he hadn't.

Mother appeared to be waiting patiently for him to continue.

"Fishing, huh? Still... I haven't time. I just haven't time. And then, where would we get the money?"

Julia saw her mother pause and take a deep breath as she gave Papa a long look. Her shoulders squared. Her eyes flashed. Julia winced. She had a feeling that Papa was about to receive his wife's complete and unedited oratory on time, money, and a trip to Savannah.

By the time she'd finished airing her opinions, many of which had been aired before in bits and pieces through the years, Julia could detect a flush warming Mother's cheeks and misty tears forming in her eyes. She'd given him the plain and simple facts. Of course it was a great distance, she'd said, but it wasn't going to get any closer by waiting to go there. It also wasn't likely, she'd pointed out, that Clifford would sell his lumber business and move to Morgan's Landing. When, she'd wanted to know, was he, or anyone else, for that matter, *not* going to have work to do? She abandoned tact, Julia felt, in reminding him that half the contents of his workshop had been in their processes of completion for years. If they waited until they were all finished, their one and only trip outside Morgan's Landing would likely be their final one—to the Memorial Hills Cemetery just outside town! And fishing? Why, if he stayed home, he merely fished out of necessity and usually felt guilty for being away from the workshop. On this trip, what was to stop him from relaxing and enjoying it for a change? And money! Would he *please* tell her when there wouldn't be a hundred other places for the money to go? The shutters needed paint and, if the cellar door wasn't fixed soon, they'd likely find raccoons down there prying open jars of canned goods! Hadn't he just fixed machinery for several farmers in preparation for harvest? There was that money. Hadn't she just ordered fabrics for ladies in Morgan's Landing who were friends and relatives of the governor's wife? Not only that—they'd ordered them in twos, not wanting to be seen at the Governor's Mansion Christmas Ball and the New Year's Eve Gala in the same dress! They'd be back in time to finish the dresses if she hired a girl to do cutting and basting. The trip was not only affordable, but the timing was perfect. It would, she reminded him, do no harm to ask the Good Lord if there were any reason why they *shouldn't* go.

"And," Mother concluded as she stopped for a deep breath, "Julia's never been to Savannah, so I suppose if you simply cannot leave your work, she and I can make the trip ourselves."

Julia began to fidget. This type of talk was bound to rile Papa. She wished she'd stood up and announced herself the instant Mother came through the door.

"You two have no business going halfway across these United States of America unaccompanied!" Papa's voice grew louder. "There's no telling what might happen. I'd be here and not be able to..."

His voice trailed off as if something in the distance caught his eye. Julia leaned forward a bit to get a better look. Papa appeared to be looking out the workshop window. It provided a clear view across the yard to the back of the house. Julia thought it likely that Papa assumed her to be in the house. Perhaps he thought she might even be able to hear his raised voice. For all he knew, Mother may have already shown her the letter.

He paused and appeared to be studying the workshop floor for a few seconds. "How about we talk about this when I come in for supper?"

Mother smiled and started for the door. "I'll start to work on that right now, but only because you're my *favorite* husband!"

As the door closed, Papa leaned back. Locking his fingers behind his head, he let out a long sigh.

Julia sighed also, preparing herself for what she must do next. Placing the book in the nested baskets, she stood and walked to the ladder, knowing that her footsteps would reveal all.

Looking over her shoulder as she started down, she met Papa's shocked eyes.

"Julia? What...? Since when do you hide out and spy on people?"

"I'm so sorry, Papa! I fell asleep up there with this book and the next thing I knew... I... I just didn't know how or when to interrupt. I'll go in the house and tell Mother."

"And so tell *me*—what do you think?"

"What do I think?"

"About Savannah. Come on now, you heard the whole thing."

"Well..." Julia hesitated, feeling a bit like a spy who had been captured. "I think your idea is best. We'll talk about it at supper."

"Julia..."

"Oh, Papa, it's really between you and Mother. I don't want to get in the middle of..." Julia paused in response to the look of sarcasm on Papa's face, realizing that she couldn't have put herself more in the middle of things if she'd tried. "I think it's a lovely invitation. I can imagine how much Mother longs to see her friend again. I think time away will do you good. And," she flashed him her brightest smile, "there was that part about fishing on some islands!"

Julia watched as Papa picked up the clock and peered down inside the casing.

"Time away... You know, I may be able to get these hands back on before supper if I had a little peace and quiet."

Taking his signal, Julia scurried out the door. Just as it closed, she heard him heave another deep sigh.

"Lord, what would I do without those two?" he muttered.

Julia felt his love come through the rough wooden door and walked on to the house to make her confession to Mother.

The next day, Papa walked down to the depot and bought three train tickets.

Autumn, 1904
Savannah, Georgia

"I FIRST CAME to Savannah last year," Julia remarked as they arrived at Madison Square and Abigail gestured toward a sunny bench.

"Let's enjoy the breeze here for a bit. We'll have a little more solitude, as well as a welcome rest for our legs. Your papa did make the trip?"

"Oh, yes. Papa came with us," Julia smiled, "but he hovered

over Mother and me the whole time as though we were in danger of being kidnapped off every corner! When he wasn't fishing with Mr. Allen, he was watching our every move. He escorted us in and out of all the shops as though we were on one of those treasure hunts where you try to be the first one back with everything on the list. It got to the point where I didn't have a private moment. I had to wait till he went fishing again to look at underthings in shops! It's so nice just to relax like this and take our time."

They sat for a moment enjoying the breeze. Blue sky blinked through the moss-covered tree branches as carriages and a few automobiles rolled by. People strolled the square, making their way in and out of houses. Some, walking more purposefully, carried parcels from shops or baskets that had been filled or waited to be filled on Market Street. Julia's nose for baked goods drew her eye to a mother who pulled a doughnut from her basket and handed it to the small girl at her elbow.

As they passed, Julia inhaled deeply. "Mmm... that smells delightful. I wonder if it's as light and airy as Mrs. Schmidt's."

"Is Mrs. Schmidt your cook?" Abigail asked. "You mentioned her earlier."

"Oh," Julia paused. Of course, someone like Abigail would assume that the Lansing family, like any other in the Hadleys' social circles, had a hired cook. Though she felt no shame concerning her relationship with the Schmidts, something seemed to hold her back from revealing it to Abigail just yet. "No, quite the opposite, actually. She's very special to me, and we do miss one another when I take these trips with Mother."

"So you came back again this year. I'm glad you did, but I'm surprised you did if your father is so concerned about your traveling. What made him change his mind?"

Julia released a little sigh, grateful that Abigail seemed willing to let the topic rest for now.

"Well, it's all due to Ruby Allen." Julia paused, searching her mind for a way to explain what happened on their first trip to Savannah in a fashion that wouldn't keep them on the park bench till sundown. It had changed their lives in an unexpected way. "We stayed at the Allens' home, of course, and after the men had gone fishing one day, she rose from the breakfast table and led us into the sitting room, saying she had people she'd like Mother to meet. She brought a large envelope over to Mother and started pulling out the contents and apologizing, as if she'd done something that might have earned Mother's disapproval."

Abigail shifted her weight on the bench to face Julia. "Oh, my! It sounds as if she had some ulterior motive for inviting you to stay."

"Oh, nothing unkind, Abigail, but she had been keeping a secret and she wanted Mother to see it with her own eyes." Julia could see that Abigail's eyes held a child-like longing for a secret that her upbringing prohibited her from asking for outright. "Mrs. Allen had saved page after page of Mother's drawings and fabric swatches, mostly her latest designs. She seemed so excited as she spread them out over the table and we couldn't imagine why."

"Why?" Abigail repeated in a whisper.

"Being so far removed from Mother, she'd been having her

seamstress create dresses for her from Mother's drawings and, though she considered them a mere imitation of Mother's lovely work, her friends had been asking where she got her clothes. None of them knew anyone with designs like Mother's. So, her ulterior motive proved to be that if she could arrange for a visit and they could meet Mother in person, they'd want dresses. Once Mother had written to say we were coming, Mrs. Allen started showing Mother's drawings to more of her friends. Not only that, she'd arranged for a tea that afternoon to gather them all together!"

Abigail gave a little gasp. "And did they want dresses?"

"They'd already chosen them, Abigail!" The memory still brought Julia almost to the point of disbelief and she found herself shaking her head. "All those drawings had penciled signatures on them of ladies who wanted dresses made. Mrs. Allen had told all those women that Mother's designs were *exclusive* and if they wanted them, they'd have to commission her to make them."

"Mrs. Allen must have felt she knew your mother well to take such a liberty," Abigail marveled.

"Well, I've rarely seen my mother at a loss for words, but Mrs. Allen's secret plot did render her speechless," Julia laughed. "She managed to snap out of it by the time the ladies arrived for tea."

"I suppose Mrs. Allen's plan produced the desired result, because here you are again, and your mother is already meeting with Mrs. Grayson. She's an important client of Father's." Abigail shifted on the bench, adjusting her hat. "The sun felt so good for a bit, but if I stay here any longer, I'll be so freckled I'll never recover. Shall we walk on? You can tell me more as we go."

After debating whether to take a direct route to Congress Street or to continue wandering through the squares, Julia and Abigail resumed their walk, coming to the conclusion that, with the whole day ahead, getting to know one another could occupy them through the morning and serious shopping could wait until after lunch. Finding another bench, this time on the west side of some colorful, tall homes that blocked the sun, they settled down again, amused by some children playing on the front lawns.

"I'll never forget the surprise of the ladies," Julia recalled, "when Mother told them that, though she was flattered by their requests, they'd need to wait three days for her decision."

"Three days!" Abigail took her eyes off the children and stared at Julia.

"Mother often says that if you ask the Good Lord a question and a door opens, you should pause on the threshold and pray again, her general rule being that if Jonah could spend three days in the belly of a whale, it can't hurt to spend three days on dry ground praying. Then, if crossing that threshold makes her unsettled, she refrains. But, if the thought of not being on the other side of the door steals peace from her heart, she goes ahead, even into unfamiliar territory. She says she learned this by walking through too many of the wrong doors."

"Well, I have to admit," Abigail conceded, "when you put it that way, it does make sense."

"Anyway, after three days, she and Papa sensed it was the

right thing to do. Ever since, Mother's quite the business-woman. She would have been content sewing for the ladies back home, but she felt she'd been guided down this path without her knowing it. It helps fill in when things get..." Julia hesitated, grasping for words that would convey the truth without causing Abigail to think of her as complaining or judgmental. "Well, I'd never criticize Papa. He's an inventor. He works hard. Please understand, Abigail. He encounters delays. Sometimes things go wrong... What I'm trying to say is that, for us, many times, it's what we call back home 'feast or famine', if that's a term they use this far south." Abigail nodded and Julia continued, "Papa repairs clocks and machinery and such, but he mostly works on inventions and things that haven't become... anything... yet."

"My, he sounds like a man with real vision! He's bound to see them come to fruition if he just keeps on trying."

The words, spoken with such sincerity, touched Julia. "Abigail Hadley, with the possible exception of my mother, I don't think I've ever met anyone with such a positive view of life. Anyway, with requests coming in for Mother's dresses, it's been easier. It's been exciting for me, too. When Papa can't take time away from his work, he's resigned to the fact that Mother must travel to meet with customers. He won't hear of her going alone, so I get to see all sorts of interesting places. When folks in Morgan's Landing heard that Mother now sews for the wealthy Savannah ladies, it made her a bit of a local celebrity. We've been to St. Louis, Kansas City, and, of course, Jefferson City, and now back to Savannah. I'm sure that in addition to Mother's established Savannah customers, at least a few more of Mrs. Allen's friends will want dresses today. I may become a world traveler yet! Of course, Mother can only make so many at a time, so I may be getting ahead of myself."

"Oh, Julia, I agree!" Abigail exclaimed. "It *must* be divine intervention. Just think of how my father's family struggled through the war and how he's worked to make a living for us. I hear him speak sometimes of what it took to make his business a success. To think that this all came about for your mother unbeknownst to any of you, due to a single letter written by an old friend! God does work in mysterious ways. When I listened to our mothers at breakfast, it reminded me of how Father sounds—how his face looks—when he talks about jewelry. He says some people paint masterpieces on canvas and some with music or great literature, but that he creates them from what lies hidden in the earth. Your mother's an artist, Julia—with a pencil and paper and needle and thread. I'm sure it makes her as happy as Father's work makes him."

It wasn't often that Julia heard Papa spoken of with such understanding and it warmed her heart to hear Abigail speak of him much as Mother did. Indeed, Abigail might be the very picture of what Mother had been like at the same age, for she certainly seemed full to the brim of dreams, inspirations and ramblings. Julia smiled and watched Abigail's eyes sparkle as she continued.

"Besides, times are changing. I'm hearing more and more of women becoming educated and pursuing professions. Why, ones I never dreamed! Father's met a couple of women who are *doctors*! It's all so *daring*! I must admit," she lowered her voice to a whisper, "that I find Nellie Bly simply too fascinating for words. Can you imagine being so courageous?"

Julia studied Abigail's faraway look. *She must be picturing herself feigning insanity and being carried away to the asylum on Blackwell's Island.*

"I've read," said Julia, "that Carrie Chapman Catt *studied law*! She was a high school principal, but, after her husband died, she actually became a newspaper reporter—not that you could make a living doing that sort of thing in Morgan's Landing. Why, her second husband signed an agreement before they were married stating that she'd be free to work in the suffrage movement for two months in the spring and two in the fall! I've heard he said it was his role to earn a living and hers to reform society."

Abigail's eyes shone. "The papers say that in areas of Australia, women have already won the right to vote and some are standing for public office! Father hasn't actually criticized that, but he looks grave when he reads the papers. I hear him saying, 'Hmmm...' as he reads. I think it's all rather exciting, don't you? I haven't said so, of course, in front of Father. When there's talk of suffragists, Mother just says that we 'are ladies and must remember that', but I think if she were certain of Father's approval, she'd want to vote, even if she refrained from these protests you hear about."

"Oh dear!" Julia's eyebrows shot up. "I've read about the goings on in Australia. I hope it doesn't come to that here. If they start that sort of thing in Morgan's Landing, *my* mother may be at the front of the march!"

Julia watched as Abigail fell silent and seemed to be gazing at nothing in particular.

"Perhaps you're picturing *yourself* at the front of the march, Abigail?"

Abigail laughed. "No, I was just remembering something you mentioned earlier. I don't mean to change the subject, but I do have a question."

"Yes?"

"I don't mean to pry, but I'm so interested in all your stories about your family and your town. I asked earlier when we were leaving the hotel kitchen and you did mention them again when we were sitting in Madison Square. Who are Mr. and Mrs. Schmidt? Are they friends? Or perhaps business associates?"

"Abigail," sighed Julia. "You and I have such different lives."

Chapter Six

Julia studied Abigail's face, unsure as to how their blossoming friendship might be affected by the truth concerning this aspect of her life.

"Remember telling me earlier that you're a lady of leisure?"

"Yes."

"Well... I'm not. Mr. and Mrs. Schmidt are my employers."

It was one thing to move in society circles with your wealthy parents, keeping up proper appearances at all times. It was another thing to venture into a man's world and make your way as a doctor, suffragist, or adventurer, a thing that provided a counterbalance and an excitement that might justify a woman's decision to part with society's norms. It was quite another thing to be ordinary. Julia had never felt ashamed of what she did back home, so why did this revelation make her feel so inadequate? *All this talk of independent womanhood!*

And now we're about to discuss Julia Lansing, shopgirl—more or less.

She and Abigail lived in two different worlds. Perhaps Abigail wouldn't understand. Atlanta society was far removed from the rural social life in a town as remote and mundane as Morgan's Landing. Having been raised with good manners, Abigail might appear friendly and polite, yet still consider Julia among the poor and unfortunate. Julia didn't like the idea of this pleasant part of her life being misunderstood.

Abigail seemed curious. "Your employers?"

"I work at Schmidt's Bakery."

Julia didn't detect any indication of shock or disapproval in Abigail's demeanor upon hearing the news. She took encouragement from it.

"I don't remember a time when I didn't love going into Schmidt's. I remember toddling along Main Street holding Mother's or Papa's hand while they went about their errands. The smell of Schmidt's perfumed Main Street. We always stopped in on our way home.

"The Schmidts—August and Helga—are German. Most of Morgan's Landing is. They immigrated with their families and grew up on neighboring farms. When they married, they struggled at farming, so Mrs. Schmidt baked bread to bring to town when she sold her eggs. Eventually, they opened up a small bakery in town. Word of mouth and sense of smell brings everyone into Schmidt's for breads, rolls, strudels, and stollens. By the time I was old enough to remember Mrs. Schmidt's kind face looking down at me from behind the counter, they'd already moved into a bigger store on Main Street."

Abigail sighed. "You're beginning to make me hungry! Now I'm starting to see why you were so interested in talking to the chef this morning. Tell me all about the Schmidts and what you do for them."

"Well, as you might suppose, I do a lot of baking and I take care of the customers as well." Julia paused. The expression on her friend's face lacked any trace of judgment. Encouraged by Abigail's evident desire to get to know her better, Julia felt her shoulders relax. Somehow, though she'd only known this girl since breakfast, she trusted her. "I'll confess something, Abigail. I'm Mrs. Schmidt's spoiled pet. She's indulged me shamelessly for as long as I can remember. I'd stare at all the bread and buns and pies and ask their names. Mrs. Schmidt would smile at me and cut a warm slice of bread or pull a roll fresh from the oven and top it with a pat of butter. 'Do you like?' she'd ask in her German accent. I always liked! As soon as I was old enough to run errands for Papa or Mother, I'd always try to hurry so I could stop by Schmidt's before going home. It mesmerized me —watching Mrs. Schmidt manipulate the dough. Mr. Schmidt would be there, carrying in heavy sacks of flour, doing chores, and making deliveries."

A trace of sadness appeared in the blush that had brightened Julia's cheeks. She paused as a memory surfaced, feeling as though Abigail stood with her, peeking through the bakery window and through time itself.

Abigail inclined her head, whispering, "Well...?"

"Mr. Schmidt is quite taken with me as well. They have two sons, Friedrich and Rudolph, but their little infant daughter died when only a few days old. Mother says that having an inquisitive little girl following their every move brought joy to them. Mrs. Schmidt told Mother once that my blue eyes and blonde curls were the very picture her heart carries of what her little girl would have looked like. They loved having me at the bakery."

"It sounds like they love you very much."

"I know they do," Julia smiled, "but there were rules. I had to have permission and not be late getting home. Otherwise, I'd suffer a week or so of banishment from the bakery. Mrs. Schmidt could always tell when I came in without permission. She'd hand me a buttered treat and ask, 'Do your Mama and Papa know where you are today?' If I acted sheepish and confessed being on another errand, she'd show me everything rising or cooling, tell me the names of each, and send me home. If I bounced through the door saying, 'Mother says I can stay a while as long as I'm not in the way!' she'd smile, reach for an apron, and tie it up as much as she could to fit me. I'd butter the tops of rolls and thump fresh loaves of bread—imitating Mrs. Schmidt—to see if they were ready to come out of the oven."

"It must have been like having a second family."

Abigail sounded wistful, Julia thought. Could she, despite having been raised with so many more advantages in life, be perhaps a trifle envious?

"I was kneading dough and rolling out for recipes with all the strength I had in my arms by the time I was eight years old.

At home, I'd show Mother and Papa what I learned. Papa would taste it, roll his eyes in delight and announce that someday I'd be a better cook than Mother and Mrs. Schmidt combined!"

Abigail laughed. "You were right. You *are* a spoiled pet!"

"Mother always clipped recipes from women's magazines or got some from someone she'd met that were of other origins and she'd help me make them. We tried all sorts of new things—French recipes, some Russian, and things for English teas. I'd take them to Mrs. Schmidt. She would be so proud of me. She'd say, 'This is good, *good*, my Schnucki! But I don't know how to make these things. I bake German—springerle, stollen, lebkuchen, or kerscheblotzer if the cherries are ripe—this is as fancy as I know.' She calls me Schnucki."

Abigail's eyebrows rose. "My! I have no idea what those are —except for stollen. Isn't that some type of cake?"

Julia nodded. "A Christmas cake. Springerle is an intricately molded cookie. They're very hard and you dunk them. Lebkuchen is like a gingerbread cookie and kerscheblotzer is a bread pudding made with cherries and topped with a vanilla sauce. They're all delicious." Julia paused, giving a meaningful glance to her new friend. "Well, German recipes can be rather... sturdy, if you know what I mean, Abigail. When I first became fascinated with delicate pastries and lighter baked goods, the Schmidts weren't very interested. We just kept them to nibble on behind the counter, but, when I was about twelve years old, I put a tray of croissants out on the counter one day. I didn't charge for them—just offered one to customers as they came in."

Julia smiled at the special memory. How nice of Abigail to listen to her ramblings. She wondered if, up until this point, Abigail had given much consideration to such things other than deciding which item to choose from a menu.

"The customers who sampled them were impressed. Some even ordered them by the dozen!" Julia smiled with satisfaction. "After that, Mrs. Schmidt would often say, 'I finish the bread, my Schnucki! You start the croissants!' She began to give me just a little money. She said I earned it. It was such a small amount that Papa and Mother didn't mind—Papa especially, as I always brought home leftovers. Everything went along just fine until I was fourteen. Then, when things changed, Papa nearly came apart at the seams!"

"What happened?"

"Well, Mrs. Schmidt's sister had a baby. It was her first and she had trouble. The baby was small and needed constant care. Mrs. Schmidt needed to go stay with them for a while. I remember coming into the bakery one day after school and there she was, behind the counter, pounding on a ball of dough with tears running down her cheeks, her soul in misery. She wanted to be at her sister's side, but the bakery was their livelihood. I knew what I had to do. I put my arms around her, told her I'd be right back, and ran home as fast as I could. I took Mother to the workshop with me. I cried the whole time. I begged them to let me have time off from school to keep the bakery open. Mr. Schmidt would stay to keep supplies on hand and wait on customers, but someone had to do the baking. My parents had reservations, but they realized the same thing I did. What if something happened to Mrs. Schmidt's sister or the baby and Mrs. Schmidt wasn't there?

"I'll never forget Mother saying, 'Sometimes the Lord doesn't give you three days to pray, does He? I suppose we need to ask ourselves what He would do and do it.'

"Papa kissed me on the forehead. He said, 'I think what Jesus would do is start baking bread. You go tell the Schmidts and I'll go over to the school and straighten it all out with the teacher.'

"I ran back to the bakery and told the Schmidts that Papa and Mother insisted. I know the Schmidts are very stoic and don't like to cry, but they both surely did that day. That was the hardest I've ever worked in my life, but it was worth it. I kept up with my lessons every night and baked all day, every day, for three weeks."

"You really meant it when you said you weren't a lady of leisure. I'm glad you could keep up with your studies. I wouldn't like to think of you sacrificing your education." Abigail gave Julia a quizzical look. "Is that what made your papa come apart at the seams? I mean, was it because you had all that responsibility?"

"Oh, no. It was what happened about a week after Mrs. Schmidt got home. I'd been at the bakery for years, but never officially employed there. You know how fathers can be if they think it might appear they can't provide for their families."

Abigail gave an understanding nod. "Yes, I know exactly what you mean."

Julia shocked herself with her imitation of Papa. "Absolutely not! Over my dead body!" She puffed out her chest in a subdued version of him, with his voice raised and eyes bulging.

"Oh, Julia! If your poor papa could see you... you really *shouldn't!*" Abigail feigned graciousness in an attempt to display good breeding, but Julia took her ill-concealed giggles as an encouragement. The mixture of playfulness and goodness in Abigail made Julia feel safe. She cast her normal reservations aside.

Pouring out her life story to a girl who had been a total stranger until breakfast this morning would have seemed impossible yesterday. *This is ridiculous! Why am I doing this?* Other than her parents, her best friend, Bertina, and, occasionally, Mrs. Schmidt, Julia couldn't think of anyone with whom she'd behaved this way.

"Mother had her doubts at first, but she was willing to look at the situation from all sides. She had confidence in my ability —they both did—and that made me feel good. I remember being perched on the settee, twiddling the fringe on a pillow. It's a wonder I didn't snatch the poor thing bare, watching Papa pace back and forth, blustering because the Schmidts had offered me a *regular* job. I knew I'd have to wait for him to get over the shock."

"So he was set against it? I'm sure *my* father would be. Sometimes I think he has my life all planned out. I can't imagine what would happen if *I* wanted to... Oh, Julia!"

Abigail gasped. "I didn't mean to imply that there's any difference..."

Julia patted Abigail's hand. "I know you didn't. I suppose all fathers are like that. Papa gave me a sound lecture on how this just isn't the way things are meant to be. 'First your mother! Now *you*! This whole town's going to get the idea that I can't support my family! Why can't you just do what you like at home, like other women?' Goodness! If I did as much baking at home as I liked, we'd all be fat as pigs in a month's time."

Abigail laughed. "Then how did it all come about? You say you're working there now."

"Reasoning... and waiting. Mother tried to tell him it wasn't the end of the world. I stayed quiet for the most part, but, when I saw a chance, I'd remind Papa of things he already knew. I'd be finished with school soon. I'm an excellent cook. I sew to a certain degree, and I'm moderately musical. I love to read and learn. I considered a nearby ladies' college, but was uncertain what I wanted to study. Besides, money for tuition would have been a terrible strain. In my heart, I wanted to be near Mother and Papa and someday raise a family of my own. Till that happens, I want to do something besides attend social functions, read books, and help out at home. I wanted something to take joy in—something that uses my God-given abilities. Working at Schmidt's was perfect, but not in Papa's world."

"But you are working there, so I assume he did come around?"

"Yes. It didn't take long. Mother has a way with Papa. She

pointed out that, though he's never failed to provide for us, his business doesn't always allow for the little extras—things women don't really need, but make us happy. My job at the bakery would provide for those. I suppose Papa's main concern was whether or not people would see me on Main Street in the bakery every day and think that his daughter had to work for hire. It was different than having me spend time there because I enjoyed it. Having the Schmidts drop a coin or two into my hand in appreciation was a whole different thing to Papa than the thought of my *having* to go to work!"

Abigail sighed. "Why do you suppose it is that people think that way? Little boys grow up imagining what they'll be and no one tells *them* to put the thought out of their head!"

"So true, Abigail," Julia nodded, "and *so* aggravating. Anyway, Mother was torn between wanting me to be happy and feeling that it might not reflect well on us. Of course, there are women who work out in public, such as the postmistress or the milliner, but they're spinsters or widows without family. My dearest friend works at her parents' drugstore. Mrs. Schmidt and her husband run the bakery together and live upstairs, so that's understandable. All in all, I think what finally began to sway Papa was knowing that even though Mother could make me all the dresses and underthings I needed, there are just some things—shoes, hats, and other such finery—that might be harder to come by at times when his inventions are... incomplete... and other business is slow. He knew I'd need things to fill my hope chest and he didn't want me turning down invitations because I had holes in my shoes."

"I should say not!"

It seemed to Julia that Abigail's shock at the idea might be mixed with a little sympathy. *I've done it now. Why have I said all these things—to convince Abigail we're poverty-stricken?*

"Oh! I mean because I didn't have the *proper* shoes. I don't know exactly what I'm trying to say, Abigail. We've got no intentions of putting on airs and making people back home feel like we're any better than anybody else, but we certainly are just as good as anybody else. It's a small town. Savannah is fifteen times the size of Morgan's Landing! And your Atlanta? It's not Saint Louis, but I still can't imagine living there. Our need for finery isn't... I mean... things are much more simple where I live."

Abigail stood, sighing. Julia watched her walk a few yards away. *You should've kept your mouth shut, Julia! You're embarrassing yourself!*

She waited a moment, her insides churning, before joining her. At last, she walked toward Abigail, dragging the silence along like a sack of coals too heavy to lift. The distance between her world and Abigail's had been measured. She'd soon discover how far apart they were.

Julia jumped when Abigail turned to face her with eyes flashing.

"Sometimes the rules that govern propriety make me want to scream, Julia! Why can't a person's decision be theirs and theirs alone? We can't let other people rule our hearts. We must let peace rule our hearts. Your true friends will know why you're at the bakery, and those who aren't—well, it simply doesn't matter what they think. We can do any number of things out of pure enjoyment or out of need, for that matter, if we should fall on hard times. You love to bake and to see others enjoy it. Our parents should be happy with what makes us happy."

Julia smiled, the weight lifting from her soul. "It's as if you were in the room, Abigail. That's exactly what my parents decided. That is, after Papa kept us in suspense by praying about it for three days. I worked after school at first, and now I go in early and stay till noon five days a week. The Schmidts are more than gracious. I take time off any time we travel or I have a social engagement. Their boys are busy working at the mill, but they stop by often and help out. They plan to buy the mill as soon as they can, and besides," she smiled, "customers are getting spoiled to my recipes and ask for them more and more. I enjoy it. I really do."

"Why Julia," Abigail's eyes sparkled, "you're a modern-day example of independent womanhood! You're an artist, just like my father and your mother, and I'm starting to think your father must be as well!"

"Goodness! And all this time I just thought I liked to bake. You know, Abigail, I was so anxious for the Allens to return so that I could get away from the hotel, but now I'm almost wishing that I had more time there. I'm sure a week isn't going to be enough time to learn all I want to learn from Chef Plouff and not nearly enough time to get to know you."

"Speaking of time," Abigail said as she gave Julia's elbow a gentle tug and they resumed their walk, "if we tell our life stories all day, we'll never get over to Congress Street to see that dresser set."

Chapter Seven

"WHAT IS THAT MARVELOUS SCENT?" Julia hurried ahead, peeking into the doorway of a shop. "Are you as hungry as I am, Abigail? If so, I think I may have found the perfect place to get a bite to eat."

Abigail read the sign above the shop. "Bernbaum's. Let's give it a try." Soon they were seated on another bench, enjoying their lunch from brown paper bags.

"My first *delicatessen,*" Julia said as she wrapped both hands more carefully around the bread in an attempt to keep the filling inside. "I don't know how I missed this on my last trip to Savannah. I'm so glad you invited me on this walk, Abigail."

Abigail swallowed a bite. "I'm glad I did, too, but you're the one who saw it first. Mmm... this meat, tomato, lettuce, onion... It's heavenly, I'll admit."

"This bread is delicious. I wonder if I could get some of these recipes."

"Is that all you ever think about?"

"Well, it's not *all* I ever think about, but I'm sure it must seem that way to you."

"I know *I* think about more than just food." Abigail's eyes darted toward the street. Julia followed the meaningful gesture, blinking as a bicycle flew past. She stifled a little gasp as she wondered if she recognized the rider and, perhaps, if he'd recognized her.

"Did you say something?" Abigail asked.

"No. Nothing. It's just that that bicycle went by so fast it gave me a start."

"The man on that bicycle. I can't be certain because he has a cap on today, but I think he was at the hotel last night. I saw him looking toward your table several times during dinner. The only reason I noticed was because my mother had just drawn my attention to your table to tell me who I'd be breakfasting with this morning. I thought perhaps you and your mother knew him, but his party left without saying anything."

Julia fought the urge to scan the horizon. "No. No, I have no idea who he is."

"He's very nice looking, don't you think?"

"I... I didn't get a very good look at him."

Julia attempted an air of indifference as she wiped her mouth and gathered her trash and stood. Abigail seemed to take her cue and followed suit.

"Let's be off. I feel myself getting closer and closer to that dresser set."

"I know it sounds piggish of me, but if you think you would be able to share half, I'd love to taste one of those bagels people keep coming out of Bernbaum's with."

Abigail chuckled. "Only for a friend, Julia."

As they walked, Julia struggled to keep her thoughts off the bicycle and its rider and attempted to distract herself by focusing on her lunch. *What's the secret to these delicious bagels? What would Mrs. Schmidt's views be on boiling bread? Was that man on the bicycle the same man—the man whose hand I held last night? Where is he now? If we keep walking this direction, will we see him again?* With a little sigh, she abandoned her futile efforts and let her eyes roam the street, hoping Abigail would assume her to be window shopping.

THE WINDOW of the shop held all manner of things strategically positioned to capture the eyes of passing ladies. While purses, gloves, hatpins, and beautiful hair combs enticed them to enter, the dresser set stood out among all the other items one might dream of having displayed on one's vanity. Once inside, they stroked the velvet case, touching the comb, brush, hair receiver, nail buffer, powder jar and other items that made up the set. Accented with mother-of-pearl, each rested in its own satin-lined indention.

"Oh, it's even more beautiful than you described!" Julia said. "Are you going to get it?"

"I shouldn't. I'll feel terribly spoiled. It's not as if I don't have a dresser set already. But, Julia, I like it even better than when I first saw it."

Julia knew Abigail would buy the dresser set. Money came easily to Abigail and, though Julia nearly always struggled over spending her hard-earned money on purchasing frivolities, she certainly didn't begrudge anyone else's ability to do so and found it amusing to watch Abigail's mental debate over it. While Abigail fondled the nail buffer and hair receiver, Julia reached for the comb. As she turned it over in her hands, she drew Abigail's attention to a tiny scratch on the mother-of-pearl that ran along the spine of the comb. The storekeeper offered to retrieve another set from stock room.

"This might take a little time, Julia. I'll wait here and you go on. I want you to see as many shops as possible before it's time to go back to the hotel. I'll catch up in a bit."

Abigail seemed determined to ignore Julia's protests, so she left the shop and resumed her stroll alone. Pausing at the window of a furniture store, she admired a large dining table. Mother would like it. Assorted chairs and small tables sat outside, marked for sale. In large letters across the window were the words, "James Woodson—Undertaker". At the bottom of the window ran a line of smaller print, stating, "Furniture and Carpentry". *Ugh! The worst thing about being in the furniture-making business.* Along with items used for practicality and pleasure in everyday life, furniture makers also met people's needs in death. Through the open front door, she could see all the way to the back, where a man worked with vigor sanding a coffin.

Smells of wood and varnish, mixed with particles of sawdust, floated out through the door, tickling Julia's nose. She backed away from the door, fumbling in her bag for her handkerchief. As she raised it to her nose just in time for the inevitable sneeze, she heard a tinkling sound and looked down to see the key to the hotel room at her feet. *It must have been in the folds of my handkerchief.* Julia stooped and grasped it, then jerked her head toward a squeaking noise. A little boy approached, pedaling his bicycle as fast as his legs could go. Julia hurried to stand before he could collide with her stooped form. The bicycle wheel rolled over the hem of her skirt as she attempted to jerk it out of the way, tumbling boy and bicycle off the sidewalk and into the street.

Julia ran to the boy, bending over to help him as he struggled to get out from under the heavy bicycle. She lifted it and placed it to the side, wincing at the sight of his bloody knees and the cut on his head.

"Oh, I'm so sorry! I was trying to get out of your way. Let me help you. You're hurt."

"I'm not hurt. I'm fine!" he blubbered, wiping his face with hands dirty from the street while fresh tears etched muddy tracks down his cheeks.

"Come now, you're not a bit fine. Look at your legs!"

The little boy jerked away. A few passersby, drawn by the commotion, paused to stare. The man who had been sanding the coffin appeared in the doorway.

"What did I tell you, Marcus Levitt?! I told you over and over not to ride that bicycle on the sidewalk. You could have hurt the nice lady! Now you will learn. *Now* you will learn!" He turned and disappeared into the store.

Julia extended a hand. "So, your name is Marcus. Come, we must get out of the street."

"Leave me alone! I'm all right!" he snapped between hiccups.

A shadow fell across them. Julia looked up as a deep voice spoke.

"You don't look all right to me. Would you hold this, miss?"

Julia took the doctor's bag being offered to her and watched as a tall, fair-haired man scooped Marcus Levitt into his arms. Carrying him to the front of the furniture store, he sat him on a straight-backed chair among benches and other items for sale. Julia put the doctor's bag on one of the nearby benches and watched. Curious onlookers continued on their way, satisfied now that a doctor had taken charge. As Julia studied him, she thought he seemed fairly young to have completed medical school.

"Let me see," said the doctor, kneeling to move hair aside in order to examine the cut on Marcus's head. His presence and authority seemed to calm the squirming boy. After examining the bloody knees, he looked Marcus in the eye. "You'll be just fine, but you need to be cleaned up. Why don't you come along over to my office and let me wash that out and put a little medicine on it. Your knees need to be wrapped."

Marcus let out a wail and tried to run away. The doctor caught him and sat him back in the chair.

"What's wrong? You're not scared of going to my office, are you?"

"No, I'm not scared," Marcus sniffled. "But you give doctors money and I don't have any money. I gotta go home!" He began to cry.

The doctor gave Julia a nod. "Oh, well, in that case, we'll do it a different way. It won't cost any money at all."

"It won't?" Marcus seemed suspicious. "Will it hurt?"

"Not if this nice lady helps us. Now you sit still." Rising to his feet, the doctor called inside the store. "Jim! Can you get me a dish pan of water and a couple of clean rags?"

"Sure, Doc!"

"I'll just bet you didn't know that I only charge for cleaning up wounds when you come to my office. Why, if you're right out here on the street like this, and if I have someone here to do part of the work, like this nice lady, your mama won't have to pay me a cent. How about it?"

"Well, if it won't hurt."

"You'll feel much better when it's cleaned up and bandaged. All my patients tell me so."

The doctor turned to Julia. "Would you mind holding him while I bandage him?"

"Of course," Julia replied.

"Now let's have the lady sit right here in the chair and you sit on her lap, just so."

Julia slipped into the chair. As the doctor put Marcus in her lap, he whispered in her ear, "Hang on to him, no matter what."

Julia nodded.

"Thanks," he said, taking the basin of water and rags from Jim. Reaching into the bag, he pulled out rolls of gauze bandage, scissors, and a small bottle of medicine. He held it up to the light. "Plenty of bandages, but looks like this is empty. Now, Marcus... that's your name, isn't it? Here's what we'll do. You sit right here with this nice lady, Miss, uh..."

"Lansing," Julia answered.

"You sit right here with Miss Lansing and get your face washed while I run to my office for some more of this medicine. Is that agreeable?"

Marcus nodded. The doctor rose, turning his attention to Julia. His brown eyes and blond hair stood out in contrast to his tanned face.

He offered his hand. Julia shook it briefly, hurriedly slipping her arm back around Marcus.

"William Hancock," he said. "A pleasure to meet you, Miss Lansing. I'm sorry we couldn't be properly introduced."

"It seems quite understandable, considering the circumstances," Julia smiled. "It's very nice to meet you, Dr. Hancock."

"I'll be right back," he called over his shoulder as he disappeared down the street.

Julia removed her gloves, dipped one of the rags into the basin, and began to wash Marcus's face. In the doctor's absence, the patient was not so docile as before. He squirmed and twisted.

"No! Stop! I wanna go home!" he fussed, trying to wriggle free.

Julia tightened her grip on Marcus, steeling herself for the fight. Though unwilling to admit defeat to Doctor Hancock, she considered the impossible task of getting his face washed with one arm while holding him securely with the other. His bloody, wagging head threatened to brush against her white blouse. His legs flailed in all directions. Her new skirt had quickly become a favorite of hers and, though she sympathized with Marcus's reluctance to let her touch his tender scrapes, Julia found herself maneuvering every which way she could to avoid blood stains on it.

"Now, Marcus, you sit still! Maybe you'd like to pretend you're Doctor Hancock and put some of this on your legs." Fumbling inside the doctor's bag on the bench beside her, she pulled out a roll of bandages. It seemed better to have it all unwound by the time Doctor Hancock returned than to have ruined clothes or a missing patient. "Settle down now, Marcus, and help the doctor!" Julia waved the bandages in front of his face.

"Here now, you're not disobeying doctor's orders, are you?" A soothing, masculine voice spoke.

Julia looked up. A man leaned a bicycle against a post before squatting in front of Marcus. His blue eyes caught

Julia's for a moment before he turned his attention back to the boy.

"Say, did you wreck your bicycle? Let's have a look at it. Did you inspect it for damage already, sir?"

The question seemed to calm Marcus a bit. "Not yet," he sniffled.

The young man took off his cap and ran a hand over his thick, brown curls before tossing the cap onto the bench.

Julia's heart began to race. *It's him!* The unexpected feeling at the sight of this stranger, whose hand she'd held the night before, made her feel a little silly.

The young man began examining the bicycle with an intense air that made Julia want to chuckle.

"Well, sir," he reported after examining the cycle, "I believe your bicycle is just fine. Looks like it's in good enough shape to get you home. I wish I could say the same for you. You're a mess. I think you need the doctor's attention."

"Oh, Adam! Adam Cole, is that you?"

A middle-aged lady hurried across the street.

"Yes, it is. Why, Mrs. Greenwood, how nice to see you!" He stood and smiled at the lady, giving her his full attention.

"I thought so. I said to myself, 'There goes Charlotte Cole's boy or I am horribly mistaken'. Or," she chuckled, "maybe I should say, 'There goes *Doctor* Cole'. We're so proud of your accomplishments, Adam."

"Well, I haven't accomplished yet, Mrs. Greenwood. I've more schooling to do before you can call me 'Doctor'. I'm going back to Boston soon to resume my studies."

"Oh, I know you'll make us all proud. I must rush, but do tell your dear mother I send my warmest regards. I must write to her sometime soon."

"I will. And now I'm afraid I need to see if I can comfort this poor accident victim."

After a few more parting pleasantries, Adam turned back to Julia and Marcus.

Marcus writhed in Julia's arms. "I want my bicycle. I want to go home."

Julia looked up at Adam as she wrestled the boy anew. "He needs medical attention first. We're waiting for a bottle of medicine to arrive so we can get these wounds cleaned and wrapped."

Adam grabbed a small, three-legged stool and sat down. He lifted Marcus's chin.

"Look at me, Marcus!"

Marcus stopped twisting at the sound of Adam's compassionate, but firm, voice.

"Have you ever been to a doctor before?" Adam asked.

"No. Mama has. And my sister, once."

"Did the doctor help them? Did they get better after they saw the doctor?"

"Yes."

"Then you know they would want you to do the same thing they did, don't you? If your mama were here, would she ask you to do what the doctor says?"

"Yes," Marcus whispered.

"And it's an extra special treat to have a nice lady like this to help you, isn't it?"

Marcus nodded.

Adam patted Marcus's shoulder. "No more thrashing about. After all, you never know... Perhaps God has sent an angel to help you. Did you know the Bible says that sometimes we entertain angels unawares?" He smiled as his eyes met Julia's.

Marcus craned his neck, staring at Julia with awe. "We do?"

"Don't you think she looks like *she* might be an angel?"

"Maybe."

Marcus quieted. Julia sensed that the fight was over. She lowered her eyes and hoped the flush that rushed to her cheeks the moment Adam referred to her as an angel would be interpreted by him as a natural result of wrangling Marcus.

"Thank you, Mr. Cole," she smiled, succumbing to the urge to look into his eyes.

"I do what I can." Adam stood, returning the stool to its place amongst the other furniture. "It looks like he's already in capable hands. I must be getting along to an appointment." He turned to Marcus, extending his right hand, and smiled when the boy shook it. "Good day, Marcus. I'll be in Savannah for a little while yet, and I know I'll see you back on your bicycle, good as new, in no time." He turned to Julia. "Good day... I'm sorry, there wasn't much of a chance to be introduced, was there?"

"No, there wasn't. I'm Julia Lansing."

"Well, Dr. Lansing, I'll leave you to your patient. It's been very nice meeting you. I'm sure you're glad to be dealing with a case where the injuries are more emotional than physical."

Julia gave a start. She glanced at the doctor's bag on the bench next to her and the roll of bandages in her hand. She could see how Adam Cole might presume her to be a doctor. An odd mixture of feelings rushed over her. This new sense of inferiority that seemed to plague her in the presence of Savannah's society elite mixed with her natural sense of humor. How could *anyone* possibly mistake *her* for a doctor? Considering that he was in medical school himself, it seemed all the more ridiculous.

Julia stifled an outright giggle. Perhaps she should venture into the entire explanation, but the likelihood that she would ever see Adam Cole again seemed remote. She gave in to a sudden urge to play along.

"Oh, yes! But I'm sure you must have some idea of the trials involved in a life spent in alleviating the pain and suffering we see in our fellowman."

Adam met her gaze with a quizzical expression. "Yes, I suppose I do. Well, good day." He put on his cap, mounted the bicycle, and rode away.

Julia chuckled inwardly at the idea that she'd been mistaken for the ultimate example of independent womanhood. Adam Cole probably came across these women all the time at school in Boston. *How funny! The closest I'll ever come to surgery will be carving designs in my pie crust.* She envisioned herself covering a loaf of rising bread dough with a piece of cheesecloth and, giving it a gentle pat and telling it to get some rest, promising to return in an hour to see how the swelling was coming along.

As Julia picked up the cloth and wiped Marcus's face, a sudden feeling of embarrassment washed over her. Why hadn't she called after Adam? She recalled his expression as he made his parting remarks and should have realized that perhaps he missed her attempt at humor. Now there seemed no way to make amends. His being at the Wentworth Hotel might bring him into contact with some of Mother's customers. Having had her fill of embarrassment with Senator Thornhill, she cringed at the thought of Adam innocently telling people she'd introduced herself as a doctor!

Marcus did not allow, however, for her to dwell on Adam Cole. He'd calmed as she washed his face and now talked of his bicycle-riding abilities. He took the bandages from Julia and began unrolling them. Julia focused her attention on him until Dr. Hancock returned with the bottle of medicine. Abigail appeared in the distance as well, carrying a parcel.

I'd better not tell Abigail about this just yet. She thought it best to get to know Abigail a bit better first. It was one thing to discuss society's steps toward women's advancement and quite another to tell foolish lies about yourself for the fun of it. Julia yearned for the peace and quiet of her hotel room.

Doctor Hancock, busy washing the wounds, seemed unaware of Abigail's approach. Julia could see by the look on Abigail's face that she wondered what sort of events had unfolded while she'd been buying the dresser set.

Abigail sat down on the bench, watching as the doctor put

a couple of rags under Marcus's legs to protect Julia's skirt. Marcus, having made a show of bravery during the cleansing of his wounds, clasped Julia's hand when the medicine was applied. She gave his forehead a kiss as tears rolled down his cheeks.

Doctor Hancock finished wrapping the bandages. "There now—good as new! You get your bicycle and run along now. Walk it home—don't ride. Tell your mama there's no charge and thank Miss Lansing for being your nurse."

"Thank you, Miss... Angel!" Marcus kissed Julia's cheek, hurried to his bicycle, and steered it in a crooked path down the street.

Julia, feeling far from an angel, felt her face redden. She felt compelled to offer some explanation.

"Someone else happened along and told Marcus that sometimes God sends an angel to help you. I suppose he's a little confused."

"Well, I don't think he's far off the mark!" William Hancock smiled warmly. "You were a great help to me, Miss Lansing. Are you on a temporary angelic mission here in Savannah, or do you live and walk among us?"

"You're embarrassing me, Doctor Hancock. I am here on a visit with my mother. We've just arrived from Missouri. We have plans to stay about a month."

"It would be my pleasure if we meet again sometime during your visit. Although, I have to confess that it would be much more enjoyable if we met socially instead of in the line of duty."

"Yes, it certainly would." Julia faltered. In the moments

since she'd parted with Abigail, events had passed in such a rush and now she felt incapable of any coherent response to the doctor's attentions. "I'd like to introduce my friend to you. Miss Abigail Hadley, this is Doctor William Hancock."

"Miss Hadley." Doctor Hancock tipped his hat toward Abigail.

Abigail nodded and offered a polite greeting, her eyes wide with questioning.

Bending over his bag, he placed the bottle of medicine and bandages inside. "I'll have to be running along, ladies, I have a... Well, what have we here?" Stooping to reach between the bench and Julia's chair, he rose again with a few items in his hands. "Say, is this what I think it is? Is it yours?"

Julia jumped to her feet. "Oh! Yes, that's mine. I suppose it got knocked off the bench. My bag must have come open when it fell."

Handing Julia her handbag and gloves, the doctor kept the remaining item in his hands, turning it over as he examined it. His eyebrows rose as he lifted his eyes from the Chicago Palm Protector to Julia's face.

"I've never actually seen one of these—only the advertisements. Have you fired it?"

"Well, of course, I've fired it. I hope you don't think I'd be carrying around a gun I'd never fired. That would be dangerous."

As he turned the weapon over in his hand, Julia caught a glimpse of the safety lever. It was still on. She offered up a silent prayer of thanks.

"I suppose I'm just a bit surprised to discover something like this in the hands of an angel," he smiled. "I hope you didn't come to Savannah thinking that you'd need it at every turn. After all, you're the one who lives on the brink of the wild west."

Julia took the gun from his outstretched hand. "We're fairly civilized out in the middle of Missouri. Most of us have manners enough to refrain from shooting people who make fun of us."

"Then I think I'd best be going before I unknowingly violate some western code and pay the price for it! Thank you for letting me take a look at it."

Wishing both ladies a pleasant day, he picked up his bag and walked away.

Julia felt the blush in her cheeks deepen at the doctor's parting smile, partly because he showed such attentiveness in front of Abigail and partly because she wondered what he'd think if he knew she'd just been leading someone to believe her to be a doctor.

Checking the contents of her bag, she stole a glance at Abigail, noting the mischief that played across her features. *Handkerchief. Money. Room key. Everything's here.* Checking the safety lever on the Palm Protector, she dropped it into the bag, brushed her skirt, and pulled on her gloves. She braced herself, for Abigail's eyebrows had risen to the point that Julia thought they might possibly collide with the brim of her hat.

"My, you certainly know how to make an impression on the men of Savannah! And I thought my purchase would be our biggest excitement for the day! Tell me, Julia, what went on while I was buying this dresser set? I saw the man from dinner last night kneeling before you and before I could *blink* he was gone and that handsome doctor was there in his place, calling you an angel! Not only that, but I find that in the middle of it all, you've tossed a gun, if that thing really is a gun, on the sidewalk! I want every detail."

"First of all, Abigail, it was my fault that little Marcus fell off his bicycle, so I was only trying to help the doctor."

Julia told the whole story, with the exception of her failed attempt at humor, as they continued along the street. Though Abigail praised her efforts in assisting Dr. Hancock and comforting Marcus, Julia took little encouragement from it. Adam Cole didn't deserve to be misled and she had no idea how to correct her blunder.

"And you can be certain of one thing, Abigail. I'm no angel."

Though Abigail remained in the mood for chatting and shopping, Julia feared that she'd ceased to be good company. When Abigail asked if she were tired and wanted to return to her room, Julia readily adopted the excuse to escape to her room and think everything through. Any optimism she had held onto in hopes that the scandal involving Senator Thornhill might fade quickly once the gossips in Savannah's society found something else to feast upon evaporated. Julia now realized that unless Adam Cole somehow kept his presumptions to himself, the next piece of news to spread like a prairie fire amongst Savannah's elite would be the fact that Beatrice

Lansing's daughter had the habit of presenting herself as a doctor.

Though not in the habit of withholding things from Mother, Julia decided to keep her blunder to herself for now. She'd gotten herself into this and considered it her duty to get herself out of it. Mother had enough things on her mind.

JULIA REMOVED her hat and shoes and lay across the bed. She'd been craving this time alone. Later, when Mother arrived and revealed their plans for the evening, she'd have to dress for supper. After staring at the ceiling for a moment or two, her eyelids fell, forcing a tear to trickle down to each ear. Her mental exhaustion far outweighed the physical exertion of exploring Savannah. In two days, she had encountered more mishaps and upsets here than she had managed to experience in two decades in Morgan's Landing. Julia let out a moan of distress and rolled over onto her stomach, grabbing her pillow and giving it punch before crossing her arms over it. If only that senator hadn't been in the bath. If only she hadn't dropped the soap. If only he hadn't aroused the whole hotel with his bellowing! Then, to stand in the middle of the hotel lobby and clutch at a strange man's hand. If that wasn't enough, she'd topped it off today with her poor attempt at humor and convinced the same stranger she was a doctor—a thing he'd very likely, in all innocence, tell anyone he happened to know in Savannah. Even if her reputation managed to survive after being deemed a hussy and a liar, she doubted she could count on Doctor Hancock to spare it from utter destruction. The fact that she carried loaded pistols around and flung them at random on the street would certainly be of interest to anyone who inquired as to what he knew of this Julia Lansing they'd seen him conversing with.

Julia sat up and leaned to her right until she could see her pitiful reflection in the mirror on the wardrobe door. "You're a wreck!" she spoke aloud with a catch in her voice. "Stop sniveling!"

Having dealt with bullies at school, teasing by the Schmidt boys, and any number of cranky customers at the bakery, Julia had usually taken it all in stride. She'd never found herself prone to emotional outbursts, nor did she have a habit of running to her room and wallowing in tears. The tears were here now, however. There was something about Adam Cole—something that seemed to worsen the misunderstanding. If she'd done the same thing to someone who put on airs or someone arrogant, she may have felt different. Among all the strangers in the hotel dining room, hadn't his been the only pair of eyes that hadn't judged her? Well, he had something to judge *now*, didn't he? Didn't he soothe Marcus with the same kindness and gentle voice as last night? And he'd referred to her as an angel! Adam Cole would soon find out that she was far from it.

Julia twisted the pillow in her hands before flinging it at the reflection that sat there looking pitiful and offering no solutions. She gasped, then closed her eyes in gratitude that the pillow hadn't burst. Having to explain to the hotel why her room was filled with feathers would have been the last straw.

Julia walked to the wardrobe, picked up the pillow, and tossed it onto the bed. "Oh, why am I getting myself all worked up over this?" she muttered as she busied herself with straightening the bedclothes. "Why these tears over a complete stranger—over words spoken in jest?"

The tears, paying no heed, ran down her cheeks and Julia crumpled over the bed again.

"Please, Lord," she whispered, "don't ever let me say any more stupid things because I feel inferior. And *please*, could I see Adam once more so I can tell him the truth?"

Julia curled up in a ball. Her head ached.

Chapter Eight

JULIA PAUSED at the foot of the staircase, making a quick search of the lobby. There being no sign of Abigail, she chose the most secluded area to wait to join her for their morning walk. She still shrank from the idea of placing herself in a position that might cause more talk than necessary among the hotel guests. Some people loved a good rumor, hoping every scandalous one would turn out to be true. A boisterous greeting from Senator Thornhill just now would only reignite the flame of gossip. Approaching a settee in the corner, Julia paused, listening to a soft sniffling sound. Tiptoeing closer, she saw a lady huddled on the settee and recognized her as the bride who had been escorted to her room along with her husband by Marty two days ago. The incident with Senator Thornhill had wiped the newlyweds' existence from her mind.

Recalling her own recent tears and embarrassment, Julia

decided to leave the poor thing to her own private sorrow. She took a step back and, after searching for another seat, settled for one a little closer to the stairs. Though the lobby clock assured her it had been a mere ten minutes, it seemed like hours before she caught sight of Abigail strolling down the staircase.

Julia rushed to her. "Good morning, Abigail," she whispered.

Abigail took a glance back up the stairs and then across the lobby. "Why are we whispering?"

"Oh, I don't suppose we need to. It's just that there's someone in the corner alcove who is so upset. I hate to have her think there are prying eyes."

As they strolled to the front entrance and out the door, Abigail glanced back. "I see her now. Do you know her, Julia?"

"Not really. If I recall, her name is Beaumont. All I know is what I overheard when Marty helped them get settled in their room. She's on her honeymoon, but it certainly doesn't seem like a very happy one."

"Poor thing. If I see her again, I'll be sure to smile and speak to her."

Exploring streets and shops they hadn't had time for the previous day took well into mid-morning when the two strolled again to Forsyth Park. After an hour or more they came to an agreement that an abundance of fresh air and the sound of the fountain's rushing water stirred their appetites. Taking yesterday's path and picking up their pace, they soon found themselves standing once again in front of Bernbaum's Delicatessen.

Next door stood a shop boasting a window full of sweets. They debated the advantages of each.

"Poor little fellow!" Julia whispered. "I see he still has both knees bandaged!"

"Why, it's Marcus!" Abigail exclaimed. "Wasn't that his name, Julia?"

"Yes," said Julia, "and that must be his mother and sister."

Marcus, recognizing Julia, broke into a smile, running to greet her as fast as his sore knees would allow.

"Miss Angel! Mama, this is Miss Angel!"

Marcus's mother smiled. "I am happy to meet you, Miss Angel. My name is Hannah Levitt. Marcus told me how you helped him yesterday. I'm glad that I'm now able to thank you."

"I was glad to help, Mrs. Levitt. I'm afraid it was partly my fault that your son took a fall. My name is Julia Lansing. I suppose that it's due to another helper's bit of Bible lesson that Marcus refers to me as 'Miss Angel'. I hope he's feeling better today."

"Oh, yes! So much that I had to hang his bicycle on a peg to keep him from riding it. He's very proud of it and wants to ride it well. It was the last gift his Papa gave him before he died." She swallowed hard. "This is my daughter, Rebekah."

Rebekah appeared to be about eight years old. She seemed painfully shy, but smiled when the ladies greeted her, as though it made her feel quite grown up.

Julia glanced up the street. Even at a distance, there was no mistaking the brisk and bouncing form. "Why, it's Mother!

Mrs. Levitt, do take a moment and let me introduce you to my mother."

Mrs. Levitt seemed withdrawn when confronted with Mother's exuberance, but Julia could see that Mother was being studied from head to toe. Mother seemed to be giving the Levitts an equal analysis in return.

"Look at their clothing, Julia!" Mother whispered after the Levitts had gone into the delicatessen. "Most people who can't afford nice fabrics sew their children's clothing up, not to mention their own, like feed sacks, but take a good look at the Levitts!"

Julia hadn't given it much thought, but the Levitts did seem to have a distinctive quality about them. She looked at Mother, who seemed to be lost in some sort of reverie.

"The little boy's clothes are somewhat threadbare," Mother murmured, "but well made. Rebekah's little dress wasn't a bit worn, but you could tell the fabric was cheap."

"Well, after all, Mother, it seems they've lost their father. I'm sure they're doing the best they can under the circumstances. I thought her little dress was very pretty."

Mother turned to her companions as though she'd just been reminded of their existence. "Oh, I didn't mean... I mean, I wasn't making rude remarks about the way they dress. What I mean is, that there goes a woman who is not only quite the seamstress, but has an eye for design. Rebekah's dress *is* pretty, *not* because of the fabric, but because of the *style* and cut. That lady understands how to make *anything* look stylish!" Pausing, she gazed into the delicatessen window for a moment before turning to Julia and Abigal with a smile. "You girls have a wonderful time. I'll see you back at the hotel for supper."

It now appeared that Mother had developed a sudden need for something from Bernbaum's. Julia stood with Abigail, watching as she scurried into the establishment with an air of purpose.

"What do you suppose your mother is going to do?" Abigail asked.

Julia stood silent for a moment. "Abigail, I really can't say."

TIME PASSED QUICKLY FOR JULIA. She rose early each morning to join Chef Plouff in the kitchen. By the time Mother and the Hadleys came down to breakfast, her latest creation would be ready for sampling. Afterward, she enjoyed her excursions with Abigail. Earlier visions of spending hours alone in her hotel room evaporated and each time Julia addressed her letters to Morgan's Landing and delivered them to the hotel desk, she hoped her best friend, Bertina Drexler, wouldn't feel slighted. Her promises to describe her daily activities in Savannah had been reduced to sporadic, one-page greetings scribbled before going to bed.

The Allens were away for nearly two weeks before word came of their return with an invitation for the Lansings to continue their stay with them. Though Julia delighted in watching Mother and Mrs. Allen chattering away like schoolgirls, she confided in Abigail that she now felt a twinge of disappointment at the thought of leaving the hotel. When word came that Mrs. Allen had made arrangements for their trunks to be moved, Julia told Abigail she'd have to miss their afternoon excursion and went to her room to help Mother pack.

Julia stared at the trunk for a moment, issuing herself a reminder that the latch had the jaws of an alligator. Placing a pair of shoes inside the open lid, she jiggled it. The weight seemed to steady it. She pulled a dress from the wardrobe, pausing at the sound of a knock at the door.

"Who is it?"

"It's me. Abigail."

Julia opened the door. "I'm surprised you're still here. I thought you would have gone out by now."

"I've come to see your mother."

Mother laid her comb and brush aside. "Yes, Abigail?"

"Mrs. Lansing. I know Julia enjoys being here in the early mornings to learn from Chef Pluff. *Pleeeouuf.* Well, you know what I mean," Abigail laughed. "Anyway, we've been having a delightful time getting to know one another, but we've only just started. Father and Mother agree that Julia can stay with me in my room and join you and the Allens any time during the day. The hotel assured Father they could move another bed into my room. If Julia stays, she'll be able to join the chef first thing every morning. I'd be delighted to have her as my guest."

Julia took encouragement from her mother's indulgent smile and stood politely by while Mother explained to Abigail that she would have to speak to Ruby Allen and be certain it would cause no offense. Abigail offered her thanks and slipped out the door, smiling over her shoulder as if to tell Julia that she felt her charms had produced the desired effect.

"Well, Mother?"

"I'll speak to Ruby when we arrive today. I don't want her to feel slighted if you aren't spending every moment socializing with her twins. They're fifteen years old now and feeling quite grown up. Perhaps if you can arrive by lunch every day that would suffice. After I explain the mishap with the senator to Ruby..."

"Oh, Mother! Must you?" Julia sighed.

"Yes, I must. Ruby's social circle demands it. You can be certain she'll understand and won't think any less of you for it. Considering how hard Ruby has worked to open doors for my business in Savannah, she's likely to agree with me that continuing to be seen with Dahlia Thornhill might go a long way toward taming wagging tongues and might even lead to introductions to more business contacts through the Thornhills' friends."

Ruby Allen proved to be understanding and Julia marveled at herself as she settled into Abigail's room. She hadn't made as speedy an exit from the Wentworth Hotel as she had planned. She managed to tolerate her encounters with the Thornhills well, as long as the senator was accompanied by the confounded horn thing.

On occasion, Julia accompanied Mother to meet with clients and enjoyed lunch or tea in the fine homes of gracious hostesses. She found it irritating, however, when a few of them viewed her mother more along the lines of hired help and had them shown to the sewing room to await their arrival for consultation and measurements. These incidents were few and far between. For the most part, they were received as Ruby's dear friends and enjoyed an open door to social connections. Still, initial meetings with new clients never failed to make Julia feel inadequate and nervous.

Some clients arranged luncheons to include friends with daughters Julia's age. Others, hosting intimate suppers, sometimes included the Allens, the Lansings, and even the Hadleys if they happened to be doing business with Mr. Hadley.

Julia and Mother seized every opportunity to show off Mother's talents. Ruby's friends responded favorably. At times, Julia would catch her mother's eye when she'd received yet another order for a dress and feel a little sorry for her. Mother seemed to have a sense of being thrilled and overwhelmed at the same time.

True to her word concerning the sad, new bride, Abigail made a point to befriend Mrs. Beaumont when Julia joined her mother on appointments. During their strolls together, Abigail had learned that Mary Beaumont's husband had taken ill and was confined to their room. He had insisted that she go out for fresh air while he rested, so she often strolled with Abigail through Savannah's now familiar streets.

Julia treasured her mornings in the kitchen. Not only could she escape the prying eyes of the hotel guests, it provided her mind a brief respite from dwelling on Adam Cole. Each day, Chef Plouff seemed more appreciative of not only her interest, but her aptitude. Julia kept a notebook in her pocket and her hands in pastry dough, learning sauces and other recipes that would be great fun to fix for meals at home. The pastries alone were going to make Schmidt's Bakery the talk of the town! Morgan's Landing was in for a treat.

During afternoon outings, however, Julia found herself surveying her surroundings, hoping that Abigail assumed her to be taking in the beauty of Savannah or window shopping. She searched everywhere for Adam Cole. She had an apology to make. If only circumstances would arrange themselves so that no one else would be able to hear. She must explain things to Adam alone. It would be improper to ask to be alone with him and she had no idea how she might manage to speak to him in public with no one else present. She might happen onto him while out for a walk, but even so, they mustn't linger in private conversation. Though the likelihood seemed remote, Julia couldn't stop her eyes from searching everywhere for him.

Chapter Nine

With only a little more than a week left in their stay, Beatrice was relieved to see a letter arrive from home. She felt a flurry of mixed emotion upon reading it. Roderick had taken the telegram seriously and had given all the details. If it hadn't been for his usual crude penmanship, it couldn't have been more clear—if you were an inventor. The explosion had, indeed, been caused by a malfunction of a steam invention. That was of secondary concern, he'd explained, due to the fact that it had merely been the latest steps in perfecting an invention that would make work faster and free him up to spend more time on his more important inventions. Hopefully, he stated, the explosion had revealed the last and final steps he needed to take to ensure the success of his steam-powered grass clipper. He would have to rebuild it, of course, but then he could devote himself entirely to the project which would be of interest to Senator Thornhill.

Descriptions of this fascinating device filled the pages of his letter, but Beatrice hadn't realized that when asking him to be specific she had loosed Roderick to unleash a stream of baffling technical terms. She poured over the letter, soon realizing she had no idea what on earth he'd invented, except for the name of it. Roderick called it a *mobile wireless communication device*. She stopped by the hotel on her way to an appointment to ask Julia's opinion of it.

"But now what on earth do you suppose it does?" Beatrice gave Julia a helpless look.

Julia smiled. "Well, I don't know, but I don't think it cuts the grass—that's already been taken care of."

Beatrice let out a frustrated *"Humph!"* It tickled her sometimes, too, these inventions of Roderick's, but she failed to see much humor in it at the present.

"I'm sorry, Mother. I was just picturing all the neighbors watching Papa strut around the yard behind something puffing out steam like a locomotive. If it really does work, and other people start ordering those from Papa, Morgan's Landing will be the noisiest place on earth!"

Beatrice offered a brief smile at the notion before her brow furrowed again. "But I get so frustrated, Julia! He says none of the dishes are broken after all, but we have no windows on the south side of the kitchen! I haven't time to be making curtains with all these orders for dresses coming in!"

Beatrice sat back in her chair, passing a hand over her forehead in distress.

"Well, even I can sew up a few curtains, Mother. Try not to worry about it."

"But what shall I tell the senator? Your father can't continue on with the *mobile wireless communication device* until he gets the windows replaced and that could take a while. It's rainy this time of year at home. I've got to tell Senator Thornhill something that will make him want to come to Morgan's Landing and see this contraption, but wait a month to do it! I don't understand any of this description of the thing!"

"'Communication'—like a telegraph, maybe?" Julia pondered aloud.

"Well, it says here that the military will be wanting lots of them out in the field. It couldn't be that—telegraphs are all strung together with wires."

"Yes, Papa says it's mobile and he mentions a harness, so I assume you *wear* it?"

"Or do you suppose a horse wears it?" Beatrice tossed the letter aside in frustration. There seemed to be no use in thinking about this until she got a headache.

"Mother, I think all we can do is give the senator the name of it, tell him that secrecy is imperative to military operations and that an operating model will be ready to inspect in thirty days... and then we'll be praying that it will be."

"Yes. You're right, my Lovely One." Beatrice sighed. "But still, this whole thing," she said, grabbing the letter and waving it in the air, "makes me feel like a complete idiot!"

"I feel as though we may be leading Senator Thornhill down one of two paths, Mother. Either this is the fulfillment of Papa's dream and something that will save lives and change the world, in which case we must get the senator to Morgan's Landing at the right time. Or the senator is going to come out of Papa's workshop, shake his head, and say that this is just about the silliest thing he's seen since the invention of the steam-powered grass clipper!"

Beatrice nodded. Much of life involved the unforeseen. They may as well resolve to view this situation as though it were the newest rose in life's bouquet and watch the petals unfurl to reveal what lay at the center of it all. She would have expressed this flowery philosophy if there hadn't been a knock at the door.

Julia opened it to reveal Marty holding an envelope.

"Letter for you, Mrs. Lansing. Whoever sent it must not realize you've checked out. It was delivered to the front desk with a request that it not be held for you. When I saw you come in, I brought it right on up."

Beatrice stared at the letter as Julia closed the door and turned to hand it to her. Letters and telegrams hadn't been in the habit of bringing pleasant, or even decipherable, tidings lately.

JULIA WATCHED, relieved to see her mother's features relax as she sat down in the chair to read the letter.

"Oh! How wonderful! I'd hoped something like this would

happen. The Graysons are inviting us to a ball in honor of their nephew. He graduated from West Point last spring and is visiting them before assuming a new military post. It will be this Saturday. I'm so glad—another few days and we would have left for home. This will be quite the elegant affair! I can't wait to see you enter in the blue taffeta."

Julia smiled at the pride Mother took in how she looked. Any insecurities she felt when looking in the mirror melted away when she looked in Mother's eyes. She knew her parents thought her the loveliest creature on earth, although they never demeaned anyone else. If only she felt a little lovelier on the inside just now.

"Will you wear your green, Mother?"

Mother nodded. "It suits me well, I think. Besides, it's the only thing I've brought that's fit for such an occasion." Mother leaned back in her chair with a dreamy sigh. "Dinner and dancing—oh, this will be such fun, Julia! The Graysons have the finest home in Savannah. They have more than enough room, so everybody who's *anybody* will be there and dozens of others besides. Of course, we'll have to spend all day getting ourselves ready for this, so let's not plan on doing anything else the day of the party."

"Maybe the senator and I should begin working out a rotation for the bath right away," Julia laughed. "You love this sort of thing, don't you, Mother?"

"Well, we don't do this sort of thing in Morgan's Landing on quite such a grand scale. My goodness," Mother gasped, springing up from her chair. "Look at the time! I've got to be out and about. There's a shop I've been hearing about that carries laces and notions. I'll be needing quite a bit to take home with me. Would you like to come along? Ruby's coming and then we're having lunch at her home."

"I've promised Abigail I'd go on a picnic just outside town. I'm afraid I won't know anyone else other than her brother, James. His friend invited us to bicycle to a plantation out there. It's all turned into quite the to-do. I told them I had no idea where to acquire a bicycle. James's friend has borrowed from here and there and arranged the whole thing. I keep picturing myself taking a tumble and embarrassing myself in front of a lot of strangers."

"You'll make lots of new friends, Lovely One. I'm sure you won't tumble. Well, just mind that you *don't*! I don't want you limping into the Graysons' ballroom in that blue taffeta. What will you wear? We didn't pack your bicycle skirt."

"I bought one yesterday. It seemed frivolous, but Abigail and James were so set on my going. I should be dressed by now. Abigail's already gone downstairs to wait for James."

"I'm not sure I'd recognize you in something I haven't made myself! Is it up to the required standard?"

Julia recognized the half-tease. "It looks nice. But if you like, I can pin a note onto them stating that they are not designed or manufactured by the famous Beatrice Lansing."

"What an excellent idea!" Mother kissed Julia on the top of her head, gathered her things, and went out the door.

Julia dressed in the bicycle skirt and a white blouse and

joined Abigail in the lobby to wait for James. He would drive them to his friend's home and they would bicycle from there.

A TALL, lanky young man with sandy hair ran down the large home's brick front steps and greeted James before turning to Julia and Abigail.

"Now, James," he said, "introduce me to these lovely ladies."

Julia watched Abigail's peaches-and-cream cheeks warm. Her eyelashes fluttered. There was no mistaking it, at least to another woman. Abigail was smitten.

James made the introductions. "Julia Lansing, a new friend of ours, and Miss Abigail Hadley, my little sister. I'd like you to meet Robert Kensington. Thank you, Robert, for letting us all meet here."

"Happy to have you," Robert smiled. "Mother's invited you ladies to come in and freshen up if you like before we ride out to Sweetbriar."

Robert busied himself with making introductions as a few other people came out of the house. Three more carriages rolled up. Julia, caught up in trying to remember new names, was unable to determine whether Robert was as taken with Abigail as Abigail seemed to be with him.

Those who lived in the Kensingtons' neighborhood had arrived on their own bicycles. Assigning the proper bicycle to the proper rider amongst those who hadn't brought their own took some time. The borrowers chose theirs by trial and error until, at last, they were on their way. Ella and Henry Barton, whose parents owned Sweetbriar Plantation, led the way as their hosts. Cool air and sunshine created a perfect day for bicycling and picnicking.

Julia discovered that, if she intended to ride anywhere near Abigail, she would have to maintain her speed in relationship to Robert Kensington's. Abigail's attempts at subtlety may have fooled everyone else, but Julia noticed that she managed to be near enough at all times to join in the pleasantries exchanged by Robert and the other guests.

The bicycle skirt proved to be a nuisance, seeming to have been designed long on fashion and short on practicality. Julia wobbled and struggled a bit at first as she tugged at it, trying to persuade its voluminous folds to stay clear of the bicycle's moving parts. It was only as they reached Madison Square that she managed to catch an intermittent view of the outdoors that included more than the first two feet ahead of her front wheel.

This might turn out to be fun after all, if I can stay upright and disentangled.

Robert Kensington gave a shout. "Hello there, my friend! Won't you join us?"

Following the direction of his wave, Julia saw a bicycle leaning against a park bench. Her heart gave a leap before sinking into a nervous, jellied lump. A man, seated on the bench, looked up from the book in his lap.

Chapter Ten

As she followed Ruby across the threshold, Beatrice closed her eyes for a moment and took a deep breath. The smell of new fabrics, laces, and notions made her happy—almost as happy as the smell of rain falling on dry earth or the smell of a hot iron on freshly laundered cotton. She opened her eyes and returned the smile of the gentleman emerging from the back of the store.

"Good morning! Good morning! Welcome! What can I do for you fine ladies today?"

Beatrice warmed to him.

"Good morning!" said Ruby. "I'm Mrs. Clifford Allen. I'm told by my seamstress, Jane Ward, that I must bring my friend to Cohen's. This is Mrs. Roderick Lansing. She's returning to Missouri soon and would like to see what you have to offer."

"I am Isaac Cohen. My wife, Sarah, and I have had the finest merchandise here for over fifteen years. Sarah!" he called. "Come and meet Mrs. Allen and Mrs. Lansing."

Sarah Cohen appeared in the doorway, carrying a basket bulging with bolts of trims and lace. Placing it on the counter, she acknowledged the ladies, brightening as though she'd been hoping for their arrival. One or two grays glimmered in the mass of dark hair she had smoothed into a bun at the nape of her neck. Her brown eyes sparkled with life.

She motioned toward the basket. "I'm glad you have come today of all days! See what has just arrived! Come. Come."

Beatrice could have spent hours in Cohen's. Images flitted through her mind—some of them visions of designs she'd already drawn out—coming to new life at the sight of a lovely new embellishment. Others, never before imagined, twirled before her mind's eye and begged to be sketched out as soon as she got back to Ruby's and sat down to her drawing pad. Oh, what she could do with all the wonderful things Sarah Cohen showed her! Her customers in Morgan's Landing had never seen such beautiful trimmings. The wide variety of choices renewed her hope of finding lace to match the snippet of fabric she'd tucked into her bag.

Ruby's fingers fluttered over the trims in the basket.

"I must have you make me a few more stylish things, Bea, now that I see these."

When the bell over the door tinkled, Beatrice and Ruby stepped aside to allow a well-dressed woman to approach the counter. Beatrice, struck by the woman's stiff demeanor, cast a questioning glance toward Ruby, who responded with an almost imperceptible shake of her head, indicating that she did not know the woman.

"I see you're open," the woman observed as she marched toward Sarah Cohen.

Sarah offered a serene smile. "Yes, and we welcome you to Cohen's. How may I help you?"

"You seemed to be locked up tighter than a jug on Saturday when I tried to come in."

Isaac Cohen moved to the side of his wife and introduced himself. "May I ask if you are new to Savannah?"

"Yes, I am."

"We are closed every Saturday, and you'll find that there are some other shops that are also closed on Saturdays as well."

"Oh?" The woman gave an irritated sniff and paused.

Beatrice felt Ruby's tap on her forearm and caught her eye. Following it, she studied the woman, who seemed to be staring past the Cohens at a small, intricate embroidery on the wall. The elegant gold twist that bound the edges and formed the image of a seven-branched candelabra in the center stood out against the deep blue background.

"Is there something in particular we can show you?" Mr. Cohen asked.

The woman brought her attention back to Isaac Cohen's face, but it seemed to Beatrice that she looked at him as though she didn't even see him.

"No. Nothing. I've changed my mind."

As the woman turned and left the store, Beatrice looked at Ruby and saw that she, too, had the impression that the woman wouldn't be likely to pay a return visit. After a moment of awkward silence, they resumed their examination of the vast array of trims.

Beatrice emitted a little squeal. Scurrying to the other side of the store, she smiled back at Sarah. "Perfect! Just perfect!" Grasping a wide bolt of lace as though it were a long, lost friend. After unwinding a length of it, she pulled a pencil and pad from her bag and began to sketch and make calculations.

When the clock in the shop struck eleven, Beatrice emerged from her reverie.

"Goodness, Ruby! I didn't mean to keep you so long. We must go. I'm sure lunch is nearly ready."

"I didn't mind a bit, Bea. It's been as much fun as when we used to sew our very first dresses together when we were girls."

"I have one more thing to ask Mr. Cohen." Beatrice carried the bolt of lace to the front counter. "Mr. Cohen, I'd like to purchase some of this lace. I've done some quick sums," she said, removing a page from her pad and handing it to him, "and I think this amount should be sufficient. I'd also like to have some in the same style, only narrower."

"I did order a narrower lace of this style, but it hasn't come. You can check again at the end of the week, but if it does not come in Friday morning, I'm afraid you cannot expect it before Monday. We close early Friday to prepare for the Sabbath and then, of course, we are closed Saturday"

"I understand, Mr. Cohen. Perhaps we should both say a little prayer that it arrives before I leave next week."

"You do not seem disturbed to discover that we are Jewish,

Mrs. Lansing. Some wouldn't consider the possibility that you and I would be praying to the same God. You're not a Jew, are you, Mrs. Lansing? Or perhaps have ancestors of the Hebrew faith?"

"No, not that I'm aware," Beatrice answered. "But I do read my Bible, and it says that your people, Mr. Cohen, are the 'apple of God's eye'. I don't suppose He'll be changing His mind about that anytime soon, as I don't believe the Lord is a promise-breaker. My Bible tells me that the Messiah brings redemption and God's favor to *me* because of His great love for *you*! Now, how could I have animosity toward someone through whom I'm blessed?"

Beatrice looked into Isaac Cohen's emotion-filled eyes. Perhaps her impromptu ramblings hadn't exited her mouth with the same degree of good intent that had filled her heart. She and Roderick had spoken of such matters through the years, but as there was only one Jewish family in or around Morgan's Landing, the topic hadn't come into much practical use.

"Mr. Cohen, I apologize. I know too little about your faith to know when I may or may not be speaking out of turn."

"My dear Mrs. Lansing, you're very kind. You've not offended me. You've shown us goodness. I, and I think I speak for Sarah as well, would like to know more about what you believe concerning my people."

Beatrice smiled. "When I come Friday morning to see if the lace has arrived, may I bring a gift for you and your wife?"

"Your words to me today have been gift enough."

"Now, Bea, are you stitching that lace onto a gown in your mind, or has something else snatched you away from me?" Ruby asked after they settled themselves into her automobile and the driver approached the corner where they would turn off the busy street.

"Ruby, I'm so sorry!"

They both laughed, for Beatrice's mind had taken dreamy excursions for as long as they could remember and Ruby often teased her about it.

"I've been pondering my conversation with Mr. Cohen," said Beatrice. "Had you known they were Jewish?"

"Yes. Savannah has quite the Jewish community. Jane tells me the Cohens attend the temple we'll pass by in just a minute or two. Savannah's Jews have been here a long time. They've done well in business and politics, so much so that they elected a Jewish mayor." Ruby narrowed her eyes and met Beatrice's. She wrinkled her nose as though she'd noticed a bad smell. "You'll always have some people, like that woman in the shop, who won't have anything to do with them—practically treating them as if they aren't human. Here's the temple now."

Following Ruby's nod, Beatrice took in the beauty of Temple Mickve Israel.

"My, isn't it lovely! I hope I can be a blessing to the Cohens. As we just witnessed, he and Sarah have been on the receiving end of ignorance and unkindness—and that woman likely calls herself a Christian."

As Julia watched Robert Kensington and Adam Cole shake hands, she felt panic rise within her. Her eyes darted around as she tried to organize her thoughts, but they swirled like a tornado as she tried to organize them on her mental list of "Reasons to Stay" versus "Reasons to Flee". If she could only grasp one, a decision might be possible.

Julia had felt a flush of excitement when she caught sight of Adam sitting on the park bench. The surprise caused her to jerk and she put her foot down to steady the wobbling bicycle. She'd been convinced that she'd likely not see him again before she left Savannah. His friendly, kind face as he spoke with Robert seemed to have grown handsomer since they'd last met. The revelation that he and Robert were friends filled her with a rush of hope that there now might be a possibility of getting to know him better. The thrill of this vanished in an instant, replaced with the dreadful thought that he might see her and greet her as "Doctor" in front of all these people. Her chest began to pound as the prospect went to battle with the thought that he might not see her at all. He might speak with Robert, walk away, and they would never meet again. Somehow it mattered. Somehow, she had to sort out the mess she'd made.

Desperate for help, Julia searched the crowd. Abigail seemed the only person she knew well enough to take into confidence in an emergency. Julia could see no way to attract her attention. With her eyes set on Robert Kensington, Abigail's attentions were already spoken for. There seemed no way of speaking to her without causing a scene. She hadn't confided in Abigail about anything whatsoever concerning Adam. Might Abigail take offense at being deemed untrustworthy of her confidence? Might she unintentionally say something in front of Adam that would make matters worse? Julia began to perspire. She pressed a hand to her flaming cheek. *I must be red as a beet!*

"Oh, God," she whispered, "please help me. Show me what to do!"

When Julia heard the Bartons tempting Adam with the picnic fare in order to entice him to come along, she didn't know whether to be glad of it or not. She closed her eyes, waiting for his answer.

"I really should be studying," Adam hesitated, looking at the group gathered before him, "but I suppose it can wait since this is a perfect day for a picnic. I accept!"

He climbed on his bicycle and joined the group.

"Excellent!" Robert smiled. "Let's be going. Meet Adam Cole, everyone," he announced with a broad sweep of an arm. "We'll finish the introductions when we've settled down for lunch, but for now, let's be pedaling. The Bartons will wonder what's keeping us from lunch."

Adam joined Robert and James near the head of the party. Julia fell back, keeping well behind Adam. Things would have to unfold in their own way when they reached Sweetbriar.

The possibilities terrified her. Three scenarios presented themselves. The first was of hopeful perfection. She and Adam would be introduced without incident. By some miracle, he wouldn't reveal that he thought she was a doctor. Later, by means of another miracle, they'd find themselves at some little distance from the others long enough for her to spill out the truth and apologize for misleading him. He would understand completely. They could each go their own way as friends.

The second scenario filled her with dread. They would arrive at the picnic. Robert would make introductions. Adam would innocently recognize her. "Why, of course," he would say, "Doctor Lansing and I have already met." All eyes, including Abigail's, would turn upon her. Abigail would shriek, "Doctor? Why, Mr. Cole, you must be mistaken. Julia may be a sweet girl, and an excellent cook, but she certainly is no *doctor!*" —which point Adam would feel he'd been deceived and he, along with all the others, would have nothing more to do with her.

The third scenario made Julia sick at heart. She envisioned Adam taking no interest in her whatsoever. No matter how she might attempt to engage him in conversation, she would be ignored. Then, at some point, in her absence Adam would tell the others that he had met this unimpressive "Doctor Lansing" before. If this happened, Abigail, James, and all their friends would know about her pretense, but she wouldn't know they knew, and wouldn't be able to do anything about it. There would be idle talk behind her back, somehow connecting this to the incident with Senator Thornhill. The stain on her character would be a permanent one.

By the time the cycling party arrived, the staff had already carried lunch out to tables under the large oak trees near the house at Sweetbriar. Normally, Julia would have been drinking in the beautiful surroundings and the architecture of the large, white plantation house with its balconies and porches all around. Mother would want every detail, but Julia barely noticed them. Feeling clammy and nauseous, she leaned against a tree, trying to catch her breath.

Abigail grasped her arm. "Julia, are you well?"

"Oh, I'll be fine, Abigail. I suppose the ride was a bit long for me. It's been a while since I've ridden my own bicycle, let alone someone else's."

"Come," Abigail sounded worried as she grabbed Julia's elbow. "Let's get you to a chair."

Abigail led Julia to a wicker chair near the table laden with food and helped her get settled. "Now, let's get you something to drink."

Before Abigail could turn to go, Adam Cole appeared with a bucket and a dipper. Kneeling beside Julia, he held the dipper of cool water to her lips.

"Drink this."

Julia swallowed the cool well water.

Adam pulled a handkerchief from his pocket and dipped it in the bucket. "Here now, hold this on your forehead, just like this. Just rest a bit."

Taking Julia's hand, he placed it over the cool, wet handkerchief, covering her hand with his own. She closed her eyes and, for a moment, she relaxed, forgetting the cause of her distress until Robert Kensington spoke.

"Why then, you two seem to already know each other!"

Julia responded to Robert's exclamation. "Once, yes. We met last week on Congress Street."

Adam smiled at her. "Yes. In the line of duty, so to speak. Helping out a small boy."

"Sounds typical," said Robert. "I know how dedicated you are to your work."

Adam turned his attention back to Julia. "How are you feeling now?"

Julia returned his concern with a smile. "A little better, thank you."

His closeness would have been more welcome if it hadn't been such a strain on her nerves. She took her eyes away from Adam's and scanned the circle of faces around her, wishing they would all depart and leave them alone so that she could make her explanations. Rather, they seemed determined to remain clustered about her as if on the verge of saying something that would prove to be horribly embarrassing.

At the prospect, her pulse raced anew. Julia sat up straight and pulled in a deep breath, determined to convince her onlookers that she needn't be hovered over like this. She wiped her brow once again with the handkerchief and stood, hoping it would signal that they could feel free to disperse.

Abigail had stepped away to the other side of the food tables and now appeared to be excusing herself in order to come to Julia's aid. Julia thanked Adam again and walked to meet Abigail before she could join the group.

"Goodness me! You're still a bit unsteady." Abigail shifted the plate she was holding to one hand as she reached for

Julia's elbow with the other. "Here, I've brought you a sandwich."

"I'm fine." Julia forced a smile as she took it. "I suppose I got a bit winded."

Abigail accepted her answer, but stood back to take Julia's appearance in from head to toe. Then, she gave a knowing glance over her shoulder toward Adam that told Julia that her feelings were not entirely hidden. When Abigail's eyes returned to meet hers, Julia saw hesitation and worry in them. She thought it likely that, if it hadn't been for the attraction that held Abigail fast to Robert Kensington's every word, her usually caring friend would have insisted on returning to the hotel so that she could put her to bed and look after her.

But for the inescapable tension, it may have passed as a perfect day. Julia watched Adam. Whether enjoying lunch under the trees, playing croquet, or chatting over lemonade, he seemed a perfect gentleman. Whenever he conversed with her, others were present and Julia's heart fluttered, fearing he might make some reference connecting her to the medical field. Neither Adam's future occupation nor Julia's present one came into discussion; though, he did inquire as to whether her little, bloody-kneed bicycler had recovered. Julia avoided the eyes of the others, explaining that she'd seen Marcus only for a moment, but felt sure he must be doing fine by now. She caught her breath and felt her clamminess and nausea return. The conversation turned to other matters, however, sparing her further embarrassment if only for the moment.

Julia overheard the men as they conversed in groups

throughout the afternoon, talking of school, chosen trades, and the inner workings of family businesses. She never heard Adam speak of medical studies, however, for when the subject turned to professions, she distanced herself, developing sudden desires for lemonade, cookies, or tea.

When in her company, Adam appeared to go out of his way to be polite to her, now and then retrieving her dropped napkin or refilling her lemonade with a smile both on his lips and in his kind, blue eyes. His genuine manner increased her longing to have her explanations over and done with. If only that could happen, her tension would evaporate and she might enjoy his intelligence and kind wit to the degree that seemed to put everyone else at ease.

When Robert announced that it was time to return to town, Adam appeared at Julia's elbow.

"If you'll wait right here, Julia, I'll be glad to bring your bicycle to you. That is, if you're sure it's wise to attempt to ride all the way back. I'm sure Robert could ask for a carriage for you."

"Oh, no! I'm fully recovered, but thank you, Adam, for being so concerned."

Climbing on her bicycle and falling in with the other riders, Julia soon noticed that Adam maneuvered to be alongside her on the right. Suddenly, the thought struck her that she'd been a fool not to accept the offer of a carriage. Perhaps, the Bartons would have let Adam drive her back to town and she might have set things straight along the way. Perhaps Adam hadn't been concerned merely for her health, but had been hoping for the time alone with her as well. Julia heaved a sigh of regret at her lost opportunity and spent the ride back to the Kensingtons' praying they might find themselves a bit ahead or behind the group at some point, affording them a private moment. Soon, however, the party clustered near the Kensingtons' front porch, saying their goodbyes.

Robert, along with James Hadley, exchanged a few parting remarks with Adam before joining Abigail at the top of the front steps. Julia scanned the group. Perhaps the others hadn't noticed that she'd stayed behind. She turned to Adam. Their eyes met and they stood smiling.

"I've really enjoyed the picnic today," he said. "To think I might have spent my day on a bench in Madison Square all alone. That would have deprived me of getting to know you better. I hope we'll have more opportunities during our time in Savannah…"

Julia waited, puzzling at his hesitation. Perhaps he wished he hadn't made his last remark.

He continued, "… but I suppose your time is occupied predominately with your work, Doctor Lansing."

Julia knew in that moment that her opportunity was at hand and was likely to vanish at any moment. Her words came in a rush.

"Oh, please, you mustn't call me 'Doctor'! Call me Julia."

"All right then," Adam relaxed, looking pleased. "As long as you agree to call me Adam."

"Adam, I have misrepresented myself. I'm terribly ashamed of it and I feel I must set matters straight."

"I'm sure that's imagined on your part. I've enjoyed your company very much. I've seen nothing today that would cause me to doubt your genuineness. In fact," he lowered his voice, blushing, "I confess that your sincerity of heart stands out in comparison to that of most young ladies one usually meets."

Sincerity—the very thing she lacked. Julia's mind seemed void of any way to make a concise explanation of her blunder. She opened her mouth, hoping something sensible would come out, but jumped as she heard Robert call from the top of the stairs.

"Adam!" Robert ran down the steps and appeared at Julia's elbow. "I'm glad you're still here. Come in and visit with Mother for a bit!"

"Thank you, Robert, but I must be going." Adam's eyes caught Julia's again. "I've enjoyed picnicking with you all and I hope we'll see each other again soon." He offered his hand to Robert. "Good day, Robert. Thank you for inviting me. Give my regards to your family." He turned back to Julia. "Goodbye, Julia. I hope we'll meet often while we're in Savannah."

"So nice to meet you, Adam," Julia offered weakly as he turned to walk away.

How wonderful his words would have sounded if they hadn't been spoken under such a delusion! They seemed a waste, directed toward her. If she'd possessed an ounce of this "sincerity of heart" he'd spoken of, she would have confessed that, as pleasant and kind as Robert had been all day, it took all the self-control at her disposal to resist the urge to pinch him good and hard for coming back down those stairs at a time like this.

Julia was often sporadic when it came to keeping a diary, but this day would have to be recorded as a marvel. None of the scenarios she'd envisioned had come to fulfillment. She debated as to whether to record the event—unless life doled out another of these frightful ordeals—as the "Best of Times and the Worst of Times", or at least the "Best of Picnics and the Worst of Picnics".

With a sigh, she started up the stairs, hoping to find Abigail ready to return to the hotel. Matters had passed beyond her control.

Chapter Eleven

Early Tuesday morning, when Chef Plouff welcomed Julia to his kitchen, she felt a sense of sadness. Only a week from today her lessons would have ended and she would be on a train headed to Morgan's Landing. He adored her. The little Frenchman smiled each day as she left, watching her as she stopped at the door to place her notebook between her teeth for a few seconds while removing her apron and brushing flour from her face and hair. He'd spoken of their eventual parting a few times, lamenting that it grieved him to think of losing his lovely pupil to a place called Missouri, which he considered to be a desolate frontier. With a sullen shake of his head, he expressed hope that its crude residents could appreciate the enthusiasm that went into their new culinary experiences. He doubted they were capable of appreciating the true works of art that were about to appear in their bakery shop window. Julia found herself yawning as she wiped the work area and began putting away the cooking utensils. She had never struggled with sleep—until now. Morgan's Landing had, at times, seemed a bit dull when she was growing up. She had struggled as she watched and defended her friend, Bertina, from bullying and tried to draw her out of her shell. She'd been teased by school-mates. Though not a common occurrence, she'd learned to deal with irate customers at the bakery. She'd ached from long days of work and she'd spent days curled up in the porch swing with a book. There had been parties and there had been funerals. Despite her struggles, however, Morgan's Landing had always embraced Julia. She had parents who loved each other and wanted the best for her. The stresses, joys, and sadness flowing in and out of her life hadn't shaken her sense of security.

Her sense of security had come with Julia to Savannah. As she recalled standing in her hotel room upon her arrival, looking down at passersby from her window, Julia remembered the feeling of peace that emanated from the town. Her anticipation at the thought of exploring it had eased away some of the anxiety she'd been having about meeting new people or perhaps even being bored.

All this had vanished with a turn of a doorknob. Now, frenzied nerves seemed to rule the day, as well as the night. Since meeting Senator Thornhill and Adam Cole, sleep had only come to Julia on nights when exhaustion reached such a peak that her mind gave in to her body's demands. Julia longed for home, her own bed, and ordinary days.

Mixed emotions ran amok each night when the darkness

and quiet enveloped her. The dress was ready for the Graysons' ball on Saturday night, but it seemed as though a million small details remained, each needing attention in preparation for an event of such magnitude. Annoying thoughts pestered her mind like little, scurrying creatures. Some, darting and shadowy, carried little signs that read, "Dread This" or "Look Out for That". Others floated past, shimmering. Their little signs said, "Won't This be Fun?" or "I Simply Can't Wait!"

She dreaded the dance card. Mother was right. Events like this didn't happen in Morgan's Landing. Only very special occasions called for a dance card back home. Most were informal with music played by those who thought to bring an instrument or by some attendee who was asked to play the piano. Julia usually danced with whomever asked and the young men back home were different. She had known them long enough to be well-acquainted with their conversational and dancing abilities. She knew what to expect. The men at the Graysons' would be not only more numerous, but more experienced. She'd met a select few through the Hadleys, Allens, and Kensingtons, but hadn't danced with any of them. Though not as tall as Mother, Julia was well aware that she might tower over some of her partners. The idea of that little card dangling at her wrist with a string of unknown names on it and of her being expected to smile and switch partners all night long was only paralleled by the thought of all the lines being blank.

Her recent misfortunes bombarded her mind each time she imagined herself in a room filled with society's elite. They would all have heard dreadful things about what happened with the senator! Some may have even seen her topple Marcus into the street. Perhaps word had gotten out that she had a habit of telling people she's a doctor. They wouldn't all be as sympathetic as Abigail if they'd heard she cooked in the hotel restaurant! *I'm such an embarrassment to Mother.* Julia's mental upheaval brought back the clammy, queasy feeling that had plagued her at yesterday's picnic.

Thoughts of the picnic unleashed a stampede of regrets. Oh, to turn back the clock and have the opportunity to tell Adam Cole the truth! Her miserable attempt had become a half-apology, encouraging his attentions toward her rather than setting things straight. *Oh, why do I have to be so prideful? Why couldn't I have blurted out the whole truth as we parted? It was Robert Kensington! He came down those steps and would have heard.* It had been, now that she'd had time to ponder it, pride that kept her from telling Mother or Abigail about Adam and asking for advice.

She craved solitude in order to think and pray, but staying in Abigail's room had left little time for it. A brief quiet time after breakfast seemed all she could manage before the day's activities began. Oh, to be alone—*completely alone.* A million things seemed to stand in the way.

Julia's thoughts inevitably returned to Adam Cole. His words seemed etched in her mind.

"That would have deprived me of getting to know you better."

"I hope we'll have more opportunities such as this during our time in Savannah."

"Call me Adam."

"I've found your company very enjoyable... your sincerity of heart stands out in comparison to that of most young women..."

"I hope we'll meet often..."

Julia wanted that, too. In fact, it was *all* she wanted. Last night, in the darkness, she admitted it. *I'm every bit as smitten with Adam Cole as Abigail is with Robert Kensington.*

Once she knew, Julia had spent the night on a pillow wet with the stinging tears of truth.

Wednesday's flurry of preparations for the ball held the tears and regrets of the quiet night at bay. Julia's selection for a gown couldn't have been less complicated, having brought only the blue moiré. Not so with Abigail Hadley. She had brought four exquisite gowns with her from Atlanta, saying that she'd had difficulty choosing which ones to pack. Julia couldn't imagine having so many that she'd have such a limitation. The shared hotel room now seemed fairly bursting with gowns, petticoats and every other thing deemed necessary to turn a lady out in style. They readily agreed when Ruby suggested at supper that evening that their finery be sent to her house so they could have more room to dress. The dresses could be pressed there as well and be perfect for the event. They would return to the Wentworth each night so that Julia could keep her early appointments each day with Chef Plouff.

Hannah Levitt and Ruby's seamstress, Jane Ward, arrived to help with the packing and by lunchtime on Thursday they had settled Julia, Abigail and their gowns into spacious bedrooms at

Ruby's house and were busy unpacking and pressing everything else.

Julia found herself much less envious of Abigail's gowns than her state of mind. Positive that Robert would be at the ball, Abigail fluttered in anticipation. No matter the topic, Abigail, with a sudden gasp, would interject, "Oh, Julia, that reminds me…" and turn the conversation once again to the guest list, gowns, or decorations.

Drawn in by Abigail's chatter, Julia felt grateful for the distraction. It helped her avoid what disturbed her most. Inevitably, after they'd covered gowns and décor, and after Abigail teased her by admonishing her to *stay out of the kitchen and, by all means, not to ask for the recipe for anything, no matter how good it tasted*, the topic would turn to dancing partners. At the mention of them, Julia thought she might become ill. If only Bertina were here! Though her anxiety would likely have rivaled Julia's, her calm demeanor would have had a settling effect on Julia's nerves.

Abigail's worries were limited to working things out so that her dance card had Robert Kensington's name written in most of the blanks.

"There must be a few dances with others, of course," Abigail chattered as she held her shoes up against one of the dresses and gave them a judicious analysis, "just for appearance's sake, and I must dance at least once with Father and once with James. I suppose I'll have to dance with that Senator Thornhill if he asks because he is, after all, a senator, but never mind all that. We need to concentrate on you."

Julia fought to keep her composure. She'd been wondering if the Graysons had invited the Thornhills. Now, with a passing comment, Abigail had confirmed it. She'd be obligated to dance with the senator as well, giving plenty of fodder for more gossip and scandal at her expense. She had never discussed the incident with the senator with Abigail and, if Abigail knew, she had never hinted at it. She emerged from her thoughts and looked up, hoping her face hadn't turned red.

"Concentrate on me?" Julia raised an eyebrow. "You mean you've had time to plan my evening out to be a perfect success as well?"

"Julia, *dear!* That's taken up the greater part of all my planning. Now, James is a wonderful dancer. You can depend on him. Some of the others we met at the picnic know the Graysons as well as the Kensingtons, so they should be there, positively lining up in rows to dance with you!"

Julia laughed, then feigned distress. "Oh, Abigail, what'll we do? I can see we're going to have a real problem."

"Oh, no! What?" Abigail spun around, dropping one of the shoes.

"I'm going to need *two* dance cards!"

"Oh, you!" Abigail scolded, pointing the remaining shoe at Julia. "Here I am, trying to make sure... now where did that shoe go?"

Julia shook her head as she watched Abigail drop to her knees and probe behind layers of hanging dresses for the shoe before deciding to join in the hunt. Though the silk gowns muffled her voice, Abigail managed to regain her train of thought.

"I've made all sorts of inquiries, trying to be sure you're the belle of this ball," she said, emerging at last with a triumphant wave of the shoe. "By the way, even though James and I had never met him, it appears that Robert has known this Adam Cole for years. He's asked his mother to use her influence with Mrs. Grayson to wrangle an invitation so that he can meet more people before he returns to Boston. I'm sure we can get his name on your card."

At the mention of Adam's name, Julia felt as nauseous as she had at the picnic, and for all the same reasons. At the ball, she would need to take Adam aside the moment she saw him and make her confession. It must be done before matters worsened—and they certainly held the prospect of becoming worse. There seemed no doubt now that he firmly believed her to be a doctor, a notion he'd gotten from her own lips. He'd expressed genuine respect for her and now she would prove herself a liar. A sudden temptation swept over her to leave well enough alone. She could go back to Missouri and he to Boston, each thinking well of one another.

A different feeling swept over her at the thought—this new thought of *never* seeing Adam again. His parting words on the day of the picnic had been enough to convince Julia that he wanted to get to know her better. If it weren't for the mess she'd created, the prospect would be thrilling. There seemed no point in toying with the notion. Every couple she'd known who carried on a long-distance courtship had at least known each other first. Girls in Morgan's Landing with beaus who were away at school or apprenticeships had courted before corresponding by letter. Besides, Adam would hate her the minute he knew he'd been deceived. Even if hate proved too strong a word, he'd lose all respect for her when he discovered how disingenuous she was.

Julia looked up as she realized that Abigail was addressing her. "Hmm?"

"I said," Abigail responded, graciously ignoring the fact Julia hadn't been listening, "I think I'm missing a pair of stockings. I'll just go have a look in the trunk room to be sure they weren't left behind."

"Oh, all right. And Abigail, I do like the shoes."

Abigail smiled and positioned the shoes beneath the hem of the dress before going out the door.

As the latch clicked, Julia turned to the mirror. "Stop it, Julia!" she whispered at her reflection. "Oh, Lord, help me! I'm about to find out exactly how much courage I lack, or... exactly what he thinks of me."

Julia jumped as the door opened again and her mother entered with Ruby Allen.

"Have we lost Abigail?" Ruby asked.

"No," Abigail answered, appearing in the doorway. "I've just been in search of stockings."

Ruby looked at the array of dresses. "Have you chosen your gown?"

"Oh, yes," Abigail said, crossing to the dress, "this one."

"It's lovely!" Ruby exclaimed. "With that settled, will you girls follow me?"

Ruby Allen led the way through the hall, opening the door to a spacious bedroom. "I've had all your petticoats and things brought in here. Abigail, I'll send your gown to the sewing room for Jane to press. You can put the rest of your things in this dresser if you like. I'm sure those stockings are here somewhere."

"Thank you, Mrs. Allen."

"Your beautiful, blue dress is in the sewing room, Julia. It's probably pressed and ready by now. It can hang there without getting wrinkled until Saturday. Then Jane will bring it to you."

"That's very kind of you. Thank you."

Julia watched her mother, who had lingered after Ruby had taken Abigail to show her the way to the sewing room. Now, reaching into the wardrobe, she pulled out a dress and spread it across the bed with a flourish. Stepping back, she smiled, looking like a little girl who, having kept a delicious secret until Christmas morning, now rejoiced to see the face of the recipient.

"Well, what do you think?"

Julia stared at the plum-colored silk. She wouldn't be wearing this dress to the ball. Then, remembering its scarred front, she ran a hand over it, wondering how Mother had managed to hide the damage done when the trunk lid had fallen.

Mother beamed with satisfaction. "I've had Hannah Levitt

work on it. I was too busy with the orders and appointments to do it myself, and I wanted to see what her work was like."

"Mother, where did you get this lace? It's the same plum color as the rest of the dress, but you got this dress fabric back home!"

"I consider us blessed. I found it in Cohen's, the shop Ruby and I visited the day you were gone on the picnic. It's a perfect match and wide enough to make an underskirt. It allowed for Hannah to gather the silk into flounces."

"I like it better than when it was brand new."

"So do I! I left it in Hannah's capable hands. Better to have her practice on you and me before she sews for my clients. I knew from the beginning that she has what it takes. Somewhere stitched up into this flounce is a little hole that looks exactly like a trunk latch! She even added a bit of the lace to the neckline to carry the look throughout the design. It's a miracle. I hope I've been some small blessing to the Cohens because they certainly have been a blessing to me."

"She's going to sew for clients?" Julia now realized that she'd forgotten to ask her mother what happened the day she followed the Levitts into the delicatessen.

"Yes. I've hired my first employee," Mother announced with an air of accomplishment before admitting, "It's a little frightening. It feels quite different from having girls in Morgan's Landing coming over to do basting."

Julia looked again at the dress and smiled at Mother. "You certainly found the right person!" Though there was no one else in the room to hear, she lowered her voice almost to a whisper. "I hate to sound like Papa, but can we afford it?"

"Well, up until these society ladies placed their orders—no. Now I can't afford *not* to have someone capable. You can see by the quality of work that Hannah is quite capable. And, I feel we'll be helping her in turn. She's lost her husband, and needs to support her children."

Julia nodded. "I know. I'd hate to see her marry some man she doesn't care for just so she can feed herself and her children."

"I've been going over my financial situation in great detail," Mother said as she returned the dress to the wardrobe. "Lovely One, our standing has changed from one that was questionable, seasonal, and subject to famine at the cancellation of a party, to one that is quite solid! Women are willing to pay a great deal of money for these gowns I'm creating. I need Hannah Levitt."

"It's thrilling, isn't it, Mother? You look happy—and maybe a little anxious around the edges?"

"Oh, Julia! The *only* thing that makes me anxious about hiring her is how on earth I'm going to tell your father."

BEATRICE SIPPED HER TEA. "I'd be getting sad by now, Ruby, if I weren't so excited about Saturday night. We've never been to anything so elegant. Morgan's Landing, as you well know, doesn't offer parties nearly so grand. Ladies wear my gowns to the Governor's Ball in Jefferson City, but that's as close as I've gotten to attending one myself. Speaking of home, we only have a few more days together. We must make the most of them, Ruby."

The life-long friends sat for a moment, watching each others' eyes fill with tears. Tuesday morning loomed ahead. They would stand at the train station, speaking every endearment that came to mind, parting for an unknown length of time.

"Well!" Ruby brightened, "you won't be gone from me as long as last time, will you? You'll be back soon for another round of fittings. I have to say, Bea, I thought this was going to be wonderful for you, and it is, but I'm starting to wonder how you're going to handle all this business unless you move to Savannah."

"Oh, Roderick would never agree to that," Beatrice exclaimed, her eyes widening over her teacup. "Besides, Morgan's Landing is home. Still, I'm afraid you're right. I'm in a pickle. All these clients are a blessing beyond anything I could have imagined and I have you to thank for much of it," Beatrice smiled, leaning forward to give Ruby's forearm a squeeze, "but I'm not sure I'm capable of handling it all. Having Hannah is a start, though, and I'm grateful for that."

"Something will work out, Bea. I know it will." Ruby tilted her head, looking toward the doorway expectantly. "I can't wait till Jane and Hannah finish dressing those two girls. I told them we'd be out here in the screen porch having our tea and to come show us their dresses. Then you can tell Jane and Hannah if there are any nips and tucks that need to be made."

Pausing for a sip of tea, Ruby continued, her tone sounding as though she were about to touch on some tender subject. "Bea, I want to ask you something."

Beatrice looked into her friend's eyes, unable to imagine anything that could be amiss between them.

"Bea, you don't have to tell me if it's something I shouldn't know about. You're doing a wonderful job of acting as though nothing is wrong, but what on earth is the matter with Julia?"

"Julia?" Beatrice's eyebrows rose. "You think something's wrong with Julia?"

"Well, I can see she's not the same girl I observed on your visit last year. She's a little older and perhaps a little more mature, but something about her demeanor just doesn't seem right to me. Has she had a broken courtship back home? Is she ill? In all our letters through the years, I never got the impression that Julia is the moody sort."

"No, she's not." Beatrice sat for a moment, her eyes lowered. This was confirmation of something that had been nibbling at her thoughts. Something *was* wrong with Julia and she hadn't been listening to her intuition.

"Oh, Ruby! I feel as though I've let Julia down, now that I hear you say this. I had an inkling that something wasn't right. I'll speak to her about it. I suppose I brushed it off as the exhaustion from the trip and the embarrassment over the incident with Senator Thornhill. We laughed it off as best we could, but that sort of thing is traumatic for a girl like Julia. Well, for anyone, really. Since then, I've been in such a flurry! I've let myself assume she's been able to divert herself by spending time with Abigail and Chef Plouff. I haven't stopped to get to the heart of the matter."

"That's understandable," Ruby soothed. "It's not too late. Why don't you try again? Julia's always confided in you."

Beatrice rested her cup in its saucer and stared into the tea, speaking almost in a whisper.

"I'd see her with a far-off look in her eyes. When I asked if she were tired or nervous about meeting new people, do you know what she would say? 'I suppose that's what it is, Mother.'"

Beatrice looked up at Ruby, shaking her head in self-admonishment.

"Now, since when have I ever let such a pitiful excuse for an answer stop me from finding out what's really wrong with my daughter? I've been so busy that I've made up my own reasons for her demeanor. I even told myself for a bit that she was worried about my being so over-extended. I know some mothers whose households are in a constant state of emotional upheaval while their daughters are growing up, but I've never had such problems with Julia. She's always taken the bad with the good and never let circumstances make her overwrought for long." Straightening herself in her chair, Beatrice pulled in a deep breath. "I'll talk to her soon, Ruby. I hope it's something that can be sorted out and set in order before the ball. I want Julia to have a wonderful time."

"I hope she will, Bea. It's just like you, though," Ruby chuckled, "to think everything will sort itself out perfectly in no time at all."

Beatrice lifted her teacup for another sip. "You just let me look on the bright side, Ruby, dear. You know perfectly well that's what I do best!"

Chapter Twelve

A DAM SHIFTED HIS WEIGHT AGAIN. He'd tried for the better part of two hours to do some serious study. Sitting on three different benches in three different squares hadn't helped him concentrate. He felt distracted, frustrated, and, for no reason he could think of, just a little bit angry.

Strapping the two books onto his bicycle, he climbed on. *Just ride! Just think! No, just get it over with!*

Within a few minutes, Adam arrived at the Kensingtons'. A tidy, courteous maid answered the door, showing him into the parlor. He tried to hide his disappointment at the news that Robert wasn't in. Adam was in no mood to speak to anyone else, but smiled, offering a gentle bow as Robert's mother entered the room.

"Good afternoon, Mrs. Kensington."

"Adam! How nice to see you. Won't you sit down? I'm

sorry Robert isn't here right now. I don't expect him back right away."

Adam sat down. He liked Robert's mother, but small talk irritated him just now. He was hardly dressed for a parlor visit and his thoughts were elsewhere. He relaxed a bit, however, under Mrs. Kensington's warm smile. Though his family's social standing had always been far below that of Robert's, he had never been treated as though any gap existed between them. Still, as he glanced down at the well-worn spot on his trouser knee, he couldn't help but slide his cap over it.

"I only stopped by to let Robert know that I won't be able to attend the ball. My train leaves for Boston tomorrow. Aunt Bethel isn't feeling well, and I need to do all I can for her before I go back to school."

Mrs. Kensington laid a hand on Adam's sleeve. "Is it serious?"

"It didn't seem so in the letter, but still, I need to go. I owe much to Aunt Bethel. She's taken me in and doted on me while I've been in school, just as Aunt Lydia has while I've been in Savannah. Those two worked everything out between them so that I could manage to get by and save money. I've no doubt she'd pay for my schooling if she could, but I wouldn't let her do that. God's provided everything I've needed so far and I know He's working all things out for my good."

Mrs. Kensington smiled. "It's nice to see a young man of your age who believes that there is a greater Power over his life than that of his own ambition."

"Well, if I didn't believe that, I wouldn't have gone to Boston in the first place."

"So many men consider life *only* in terms of how they can use their own brains and muscle in order to build wealth. They get so caught up in it that they forget 'from whence cometh their help'."

Adam sighed. "Oh, I'm very aware of 'whence cometh my help', Mrs. Kensington. I needed a big dose of it in finding a way to use the brains and muscle I've been blessed with to make enough money to finish. I am close to finishing, but if I'd kept up at odd jobs after classes, I'd have been in school forever. I needed something during this break that's steady and pays well. I couldn't find anything in Boston. The only manufacturing plant with an opening was Bailey's."

"Bailey's? Is that soap?"

"No, automobiles. I'm interested in how they make those electric roadsters, but Aunt Bethel wouldn't hear of it. Bailey's is all the way across town. Her favorite nephew would have had to take a room in a cheap boarding house that didn't meet her standards. She doesn't share my interest in all the progress being made in machinery and scientific study. She thinks the automobile is a passing fancy."

"Your aunt may not have a great understanding of automobiles, Adam, but it sounds like she is an expert at looking out for her favorite nephew."

"She does her best," Adam laughed. "She wrote to Aunt Lydia and, since I do well at construction, here I am—working for Cousin Frank. It's allowed me to save enough to finish school, but as I said, I must leave tomorrow morning. Please give the Graysons my regrets."

Adam stood and Mrs. Kensington followed suit.

"I will, Adam. It's been good to visit with you. I'll tell Robert you stopped by. Remember, if you need anything, please write."

"Thank you for your kindness. Tell Robert I'm sorry I missed him."

Adam had spoken the truth. He was sorry he'd missed Robert. Unless circumstances changed, he wouldn't get to say goodbye to him, nor would he be able to find a way to see Julia again.

Returning to his bicycle, he climbed on and left the Kensingtons' house behind. At the end of the block he paused, then turned left. He increased his speed, not knowing where or how long he might ride.

The breeze in his face brought the usual, wonderful smells of the old town more quickly to Adam's senses. It should have been therapeutic, but not today. Fragrant flowers filled the gardens he passed. Fresh pine stacked behind the furniture store gave off a fresh scent. Neither offered a calming effect. With his train leaving so soon, Adam's hopes of seeing Julia again had dwindled to an impossibility. *Why did everything have to be such a struggle?* He rode on, not caring where the bicycle might take him.

Leaving school to work and save money had been a struggle. Going back would be a struggle. Staying in two different towns far from home had been a struggle, but Adam felt a strong calling to see things through in order to live a life of purpose. He missed his family back in Kansas City, but with little money for tuition for the type of school he needed to attend, the only way to afford his education had been to find a school where he could stay with relatives. That was how he'd ended up in Boston, living with Aunt Bethel. Aunt Bethel loved him. The sweet old lady tried to make him comfortable in her modest, little home. While Adam was at school, she busied herself with church activities and ladies' auxiliaries, hurrying home in time to prepare good meals for him.

At first it seemed an answer to prayer. Free room and board with Grandpa's sister made what little money he had stretch further toward tuition and books. Then, when he'd come so close to completing his studies, it had run out. Adam had reluctantly appealed to the school administration for permission to take time off before the semester's end in order to find work and pay for his remaining tuition.

After Aunt Bethel had written to her sister, Lydia, in Savannah, the arrangements were set. Adam would work every day he could for Frank Morton, Great Aunt Lydia's son. Frank, a builder, understood the situation and had offered him temporary work on his crew as they constructed new homes. The bicycle he'd found in Aunt Lydia's shed had carried him to construction sites each day after he reported in to Cousin Frank. Once Adam showed his skill at detailed tasks, he had been reassigned to interior trim work and given a raise. Saving almost every cent he made, tuition was no longer a worry. In celebration, the Mortons had taken him to dinner at the Wentworth Hotel where Julia had reached out and taken his hand. While riding the same bicycle, he had stopped to comfort a small boy on the street and found him in Julia's arms. That was how Robert Kensington stumbled across him on a park bench and invited him to a picnic. And, that was how he found himself now—on the bicycle, restless, distracted, frustrated, and downright miserable.

With his dreams so close to becoming a reality, why the urge to ride this stupid bicycle down to the Savannah River and throw it in? There didn't seem to be any logical reason why he'd become so taken with a girl he'd only come in contact with on a few occasions. On the other hand, there didn't seem much of a chance that she would respond to his attentions anyway. Why should she? Being one of those modern, career-minded girls, she wouldn't likely take up with someone just starting out without a penny to his name. He certainly wouldn't be able to keep her in the lifestyle she was accustomed to, for each time he'd seen her, she'd been dressed like a princess! If her family held the social standing of her friend, Abigail, then Julia Lansing was far beyond his reach. Besides, being a doctor, she'd return soon to wherever she practiced. From the snippets of conversation he'd overheard at the picnic, it was some town out in the middle of nowhere back in Missouri. He knew full well that Missouri was a large state. The sensible thing to do was to dismiss the silly notion of ever being near Julia again.

"Ouch!" Julia's hand shot up to rearrange the hairpin that Abigail had inserted.

"Careful, Julia! I had that curl just where I wanted it."

"Yes, but the hairpin is definitely *not* where I wanted it!"

Abigail responded to the good-natured reprimand with an artificial pout over Julia's shoulder in the mirror. "Well, I suppose you'll have to hire a new hairdresser, Miss Lansing. I'm doing my best."

Julia smoothed the hair at the nape of her neck. "Yes, you are! It looks so nice." Julia turned from the mirror to study Abigail's tiny frame. "Let me have another look at you. Abigail, I must say it again—you look radiant!"

She'd never seen anything quite like the pale green gown. The low, straight neckline extended from one armhole of the satin bodice to the other. Its sheer, cream-colored overlay had a hint of shirring. Twin cascades of embroidered roses grazed Abigail's shoulders with the palest of yellow and lavender. Slim ribbons of green satin created a bit of sleeve over her delicate arms, looking almost as if they were attached to the dress by a single thread.

Abigail lifted her skirts gently and turned her back to the mirror, twisting to look over her shoulder. The full, cream-colored satin skirt, covered with floral embroidery, swished as its train fell into place behind her. She released the fabric and smiled, smoothing the lace inset that fell from her waist to the floor, peeking from beneath the curved opening in the satin overskirt. Large roses of pale yellow, appliquéd along the edge, encircled the skirt like a wreath.

"Adjust the bow, would you, Julia?"

Julia untied the wide ribbon of pale green satin that encircled Abigail's waist and retied it near her left side, leaving its ends trailing down over the skirt.

"This suits your peaches-and-cream complexion."

"It's from the House of Worth," Abigail smiled. "Mother bought it for me last year in Paris. Your mother will be making things like this someday, Julia, and then she'll be charging just as much. I do wish she'd bring her unique designs to Atlanta!"

"Here we are, miss." Hannah Levitt entered with Jane Ward. Together, they carried the blue moiré across their arms, lowering it gently onto the bed.

"You'll be the belle of the ball, Miss Abigail," said Jane.

"Thank you, Jane, although I doubt anyone will be giving me more than a passing glance once they see Julia's blue eyes with that lovely gown. You're so tall and graceful, Julia."

"Oh, Abigail!" Julia blushed.

Hannah and Jane lifted the rustling mass of blue, slipping it over Julia. Once buttoned, tied, fluffed and smoothed, Julia turned to the mirror. It couldn't be compared to Abigail's in terms of appliqués and embroidery, but Julia smiled, pleased with her reflection.

Jane stepped back and crossed her arms in satisfaction. "Your mother's a genius when it comes to fitting a dress, and her work is so fine."

"Oh, Julia!" Abigail spoke in an awed whisper. "It's as though this dress has been waiting for you, and no one *but* you, to wear it!"

The gown's fitted midriff came to a point at the basque waist. Julia adjusted the loose, horizontal pleats that lay across the bust, forming a sweetheart neckline, its top edge revealing a sheer inset of a slightly darker blue. The same sheer fabric lay in narrow straps over her shoulders.

Hannah and Jane bent to take hold of the ruffled hem. Lifting the skirt, they let it fall again, watching as it slowly spread into its wide silhouette. Julia reached up, running her fingers over the scalloping garlands of blue roses attached to the armholes of the dress, held only by the tips of sheer leaves of darker blue that peeked from beneath each rose. Draping over her upper arms, they stood out in striking contrast to her ivory skin.

Hannah Levitt broke the silence. "With your mother's training, Miss Julia, I hope to do so well at choosing colors. The dress is like your eyes—the color of the sky on a perfect day."

"Thank you, Mrs. Levitt."

Hannah opened the door. "Let's not keep Mrs. Allen and your mother waiting, ladies. They want to see how well you've turned out."

Abigail picked up her skirts, leading the way toward the staircase. "I wish Mother had finished her shopping. She could have stopped by to see how we looked."

As they crossed the grand entry hall, Julia felt they must look like a pair of princesses with their ladies-in-waiting following close behind.

Abigail stopped short. "Listen!"

"What are we listening for?" Julia asked.

"Those voices. I thought your mother and Mrs. Allen were in the parlor."

"No, Miss Abigail," said Jane. "They told me they'd be in the big, screened-in room, straight ahead, since it's so nice out today."

Abigail shook her head. "But two sides of that room face the streets! The whole town is going to see our dresses before Saturday night!"

"Oh, Abigail, you silly thing!" Julia swished around her, leading the way.

THE SMALL, leafy branch on the street in front of him was something that Adam wouldn't normally have given much thought. He prepared to whip around it, but at second glance he realized that this branch seemed to be begging for trouble. Since leaving the Kensingtons', the physical exertion had done little toward easing his mind. He rode straight over the branch, enjoying the sound it made when it snapped in half.

The two seconds of gratification as the halves parted gave way to a new frustration. A twig, having snapped off the branch, now waved from the spokes. Its tip touched the frame with every revolution of the wheel, taunting him.

"I knew it! Just one more aggravating thing!" Adam muttered under his breath. The twig could stay there for all he cared. He had no intention of stopping to pull it out.

He turned onto a lazy, residential avenue. The *tick, tick, tick* of the twig against the frame fed his anger with its clock-like rhythm. He sped up, hoping to dislodge it, but it only ticked faster. Slowing down, Adam leaned over the handlebars to see what prevented the twig from falling out. The rhythmic ticking slowed, making him wish he had this same control over his own time and destiny.

How wonderful it would be to slow down events, stay in Savannah and see Julia again. He'd be sure to express himself better and find a way to keep in touch with her while he finished school. He'd slow down that train and go to the Graysons' ball. Robert had said the Hadleys and Lansings would be there. He could speed up his remaining time in school and re-establish contact with Julia before she met someone else.

Intolerance for the twig now bordered on the point of hatred. Spotting a stone wall surrounding a large, elegant home on a corner lot, Adam made a quick right turn onto the side street next to it. The wall, topped with wrought-iron fencing, would be an ideal place to lean the bicycle and rest for a minute or so.

Adam grabbed the twig, jerking it back and forth. Pulling out his pocketknife, he squatted down for a bit of surgery, reminding himself that his goal was to fix the bicycle, not to carve it into a million pieces out of the aggravation that gnawed his insides. Once the twig surrendered, he sat down on the stone wall, leaning against the iron fencing. *None of this is doing you a bit of good. You may as well accept your circumstances.*

Muffled voices coming from inside the house sounded pleasant and serene. The tinkling of china dishes made him feel less agitated. The sound of people enjoying a visit with family or friends reminded Adam that not everybody was miserable. Perhaps the world wasn't such a rotten place after all. More voices joined the group. These people probably had sorrows of their own, but that didn't mean they couldn't enjoy the simple pleasure of sharing a little time together.

Hearing a gasp, Adam turned, looking through the iron posts toward the sound. As the volume rose, making the excited chatter of women's voices audible, Adam Cole saw a vision.

JULIA SWEPT THROUGH THE DOORWAY, followed by Abigail, Jane and Hannah close behind. She smiled at her mother, waiting for her reaction.

"Oh!" Mother stood, beaming. "I've fitted that dress to you before, but never with your hair styled so. It's lovely, just lovely!" Putting down her teacup, she grasped Julia's hands. "Let's have a look! Turn around. Turn around."

"Mother, you're getting silly!" Julia giggled as she let her mother spin her around a few times.

"And, look, Ruby!" Mother squealed. "Look at our Abigail! Perfection! You're both visions of perfection!"

"You certainly are!" Ruby gave both girls a squeeze. "I don't know when I've seen anything so beautiful!"

Chapter Thirteen

I DON'T KNOW when I've seen anything so beautiful! Adam pressed his cheek against the iron post and stared. He drank in the vision of Julia in the blue dress—laughing, smiling, and twirling. Her cheeks flushed. Her eyes danced. Her ivory shoulders rose gracefully from the wide neckline and curved into a long neck encircled by a delicate chain and pendant. It continued upward to a pair of earrings perched on the lobes of the prettiest ears he'd ever seen. Adam hadn't taken particular notice of girls' ears until now. The sight of them led him right to her blue eyes. *Have they always been this blue?* He could see their color from the street—he was sure of it.

Other people surrounded her. Adam didn't know who they were and he didn't much care. Though his brain functioned little apart from drinking in the vision of Julia in such splendor, he had a notion he'd seen the petite girl beside her somewhere before. Yes, she was Abigail, the girl who stirred such an interest in Robert on the day of the picnic. One of the other ladies seemed so like Julia in her movements and expressions that Adam could only assume her to be a close relative. He had a dim realization that passersby may think it odd to see a man with his face wedged between two iron fence posts and hoped no one thought he'd gotten stuck. Nevertheless, Adam sat transfixed, watching as though he'd bought a ticket to the event.

Quite a bit happened that seemed to fall into the category of things understood only by women. Amidst a flood of favorable comments raining down on the two girls, there occurred what seemed to Adam an incredible amount of fluffing, tweaking, smoothing, and suggestions for minor improvements. He failed to see any point in all of this, as nothing needed to be improved upon, but if it kept Julia in front of the windows, the other ladies could spend hours analyzing her for all he cared.

"OH, YOU LADIES ARE TOO KIND!" Abigail blushed. "I don't know when I've been so excited to go dancing."

"Yes," Ruby teased. "It seems you're not the only one. I've heard Robert Kensington is looking forward to it."

Abigail could no more control her smile than she could the deepening blush of her cheeks. It would appear everyone had noticed the attraction. She hoped that she and Robert wouldn't be the objects of a roomful of staring eyes all evening at the ball. She'd been attracted to various handsome men, but had never felt the way she did around Robert. He seemed to exude strength and honor. The moment he first smiled at her, his eyes had conveyed a spark that kindled something in her heart she'd never felt before. Abigail had made a decision. Robert Kensington, unless he proved to have some opposition to the idea, was the man for her.

Elizabeth, Mrs. Allen's daughter, squealed as she fluttered into the room. "We just heard!"

Her twin, Eleanor, following close behind, sighed with satisfaction as she looked at Abigail and Julia. "We heard you were trying on your gowns. We had to see!"

Abigail nodded at each girl in turn. "Hello, Elizabeth... Eleanor." It pleased her to see the likable pair exchange smiles of amazement when she greeted each by their correct name. She'd learned from Julia how to identify them by the slight difference in the tilt of their noses, though she found the knowledge of little use unless she engaged both twins at the same time. Taken separately, she merely needed to converse for a few seconds to discern whether she'd encountered the animated and excited Elizabeth or the calm and placid Eleanor.

"How did you...?" Elizabeth began.

"Now, now," Abigail teased. "We all have our little secrets. Besides, in an hour's time I might get it all wrong again." Picking up her skirts, she twirled again for the girls. "Do we have your approval?"

"Oh! You look beautiful!" Elizabeth circled Abigail and Julia, patting their delicate sleeves and running a finger over the embroidery. "Did you ever see such a dress, Ellie? I'm pining to be there, Mother, to see these dresses dance!" She clasped her hands under her chin, smiling at the two older girls. "You'll be the most beautiful ladies at the ball." Turning to face Julia's mother, she gushed, "I'm sure you and Mother will look just as lovely, Mrs. Lansing. I'd love to be there."

Though she smiled, Ruby's voice carried a hint of reproach. "We've already had this discussion, Elizabeth. You girls are still a bit young for this sort of thing. We all have our time to shine. Yours will be here soon enough."

Elizabeth gave a little sigh and turned to face Abigail, appearing to abandon any efforts to change her mother's mind. "Oh, Abigail, what darling shoes!"

"Thank you."

Abigail, fidgeting under the scrutiny, waited. Mrs. Lansing seemed to be studying her feet with an analytical eye.

"Are you wearing those Saturday evening?" Mrs. Lansing asked.

"Yes," Abigail replied as she looked down at her toes. "I see you've noticed my hemline, Mrs. Lansing. It isn't the shoes that make the dress puddle like this. I've eaten so much rich food and sweet treats on this trip. I expected this dress to be snug, but the exact opposite is true. Julia and I have walked and explored and ridden bicycles. I think I've lost a pound or so. It feels fine everywhere. It just hangs a bit long."

"Let's go upstairs. I'll pin it up a tad and Hannah can take it up. We'll do it at the waist. We don't want to bother that lace edge on the bottom."

"May I pour myself some tea and take a cookie upstairs with me?"

"Oh, girls! What am I thinking?" Ruby exclaimed. "We've been sitting here enjoying ourselves. You must be hungry by now."

Abigail reached for the teapot. "I'm too excited to eat more than a bite or two!"

"Oh, no you don't! You'll spill all over your dress. I'll carry the tea. Eleanor, would you bring the cookies?"

Julia looked around the breezy, screened-in room.

"Would you mind, Mrs. Allen, if I had my tea and cookies out here while Abigail's being pinned? I'm a little too warm and this room is such a beautiful place to catch a little air. You can send for me when Abigail's finished and then I'll take my turn."

"Your turn?" Mother scanned her from head to toe. "Is something wrong with the dress?"

"Oh, no! It's my petticoat. It's come apart in the back somehow. I caught my toe when I stepped into it. Nobody would ever notice, but I don't want it to get any worse."

"Well, you stay here, have your tea and cookies and cool off, but whatever you do, *don't sit down!* You're perfectly pressed and ready. We don't want any more wrinkles!"

"I'm afraid I won't relax much if I don't. How's this?"

Approaching the wicker footstool, Julia picked up her skirts and petticoats and, backing up to the footstool, lifted the mass of material over it. She sat down in a big puff of fabric, smiling at everyone. "Now would someone please hand me a cup of tea?"

Julia watched her mother fuss about with table linens and teacups.

"Very well, but let's not take any chances," Mother cautioned, tucking a napkin into Julia's neckline and spreading another over her lap. After scooting a small table near Julia, she put a few cookies on a plate and poured a cup of tea. "Be careful!"

Julia nodded. The others filed out of the screened-in room and crossed the main hall. Julia held the plate directly under her chin and nibbled a cookie. As voices faded away on the stairs, she closed her eyes, listening to the peaceful sounds of the neighborhood. Placing the plate back on the table, Julia reached for her cup of tea. Beside it on the table lay Mother's handbag. Julia studied it for a moment before giving it a gentle poke. It felt heavy and solid. Twisting the latch, she took a peek inside. *I thought so. Mother's keeping her promise.* Julia had seen all of the Chicago Pocket Protector she cared to lately. She fiddled with the clasp. The handbag, refusing to cooperate, inched away from her fingers, landing on the floor with a thud. Jerking her hand back with a gasp, she jostled the teacup, nearly dumping the contents. As she raised the teacup to her lips, she saw that her hand trembled. A wave of thankfulness passed over her at the thought that the gun, if it had landed on the hard floor and jarred the safety lever loose, might have gone off. The harmless-looking bag lay out of her reach now, resting behind her on the mound of skirt and petticoats.

The tea brought calm. Julia finished it and placed the cup back in the saucer. An odd feeling stole over her, giving her the distinct impression that she was being watched. The low foot-stool kept only her head above the bottoms of the windows. The gardener had finished work in the cool of the morning. No one else had been on the grounds, which were elevated above the street. Anyone who passed would have to climb the wall to see into the screened-in room. Still, Julia couldn't escape the feeling that someone observed her every move.

WHEN JULIA SAT, Adam stood. He watched the other women file out of the room. *She's alone!* He took a quick look around. There didn't seem to be anyone in sight. The street alongside the house seemed to be deserted and, though a little light traffic passed in front, no one turned the corner. People might be looking from windows of three or four nearby houses, but then again, they might not. A great opportunity afforded itself. Adam felt certain of it. However, he couldn't imagine what it might be. *What am I to do? Climb the nearest tree and start singing love songs?* Still, he must do something, even if it was merely to gaze at Julia as long as possible. And she, that gem of loveliness who didn't know she needed to be gazed upon, must be sitting on the floor! Though her reasons for doing this confused him, he didn't dwell on it. It took one second for

Adam to realize that the others could come back into the room with Julia at any moment, another to decide he didn't care, and three more to climb the iron fencing above the wall and hop off the top into the Allens' side yard.

Instinct told him to call out to her. He cautioned himself against it. Others might hear. It seemed best to employ stealth. He would draw near, then follow one of his two inclinations by either sneaking to the corner of the house, crouching silently below a window where he could look at Julia for as long as possible or—the bold alternative—whisper her name, enter through the screen door, and pour out his heart.

His heart, in quite a desperate state, needed a good deal of pouring out. A realization had accompanied the jolt Adam felt when his feet returned to earth. This must be *the* dress!

Julia would be going to the Graysons' on Saturday night looking just as she did now!

Adam repented of anything bad he'd ever said or felt about elegant parties and dances. This one, confound it, would be the ball of the century! He wanted—no!—*needed* to attend! Julia would walk into the Graysons' ballroom looking like she'd been sent from Heaven, turning every man's head. They'd all clamor to dance with her! Every name of every well-off, well-educated, fancy-pants would end up on her dance card. She would be twirled around in that dress with that neck and that smile and those ears and those eyes... *and I'll be headed for Boston! This is it—it's now or never!*

JULIA LISTENED to the sounds of birds and the distant traffic. A screen door slammed somewhere along the street, and she heard a thud out on the lawn that sounded like a rather large cat jumping down from a tree. Her eyes darted from window to window, but she saw nothing that might account for this funny feeling of being observed. Jane or Hannah would come to get her soon for the mending. She longed to lean back and relax, but dared not wrinkle the dress. Julia twisted, peering at the chair behind her. Would her elbows reach the cushion? It wouldn't be like a nap in a feather bed, but if she could manage to stay on the footstool and lean back on her elbows for a bit, she might stretch her legs. *It's bound to be more comfortable than staying bunched up like this.*

Twisting to the right, she grabbed the big wicker chair, pulling it closer. It wouldn't do to move it more than an inch or two, for it would crush the billowing mound of silk resting between the chair and the footstool. With some effort, she managed to plant her right elbow onto the chair cushion. Twisting to the left, Julia struggled, trying to reach the chair with her left elbow as well. What had held such an appeal in theory proved to be nearly impossible in practice. As a child, she'd once spent half a day with two straight-backed chairs, trying to keep her feet on one and her head on the other while holding her body parallel to the floor between them. This felt like a similar challenge. Remembering that balance and leverage were key in these matters, Julia lifted each leg slowly, one at a time, in front of her. She enjoyed the stretch for a few seconds before getting back to business. She needed to plant her left elbow on the chair cushion. The need arose to stifle a case of the giggles. Pausing, she re-gained her composure. *I'd be a sight if someone was watching!* Each swing of the elbow caused her feet to rise higher, rotating in small circles. She'd be resting comfortably any second now, enjoying the pride of her accomplishment.

ADAM PRESSED his back against the side of the house. During his bold dash across the lawn, he'd decided on middle ground. He wouldn't stare at Julia in silent admiration, nor would he pour out *all* his feelings. He must somehow, however, express himself to the degree that would achieve one goal—she must agree that they would be corresponding regularly once he returned to school and Julia went home. He must stake his claim before she danced with all the eligible men at the ball. No matter how career-minded and modern Julia might be, if she set out to look this beautiful, the men at the ball weren't likely to keep their distance! She must know that he was throwing his hat in the ring. If he couldn't have Julia, it wouldn't be because he hadn't tried.

Adam took a step away from the house. Fear and timidity pushed him back. *What on earth are you thinking? You're not this way with girls!* He was polite. He had manners. He could converse with some degree of ease, but this tactic took him into unknown territory! *What if...? What if...? Adam Cole, are you a man or are you a mouse?*

"Julia!" The crisp, loud whisper exited Adams lips as his

head popped in front of the window. Then he saw her—the girl of his dreams—with her right elbow buried in the cushion of a chair and her bent left arm flapping like a chicken wing. Both her feet, sticking out from a mass of petticoats, made circles in the air. How the middle of her managed to hover in mid-air was a complete mystery.

Adam would have spent more than a half-second analyzing the spectacle if it had continued along the same lines, but it didn't. Julia's body began a series of activities that erased his first impressions. She shrieked as both arms flew up, knocking the wicker chair back. Julia's head landed on the chair cushion. Something in the middle gave way, bouncing her onto the floor and sending both legs straight over her head. Puffy clouds of blue silk and white petticoats floated down over her head. Though a bit muffled by all the layers, Adam had no trouble understanding the voice that came from beneath.

"You ought to be horsewhipped! Do you know that? Spying on people when they're minding their own business! I've a good mind to tell the Allens what a pest you really are and you'll see, then, if you don't get run off this property and are never allowed to return!"

Adam shrank back for a moment, but pushed aside his urge to flee as Julia continued to flail her arms as if making an attempt to come to the surface. He entertained a fleeting notion that he might have startled her as she performed some sort of exercise. He dismissed this idea as he realized she seemed unable to get up. *She must be ill!* Perhaps she had some chronic condition which threw her into these episodes from time to time.

Perhaps in whispering her name he'd caused her to fall and be injured. Whatever the cause, she needed his help. And she was right. He had been spying on her and he did deserve to be horsewhipped. He had to do something! Adam maneuvered himself through the shrubbery and hurried around to the screen door on the other side of the porch.

Julia's heart pounded. *Surely no one said my name! No! Someone* did *say my name! But who?* Had the whisper belonged to a male or female? She concluded that it must be the boy who ran errands for the gardener. She'd encountered the youngster a time or two and it had seemed to her that if ever there was a boy with a twinkle in his eye and the capability of playing nasty jokes on people, this was the boy. As she drew her knees to her chest in an effort to catch her heels on the footstool and kick it away, Julia's view of the ceiling disappeared beneath the mountain of fabric that floated down over her. Embarrassment mixed with her aggravation as she pictured him peering through the window while she, bottom end up, had her underthings waving in all directions like a load of wash on a windy day. She shouted things at him that, even in her fury, she could hardly believe were her own words. She planned to have a few more things to say to him as soon as she got up.

She couldn't seem to manage it. Something held her in place. Pinned between the footstool and the chair, she reached for the footstool and pushed. It wiggled, but wouldn't go away.

The chair slid backward. Julia's head slipped off the seat. She landed on the floor with a thud. Drawing her knees up again, she delivered a series of kicks to the footstool, but couldn't knock it away from her body.

A small ripping sound brought the truth to her ears. The leg of the footstool had gone through the rip in the petticoat. *Petticoat? I'm ruining the dress!* Already having damaged one dress, Julia panicked at the thought of destroying this one. *No, not the blue moiré!* Tears made their way toward her ears as she whimpered. Several more desperate attempts to dislodge the footstool proved futile. She would require much longer arms in order to grasp it at any angle that would enable her to remove it.

"My dress! My dress!" she whimpered.

Julia considered shouting for help, but reconsidered. She must become much less exposed before anyone saw her. There seemed no alternative but to roll over, get onto her knees, and stand. She felt a pang of grief. What this might do to the dress Mother had labored over horrified her. *Wicker! This room is filled with the awful stuff!* Rolling against it could snag the silk beyond repair. A plan formed in her mind. *Gather up your skirt and hold it over your head before you stand.*

"Oh! Oh! No! Mmm... uh! Mmm... ush!"

In order to stand, July knew she must first roll over. The footstool, as though it had an agenda of its own, seemed to oppose each of her attempts to do so. Traveling the room like a croquet ball gone amok, Julia collided with every piece of furniture and repelled away. Finally, the struggle brought her to her hands and knees. She caught her breath as she heard the sound of running feet beneath the windows and stiffened in fright as she heard someone attempting to open the screen door.

"Julia! Julia! The door's latched! Julia, if you can, let me in so I can help you!"

Adam's voice shocked her into a motionless pose. *I know that voice. It can't be! No, it just can't be.*

The thought of sinking back onto the floor, leaving the skirts and petticoats over her head, was tempting. From her hiding place, she could whisper that she was fine and send him on his way. Then he uttered something ridiculous.

"Julia! I want to help you! Shall I go in through the front door and call someone?"

"Thank you, but I don't need any help." Her voice became soft, but formal.

Two options presented themselves. Julia toyed with the tempting notion of keeping the fabric over her head and insisting that Adam leave. It would spare her the added humiliation of allowing him to see her face. This idea lost its appeal, however, the instant she remembered everything else he could see. Only the alternative option remained. She would rise from her hands and knees and face Adam. After offering him a gracious smile, she would inform him that she was "fine, thank you very much", though she'd taken a bit of a tumble. She would excuse herself, as she was needed in the sewing room, make a swift turn and leave, taking her shame and embarrassment with her.

The first half of her performance unfolded as though she'd been rehearsing it. After managing to get to her feet, she released her skirts in hopes they would fall in a manner that would return her to some degree of modesty. Taking a deep breath and forcing herself to look into Adam's baffled face, she made her curt explanation and turned to go. However, the footstool now returned to make a pest of itself. With one of its legs still stuck in the petticoat, it followed Julia everywhere, weaving in and out between her legs like a playful puppy. She stepped on some hard object. It shot from beneath her foot and slid across the floor behind her. Julia caught a glimpse of it and gasped as Mother's bag popped open and the Pocket Protector rattled onto the floor and lay spinning in circles behind her. Stumbling forward, she threw out both hands. With her face pressed against the screen, Julia looked into Adam's eyes, now about four inches from her own. She detected concern and perhaps a hint of amusement in them.

"I think I might need help."

"Just as I said. The door is latched. You'll have to let me in, Julia."

Chapter Fourteen

PLACING one hand against the door's edge to steady herself, Julia released the latch with the other. Adam's tug at the handle brought her tottering forward into his arms. He lifted her upright and, stepping into the screened room with her, grasped both her arms and held them in a firm grip. Julia didn't attempt to release herself for fear of falling again. How she'd longed to see Adam again—but not like this. She could feel her cheeks, already heated from her ordeal on the floor, reddening to a deeper shade as she watched his eyes. They did not look into hers, but roved over her silhouette, as though he were standing in a museum marveling at some newly discovered oddity. After a moment, he seemed to return to himself and blushed as he cleared his throat.

"There seems to be... a bit of a, well... uh," he stammered, "I suppose you would say a bulge or protrusion in the... well... in your rear portion."

As Adam finished speaking, his eyes darted from hers and his lips tightened as though he were struggling to suppress a rising mirth. Julia couldn't find any amusement in the situation at all.

She jerked her chin. "It's a footstool."

"It's a *footstool*?"

"Yes," said Julia, pulling one arm free from his grasp and reaching back to lift her skirts a bit. "A small, wicker footstool."

Adam leaned to one side and examined the evidence. "I see that." He brought his eyes back to hers again. "But why would anybody tie a footstool to their...? I mean, under their...? Oh, I'm sorry, I suppose it's none of my business what girls do with..."

Julia released her skirts with a huff and tried to step back. As her heel caught the rung of the footstool, her arm shot out and Adam grabbed it again. "Well, I certainly didn't *put* it there! Well, I did put myself on it in the beginning, but it's caught up now in my... well, you know, my... *underthings*," Julia finished in a whisper.

Adam's blush returned, deeper than before. "Would it be possible... and I hope I'm not being too forward... but if you'll just take both hands and hold tight to my left arm, I'll reach round and see if I can't pull it loose from your... material."

Adam held his arm aloft and Julia took hold of it while he bent down to reach for the footstool. She struggled to stay upright as she moved with the sway of his body as he groped for it and winced each time she heard the petticoat rip further. Suddenly, Adam stopped swaying and the sound of the footstool knocking about came to a stop.

"Hold steady," Adam urged. "I think I've got a good grip on it."

Julia stiffened. "Adam," she said, "that's my leg."

Adam straightened to his full height so suddenly that Julia staggered back. Encircling her with his arms, he pulled her back to him, pressing her against his chest. Instinctively, she passed her arms around his waist and clung to him.

"I'm so sorry!" he panted, his breath falling hot against her hair.

Julia could do no more than manage a weak nod of acceptance to his apology as her head lay against his shoulder, feeling his heartbeat as it pounded against hers. Inner voices tugged at her, one telling her to flee from this mess she'd gotten herself into and the other urging her to tell Adam to never let go.

"Julia?"

"Yes?" Julia pulled her head away from his chest and looked into his eyes.

"I'm... I'm... so..."

Adam brought his lips so close to hers that Julia began to tremble. *Don't kiss me, Adam. Don't kiss me till I've told you the truth.*

Adam hesitated, then inhaled and straightened his back.

"Let's concentrate. I'm only trying to help you."

"I know."

"This could all be over in a matter of seconds if... I mean... what I need to do is... that is, if you would allow me..."

Julia leaned back and nodded. "Just tell me what we need to do to get this over with."

"I need to... well, I need to have the use of both hands and... I need to... to see... underneath."

Adam reddened to such a degree as he spoke that Julia felt almost as sorry for him as she did for herself. She gave a quick nod and closed her eyes, preparing for what might come. As she did, her mind transported her in a flash to the Wentworth Hotel where her attempt to take a bath had ended with discovering Senator Percival Thornhill completely naked in the bathtub. At least there were no prying eyes in this instance—or were there? Three sides of the screened-in room faced the outside world. Julia glanced up and down the street, but saw no one.

"Now," Adam explained, tilting her sideways, "if we could just lie down..."

Julia gasped, jerking herself upright. "No, we can *not* just lie down. That is out of the question!"

"Yes, I see what you mean. I... I... oh, never mind," Adam stammered. "Wait! Let's give this a try. If I bend over," he said, "you can use my back to steady yourself."

Adam began to bend at the waist and guided her wrists up and over his left shoulder. Understanding his meaning, Julia nodded and bent over as well, draping herself across his back. She caught her breath as she felt the air waft up under her petticoats and Adam's hands brushing against her legs as he pulled the fabric away with one hand and maneuvered the footstool with the other. He soon rose with a triumphant smile, holding the footstool up in front of her as if it were a trophy. As she glared at it in disgust, he let it drop to the floor.

Julia took a step back. Her chest tightened as she looked into Adam's face. There didn't seem to be enough room inside for the feelings that surged within her. She couldn't have made herself more idiotic and silly in Adam's eyes if she'd performed this scene before him dressed as a circus clown. The moments she'd longed to spend alone with him had arrived with far too much fanfare. All she had dreamed of was a few quiet moments to explain herself in some coherent way and now there seemed no way to begin. She looked around. Strewn linens and displaced furniture littered the once beautiful room. How would she ever get it back in order before Mrs. Allen saw it? A pack of wild dogs couldn't have done more damage. And what about Mother? She'd been so proud of this dress! The degree of damage it had suffered was yet to be discovered. Her eyes darted over the skirt, checking for damage before rising to meet Adam's once again. His feelings for her matched her own—she was sure of it. It should have made her happy, but now her only desire was to find a place to settle down alone for a good, long cry.

Brushing the mass of disarranged curls from her face, Julia stood tall in an effort to regain a smidgeon of dignity.

"Thank you, Adam. You see, I was just so startled when you spoke. I'd been trying to... to... Oh, never mind..."

"You don't have to explain anything to me. I only thought you must be having some sort of... trouble and I wanted to be of help." He softened his speech into something of a whisper. "I'd do anything to help you. Oh, Julia! There's something I must say to you!"

"I have something to say to you, too, Adam," Julia gulped, "but this has made it so difficult! I'm so embarrassed! It'll have to wait till I can..." Julia stopped, unable to speak. Tears rolled freely down her cheeks.

Adam nodded. "I understand."

"Miss Julia! We're finished with Miss Abigail. You just come on up and..."

Jane Ward stopped short as she entered the screened-in room. The sight of Julia, once the image of perfection, now with her hair disheveled and torn petticoats dragging, rendered her dumfounded. The girl looked as though she'd been through a wrestling match. A footstool lay overturned, the tea things toppled over, and every article of furniture had been shoved into a new location. A strange man stood in the doorway, his hair and clothes disheveled. She'd heard of such bold attacks in larger cities, but a daylight assault in Savannah's most respectable neighborhood was not to be tolerated.

"You! *You!*" she hissed. Jane flew across the room and began beating the stranger about the head and shoulders with the footstool.

"Jane! Jane!" Julia pleaded. "Please! Listen to me!"

Six hands gripped the footstool in mid-air. Jane's eyes

darted back and forth across the top of it, glaring at the intruder. She took a step back, scanning the room for a better weapon. She spied a small, odd-looking pistol on the floor. Julia must have knocked it from the attacker's hand during the struggle. Stooping, she snatched it up and pointed it at him.

"I've never handled one of these before, but I can sure give it a try. You'd better run as fast and far as you can, because the law will be after you in the time it takes me to put a hole in you and truss you up to a tree! Breakin' in here and molesting young ladies... You ought to be horsewhipped!"

"So I've already been notified. Ow!"

The man winced at her swift kick to his right ankle as he raised his hands in surrender.

"Jane!" Julia shrieked. "Calm down! Put that thing away! It might go off! This gentleman is a friend of mine. He is not here to do us harm. He came along when I was having a struggle and helped me. That's all."

"You mean to say you *know* him?"

"Yes! And he's a perfectly respectable gentleman. I let him in so he could help me. It's all rather complicated, but you must understand. He was just leaving and I'm coming upstairs to have my... garments repaired."

Jane took a step back and lowered the gun as an unspoken and fragile trust formed amongst the three.

The man stepped toward the door, then paused. "I'm so sorry for all this trouble. I'll be going now. I should straighten this room..."

Julia touched his sleeve. "No! Thank you! It's best if you go."

"Yes," Jane snapped. "It'll all be tidied up. You can just go on about your business."

The man had barely stepped through the door before Jane's hand shot out, latching the door from the inside. She turned to go, stopping in the doorway to wait for Julia. She looked down at her trembling hands. *Great day in the mornin'! I've come near to killin' a man!* She peeked around the doorway. The intruder remained at the screen door.

"I guess this is goodbye, Julia," he said.

"Well, surely we'll have a better time to talk when I'm more... well, perhaps at the ball."

"There is no other time. I leave tomorrow for Boston. I was invited to the Graysons', but I won't be able to go. I saw you in that dress and I wanted... I thought..."

Having stood by politely for a bit, Jane could take it no longer. She'd see Julia safely upstairs. She'd see the intruder disappearing into the distance. She stepped back into the doorway.

"Miss Julia, they'll be waiting for us."

Julia nodded. "I'm coming, Jane."

Jane once again retreated a few steps. Her protective instinct kept her near the door, listening, although Julia seemed to be on friendly terms with the man.

"I'd hoped you would be there, Adam, so we could chat."

"My train leaves at noon. I may ride through the squares in

the morning before I return the bicycle. I'm going to miss doing that. This is a beautiful town."

"Yes. It's lovely. I've enjoyed walking the squares most mornings myself."

"I've been in hopes, Julia, that after we both leave Savannah, perhaps..."

Jane marched forward and clasped Julia's wrist, pulling her away from the door, lest she be foolish enough to undo the latch and let the man in again. She would take no risk that he would say anything inappropriate or pry any personal information out of the poor girl, who seemed to have had all her senses rattled.

"I believe I already heard you tell this young lady 'Goodbye'," she snapped.

"Goodbye, then," Adam whispered.

Julia blinked, swallowing hard. "Goodbye, Adam."

Chapter Fifteen

Julia followed Jane toward the entry hall, but stopped as Adam's simple statement struck her like a blow. *Leaving tomorrow.* Unable to resist a backward glance, she caught a glimpse of Adam as he dropped to the ground on the other side of the fence. *He climbed the fence?* She wondered at the reasoning and circumstances behind this before her eyes passed over the innocent-looking footstool. It sat there, looking as harmless as it had before it had wreaked havoc on her life. She crossed the hallway to the stairs, repressing the urge to walk back into the room and give it one final, good, swift kick. *Heaven only knows what revenge it may take if I did!* If ever there was a footstool that managed to emerge from a life of obscurity, this one certainly had found its place in the record books!

Jane, having paused to wait for her, stood at the foot of the stairs.

"Jane, for Heaven's sake! Are you still holding that awful thing?" Julia rushed across the hall. "Here, give it to me."

Taking the Palm Protector from Jane's hand with two fingers, Julia slipped her hand into the folds of her skirt, pinching the fabric around the gun to conceal it. She stole a sidelong glance at Jane as they continued up the stairs.

"How did you even know what it was? It looks less like a gun than anything I can imagine. Heaven knows what might have happened!"

"Before I came to sew for Mrs. Allen, I cleaned house for some other folks. The gentleman had one of those. Sometimes, while I'd be cleaning the library, he'd be cleaning that funny, little thing. I asked him about it one day and he showed it to me."

"Well, it doesn't belong to the gentleman who was just here. It's mine... Mother's... Papa's, really. Mother had it in her bag." Julia abandoned her efforts to explain with a sigh and steadied her voice. "Jane, I would like to say something and I want to make myself very clear to you."

"Yes, Miss Julia?"

"What happened was an innocent thing, but it embarrassed and upset me and I'd like to be the one, and the *only* one, to explain my appearance. I'm asking that you speak of this to no one. Do you understand?"

"Yes, Miss Julia."

"I'll explain it as best I can."

"I understand, Miss Julia. I expect you don't want people telling any more stories after all that happened with that senator and the bath... Oh! I'm sorry! I ought never to have said such a thing!"

"I know, Jane. I know how people talk and that's why I ask you this."

"I won't say a word, Miss Julia. I won't say a word."

As they approached the sewing room, Mother emerged, no doubt to come searching for her.

"*Uh!*" Mother gasped as she caught sight of her.

"Mother, I've had an accident," Julia responded flatly.

"I should say you've had *something*! You look like you've been through a threshing machine! Are you hurt? You don't look injured. What *happened*?"

Jane stepped ahead toward the sewing room door. "I'd better get back to these alterations before Mrs. Levitt thinks I'm shirking my duties." Giving Julia a look that conveyed she wished her well, she disappeared behind the door.

"I took a fall from that footstool I was perched on and it got caught up in this petticoat that has the rip in it. I got all tangled up in furniture and petticoats before I could get free of the awful thing." Julia's chest began to quiver as she tried to measure out her words. The urge to tell Mother everything was only outweighed by the fear of collapsing into a fit of hysterics that the whole household would witness. "That's the basic story, except that I couldn't be more embarrassed. I've made a mess of the screened-in room and to make things as bad as they could possibly be..." Julia broke into tears. "... I know I've ruined this beautiful dress! It's been all over the floor, catching on all that wicker and I'm *so sorry*, Mother!" Her words trailed off, ending in a pathetic squeak.

As her mother passed an arm around her waist and pulled her close, Julia leaned into the embrace.

"Now come along, Lovely One. Let's get to the sewing room, take it off, and inspect the damage. It's a good thing I sent Jane down when I did."

If only you'd waited five more minutes, Mother.

The sewing room door opened. The other women appeared. Upon seeing Julia's state of distress, they politely withheld their questions after hearing her simple explanation. They offered to undress her amid reassurances that the end of the world wouldn't likely occur within the next five minutes. As Jane's fingers nimbly moved down her back, unbuttoning the dress, Julia drew her elbow back, giving Jane a nudge.

"Did I pinch you, Miss Julia?" Jane asked, pulling her hands away.

"Oh, no," Julia replied, turning to give Jane a look of desperation. "I might just need to sit a minute once we get *this* off." She thrust her right hand, still buried in the folds of her skirts, toward Jane.

Jane's eyes widened, then filled with resolve. "Let me finish these last two buttons and slip the dress off before we get you to a chair."

With the unbuttoning complete, Jane stepped to Julia's right side, shielding her from the view of the others. Julia inclined her head toward Jane's, questioning her with her eyes. Jane offered the slightest smile as she lowered her right hand and pulled one of the pockets of her sewing apron forward. Julia slipped the Pocket Protector into it and released a grateful sigh as Jane motioned to Hannah and they lifted the dress over her head.

Once the tattered petticoats were removed as well, Ruby stepped forward, offering a dressing gown. Julia slipped into it and sank into a chair by the window. She caught Jane's eye once again. *Now what?*

Jane approached her and, reaching behind Julia's back, began fluffing the throw pillow behind her. "Now, is that a little more comfortable for you, Miss Julia?" She smiled and before stepping away, reached into her pocket and slipped the gun under the seat cushion.

"It's just what I needed, Jane. Thank you!"

Abigail drew another chair alongside Julia and sat down to administer comfort. Jane and Hannah helped Mother inspect the damage.

Upon examination, they determined that the dress needed only brushing, steaming, and pressing to make it perfect once more. Julia refrained from explaining that this was likely due to the fact she'd had it pulled up over her head and it was inside-out at the time. The petticoats had taken the brunt of the assault. Being on the outside, they'd been snagged by the wicker and had received a good many smudges. The rip, now a gaping hole, needed mending. Thankfully, this could be done in time for Saturday night.

Julia managed a weak smile as she listened to Mother's attempt to look on the bright side.

"I must say... You can certainly count your blessings, Julia. You didn't break any bones in a fall that nearly tore up the house, though you were all but sitting on the floor when it happened. This is one journey that's certainly taken a toll on your wardrobe! Isn't it wonderful that such a girl has a seamstress for a traveling companion?"

BY THE TIME they'd settled back into their room at the Wentworth for the night, Julia had calmed somewhat. Abigail had been full of sympathy concerning the mishap and then had chattered away about what occupied her mind most—Robert Kensington.

As Julia sat on the edge of her bed and brushed her hair, she tried her best to engage in Abigail's excitement about the ball, but felt as though the day's events had stolen her joy.

Abigail sat down on the bed beside her. "I know just what you need, Julia dear—a good cheering up. I have a little surprise for you, and now seems the perfect time!"

Abigail stood and moved to the wardrobe. She removed a white, hinged box covered with beautiful carvings. She carried it to the bed and seated herself beside Julia.

"You've had quite a day, Julia. I was saving this for Saturday, to give you while we're dressing, but I want you to have it now. You'll be going home next week and we don't know when we'll see each other again. I know we'll write and we'll be friends for the rest of our lives, but I've been so sad when I think of parting. I've been trying to think of something I could give you to remember me by. I do have a brand new dresser set after all—I wanted you to have my other one—if you think you'd like it."

Julia looked at the box in her lap. Words failed her. She'd seen most of these pieces in Abigail's room during her stay, but never the whole set together in its case. She couldn't imagine Abigail's fascination for the new dresser set when she already had this one, for it was sterling, engraved with vines and flowers. Each piece lay cradled in its own nested position in the box— the brush, comb, powder box, hair receiver, clothing brush, mirror, nail buffer, and button hook.

The day's events had already churned Julia's emotions and left her exhausted. This lavish gift from her sweet friend pricked a heart already full to the brim.

"Oh, Abigail!" The tears came, an unstoppable flow. "It's lovely! It's so lovely!" Julia stayed in her room all evening, crying herself to sleep.

Chapter Sixteen

Julia rolled onto her back and blinked as Abigail raised the shade, letting in the morning light. *It's Friday.* She bolted upright. *Adam leaves today. Do something!*

What that something might be, she hadn't a clue. Chasing this mystery around in her brain distracted her, making it difficult to carry on a conversation with Abigail as they dressed for the day. She hurried to finish buttoning her skirt when she heard a brisk rap at the door.

"Yes?" Abigail called.

James's voice called out. "Good morning, Sister!"

"Just a minute." Abigail tucked away a few unmentionables, glancing at Julia to be sure she'd finished dressing before opening the door.

"Good morning, Julia."

"Good morning, James."

"Well, don't you look full of vim and vitality today, Big Brother!"

"I should be. I'm taking two lovely ladies bicycle riding this morning."

"Oh! Tell me everything! Who is it? It can't be anybody with an invitation to tomorrow night. I can't imagine anyone silly enough to go out and get a sunburned neck before dancing in a wide neckline."

James wore a pout. "Does that mean you refuse to go with us?"

"You mean Julia and me? Oh, no! Not today. We couldn't possibly, could we, Julia?"

Julia, half listening, looked up at the sound of her name.

"Oh... bicycles? Well... I suppose this might not be the best time..." she paused, remembering that Adam had spoken of riding before he left. She continued as her thoughts took shape. "If we did go, and only rode around the squares, we could rest whenever we want. If we went this morning, we'd avoid the afternoon sun. We shouldn't get pink doing that, Abigail."

No! Why did I say such a stupid thing? Just let him go! It's useless. We barely know each other. Things—stupid things—had been said and done. She'd made a mess of everything. It couldn't be fixed. The sensible thing would be for him to depart on a train to Boston and for her to leave on another to Morgan's Landing. *Why? Why did you tell James you wanted to go? If you can't think straight, Julia, just keep your mouth shut!*

Abigail turned to the mirror. "I don't know... maybe we shouldn't."

James stepped behind her, leaning to put his chin on her shoulder. "Imagining the freckles multiplying on the end of your nose? That's all right, Sis." He turned to go. "I'll just go down to the lobby and tell Robert you're not interested."

Abigail blushed, swatting James with her gloves. "What! Oh, James—you, *you*... you're the worst pest in the world! Why didn't you tell me Robert was downstairs?"

"I shouldn't have thought that would've mattered," James grinned, letting her pull him back through the door. "Besides, you didn't ask."

"You go down those stairs and tell Mr. Kensington that we will be ready in ten minutes."

Looking at Abigail's face, Julia hadn't the heart to ruin the foursome. She smiled at James. "We'll be down shortly!"

"Ten minutes?" James crossed his arms in protest. "What about coming with me right now?"

"We can't wear these clothes on bicycles! Shoo! Out!" Abigail pushed James out the door while he pretended to let her. Closing it, she beamed at Julia. "Sounds like the perfect way to get my dance card all filled out for tomorrow night!"

The cool morning made the ride perfect. Cycling at leisure, they paused often to sit on benches. Robert stopped twice for treats, making every effort to impress Abigail.

Faraway music came from the direction of River Street. It sounded like a hymn.

"Sounds like a boat has arrived," Robert explained. "Folks sometimes sing to the travelers as they disembark, hoping for a few coins in the hat. Shall we ride that direction and enjoy the music?"

As they mounted their bicycles, they heard a rattle and an excited greeting.

"Miss Angel!" Marcus Levitt pedaled toward them.

"Marcus! How are you?" Julia paused, waiting while he stopped next to her bicycle, giving her a wide smile.

"I lost two teeth!"

"Well, that's fine!" Julia congratulated him. She motioned to the others. "Go on ahead. I've been hoping to see my friend again before I left Savannah. I'll join you in five minutes. You go while they're still singing." Julia turned to Marcus. "I see you're all healed up and back to riding as fast as you can go!"

"I'm faster because I'm bigger. I had to raise the seat!" He tightened his grip on the handlebars and stretched himself high on the seat.

"Oh, my! I thought you looked as if you'd grown at least an inch." Julia said, tousling his hair. "I know your mother is happy to have a boy like you. I've seen her quite a few times lately. She's a very nice lady."

"She's happy a lot now. She sews and makes money."

"She's helping *my* mother with sewing. Did you know that?"

"I didn't know that lady was your mother. I like her. She gave me a muffin!"

"How nice. I was hoping to see you. I'd like for you to do something for me."

"What?" Marcus leaned forward and looked at Julia with a seriousness that tickled her. She put her face near his.

"I want you to be a good boy."

"Aww… that's what everybody says all the time!"

"I know, but I was thinking about how hard your mother works. I have a father who takes care of us in many ways, but sometimes I see my mother working hard and it makes her tired. Will you promise me you'll help your mother, Marcus? Do your schoolwork and chores without complaining and be nice to your sister. Do whatever you can and, when you get bigger, you can do all kinds of grown-up things to help her."

"When I get all grown up, I'm gonna be a doctor and take care of her when she's sick!"

"You do that, Marcus, and she'll be proud of you, and so will I." Julia put out her hand. Marcus gave it a vigorous shake.

"Goodbye, Marcus! Now show me how well you can ride— but not too fast!"

"Goodbye, Miss Angel!"

Marcus sat tall on the seat as he rode away in the direction he'd come. Julia climbed onto her bicycle and, smiling over her shoulder, waved as she watched him go.

"Hello, Miss Angel!"

Julia jumped, as taken aback at the sound of his voice as she'd been the day before. The bicycle proved to be a better stabilizer than the footstool as she spun around to find his kind, blue eyes closer to hers than she expected. She wobbled, but remained upright.

"Adam!"

~

ADAM SWALLOWED HARD. Though he had spent a sleepless night with his mind grasping for any plausible scenario that might bring him to this moment, none of them had prepared him for it.

"I'm so glad you've come my way. I didn't think I'd see you again."

"I didn't either. I hadn't any plans to go cycling this morning until just a bit ago, but I'm glad to see you, too."

"I'm in a terrible rush—I'm just returning the bicycle before I have to get my bags and catch the train."

"Yes, you mustn't miss your train."

Adam paused, his regrets over his botched attempts at wooing flooding his mind. He'd thought of little else since he'd last seen Julia.

"I... I... don't know how to say this, but about what I did yesterday..."

"Oh, Adam, please! Let's just forget that ever happened. It just ruined everything."

"Did it?"

"No. *I* ruined everything. Everything since the day we met."

Precious time ticked away. He only wished he had time to tell her how she'd been nothing but perfection since the day they'd met. "Julia, my train... Pardon me." Adam paused, pulled his watch from his pocket and glanced at it. He spoke in a rush. "Look, I know we live miles and miles apart. In fact, I'm not really sure where you *do* live. I also know that... that I think you're wonderful. I saw you in that dress yesterday and all I could think about was the ball! All I could see was you in that dress dancing with all those other men, especially that Doctor What's-His-Name! I wanted to tell you before I left how I admire you. I know I'm only a student and you're professional-minded and all that sort of thing, but you seem the most genuine, sensible girl I've ever met and if I..."

"Adam! Stop it!"

Adam realized he'd been mistaken. Though tears had welled up in her eyes as he spoke, Julia hadn't been moved at his words. Her face looked as though what she'd heard was about to make her choke. His hurried, pathetic excuse for wooing in the middle of a public street must have angered and disgusted her.

"My apologies. I suppose I was wrong to assume that the obstacles that stand between us can be overcome by..."

"The obstacles that stand between us certainly can't be overcome by the time the train..."

Adam saw Julia's head jerk toward the direction of the sound as the train whistle blew.

"No, I'm sure you're right. Goodbye, Julia."

"Goodbye, Adam."

Adam straightened his handlebars and sped away. Thankfully, Aunt Lydia didn't live too far from the station. He had only time now to toss the bicycle onto her porch, grab his bags, and run for the train. Nothing held him in Savannah any longer.

JULIA CAUGHT up to the other three cyclists on River Street. As she climbed off her bicycle and released the handlebars, she saw that her hands were shaking. Taking a seat by Abigail on one of the benches, she found herself barely aware of the music playing as she tried to come up with some excuse should they notice her red eyes or shaky voice. When the song ended, Julia feigned exhaustion and was relieved when James and Robert offered to cut the outing short. She could see, however, that though Abigail readily offered to return to the hotel, she suspected that something more had caused such a change.

Once in their room, Julia paced while Abigail sat on the bed, watching in fretful suspense. Julia knew she owed Abigail an explanation, but hadn't a clue as to where to begin.

"Honey, what on earth?"

"Oh, Abigail, I'm such an idiot!"

"I just don't see what that little boy could have done to put you in such a state!"

"It wasn't Marcus." Julia sat on the side of the bed and put her face in her hands. "It was Adam."

"Adam who? Oh! You mean Adam *Cole*? You saw Adam? I got the distinct impression that Adam is quite smitten with you. He's got an invitation for tomorrow night. It's been in the back of my mind all week that it wouldn't surprise me one bit if he wasn't madly in love with you by the end of the evening."

Julia threw herself onto the mattress, sobbing.

Abigail leaned over her, her face full of concern. "Well then, he's done something dreadful—is that it? You saw him today. That much you've told me. Julia! For Heaven's sake!" Grabbing

Julia's shoulders, Abigail pulled her up into a sitting position. "Now, you hysterical girl, you're going to tell me what he's done to you!"

"He didn't *do* anything. He just told me how he felt."

"But how has that managed to put you in such a state? I might have been preoccupied with my own emotions lately, but even though you'd kept so quiet about it, I could see that you were taken with him. I thought you were being private and not wanting to let on. Wait a minute!"

Abigail pushed Julia's shoulders back and looked into her eyes. "He hasn't insulted you or something? Goodness! What do you mean he told you how he felt? He didn't tell you he has feelings for someone else, did he?"

"Yes, Abigail. He told me all about his feelings for someone who is the *total opposite* of me! I was so stunned and scared and numb. He just rode away and I let him. He's gone, Abigail! He's gone."

"Who is she? Come on now, let me get you a glass of water and a hanky. You're going to tell me all about it."

Julia spilled out all the facts at once, certain that Abigail must feel as though she were drowning in a flood of blubbering details.

"So you told him you were a doctor? *Now what on earth for?*"

"No, I didn't *tell* him I was a doctor! You're not paying attention, Abigail! He *thought* I was... he *assumed*. And me? I didn't do anything to correct him. It was rather a convenient private joke of mine. It seemed harmless, surrounded by all these Savannah Somebodys, to let one of them think I wasn't a Nobody from Nowhere. I thought I'd never see him again."

Julia wiped her eyes again and blew her nose. "Thank you," she whispered as Abigail held out another handkerchief. "After that, I found out I had more pride than all the Somebodys put together. I couldn't bear to explain myself with anybody else around to hear what a nitwit and liar I was. A time to explain privately never presented itself. Now I find out he's become attached to the person I pretended to be. Every time he saw me, he would tell me what a genuine person I was. I wanted to tell him the truth. It just never happened. I don't know why I should be so upset about it. I barely know the man! We'll never see each other again, anyway." Julia blew her nose again, then looked at the ceiling as if questioning the heavens. "Why couldn't I have met him earlier in the day? What was I supposed to do—blurt out 'I'm not a doctor. Now hurry and catch your train'?"

With a heavy sigh, Julia let her head fall to rest on Abigail's shoulder. "He just rode away, Abigail, and I let him," she sniffed. "I may not ever get to ask Adam to forgive me for this, but I can, and have, asked God to forgive me. I guess I've got to wait till I can stop being angry at myself. I feel like such a *fraud*!"

Abigail's voice softened as she stroked Julia's shoulder. "Oh, come now, you're not a fraud. I may not have known you for very long, but I know you well enough. You just found yourself in a predicament, that's all. Perhaps, if you'd confided in me, we might have... oh, never mind. It's all water under the bridge now."

Julia dropped her face into the handkerchief that lay open in her hands, her voice lowering to almost a mumble. "Oh, I'm not even sure why I *care* so much, Abigail."

Abigail put an arm around Julia's shoulder. "I think you care the same way I care about Robert. It's difficult to explain why. Love grows—I know that—the way it has with our parents over the years. But sometimes it does sprout up with a bang! I'm not going to say that I *love* Robert Kensington. That hasn't had time to develop yet. But I *am* going to say that if he vanished after that ball tomorrow night and I never saw him again, I'd take it mighty hard. I knew from the moment I saw him that he was someone I'd be willing to allow myself to love if things fell into place and he turned out to be as wonderful as he seemed. I believe you've opened up your heart enough to see if it would be in safe hands if entrusted to Adam Cole. Am I right?"

"Yes," Julia snuffled.

"Just you rest. Take a good, long nap. After that, there's a little something else you're going to have to attend to." Abigail smiled at Julia's puzzled expression. "Your mother can read you like a book, Julia. You've got to tell her, or she's going to think something's terribly wrong."

"I know. I always tell Mother everything. But, she's been so happy, and so busy. I'll tell her. I *will*. She's so excited about tomorrow night. I'll wait till after the ball. That way, I'll know at least one of us is having a good time."

Chapter Seventeen

Julia crawled out of bed. Her legs felt heavy as she walked across the room. She looked at her reflection in the mirror, forcing a smile. She'd hold true to the promise she'd made to herself. She'd be happy and cheerful today. Everyone had been looking forward to this social event. They deserved to have a wonderful time. Abigail awoke, giddy with anticipation, and full of happy chatter as they dressed.

After a hurried breakfast and a short wait for Ruby's driver, they were on their way. Mother would be waiting at the Allens', likely with a written agenda, ready to make sure they left for the ball looking the very image of perfection. The mad rush made it necessary for Julia to concentrate on preparations for the evening. Thoughts of Adam seemed determined to dart to the forefront of her mind. One at a time, Julia snatched each one back, forcing them into submission. Adam, along with her regrets, would have to wait.

BEATRICE HATED the thought of a dark cloud hanging over the evening ahead. From the moment Ruby's driver delivered the girls from the hotel, she'd kept a close eye on Julia. Both girls had set about their toiletries as though they hadn't anything on their minds other than the ball. Abigail seemed especially giddy. Beatrice joined them for a bit once they settled in and listened as they sat, buffing their nails and chatting about how Abigail would style their hair. She decided to postpone her talk with Julia in order to avoid putting a damper on the day. Later, she would pull her aside and ask questions about whatever troublesome thing it was that Julia obviously had been preferring to keep to herself. Her daughter always confided in her, so this must be something serious.

She found Ruby in the drawing room reading the morning mail. Beatrice settled herself in a chair and consulted her list, trying to clear her mind to focus on the preparations at hand. Gowns were pressed and ready—even Julia's. The incident with the dress puzzled her. The petticoats had required major repairs. How Julia could have managed to do such damage while nibbling cookies and sipping tea in a room all alone remained a mystery. The undergarments had looked as if Julia had been attacked from the underside by a wild animal. According to Ruby, the screened-in room had been found in complete shambles. Jane professed to know nothing about it, except that Julia had fallen, becoming entangled in the furniture. The whole muddle would, no doubt, make sense tomorrow when she talked to Julia.

"Going over your checklist again, Bea?" Ruby smiled as she placed a letter back in its envelope and picked up another from the stack.

"You know I am," Beatrice laughed. "I look at all these checkmarks and somehow I'm still certain something's left undone."

"I think it's all been finished since yesterday, hasn't it? I believe picking up your last bit of lace at Cohen's was the last thing on your list. I'm so glad it arrived before you had to go home."

"Yes, and I'm glad Mr. Cohen felt he could accept my little gift. I had no idea when we brought that copy of *Thomas Wingfold* with us that I'd be leaving it behind in Savannah. He seemed touched by it, didn't he?"

"Yes," Ruby nodded, "and he did say he wanted to understand our faith. I think any of George MacDonald's stories would help him do that."

"Well, I want to learn more about his as well," Beatrice admitted. "I left a slip of paper inside with my name and address in hopes Sarah Cohen will write to me."

"Well, Bea, we do as we're led, and after that," she smiled, pointing a finger upward, "it's all up to Him."

Ruby turned her attention back to her mail for a moment.

"There's one in the stack for you," she said, passing the envelope to Beatrice.

Beatrice studied the handwriting on the envelope with mixed feelings. She missed Roderick, but disturbing news would be unwelcome, especially today.

She opened it, sighing after a moment.

Ruby's brow wrinkled. "Something the matter, Bea?"

"No. It's just that it slipped my mind that I'm supposed to be corralling Senator Thornhill for Roderick. Remember the invention I told you about?"

"Yes, but I didn't understand a word of it."

"Neither did I! But now Roderick says he's got the whatever-it-is well on its way to completion. I'm to bring Senator Thornhill out to inspect it. Do you know how busy that man is, Ruby? Dahlia says his schedule is enough to boggle the mind. I'm in the same pickle as before. I've got to describe something that I haven't an inkling about in some way that induces the senator to make a thousand-mile journey just to look at it. Roderick never uses enough words! I can't tell you how this frustrates me!"

Beatrice waved the letter toward Ruby, who took it, puzzling over the contents.

"What's the M.W.C.D.?"

"If it still means what it first meant, it's the Mobile Wireless Communication Device."

"What on earth is *that*?"

"See what I mean?"

The door burst open. The twins rushed in, Elizabeth's face red with frustration and Eleanor's downcast and sullen.

"Mother!"

"Mother!"

"Yes? And yes?" Ruby laughed before lowering her voice. "Now you girls know better than to interrupt me when I'm in conversation with someone. What is so important that it can't wait? Let's not burden Mrs. Lansing with your troubles."

Both girls began prattling at once. Beatrice couldn't help but smile as Ruby rose from her chair and took them both into the hall. Though the door closed, she could make out that the flurry of activity over the ball had become too much for them, that they'd been banished from the dressing room by Jane for being pests, and that they were begging to at least be able to watch the hairstyling and final preparations.

Ruby returned, giving Beatrice a smile and a shake of her head. "I remember being so excited to find I'd just had two babies, Bea! It has its challenges, though. Everything a girl wants, needs, and feels has always been present in double measure. I suppose you couldn't help but hear. I promised to intercede for them and sent them away with high hopes."

"They really are dears. I can tell by your letters how much you enjoy them."

"Letters... yes... where were we?" Ruby picked up the letter again. "'Schedule the arrival of S. T.'—I suppose that's Senator Thornhill—'as soon as possible.' What's this? 'I've had the M.W.C.D. running, though many adjustments are needed. Stress importance of MUSE.' He has that in capital letters. It *must* be important. 'Absolutely no information on TOPS'... there he goes again... 'of the invention. Come home next week as promised or I don't know what you can expect to find. I am so lonely for my two girls that I barely have an appetite for Mrs. Schmidt's daily delivery or Dora Klein's dinner basket. The whole town will be feeding me out of pity if you don't come back to me. Yours, Roderick.' Why, Bea, that's sweet, even if it doesn't make any sense. What's this big, important MUSE?"

"I haven't a clue."

"Well, I'm surprised that in the midst of all this work on his invention that Roderick has time to work on inventing toys. That is, if that's what he means by tops—children's toy tops?"

"It's the first I've heard of it. But you never know with Roderick. One day he may be working on something to change the world and the next day it's something to comb the cat." Beatrice sighed. "Tonight will likely be my last chance to talk to Senator Thornhill and Julia will dance at least one dance with him. I'd better show this to her. Maybe between the two of us we can come up with something to tell him that brings about the desired result."

Ruby giggled. "But, Bea! What *is* the desired result?"

"I haven't a clue!" Beatrice chuckled, then looked at Ruby with a touch of fear in her eyes. "I can't let him down, Ruby. This is the most important thing Roderick's ever done. Somehow, tonight, I've got to get Percival Thornhill to give me his word that he'll come to Morgan's Landing. If, as I predict, he misses every other word I say, it will take a miracle to flatter, coerce, and persuade that *blasted* senator! Pardon my language."

HANNAH, keeping her promise to report to the Allens' just after sundown when the Sabbath ended, stood with Jane and the twins at the foot of the stairs and watched the elegant party descend and make their way to the waiting automobiles.

After shooing the twins off to bed, Jane turned to Hannah.

"I suppose we'd best tidy up that dressing room," she remarked with a sigh as they started up the stairs. "Tired as I am, I have to admit I'd like to be there just to see those dresses dance. And the food! I'm sure it will be a feast fit for a king."

"I'm not about to pretend, Jane, that I wouldn't like to see it myself," Hannah said. "So many grand people in elegant clothes, dancing and laughing. It's something I've never seen the likes of—ever in my life."

"From what I can tell, it might just be that Miss Julia and her mother have never seen the likes of it either. Mrs. Allen is a rich lady, but she's not one to put on airs. When she'd show me Mrs. Lansing's drawings and have me sew for her, she spoke of her upbringing. I take it those two ladies grew up doing for themselves. The Lansings still live in that little town in Missouri, and I don't think they live near as high on the hill as the Allens do. They may go to dances and parties back home, but something tells me those couldn't hold a candle to this. And land's sakes, I surely do hope that girl manages to keep herself upright with both her feet on the floor all evening!"

"Jane, you were in the screened-in room with all that *balagan*! What happened?"

"*Bagalan?*" Jane wrinkled her brow, then smiled. "Oh, never mind—I won't try to say it, but I know what you mean." She shook her head. "No, I didn't witness whatever tore up that room. I only came upon the aftermath. All I can say, Hannah, is that I believe, given time, the thing you'd come up with if you dug to the bottom of Miss Julia's mess of trouble is a *man.*"

CLIFFORD ALLEN ASSISTED the ladies as they alighted from the automobile. Julia thanked him and tried not to appear fidgety and she fluffed her skirts and raised a hand to smooth her hair one last time. After offering an arm to his wife, Mr. Allen turned and extended the other. "Beatrice?"

Mother slipped her hand into the crook of his elbow. "I'm so glad you made it home from your business trip in time to escort us, Clifford. It wouldn't have been the same without you." She looked over her shoulder at Julia and Abigail. "Come along, girls. James and your parents may have already arrived, Abigail. If not, I'm sure they'll be here soon."

"Oh, this *is* lovely!" Abigail gave a sigh of appreciation as they made their way up the stone staircase.

Julia took in the grandeur of the Graysons' home, wishing she had Abigail's ability to treat the situation as though they'd merely arrived at another picnic at Sweetbriar. She fought to remember her manners as she tried to manage the massive front steps without gawking.

Once inside, Julia again cautioned herself against allowing

her jaw to drop. Abigail, however, carried herself with ease, as though nothing other than fun and games lay ahead. Catching her mother's eye, Julia leaned in to whisper in her ear.

"It's beautiful!"

"I didn't do it justice in my description, did I?"

A servant in immaculate attire greeted them in the front hall, taking their wraps. Another welcomed Jeremiah, Rose, and James Hadley, who entered a moment later and joined their party. Yet another requested that they follow him to the ballroom.

Though the grand entry hall hummed with conversation and strangers seemed to appear out of nowhere at a dizzying rate, Julia focused her attention on the polished wood and honed marble that seemed to glow in the light of the gas lamps and candles that flickered everywhere. Crystal and silver caught her eye no matter where she turned.

Mrs. Grayson greeted them in the ballroom, wearing a gown of pale gray, embroidered satin. Julia recognized her mother's creativity.

Drawing Clifford's and Jeremiah's attention to the whereabouts of her husband, Mrs. Grayson suggested they join him in a group of men that had gathered around him on the other side of the room. She then turned to address Julia, Abigail, and James.

"We'll go in to supper soon and come back to the ballroom for dancing afterward. I'll introduce you to some of our younger guests in just a moment."

Abigail and James offered their thanks and Julia followed

suit, keenly aware that she'd only come to know someone of Mrs. Grayson's social standing because of Mother's connections over the last year.

"It was kind of you to invite me, Mrs. Grayson," she said.

"I haven't seen you since your Mother's visit last year," Mrs. Grayson smiled, "and then only once at the Allens' when Ruby first showed us her designs. You look as lovely as your Mother tonight."

"Thank you."

Mother smiled. "Your home looks especially beautiful tonight, Mrs. Grayson."

"Thank you. I must say I have received nothing but compliments on my gown, Mrs. Lansing. Many of the ladies in this room have spoken very highly of you." She paused, looking around the room with an approving eye. "I'm glad the young people could be here to celebrate with us. We're so proud of our nephew, Paul. As you've heard, he's graduated from West Point and come back to us—as we like to tease him—to the South where he belongs!" Turning, she motioned to a handsome man in dress uniform, who then appeared at her elbow. "Paul, I have some friends I'd like you to meet."

Julia had to admit that Paul Grayson took her breath away. His dark masculinity intimidated her. His eyes, black as his hair, were soft and friendly. He towered above her, displaying a perfect smile made more striking by his tanned face. *He must be six and a half feet tall.* The guest of honor would, no doubt, receive plenty of attention this evening.

With a slight bow, he exchanged greetings with Julia and Abigail before turning to shake James's hand.

Feeling a brush against her elbow, Julia glanced at Abigail, whose eyes twinkled as though they were sending secret messages. She turned, lowering an ear to catch Abigail's whisper. "Well now, Julia! *This* ought to take your mind off your troubles!"

Julia blushed a bit, then smiled as she watched Abigail eyes roam the room. Within a half second, it appeared that Paul Grayson had already ceased to exist in Abigail's world. She seemed to be looking past him, through him, and around him. Julia knew why. The lanky Robert Kensington was bound to be here somewhere.

Offering Julia his arm, Paul gave a nod to the far end of the ballroom. Leaving Mother and Mr. and Mrs. Hadley to chat with Mrs. Grayson, the three walked with him toward a cluster of young people. Having searched her mind and found it empty of small talk, Julia felt a wave of relief when Paul spoke first.

"Mother's spoken highly of the Lansing ladies. I'm delighted to have you with us this evening. So, Miss Lansing, I hear you and your mother are visiting all the way from Missouri."

Questions about her life back home brought a nervous flutter back to Julia's stomach. But then, a new thought entered her mind. *I'll be back in Morgan's Landing soon and none of these people will matter.* Other than her life-long bond with the Allens and her new relationship with the Hadleys, she had no ties here. Adam had left Savannah, taking with him the danger that her giant, pretentious fib might come to public exposure. In the days ahead, she'd struggle to dismiss her feelings for him —to stop *thinking* about him, but for tonight there seemed no reason she shouldn't relax and enjoy herself. She inhaled a breath of fresh air.

"Yes, we've had a wonderful visit. Everyone in Savannah has been so kind to us. But I have to admit to being homesick."

As the words exited Julia's mouth, she wished she hadn't uttered them. The thought of someone like Paul asking her to tell him all about her life in Morgan's Landing made her feel every bit as inadequate as she had when she'd first met Abigail. The dinner announcement offered a reprieve as the crowd began moving toward the dining hall. Julia took James's arm. They walked alongside Paul as he escorted his aunt into the dining hall. Paul offered Julia a charming smile. "I understand my aunt helped James and Abigail fill out your dance card."

"I believe so. You see, I really don't know anyone except for the Allens and those we've just met—the Hadleys, Kensingtons, and Senator and Mrs. Thornhill."

"I believe I'm penciled for at least one dance. I'm glad."

"I'm glad, too."

Julia had thought it impossible to find herself in a room more glittering than the ballroom, but the long row of gleaming china, crystal, and silver place settings took her breath away. Several candelabra, each one surrounded by a lush display of fresh flowers, lit the center of the table and offered up a delightful fragrance. Mother hadn't exaggerated—Morgan's Landing hadn't seen anything compared to this.

As Paul seated Mrs. Grayson and went to join his uncle near the other end of the table, Julia allowed herself to be seated, grateful to find herself across the table from her mother.

A multitude of servants appeared and reappeared at Julia's elbow throughout the meal, offering delight after delight. Seated next to James, Julia found herself distracted from her food by the gentleman on her other side who seemed intent that they understand the intricacies of his shipping business. Ruby, seated across the table next to Mother, caught her eye and, after giving her a knowing smile, joined the conversation and began making an effort to change the subject.

Grateful, Julia turned her attentions to James. He seemed especially animated tonight, just as he had ever since he'd come to the hotel room to invite her and Abigail to go cycling. He looked handsome tonight with his pale curls smoothed back and his hazel eyes sparkling. The overly serious demeanor seemed to have lifted in the last day or two and Julia found this fascinating. She reversed her previous judgment that he looked too old for his age. Tonight, James seemed young and, though she could hardly have imagined it, carefree.

He surveyed the gathering with a calm smile. "I'm seeing your mother's creativity at its best, Julia. It's my opinion that the ladies wearing that unmistakable Lansing design outshine all the rest."

"Thank you! Since I am one of those ladies, I'll accept that compliment as directed to both Mother and myself. Speaking of shining," Julia said, glancing up the row of guests to where Abigail and her parents sat nearer to the Kensingtons and their hostess, "I'm admiring your mother's and Abigail's jewelry, James. Your father's talents shine also."

"Well, if you don't mind my boasting a bit, I'll claim an ounce or two of credit."

"Really? Did you design them or make them—or both?"

"I designed the jewelry Abigail is wearing. She asked me for something elegant, but a bit more youthful than some of our usual designs."

"You've done a wonderful job, but the jewels can't out-sparkle Abigail's eyes tonight."

"So I see." James followed her nod, observing Abigail and Robert. "I think my family's connections to Savannah are about to take on a much more personal nature." He lowered his voice to almost a whisper. "If I take your meaning correctly, I have to agree that something other than jewelry has captured my sister's attention tonight."

"If you don't mind my asking, James, are you happy in the jewelry business? I think everyone should do something that gives them something to look forward to when they open their eyes every morning."

"Five years ago, I'd have given a negative response to that question. You know how it goes—I wanted to strike out in some new way, amazing everyone with my adventurous endeav-ors. But time will tell, as they say, and time has told me that I have my father's eye for fine detail and his appreciation for what comes out of the earth. I enjoy it. I don't have his keen business sense, but I suppose it will come in time. At least, I hope so."

"That's wonderful! I'm glad you find it fascinating."

"Oh, I do. If you like, I could go into great detail about the shipping side of the business," he said, feigning seriousness. "You see, first the ore..."

Julia laughed. "Oh, James, don't you dare!" she whispered.

AT EVERY OPPORTUNITY, Beatrice snatched a glance at Julia and James. They seemed to be enjoying one another. Julia, at last, looked happy. Beatrice found herself puzzling over this, wondering if perhaps James had anything to do with Julia's lackluster mood during this trip. If he had been attempting to start a courtship with Julia while she'd been busy with clients, Julia would have said something. Perhaps the opposite had occurred. Julia might have been interested in James and hadn't realized until tonight that he returned her affections. James's sweet disposition, his financial position and the fact that his family had become such good friends made him a fine prospect as a son-in-law. Yet, Beatrice's heart sank at the thought of how far away Atlanta, and therefore the Hadley business, was from Morgan's Landing. Surely Julia hadn't been struggling with thoughts of moving away from home! *Oh, what am I thinking?*

Turning back to her dinner companion, Beatrice attempted to immerse herself in the feast of reason and the flow of soul that surrounded the topic of the shipping industry. After a few moments, she realized the futility of her efforts, shrugged at Ruby, and gave up the struggle.

As THE SOUND of music began to waft from the direction of the ballroom and their hostess announced that the dancing would begin, Abigail fought the urge to leap from her seat. Taking her father's arm while her mother took the other, they made their way to the ballroom and joined Julia and James. She felt no need to glance at her dance card, for she had it memorized. She'd memorized Julia's as well. Julia would begin with James, a proficient dancer and someone she knew. Though Abigail hadn't met Paul Grayson until tonight, she'd had the foresight to enlist her mother's influence so that the guest of honor would be next on Julia's list. Abigail smiled with satisfaction. She'd done as well for Julia as she'd done for herself. Once she'd had a turn about the floor with her father for good measure, she'd end up where she belonged—in the arms of Robert Kensington.

The moment her father had given a polite bow and released her hand, Robert appeared just as she knew he would.

"Miss Hadley, may I have this dance?"

Abigail made a pretense of checking her card. "Why, yes, Mr. Kensington, I do believe this dance is yours."

Once swept into his arms, Abigail felt as though her feet barely touched the floor. After a few moments, she tore her eyes away from Robert's and nodded toward Julia. "Robert! Look! Julia's dancing with Paul. Don't they make the handsomest couple you ever saw?"

"No, they make the *second* handsomest couple I ever saw."

Abigail blushed with pleasure as Robert twirled her around the floor. "Oh, yes. I noticed those other people. I thought they looked quite happy. They dance divinely."

"I think they should dance every dance together."

"Oh, Robert! That isn't how it's done. What would everybody think?"

"I suppose they'd think that those dancers were very special to one another."

Abigail lifted her eyes to meet Robert's eyes as his hand tightened around hers. Her heart, as well as her diary, would record this night as the night she *knew*.

Chapter Eighteen

Breathless from dancing, Julia excused herself and walked to the refreshment table. She paused there, watching the other dancers, and thrilled once again at the sight of Abigail and Robert, twirling as though they were the only two people in the room.

Julia hoped to always remember how her mother looked tonight, smiling and quite the vision in shades of green. The rich color stood in striking contrast against Mother's fair skin. Velvet rose leaves, appliquéd across the bodice, embellished the deep green satin, continuing down each side of the open over-skirt and around the train. The pale green lace of the underskirt also trimmed the neckline and formed the shoulder-skimming sleeves that stopped just above her elbows. The dress had been in the making ever since their last trip to Savannah.

Mother seemed to be accepting every request for a dance. First Mr. Allen, then James, followed by Jeremiah Hadley, and wasn't that Mr. Barton as well? Julia wished Papa could see her, looking so beautiful, having the time of her life. On second thought, it was just as well he couldn't. Papa may have cracked under the strain. The sight of his wife being swirled about the ballroom by all these men in a dress such as this would have had him frothing at the mouth with jealousy. In Morgan's Landing, Mother spent more time dressing other people for fancy events than she did herself.

Julia had caught sight of Senator Thornhill again. Each time he'd come into view or she'd heard his voice booming as the music stopped, the mishaps of the past month had replayed in her mind. She'd offered up more than one silent prayer of thanksgiving that such things had managed to take an evening off. The ball would be a highlight of her trip—a dazzling gem she could bring to mind in the days ahead when other memories needed to be pushed aside. She returned Mother's smile as she saw her approaching.

"Mother, you couldn't look prettier. You seem to be having a marvelous time!"

"Oh! Yes! My!" Mother smiled, pausing to catch her breath. "I've not danced like this in years! I've met so many new people at once that I'm having difficulty keeping their names straight. You've certainly made an impression on everybody, Lovely One."

"Oh, I doubt I've impressed *everybody*," Julia laughed. "I've been having a nice time with James. He's been sweet to keep me occupied. He's much more talkative and attentive tonight than he's been since we've met."

"I noticed. What about Paul Grayson? You've danced with him several times." Mother gave a slight nod in Paul's direction. "He's dancing with that French girl now. Ruby says her family has business connections with the Graysons and that both families would consider a marriage between them most desirable."

"I hope if they do marry, it's for better reasons. You should spend your life with the person you really want."

"I'm not sure Paul knows what he really wants."

"What do you mean?"

"I mean, I've seen him *standing* near Martha Gueron and *speaking* to Martha Gueron, but he's been *watching* Julia Lansing."

"Oh, don't be silly, Mother! But... well..."

"Well?"

"He did ask for the last dance, but I'd already promised it to James."

"I find that he who dances last often means to dance their way into someone's heart."

Julia wanted to avoid any such nonsense with either James or Paul.

"Mother, you'll let me know if you get too tired or the Allens want to leave? I certainly don't have to stay if the others aren't up to it."

"Don't you worry about me! I'm just getting started. Another cup of punch should keep me going."

Turning to the punch bowl, they extended their cups toward the attendant.

"There you are at last!" At Senator Thornhill's greeting from behind, they leaped skyward, clutching at one another for support. Their response paled in comparison, however, to that of the pourer of punch, who lost his grip on the ladle before disappearing behind the table. Reappearing, and now a vivid crimson, he gushed apologies to Mother and Julia as he blotted their hands and arms. He then turned his attention to stanching the flow which streamed onto the floor from the tablecloth and his face.

Julia pitied the poor fellow and assured him that they would explain to Mrs. Grayson that it couldn't be helped. She turned as the voice boomed again behind her.

"Which of you lovely ladies is going to be my partner for this dance?"

The Thornhills hadn't been seated near them at dinner. Since then, he'd occupied himself with a group of men talking politics. After dancing with his wife, Mrs. Grayson, and Rose Hadley, he apparently thought it was time he treated Mother and Julia to a turn around the ballroom.

Julia looked at her mother. It appeared she still hadn't recovered her wits. Her expression, as she continued to blot punch from her hair, hinted at frustration. Julia stepped forward, knowing that Papa's future depended on the senator.

"This dance is taken on my card, Senator, but I don't see the gentleman right now. I'm sure he won't mind if you take his place."

"Yes, go ahead and enjoy yourself," Mother beamed at her, "you *dear* girl!"

As the senator led Julia around the ballroom, she saw her mother make a quick exit. *Freshen up, Mother, and prepare yourself. You're next.* Steeling herself for the task at hand, Julia smiled at the senator. She knew full well that her mother's persuasive powers far outweighed her own. She must keep the conversation light and, once Senator Thornhill was primed and ready, she'd hand him over to Mother and let her do the convincing.

WITH THE LAST dance at hand, Julia looked around the room, trying to imprint the picture of the ballroom and its elegant occupants on her mind for the future. This had been a night to treasure. She'd had as much fun dancing with Mr. Hadley, Mr. Allen, and several other older men as she had with James, Paul, and others her age. She hadn't come to be romanced, but to savor the extravagance of it all. Her reflection smiled back at her from one of the enormous mirrors on the opposite side of the ballroom and she resisted the urge to turn and preen before it. Would there ever be another occasion befitting of this dress? When she returned home to roll out dough in Schmidt's Bakery every day, she planned to relive this night. With only one more dance to add to her memories, Julia looked around the room. *Where are you, James?*

"May I?"

Julia found Paul Grayson at her elbow.

"I'd love to, but I've promised James Hadley."

"I don't see him anywhere. Do you?"

Julia scanned the room again. "No. I just don't understand where he might be, though."

"We shouldn't let the last dance go to waste. I'm sure he'll feel free to cut in when he returns."

The smooth voice and winning smile had their effect. Julia took Paul's outstretched hand. Of course, James would return in a moment and they would finish the dance, but for now, she'd add this memory to her store of treasures. She relaxed into Paul's embrace as he pulled her close—closer than he had when they'd danced earlier. As his face drew near, she let her eyes dart away, but then pulled them back and let them roam over his face. His black hair and eyes, his gleaming smile, his swarthy complexion—now showing just a hint of beard stubble after hours of dancing—these belonged in her treasure store before the night's end.

JAMES HADLEY LEFT the library and entered the main hall. The moment he saw Julia, he realized his error. She stood, smiling up at Paul Grayson as he helped her with her wraps. He'd missed the last dance. Paul had taken his place—but then again, someone had to. He had no excuse for his ungentlemanly behavior. He'd let Julia down. If it hadn't been for Paul Grayson, Julia might have missed the last dance as well. A brief notion that perhaps he should thank Paul passed from his mind as quickly as it had come. All that mattered now was determining how much he'd offended Julia and how to apologize.

"James!"

Julia had seen him. He didn't detect a rebuke in her greeting.

"I've missed our dance, haven't I?"

"Yes. I didn't see you anywhere."

"I'm sorry, Julia. A few of the men were discussing jewelry designs with Father. He called me into the library. I suppose we talked longer than I realized."

Paul smiled. "That's all right. I offered my services. Miss Lansing didn't go without a partner."

"Well, you're here now, James," Julia smiled as she adjusted her wrap around her shoulders. "I'm glad nothing serious detained you. It'll be recompense enough if you'll escort Abigail and me back to the hotel."

Relieved, James put out his arm. "I'd be pleased, Miss Lansing. The Wentworth Hotel, as a matter of fact, is where I am staying."

"Whatever the misunderstanding," Paul interjected, "I enjoyed myself, Miss Lansing. I'd be honored to see you safely out to the automobile."

"That would be nice." Julia hesitated, but took Paul's arm and they went out.

James proceeded to follow them out to the porch and down the staircase toward the street but was hindered a bit when he stepped aside to let a few ladies go ahead of him.

"James! Where on earth have you been?" Abigail appeared at James' elbow. "I thought you were Julia's last dance."

"So did I."

PAUL OPENED the door and assisted Julia as she seated herself in the automobile.

"Thank you, Paul. The others should be here any minute, so you needn't stay. I'm sorry about the mix-up. I've never known James to be inconsiderate. If someone hadn't monopolized his attentions, he wouldn't have missed the dance. I don't want you to think he mistreated me."

"That jewelry discussion in the library was quite in-depth."

"You were there, too?" Julia asked in surprise.

"I was in the library when his father and some friends came in. Mr. Hadley was telling them all about his designs and how James designed Abigail's jewelry."

"Oh, I see. But you weren't there when James was there. You and I were dancing."

"Well," Paul paused, the corners of his mouth turning up in mischief, "after I suggested they meet James and get his ideas on new designs, I only saw him as I was leaving. I had to hurry back. I wouldn't have wanted to miss the last dance, now would I? Good night, Julia."

"Why, *Paul*!" Stunned, Julia stared at Paul as he climbed the stairs. She didn't know whether to be flattered or furious.

A familiar feeling returned, creeping over Julia just as it had in the Allens' screened-in room. *Someone's watching.* The guests, busy with their goodbyes, were climbing into carriages and automobiles. None of them seemed to be showing her any particular attention. Lifting her eyes, she saw Martha Gueron at the head of the stairs. Julia looked away, shivering under one of the meanest stares she'd ever received.

Chapter Nineteen

BEATRICE SAT down on the trunk lid with a huff. "Well, as always, things come out much easier than they go back in. How will we ever get this lid shut, Julia?"

"You're the one who's an expert at making things fit, Mother," Julia grunted as she pressed the latch again in hopes they'd hear a click. "I think it might be due to the extra laces and trims you bought at Cohen's."

"Yes, I suppose so." Beatrice stood with her hands on her hips, surveying the trunk. Since the ball, the sadness of parting had dampened the thrill of going home again. However, now that Monday had arrived, Beatrice had been forced to push both feelings aside in order to concentrate on preparations for going home. The remainder of Julia's things had been brought from the Wentworth to Ruby's where they could work together at making everything fit in the trunks. She and Julia had packed and repacked, squeezing in new things and pulling out items they might need before the following morning when the trunks would be locked and taken from Ruby's house to the depot. "I think I'll empty it and start over. Come sit with me for a minute first."

Beatrice propped the bed pillows behind them. They nestled onto the bed, legs outstretched.

"Are you tired, Mother?"

"No, I want to ask you something. I should have asked weeks ago, and, for that, I apologize. Julia, something is wrong and I want you to tell me what it is."

Pausing, Beatrice studied Julia's face. When Julia kept her eyes lowered and offered no immediate answer, she pressed on.

"Last year in Savannah, you were bright and cheerful every moment, at least when you weren't frustrated at your father for hovering over you. I've been so busy this time and you had a new friend in Abigail. I told myself you were blissfully occupied. I didn't realize until Ruby mentioned it. She noticed you weren't the same girl who visited last time."

Julia's eyes met hers. Beatrice saw in them the affirmation she needed. Still, the only reply she heard was a quivering sigh.

"A certain cloud comes over your face at times, but I didn't stop to see what might be troubling you." She squeezed Julia's hand. "What is it? I may not be able to help, but you *must tell me*. You seemed to enjoy the ball. I admit to wondering if you hadn't fallen in love with James Hadley. Is that it? Have you had feelings for James and felt he wasn't interested? He certainly seems interested now."

"James?" Julia shot up from her reclining position. "What on earth gave you that idea?"

"Oh, just that you seemed to be enjoying his company Saturday night. Is it something else?"

"It's something else, all right. I don't know where to begin, Mother. It's not James. It's Adam Cole."

"Now, who on earth is Adam Cole?" Beatrice's eyes widened. She searched her memory for any such name amongst the people she'd met in the last month.

"Do you remember our first night here? We dined at the hotel with the Thornhills."

"Of course."

"There was a young man with curly hair in a party across the room dining with a young lady in pink and some older..."

"Yes! Nice looking people? They left before we did. But it was no one we knew."

"I spoke with the young man in the lobby earlier when I held his hand..."

"What!" Beatrice's eyebrows shot upward. She tried to replay the events, but couldn't imagine any time when they'd been separated that evening. Her shy daughter, having been reduced to a nervous wreck by her encounter with Senator Thornhill earlier, couldn't possibly have elected to slip away from her and started holding strange men's hands. She sat upright and looked into Julia's face.

"Well, it was an accident..." Julia responded, her voice sounding weak and pitiful.

"You *accidentally* held his hand?"

"Yes. Oh, I'll explain about that part later. I met him the next day and a few times since. His name is Adam Cole and he's a medical student in Boston."

"Why haven't you told me, Julia? You've told me every other detail of this trip—all the recipes you've learned, the places you and Abigail have shopped, the other people you met."

"Because I wanted to burst into tears every time I remembered it!"

"What *happened*?! Has he treated you badly?"

"No. I treated *him* badly. I lied to him! Right out there on the public street! Now he's under all sorts of false illusions about me."

"Nonsense!" Beatrice knew her child better than this.

"But I did! I practically told him I was a doctor!"

Beatrice's eyebrows returned to their upward position. "*Now what on earth for?*"

Beatrice withheld further comment, her heart aching at the muffled weeping coming from beneath the blonde curls that had just descended into her lap. She patted them.

"That's what Abigail said!" Julia squeaked.

THOUGH THE DETAILS—POURED out wholly and without restraint—made the situation sound worse, Julia felt a sense of relief once Mother knew the whole story.

"So, what you are saying is that you really admire Adam Cole?"

"I know it sounds silly, but I'm convinced he's the sweetest, kindest man I've ever met."

"And you think he has feelings for you that have, as they say, ripened into something deeper and warmer than mere friendship?"

"That's the worst part. He tried to express his feelings before he left—to tell me how much he admired me. He even admitted to being upset that I'd be at the ball dancing with other men. I'm sure he climbed the Allens' wall just to be near me, Mother!"

"Climbed the..." Mother began. She paused with a faraway look in her eye as though she were trying to piece this bit of news into the rush of information she'd just received. "Well, now that I think of it, I suppose he had to get up to the window somehow. Goodness!" she sighed, "it's a relief to finally know what happened to Ruby's screened-in room. Was that the last time you saw Adam?"

Julia wiped her tears and sniffed. Taking a deep breath, she went on, "The day he was to leave, we met on the street. He was about to ask if we could correspond. Then, he said I was so genuine and sensible. I saw him check his watch. I knew I couldn't explain before he had to catch his train. Nothing I could've blurted out in that fragment of time would have left him with a favorable opinion of me. I just stood there, looking at him. Then, the train whistle blew and he just rode away."

"So you had *no* opportunity this past month to tell him the truth?"

"Not in private. Every time I tried, someone else came on the scene. I just couldn't find a way."

"Not that I want my daughter living far away from me, which would be likely if she had a big-city doctor for a husband, but couldn't you have had someone else explain? Besides, wouldn't he have found out from Robert Kensington sooner or later?"

"Oh, don't say that! If that happens, he's sure to think the worst of me. It was something that I needed to do myself," Julia closed her eyes, sighing, "but I never did."

She relaxed under the sympathetic touch as Mother's hand began stroking her hair again.

"If it's meant to be Adam Cole, somehow God will bring him back into your life."

"I'd be happy if God merely brought him back long enough to hear me explain. I get so upset every time I think about not having set things straight. I have no contact with him, and it would appear extremely forward of me if I tried to establish any. I suppose it's all over."

Beatrice pulled her into a tight squeeze. "Then how about we *go home*? We'll pray that, if things are meant to be between you and Adam, your paths will cross again. Perhaps you'll get a second chance."

"That sounds wonderful, Mother! Let's *go home!*"

Mother pointed at the trunk. "We can't leave tomorrow if we don't pack today."

Julia looked at the trunk and sighed. "All right, but once it's repacked, I'll sit on the lid and you try to latch it."

Packing took the greater part of the day. That evening, as they relaxed for one last visit in the Allen's parlor, Julia savored the time. Now Mother had no more appointments or pressures put upon her. She had nothing to do but spend this final evening with her childhood friend. Julia thought of Bertina Drexler, her best friend back in Morgan's Landing. How bittersweet it felt to think that she'd soon have the joy of being reunited while Mother would only have begun missing her best friend.

As she settled into her room all alone that night, Julia blinked back the tears she'd been holding just beneath the surface ever since she'd stood with Abigail and watched the last of her things being taken from their shared hotel room. They'd shared a long embrace and it would have to last for months and maybe even years. Turning over onto her side, Julia's thoughts turned to Papa. His welcoming hug would squeeze her till her ribs ached. She'd bake him something special and smile as he told her he'd never tasted a better pie. Morgan's Landing would welcome her in its own way. She'd soon walk its brick paved streets, its shaded lawns, its bustling Main Street. Thoughts of it carried her straight to Schmidt's Bakery where the smell of hot rolls wafted into her dreams.

The Allen household rose early Tuesday morning and began a flurry of efforts to arrive at the train station on time. They found Hadleys there, waiting to say a final goodbye, just as they'd promised. Abigail promised weekly letters. James wished Julia a safe journey and blushed as he told her how much he'd enjoyed getting to know her. Beatrice and Ruby wept openly. Clifford looked on, blinking back a tear or two, all the while ignoring the twins as they chattered away, begging for a trip to Missouri.

Julia's tears had begun when she'd stopped at the hotel for one last visit to the kitchen. Chef Plouff, holding her hands in his own, had kissed them before grasping her shoulders and kissing each cheek. Julia hadn't understood more than five or six words of the French he'd gushed over her, but she knew she'd left with the blessing of a true friend.

When the first whistle blew for the train's departure, the time for farewells ended. Julia and Beatrice moved with the other passengers onto the platform. As Julia turned to give Abigail a final wave, she noticed Hannah Levitt rising from a nearby bench. Marcus and Rebekah stood beside her, next to what appeared to be their baggage. Marcus strained against his mother's grip as she tried to keep him from running to Julia.

"Marcus! What are you doing here?" she said as he stopped in front of her.

"I'm going to your house, Miss Angel!"

Julia looked from Marcus to his mother, who offered no contradiction. She turned to Mother. Nothing in her face indicated that she found anything extraordinary in his claim.

"Of course, Julia. Don't you remember discussing Mrs. Levitt's sewing abilities?"

"Well, yes, I remember you speaking highly of her and

saying that she was someone you would trust to do quality work.”

“And then I told you I hired her.”

Julia turned away from Hannah Levitt. “*Hired* her?” she whispered.

“You mean I didn’t tell you?”

“Well, yes… but… No, Mother, I’m afraid this is the first I’ve heard of them going to Morgan’s Landing! I thought you meant you hired her to sew for the Savannah customers.” Julia turned to Hannah with a nervous laugh. “I suppose Mother’s been so busy that I’m the last to know.”

“I’m sorry,” Mother said. “I guess I talked so much about it to Ruby and Hannah, and myself, that I thought *we’d* discussed it.”

“Does Papa know?”

“Well… no. After I decided it was an absolute necessity, there just wasn’t time to write. I’m sure he can be made to see the need of it.”

Julia gasped. Grasping her mother’s arm, she led her a few steps away. “Mother!” she whispered. “You haven’t told him? I can hardly believe you kept it from me. I can’t imagine Papa’s reaction!”

“Well, I *am* truly sorry. Besides, you’re a fine one to talk! You’ve kept a few secrets of your own these last weeks.”

Julia looked up as the conductor opened the door of the train car. They would have to discuss this later. After managing to find seats that would allow the Levitts to sit facing them, she helped Hannah get the children settled before taking a seat next to Mother.

"Oh, Mother. I just remembered the senator. You danced with him after I did. What did you say? What happened?"

"Oh, *that*," Mother waived a dismissive hand, as though her deed could have been accomplished by a child of six. "It's all taken care of. I'll tell all about it on the way home."

Julia had planned to pass away the hours by reading, watching the scenery, and banishing her lingering regrets. Marcus and Rebekah, experiencing life on the rails for the first time, allowed little time for contemplation. They delighted in the sights, smells, and food that the train had to offer almost as much as the ever-changing discoveries passing by the windows. The revelation that not only did sleeper cars exist, but that they would occupy one, made them giddy. Their barrage of questions and pleas to look out the windows kept Julia's mind off her disappointments. When exhaustion prevailed over enthusiasm and they napped, she tried to sort things out.

Home. I'm going home. Life will be just as before. I'll survive. Julia thought of her parents. They often reminisced about their courting days. Ruby had introduced them at a school Christmas program. Though he hadn't expressed it in words, Papa's attentiveness had made it evident to everyone present, including Mother, that he'd taken an interest in her. Later, he'd appeared on her doorstep at least a half dozen times, only to be told by her mother that she wasn't at home. He began to wonder if the girl he'd come to court had hidden each time he'd come, having told her mother to send him away. Mother hadn't been home, however. She'd taken a sewing job. Grandma, a woman of few words, had omitted that small detail. Perhaps she hadn't been ready for her daughter to have a suitor. A few weeks later, while visiting a mutual friend, they met again. Once Papa had his explanation, he wasted no further time in courting the girl he loved. Julia pondered their romance. How near they'd come to never marrying! They both would have survived if they'd never seen each other again; but while they'd been apart, they'd each known they'd met someone special—someone they wanted the opportunity to grow to love.

That's what Abigail had said about Robert. Julia smiled at the memory of the adoration in their eyes. *My time will come. If it's meant to be Adam Cole, somehow God will bring him back to me... somehow.*

When the train blew its whistle and slowed, Julia looked out the window. They wouldn't stop in such a small town, but the whistle had its effect. The children sprang to life again, refreshed by their hour's sleep. Hannah stirred a bit and returned to her quiet pastime of watching the scenery disappear as she faced the back of the train. She seemed content to offer her children a gentle caution against speaking too loudly and let Julia field most of their questions concerning their new surroundings. Julia heard her mother sigh and watched her close the sketchbook she'd been making design notes in and slip it into a bag. As Mother looked up, Julia offered her a weary smile. Mother's eyes seemed to convey that she understood the desire to be lost in her own thoughts. Mother's exhaustion and homesickness were evident. She had to be every bit as frustrated with the quantity and variety of Marcus and Rebekah's ques-tions as Julia was, but, taking a deep breath, she brightened and soon became animated and looked as though she enjoyed allowing the children to be the distraction she hadn't allowed herself to entertain while she'd been in Savannah.

Julia rolled her shoulders and tried to follow her mother's example. After all, nothing mattered now except going home. Details, and there must be a million of them, had to be spinning in Mother's head, looking as complicated as the notes and draw-ings in the sketchbook. Mother had a way of trusting that such things would iron themselves out over time. She'd think of busi-ness after she'd rested in her own bed, cooked a wonderful meal for Papa, and told him all about the trip. She seemed so relaxed now, playing guessing games with Marcus and Rebekah and telling them stories about their new home.

After a final change of trains, the last leg of the journey brought familiar scenery. Things began to look and feel like home. Morgan's Landing, now more than ever, seemed a sweet refuge from all life's troubles. Julia longed to be surrounded by familiar things and the people dear to her. Papa's sweet, whiskery kiss of greeting as his mustache tickled her face, her own bed, the smell of the bakery, the muddy river flowing by—they all called her home.

HANNAH LEVITT VISITED with her companions, her inner thoughts a jumble of hopes and anxieties. The move offered the hope of starting afresh. Since Benjamin's death, keeping a roof over the children's heads had been a struggle. Sewing, cleaning, and other odd jobs provided what little they had, but steady work would be a relief. Beatrice Lansing had a talent she wanted to study. From what she'd observed, as long as ladies had money in their pocketbooks, Mrs. Lansing would be busy dressing them. Working for her would help her learn the trade. She'd accepted the charity of her community long enough. People had been kind to offer her sewing jobs they probably could have done themselves. They'd often brought food, claiming that they'd prepared more than was needed. Though she felt immense gratitude for their kindness, she would stand on her own two feet now. There would be room and board until she could afford her own place to live. Her employer's confidence in her made her feel good inside.

At times, fear of her new and unknown home enveloped Hannah, but she had boarded the train and there was no turning back now. In Savannah, she'd been surrounded by faith, friends, and poverty. Now, she must go, even if there were no other Jewish families within miles of this place called Morgan's Landing. Though there could never be another man in her life to compare to her first love and she missed Benjamin each and every day, Hannah was not opposed to marrying again. She found it difficult to imagine, however, that there might be a man in this far-away, western place who would want a Jewish woman and two children.

Chapter Twenty

Roderick Lansing ran a hand over his fresh haircut and shave. It wouldn't do for his girls to think he'd turned completely uncivilized in their absence. His mustache, a bit waxed, smelled of witch hazel. He held a bouquet of chrysanthemums. Though not the ideal flower of choice, they'd have to do. He hadn't thought of them until he was in the buggy on his way to the depot. Beatrice should have something special. He'd stopped at Dora Klein's house. The elderly widow had developed quite a soft spot for him and had been bringing him meals. Not only had she snipped a nice bunch for him, but she'd tied a ribbon around the stems. He stood on the brick walkway in front of the depot, satisfied with himself as a one-man welcoming committee.

For the last five miles, the Levitts had been devouring the sights of their new home, while the Lansings feasted their eyes on familiar scenery, noting that all was as they'd left it.

As the train slowed and the conductor announced Morgan's Landing, Beatrice began gathering her things. Feeling a tap on her knee, she leaned forward.

"What are you going to do?" Julia whispered.

"*Do?*"

"About Papa!"

Beatrice followed Julia's nod toward the Levitts, realizing that Julia had been pondering, just as she had, what might be the least shocking method of breaking the news to Roderick that their household had doubled in size. She turned to Hannah.

"Hannah, I can't wait for you to meet my husband, Roderick. I'm afraid, though, that we may be a bit emotional after having been apart for so long..."

"I understand, Mrs. Lansing. That's only natural. I'll wait here with the children while you greet your husband."

"You're a dear, Hannah. Thank you."

Beatrice smoothed the hair at the nape of her neck. Removing her hatpin, she straightened her hat and then reinserted it before giving the brim a gentle wiggle to be sure it was secure. She saw that Julia and Hannah were doing the same and that Marcus had gone in search of his own hat. Groping under the seat, she soon retrieved it and handed it to him. Turning her attention to Rebekah, Beatrice offered her a reassuring smile and reached out to gave her arm a squeeze. Rebekah returned the smile, though her eyes remained wide and she pulled her doll, Dinah, into a tighter embrace.

As the train stopped, Marcus stood and peered out the window. "Who are you waving at, Miss Angel?"

"That's my Papa, Marcus," Julia answered. "See, he's waving at me now, too."

"Your Papa?" Marcus ran to another window to get a better look.

Beatrice picked up her traveling case and, with Julia following, made her way up the aisle to exit the car. Her separation from Roderick had lasted far too long. She searched the faces of those who had gathered to meet the train, her pulse quickening as she looked for the one she loved. As they stepped onto the platform, she braced herself to tell Roderick the news that could wait no longer to be told. She squeezed Julia's arm.

"I'm going to need all the help I can get."

"I'll do my best. We've had extended house guests before, but what Papa will be concerned about is the fact you're planning to *pay* her."

"Well, there's that..." Beatrice's brow crinkled, "... and then there are the crates."

"Crates? What crates?"

Beatrice gasped as Roderick's arm encircled her waist. He pulled Julia close with his other arm, squeezed them both tight and began kissing their cheeks.

"Oh, Roderick dear, I missed you so!" Beatrice sniffled.

Roderick released Julia, put both arms around Beatrice, and lifted her off the platform.

"I promised myself that I would and I will!" he said, kissing her on the mouth.

Beatrice blushed with pleasure as she rearranged her hat. "Roderick, we're right out here in front of everyone!"

"These are for you!"

"Oh! Mums! But where did you get them? Mine didn't make it through last winter."

"Dora Klein. She's fed me for a solid month and now I'm her pet. Do you have something new here? Some sort of new-fangled corset or something?" Roderick massaged her ribcage.

Beatrice brushed his hands away. "Now you know you shouldn't talk about such things out here in public. Roderick, *please!*"

He released her, turning his attentions to Julia.

"How's my girl? Miss me?"

"Oh, Papa! I missed you more than you can know." Julia took his arm. "I can't wait to get home and fuss over you. I know you must have lived like an old bachelor this whole time. I'm sure the house is a mess."

Beatrice tugged at his arm. "Roderick, there's something important I need to tell you about."

"Oh, it can wait. Let's get your trunks. We'll go home and you can tell me all about everything. There's bound to be more than we can cover standing here at the station."

"Oh, there's more!" Beatrice spoke in a rush. "There are a lot of extra bags, Roderick, and the reason for that is..."

A small body wriggled in amongst the three. Beatrice lowered her eyes and found Marcus tugging at Roderick's sleeve. Roderick looked down into his smiling face, which bobbed up and down with excitement.

"You're Miss Angel's papa! Miss Angel's papa!"

"I'm sorry, son, I think you have me mixed up with someone else."

THE NEXT SEVERAL moments seemed to pass in a blur. One moment he'd been welcoming his family, anticipating a quiet reunion. In the next, Roderick felt as though he'd been spun in circles and didn't know quite where he was. Beatrice rambled, apologizing for something. A strange lady with a little girl apologized for something. Julia professed that she was, indeed, "Miss Angel" and a little boy, whose name was apparently Marcus, told him how happy he was to come and live with him.

He looked around. A porter had amassed more trunks and bags than he had room for in the buggy. He watched in horror as his wife tipped the man, asked that the baggage be delivered, and hired an extra carriage, pulling money out of her bag and giving it away like there was no tomorrow.

A temporary muteness, induced by the shock, wore off after a minute.

"Beatrice!"

"Yes, dear?"

"Are these people...?"

"The Levitts, dear."

"Are these Levitts... and let me say that it is very nice to meet you, Mrs. Levitt... moving into *our* house? Not that you're not welcome in my home, Mrs. Levitt. If you are friends of my wife and daughter, you are welcome... Beatrice! What is *happening*?"

"We met the Levitts in Savannah, dear. They've come to make a new start. Hannah is widowed. There wasn't much of a way for her to provide for her children in Savannah, so they're going to give Morgan's Landing a try."

"Oh! Well, that's fine, but what opportunity would there be here that wouldn't be in Savannah?"

"Well, not much of anything if I hadn't hired her."

"*Hired* her?"

"Help me in the buggy, Roderick. I'll tell you all about it on the way home. Hannah, you and the children will have to come along when they bring the baggage."

As Roderick climbed into the buggy, he looked over his shoulder. Julia sat on the back seat, looking innocent and saying nothing. A knot formed in his stomach as he headed the horse toward home. The pleasant reunion had been ruined. He struggled to remain calm. His wife had gone to Savannah, Georgia and lost her mind.

It wasn't as though he exploded. It was only natural that he demand to know what in tarnation made either Beatrice or Julia think that they could hire anyone for anything, let alone drag an entire family across these United States with no prospects for the future and—"To put the butter on the spinach—you didn't even consult me!"

"Roderick, there wasn't time. I only made the decision two days before we left."

"Well, at any rate, we can't afford a housekeeper."

"Hannah's not a housekeeper."

"Well, then, what *is* she?"

"She's a seamstress."

"A seamstress? We have no business hiring a *seamstress*! You've been getting along just fine with a little help from the girls who come in to do your basting, or whatever-it-is you call whatever-it-is they do. You can't bring someone all this way to work off and on for a pittance."

"You said '*we have no business*'. But, Roderick, that's just it! I *do* have business, and more than I can handle. Promise you'll just let me show you something when we get home. You'll see. Right now, I want to enjoy seeing my home again. Ah! Ah! Ah!" she said as his lips parted to speak. "Don't say a word! Except, of course, you *may* tell me how much you've missed me."

If it hadn't been for that, Roderick may have elaborated further on his wife's ridiculous idea, its total lack of practicality, and how he felt justified in taking offense at not having been informed, but there she sat, beside him again, the love of his life. Her trim figure—though he had to admit that perhaps she'd put on a pound or two around the middle in the last month—her wild mass of curls escaping from its combs and pins after the journey, the way she smiled at him as though nothing bad had ever happened and nothing ever could. She was a welcome and wonderful sight after a month alone in the workshop. He'd save his sermon for later. For now, he'd try to enjoy the ride.

THE WHITE HOUSE at 324 Beech Tree Street stood with its dark blue shutters, welcoming its family. The familiarity of the maroon roof and gingerbread trim filled Julia with happiness. She looked up at the northwest window on the second floor. It had been her room all her life. She struggled to decide upon a course of action. Two appealing ones teased her. She might dash upstairs and fling herself onto her own bed where she could stretch out and enjoy the silence and her own familiar things. Or, she might stop awhile on the front porch to savor the sounds, smells, and sights of the neighborhood. Both, however, would have to wait until all this unpleasantness was settled. Papa had a tendency to bluster when sudden changes were thrust upon him. Julia felt it her duty to stand by her mother in a show of support. Following her parents up the porch steps and through the front door, she shrank into a corner chair in the parlor and listened, hoping Mother could soothe him. She certainly seemed to be putting in a sincere effort as she extended a hand and a smile toward him.

"Come, dear. Let's go up to the bedroom. I'll explain everything."

"I think I'd like to stay right here and hash this whole thing out. I have a pretty strong notion that Julia knows more about this than she's letting on. She likes to remind her papa every once in a while that she's an adult, so I think I'll have questions for both of you!"

"Well, it simply can't be done right here and now. If you want me to explain, you're just going to have to cooperate."

Turning on her heels, Mother disappeared up the stairs. The door to their room clicked shut.

"Oh, confound it!" Papa pointed a finger at Julia. "I'll talk to you later."

Julia stood and moved to the double parlor windows to watch for the Levitts and their belongings. She tried her best not to listen. If this proved to be anything like the stressful trip from the depot, there were bound to be raised voices.

RODERICK WAS TAKEN ABACK as he opened the bedroom door. Beatrice had slipped off her jacket. Her fingers trembled as she unbuttoned her blouse. Her eyes sparkled.

"Oh, Roderick! I know you'll be thrilled. If I didn't think you'd be pleased, I would never have done this."

"Now, don't you go trying to sweet talk me, Beatrice. I've missed you just as much, if not more, as any man who hasn't seen his wife in over a month, but I think it can wait until you break the news—whatever the news is—and I'm starting to suspect it must be colossal!"

"Oh, for Heaven's sake!" Beatrice laughed, blushing. "I'm trying to show you something!"

"That much I gathered."

"Oh, stop it!" Beatrice delivered a light kiss on his lips.

"Remember when you announced to everyone at the depot that you thought I had a new corset?"

"Yes...?" Roderick stood with his hands on his hips and watched as Beatrice unfastened the mysterious garment.

"Well, I had to rework my old one in order to make room for this."

After spreading the corset out over the bed, Beatrice motioned for him to come closer. He watched as she slipped her fingers into the corset lining and removed a small stack of currency.

Roderick chuckled. "Did you think someone might steal your lunch money on the way home?"

"But it's full!"

"Full? What's full?"

"The corset. I've put a stack of bills between every stay."

As Beatrice emptied the corset of its secrets, a pile of money accumulated in the middle of the coverlet. Roderick sat down on the bed, running his fingers through it.

"Why, there must be..."

"Six hundred dollars."

"What?"

"They're only the deposits."

"*What!*"

"Roderick, these wealthy ladies think nothing of paying two to three hundred dollars for an evening gown, and what they pay for a mere day dress or traveling clothes would still make your head spin. The prices I've charged here and in Jefferson City wouldn't buy some of these ladies a nightgown."

Roderick stared at her.

"Ruby has been showing my drawings to more of her friends. They wanted appointments, and the next thing I knew I had expensive orders to fill. It didn't make good business sense to come home without having them make deposits. The more orders I had, the more I realized that I couldn't handle the work without someone capable. Hannah sews better than Julia or my basting girls. Besides, Julia's heart is in the kitchen. I met Hannah Levitt by sheer Providence. She's been a great help. About two days before we left, I panicked at the idea of continuing without her. I had to decide. I can't manage without her. She sold some things, packed the rest, and came home with us. We'll have the girls basting. Hannah and I will do the cutting and fine needle work."

Roderick ran a hand through his hair and exhaled. It seemed Beatrice had her reasons, but they all seemed to swirl around in his head, mingled with shock.

"I still wish you'd told me, Beatrice. It's the way we've always decided on important matters."

"If I'd told you about it every step of the way, would you have been encouraged? Would you have felt as you do now, sitting next to this pile of money? Or, would you have told me it was a hare-brained idea and nobody in their right mind would pay that much for a dress? Would you have told me to put the thought out of my mind and come on home to do exactly as I'd been doing?"

Roderick sat in silence. His wife knew him well.

"Of course," Beatrice continued, "I'll have to go back."

"Go back?"

"For final fittings and, if all goes well, new orders. I'll take Hannah so she can learn how to do that for me in the future."

Roderick looked into Beatrice's eyes. They held the light of fulfilled hope. His own hopes, however, sat strewn all over his workshop, waiting for the day when they would be tried and tested.

"Well, I guess you're doing better in business than I am."

"Oh, don't be silly. This will give us money to buy everything you need to perfect your inventions. You can bring all your plans into reality."

"I guess the first thing I need to bring into reality is a good oiling and repair of that poor old excuse for a sewing machine I fixed up for you out of parts and pieces. You'll need all the speed you can get."

"Mmmm... There is that." Beatrice seemed to be looking past him, as if the designs in the wallpaper had gripped her attention. "There's no hurry, dear. Let's get settled in and enjoy ourselves for a day or two. You'll need to spend your time preparing for Senator Thornhill. I'm happy to say that he is coming to see you immediately after his next round of important meetings. He should arrive in Morgan's Landing within the next couple of weeks."

Roderick stared into the distance. "Mmmm... There is that," he echoed. "It's definite? He's coming? Was it difficult to talk him into it?"

"It's difficult to talk to him *at all*! The man is deaf as a doornail! Prepare yourself for quite a time. Whatever you discuss with him in your workshop won't be a secret for long. I had no idea what to do. We were dancing at the Graysons' ball and…"

"Dancing? You danced with Thornhill?" Roderick narrowed his eyes to study his wife. "Who else did you dance with?"

"I danced with every man in the place, if you must know," Beatrice cooed with a flutter of her eyelashes. "That's what you get for staying home. What's more, I'd estimate that nine out of ten of them proposed before the night was over. Why, Clifford Allen had to beat them off with a stick when they all wanted to escort me home."

"Oh, all right…" Roderick sighed in exasperation. "What did you say to Thornhill?"

"Well, we were dancing and I kept praying for the right words. It was my last opportunity. I didn't want to leave you trying to accomplish everything through a letter-writing campaign. I've seen your letters. Then, it came to me—that proverb: 'Even a fool, when he holdeth his peace, is counted wise: and he that shutteth his lips is esteemed a man of under-standing.'"

"And so?"

"And so I didn't say anything! I danced and smiled. I leaned in a few times and said, 'You'll need to see my husband as soon as possible.' When he would start to question me, I'd say, 'Shh-hhh! The time is now!' I'd wink at him and say the same thing over again. By the time the song ended, he thought I knew everything there was to know about the invention. He promised to be here as soon as he could manage it with his hair in a braid!"

Roderick took his wife's face in his hands, kissed her lips, and looked into her eyes.

"You're something!" He laughed.

"I'm glad you think so. You don't know how flattering it is to be in the middle of telling a man all the news pertaining to his life's work and have him be more concerned about the fact that you've been dancing with other men. It makes me think very highly of you, Mr. Lansing."

Roderick slipped his arms around her waist, nuzzling her neck as he pulled her down onto the pile of money.

"I'll show you just what I think of *you*, Mrs. Lansing!"

He kissed her mouth, her face, her neck, and would have continued to do so if it hadn't been for the sudden voices coming from downstairs and the sound of trunks thudding onto the parlor floor.

Chapter Twenty-One

Julia stretched, turning over with a grateful sigh. The autumn chill made the warmth of the covers seem a blessed gift. She blinked several times before allowing her eyes to focus on the wedge of light that entered her room at a slant. Tilting her head back, she watched dappled sunlight play amongst the flowers on the wallpaper next to her bed. It would have little time to frolic before falling upon her nightstand and disappearing across the floor as the eastern sun rose over the rooftop of the house. It had been good to sleep in her own bed again. Julia gave a little start as she brushed against Rebekah. She'd forgotten she had a guest. The little girl, exhausted from two days on the train, appeared to have slept without moving. Shifting her weight with care, Julia hoped to let Rebekah sleep as long as she could. Though the Lansing household might not spring fully to life just yet, their first day at home promised to be busy for everybody.

On the train, Julia had gathered enough to know that, at eight years old, Rebekah could read well and considered herself mother and guardian to Dinah, the rag doll she kept clutched to her chest at all times. She seemed content to observe her world and let her outspoken little brother ask all the questions. Had this thin child, with her dark hair and eyes, always been this shy or had the loss of her father made her withdraw and disappear into her own world? Julia hoped she'd find friends among the children in Morgan's Landing.

Julia could have lingered in bed for hours. Leaves frolicked past her window on their way to the ground from trees all up and down the street. Rays of sunlight promised to warm the autumn day. Sugar maples in the front yard blazed with orange splendor. These gifts were to be treasured, for the Missouri weather might change within a day's time, making it impossible to prepare. Today might be spent without need of wraps, feeling a bit too warm in the sun, while tomorrow may call for a fire in the stove and shelter from chill winds. The glories of such days would fade soon enough into a bleak, colorless winter. The thought of hearing the leaves swish around her ankles as she walked in a world of yellow, orange, and red enticed Julia to crawl from beneath the crisp, cotton sheets. If Mother didn't need her this morning, she'd take a walk and see if Morgan's Landing and its people were just as she'd left them a month ago. Julia had no trouble deciding on her first stop.

Breakfast proved to be a bit frustrating as Julia attempted to fix Papa a nice meal with what little ingredients he had remaining in the house. While cooking and setting the table, she listened as Mother sat at the table with Hannah discussing her own family's customs concerning food preparation. The adjustments that would be required in the days ahead would involve more than merely having extra people in the house.

When Hannah insisted that she and Rebekah would wash and dry the dishes, Julia thanked them and gave Mother and Papa each a peck on the cheek before stopping in front of the hall mirror to tidy her hair and dash out the door.

As the screen door closed behind her, Julia gave a quick glance to the left. The porch swing and the wicker chairs beckoned to her and she made a mental note that when she returned she would find a good book and settle there if Mother didn't need her help right away.

A few of the brick-and-white houses that lined Beech Tree Street had had their porch trims painted in her absence and showed off their new colors nicely. The Methodist Church, across the street on her left as she passed, stood stately as ever. Across its wide side lawn and set back a bit, its parsonage sat, looking the same as ever and a bit lonely, as if it were too shy to step forward like the rest of the houses. Another wide, fenced-in lawn next to it belonged to Dora Klein, the sweet, old lady who had been so kind to Papa. Dora, stepping onto the front porch to shake a rug, called out a welcome and returned Julia's wave. Julia, though happy to see her, made a quick survey of the area and felt relieved that the elderly lady's dog was nowhere in sight, for Dora, as sweet a lady as one could hope to find, owned the biggest pest in town.

Just past Dora's, Julia gave a glance toward the Roth Hotel and the river that lay just north of it. Though it called to her, the river would have to wait. She turned right, heading south along Main Street, feeling as though the heart of Morgan's Landing reached out to embrace her own. She paused beneath the beautiful stained-glass awning as she always did when passing Mueller's Jewelry Store to take a lingering gaze over the gems on display. Mrs. Mueller, tidying the window, greeted Julia with a kind smile. Familiar bakery customers and church friends soon began offering greetings as she continued up the block. A glance across Main Street told her that the doctor's office, the hardware store, and the law office, among others, still operated behind their brick storefronts as usual. A few store owners who had stepped out to sweep their walks or check their window dressings offered a wave or welcomed her home. Keeping to the west side of the street, Julia crossed Hickory Street, pausing at the corner to tidy her hair and straighten her collar before approaching the door on her right. As she had done nearly every morning for so many years, she stepped forward, placed her hand on the brass plate, and gave it just the right amount of push.

Helga Schmidt glanced up at the sound of the bell, her face brightening.

"August! August! Come!"

The sturdy German woman motioned with floury hands for Julia to come behind the counter. Mr. Schmidt appeared in the doorway to the storeroom, watching as his wife embraced Julia, trying not to touch her with the doughy mess. Julia saw tears in his eyes.

"Our girl has come home."

Mrs. Schmidt's voice broke. "My Schnucki! My Schnucki!"

"Oh, Mrs. Schmidt! I'm glad to be home. I've missed you so! What are we baking today?"

Mrs. Schmidt dabbed her eyes with her apron. "Nothing that you are going to help with, my Schnucki. Sit down here and tell us all about this place you've been—where is it?—Georgia. I will roll the dough while you tell me about faraway places I may never see. First, have a little something."

"Mmmm..." Julia watched Mrs. Schmidt swoop up a piping hot roll and slather it with butter before handing it to her. As she savored the love gift, she told the Schmidts about the beauty of Savannah, the Wentworth Hotel, and the grandeur of the ball. She described many of the people she'd met, with the exception of Adam Cole. That chapter of her diary needed to remain closed and locked.

Julia spoke with passion about Chef Plouff and his creations, glad that Mrs. Schmidt seemed fascinated by her experiences. More than once, however, a baffled expression in Mrs. Schmidt's eyes reminded her that much of her chatter about French food left Mrs. Schmidt perplexed.

"I just can't do it justice in *talking* about it, Mrs. Schmidt, but wait a few days. When we get the house settled, I'll be back at work. Then I can show you everything I've learned and see how you like my new recipes!"

Julia left the bakery sooner than she would have liked. She hurried past the barber shop, crossed the alley, and then gave but a moment's glance at the window of Carlson's Millinery. Browsing through hats and other finery could wait. Crossing Oak Street, she quickened her pace as she neared her next stop. The door of Drexler's Drug Store flew open before Julia could touch the handle. She felt herself being pulled into the store and into the arms of Bertina Drexler.

"I've missed you so much. I heard you came home on yesterday's afternoon train. I would have stopped by in a little while if you hadn't stopped in."

Julia smiled at her best friend. "I missed you, too, Bertina. I'm sorry I only wrote a few letters from Savannah. We had so much to see and do and not many spare moments."

"Oh, that's all right. Now you can tell me about it in person. Sit down and I'll get you an ice cream sundae—my treat. I'll even make it myself." She waved away the clerk from behind the soda fountain.

Having befriended Bertina at first out of compassion when the Drexlers had moved to Morgan's Landing years ago, Julia had come to cherish her. The tall, plain ten-year-old, plagued by excessive shyness, had kept to herself. Joining her at lunch and recess, Julia had defended her from the boys who teased her for towering above her classmates and the girls who snubbed her for having the highest grades in the class. Her brown hair, skinny limbs, and lonely eyes had reminded Julia of Old Ned, the dog that remained chained to an old anvil at the blacksmith's shop. Julia had vowed to break the chain that held

Bertina if she could do it by being her friend. Their childhood friendship had grown into a deep bond.

Julia marveled over the changes in Bertina and the things that remained the same. Still quiet and studious, Bertina no longer gave others the impression that she was unsure of herself. She held her own in conversations on topics concerning mathematics, politics, and commerce. Julia thought it fun to watch men's reactions when they engaged in conversation with Bertina. The ones who hadn't known her as a child were shocked to discover the confident mind behind the reserved exterior. The ones who'd grown up teasing and tormenting her now wished for a way to make amends, for though she had no inkling of it, she'd grown into a tall, willowy beauty with masses of thick, brown waves and well-defined features. The lonely eyes now shone with depth and confidence under their dark, arched brows and thick lashes. Julia thought the straight line of Bertina's nose gave her a royal dignity and considered her teeth a perfect string of pearls.

Bertina's confidence seemed limited to her intellectual attributes. She'd returned to Morgan's Landing after graduating with honors from Hardin College and Conservatory of Music without the slightest inkling that men were now afraid to approach her. Julia knew that despite all the compliments and encouragement she'd bestowed on her best friend, each time Bertina looked in the mirror, a gawky, skinny, shy little girl looked back at her.

Between spoonfuls of ice cream, Julia chattered about

Savannah until she glanced at the clock behind the counter and realized a half hour passed.

"Oh, my! I must go! All I want to do is walk around and soak up Morgan's Landing and everybody in it, but I know Mother needs my help at home. Come by this evening and I'll tell you all about the whole trip."

All about the whole trip? Are lies becoming a habit? As the door of Drexler's Drug Store closed behind her, Julia knew she wouldn't tell the whole truth. She wasn't ready to talk about Adam. She'd tell her best friend eventually, after the pain and embarrassment faded. If it were to be told without tears, it would have to wait. She'd cry no more tears over Adam Cole.

Once again on sunny Main Street, Julia turned northward, then stopped. Surely if she hurried, she could manage to make one more stop. Reversing her course, she scurried south, but soon found herself peering in shop windows, taking note of new items and those that remained unsold. It made her feel rooted in Morgan's Landing again. As she passed Himmel's furniture store, the smell of sawdust through the open door brought back a flood of memories—the accident with Marcus, Dr. Hancock... and Adam. She crossed the street and continued south to where the front door of the Thalberg Opera House stood open. Stepping in, she picked up a program of upcoming performances. With her errand complete, she continued along the west side of the street northward toward the river.

Each friendly face and welcoming greeting seemed to make the burden on her heart weigh a little less. Julia paused at the corner of Beech Tree Street, where a left turn would lead her home. Scolding herself for her weakness, she answered the call of the river. Circling the Roth Hotel, she stood at the railing overlooking Front Street and the Missouri River. The breeze that toyed with her hair and her sleeves brought with it the familiar fragrance Julia had come to associate with visits to the river. The freshness of living things mixed with the pungency of mud and fish blended in a way that, though Julia couldn't quite call it pleasant, drew her to its banks and invited her to stay.

Slow-moving and brown, the river comforted her. Waves lapped higher on its banks now than in the long, dry summer. It moseyed along with a definite direction, but no cares. Julia envied it. If only she could just find the right direction and leave her own cares behind.

That's what I'm going to do—as soon as every little sight and smell stops reminding me of Adam Cole.

Chapter Twenty-Two

At a familiar "Yoohoo", Julia smiled and leaned to look through the kitchen doorway to see the very guest she'd been expecting to arrive on their first day at home. She saw her mother rush into the hall and motion toward the screen door.

"Come on in, Gretel!" Mother called.

Though Gretel Hunt's feet were planted politely on the porch, her smiling face had already poked through the screen door. "I got here as soon as I could. I want all the news. How was your trip?"

The friends settled into comfortable chairs in the parlor. Drawn by the sound of their chatter, Julia and the Levitts stepped in from the kitchen. Mother made the introductions and Julia watched as Gretel won the hearts of the newcomers. Gretel soon had the Levitts answering a variety of questions about themselves that neither Julia nor her mother had thought to ask. Without any apparent thought that her questions might be prying, Gretel drew from the Levitts information about their family background, their way of life in Savannah, their Jewish customs and, though she professed to being a poor seamstress herself, managed to quiz Hannah as to how she managed to create such expert work as she and the children displayed.

Her petite frame, as she relaxed in the parlor chair, gave the illusion of being unaware of anything but the conversation. The flowered cotton dress against her olive skin and the easy way her wide-brimmed straw hat rested on her silky, dark hair gave the impression that she'd been flower-picking when it occurred to her that, having made tea cakes, why not tuck a few blossoms into her hatband and stop by for a chat? Julia knew better. In the years since Ruby had married Clifford Allen and moved away, Gretel had been her mother's best friend in Morgan's Landing. Mother had been right all those years ago. Gretel did have kitten-like features that hinted at a playful nature. As Julia watched the Levitts warm to her, she found herself wishing, as usual, that she had Gretel Hunt's same ease at making new friends.

Though she might appear spontaneous and playful, Gretel kept an eye out for the needs of others. She had come not only to welcome Mother home, but to make the Levitts feel welcome as best she could.

"Beatrice, you and Julia and Mrs. Levitt just sit. You must be exhausted after that trip. Tell me all about Savannah while I pour. Marcus, you look like a strong boy. Would you help Mrs. Lansing by coming around with that heavy tray? Rebekah, what a sweet smile you have! If you'll look in the buffet drawer in the dining room, I'm sure you'll find some napkins we can use. You're such a help."

Enlisting the help of Marcus, Gretel took care of everything. Both Julia and Mother relaxed and let her have her way. One didn't serve Gretel. Gretel served others. This always happened when Gretel came for tea.

By the time Gretel left, Julia could tell that she'd gleaned enough information to form a plan. She promised to return the following morning to help Mother and Julia make the attic room presentable for its new occupants after calling on a few friends to let them know that the Levitts were new in town.

"I like her!" Marcus announced as her footsteps faded away down the front walk.

Mother nodded. "Everybody likes Gretel Hunt—anybody who has an ounce of sense."

When Julia placed a finger under Rebekah's chin, the little girl lifted her eyes.

"You liked Mrs. Hunt, didn't you, Rebekah?"

Rebekah nodded. "She's sweet."

Hannah stroked Rebekah's hair. "We'll be blessed to meet more like her. I feel as if I've spent the afternoon playing games!"

Over the next two days, the occupants of 324 Beech Tree Street bustled about in an effort to make room for everybody. The larger of the spare bedrooms on the second floor would now be in even greater demand as a sewing room. Rebekah could continue to sleep with Julia for now. The smaller spare bedroom would barely accommodate one person once they got it prepared, but Hannah assured them that she and Marcus would squeeze in together with no problem. The Levitts would take up residence in the attic as soon as Papa could make improvements.

Gretel appeared, as promised, bearing food she'd collected from her neighbors, insisting that it had been no trouble at all. However, this left Julia, along with Mother, to the task of determining the ingredients of each dish and consulting Hannah as to whether or not it could be eaten by all the members of the expanded household. Hannah expressed her appreciation and worked hard at bringing the kitchen up to her requirements and organizing the pantry.

WHILE THE LADIES cleaned the attic, Roderick did what he could to make it snug against the coming winter. He promised Hannah a small heating stove as soon as he could find one.

Passing Beatrice in the upstairs hall, he snatched a moment to pull her as close as he could, considering the bundle of bedding she held in her arms. He gave her a peck on the cheek.

"How's my wife?"

"Overworked. How's my husband?"

"The same. That Marcus is really something. I don't know whether I'm sorry or glad to have his help. He's so full of questions, I can hardly hear myself think. I can tell he misses having a papa. It would be an aggravation if he wasn't such a helpful little fellow. He does anything and everything I ask him, and a whole lot of things I *haven't* asked him. He couldn't be stuck to me tighter if he were a mustard plaster."

"I expect you're just what he needs."

"*You're* just what I need."

Beatrice smiled and brushed her lips against his. "I think what you need imminently is a good meal. I'll warm something up just as soon as I make up this bed. It'll take me no more than ten minutes."

"I'll try and manage till then," Roderick sighed, releasing her from his arms. "I've worked up a powerful appetite in that attic."

Half an hour later, everyone sat in silence at the dinner table, straining to hear the conversation at the front door. It sounded as though a package may have arrived. Roderick surveyed the others at the table with an inquiring eye. Their collective shrug revealed that no one expected anything.

Julia returned to the table. "The man says he has two crates for you, Mother?"

"Crates? Crates of what? Oh! The *crates*!"

Laying her napkin aside, Beatrice excused herself and dashed down the hall.

Befuddled, Roderick rose to follow her. He stopped in the parlor, stumbling as Marcus collided with the back of his legs. He examined the late arrivals. Julia, Gretel, Hannah, and Rebekah looked as puzzled as he felt. They gathered around the crates, watching as Beatrice thanked the man. To Roderick's dismay, she handed him a tip.

Beatrice spoke with a tremor. "Goodness! We've been so busy I'd completely let it slip my mind that I'd left instructions at the depot for them to bring these straight over when they arrived."

"I think it slipped your mind to tell me they were coming at all." Roderick's eyes narrowed. "I'll get the crowbar. Do you mind, Beatrice, if we ask what's inside, or does everybody else know besides me?"

Again, he studied the faces of those present. Everyone looked innocent except for the one who had given him his most recent shock. Hannah Levitt looked as though she wished she'd stayed in the kitchen.

"I'm sure *I* don't know," said Gretel.

Marcus tugged at his sleeve. "I'll get the crowbar! Where is it, Mr. Lansing?"

Roderick ignored the well-meaning offer. He had other things on his mind. He drew in a deep breath and turned again to Beatrice. "Would somebody please... What is it?" he paused in exasperation as he felt a tug on his trouser leg.

"Mr. Lansing?"

"Yes?"

"What's a crowbar?"

"Don't worry yourself with it, Marcus. I'll attend to it."

Marcus busied himself with peering through the cracks in the crates. "I can't tell what it is. It's dark in there."

"I haven't a clue, Papa," said Julia.

Rebekah slipped behind her mother's skirts. Hannah remained silent.

"They're my machines," said Beatrice.

"Machines?" Roderick, Julia, and Gretel spoke in unison.

Roderick jerked his head toward the crates and then back to his wife, who stood there looking as though she'd been in the habit of receiving daily deliveries of machines.

"What kind of machines?" he asked.

"Well… my new sewing machines."

"Your new…" Roderick had congratulated himself over the last two days on his adaptability after the sudden appearance of the Levitts and the news that they were moving into his house. This stunned him. He had the same feeling he'd had at the depot. He turned away, stifling the temptation to lose his temper. Apparently, hiring Hannah and moving her entire family into his house had been only the beginning of things Beatrice intended to undertake without consulting him. "I'll be right back with the crowbar."

"I'll come with you!" Marcus offered.

Hannah put out a hand. "No, Marcus. You'll be coming to the kitchen with us to tidy up from lunch. Come Rebekah."

Gretel followed. "Oh, yes. Let me help you."

"I'll come, too," said Julia. "Many hands make light work. Remember, Marcus, there's an apple pie!"

BEATRICE SIGHED as the deserters left her. They might not have proven to be of any help in explaining this surprise, but still, their presence would have given her a certain sense of support. She uttered a quick prayer, pleading for a way to soften the blow. When Roderick returned with the crowbar, she waited for him to speak. He didn't.

She watched as he pulled the nails from the crates, removing the tops and fronts. While he pulled the packing away from one machine, she unpacked the other. They stood back, surveying the two oak cabinets.

"I had to do it. I had the money, Roderick—every penny. The money I showed you was what was left *after* buying the machines. I just couldn't see how in the world Hannah and I were going to manage without them."

She hated it when Roderick brooded in silence.

"How much did these cost, Beatrice? And *why* did you buy *two*?"

"Eighty dollars. And I had to buy two."

"Do you mean to tell me these sewing machines cost *eighty dollars apiece*?"

"Oh, no! They cost eighty dollars together. They were forty dollars apiece!" Beatrice winced. Half the price failed to produce half the shock.

"People just don't go out and do this sort of thing, Beatrice! Why didn't you consult me? Is there anything else you'd care to inform me about before there's another knock at the door?"

"Yes, there is."

Beatrice lifted the lid of one of the machines. "It opens just like this. Look, Roderick! I want you to see the difference."

The fact could not be denied. The beautifully finished oak cabinet housed a grand-looking display of mechanical wonder. The black machine with its fancy, gold decorations made a good first impression. Gold patterns swirled over the base and sides of the machine. The word "Minnesota", emblazoned across the front, proudly proclaimed its manufacturer.

Roderick sounded sarcastic. "I suppose it cuts the material, sews the dress, and then wraps it up in a box and ties a ribbon around it."

Knowing his love of invention and mechanical design, Beatrice determined to remain sweet. She approached the nub of the matter. "You know that machine you fixed up for me to use?" she asked, stifling the urge to call the contraption the string of names that came to mind every time she tried to use it.

"That is a solid machine. You won't find one more solid," Roderick said in defense of his project.

"Yes," Beatrice nodded. "I lost count long ago of the solid parts that have fallen off that machine. If you'll recall, it won't stay together for more than an hour before something flies off! Also, all it does is sew a straight seam."

"I thought straight seams were ideal."

"That's not the point. Look at these."

Removing a small box from one of the drawers, Beatrice opened it. Inside were a number of shiny metal parts and pieces. She knew Roderick had no idea what any of them were.

"These are the attachments. These new sewing machines do everything for you! It's all in the book. See?"

Roderick took the manual from her hand and began thumbing through the pages.

"It says here that it does the hemming for you, and the gathering, and all sorts of things."

"Yes! You just screw on whichever one of these attachments you want, and it holds the material and sews it at the same time! Right here," she said, pointing at a lever, "you adjust the length of the stitches. If that little thing works like I hope it does, this will even do basting for us! Do you know how much time that will save?"

Roderick tilted the machine back, examining its underside.

"But, Beatrice, wouldn't *one* have served you just as well? Seems that if you are going to be able to sew this fast, you'll have all the time you need."

"I thought along those lines at first before I realized that Hannah and I would have to take turns using the machine. I had six hundred and eighty dollars, Roderick! I paid for them, ordered them, and had them shipped out from Kansas City. I considered it a wise decision, and I hope you're not going to tell me that I didn't do the right thing."

Roderick sighed and leaned against one of the crates. Beatrice waited. She knew her husband hated rapid change unless he'd been the cause of it. His knowledge of the dress-making business amounted to nothing. She'd done well on a small scale up until now. She felt more confident in making her own decisions than in her husband's reactions to them. It might take a day or two, but once the shock wore off, he would concentrate his efforts on preparing for Senator Thornhill's impending visit and leave her to her own work. She felt a sense of relief as she saw him straighten and give the machine a firm slap as though it were a fine piece of horseflesh.

"I suppose that even though these each weigh about a ton, you'll want me to carry the little beauties upstairs to the sewing room," he said with a half-smile.

"I suppose I would," said Beatrice.

Chapter Twenty-Three

THE LANSING HOUSEHOLD settled into a blend of old routines and new ones.

It surprised Julia to see how well Papa adapted to having children in the house. He'd helped Hannah see to it that Rebekah and Marcus were enrolled in school, which kept them occupied most of the day while he needed quiet to prepare for the senator's visit. The mobile wireless communication device was, in essence, complete, but at times it still refused to function without some degree of coaxing. After spending most of his waking hours in the workshop, Julia noticed that Papa often remained in a silent and thoughtful mood when he came in for meals, unable to relax under the strain and uncertainty even on Sunday afternoons, when he could usually set his cares aside. Though he'd waited years for this moment, it seemed he now dreaded it. After three weeks had passed, a sense of tension permeated the air. The senator might arrive in another week, just as he promised. The thought that he might arrive before Papa was ready made everyone jittery. The idea that the senator might have a change of plans and not show up at all filled everyone with an unspoken dread. Julia prayed for Papa, knowing that fear of failure might threaten to paralyze him. Each time she entered the workshop, she saw him struggling against it as he forged ahead, continuing to make adjustments and correct imperfections. At times, he stared at the thing as though he were amazed at his skill and inventiveness. At others, he shook his head as if he failed to comprehend why anyone would be interested in it at all.

Mother, preoccupied with her business, handed the operation of a household that depended on separate sets of dietary customs over to Julia. Together, she and Hannah rearranged the kitchen, separating the food to Hannah's satisfaction. Julia found the Jewish laws and customs interesting, but wrestled with the challenges they added to the preparation of every meal. Hannah seemed happy to fix breakfast every day and worked with Mother on the mid-day meals, while Julia prepared supper with Hannah's input.

A few times a week, before leaving for the bakery, Julia made a point of cooking a little ham, sausage, or bacon in addition to Hannah's breakfast. Hannah didn't seem offended, and it kept Papa from utter despair.

Once having resumed her morning routine, Julia realized how much she'd missed the bakery. The bell on the door tinkled often, bringing a warm greeting from someone eager to welcome her home. Crisp weather carried the smell of bread and drew customers in to linger for a chat near the warmth of the hot ovens. Julia kept her notebook in her apron pocket, making notes as she practiced the recipes she'd learned from Chef Plouff. She planned to compile these into a letter, asking him for suggestions in areas she felt she didn't measure up to his standard.

Though Mrs. Schmidt showered Julia's new recipes with flattery, she had little desire to learn the techniques. She allowed Julia to set out samples. One by one, the French delights began to take their place beside the German baked goods.

Reuniting with Papa, the Schmidts, and Bertina warmed Julia's heart. Morgan's Landing, its familiar faces, the smell of the river, and the crisp autumn air brought a comfort that she hoped would soon erase the thoughts that clouded her mind.

With each new recipe, however, Julia thought of Chef Plouff, the Wentworth Hotel, and how she'd first seen Adam there. Thoughts of Abigail brought back memories of the day she'd poured out her heart after Adam left. The Levitts' daily presence drew her mind to the streets of Savannah. What a mess she'd made of things each time she'd seen Adam! The bell on the bakery door, jingling like a bicycle bell, now made her jump with a silly expectation, as if Adam might walk in. What she might say in this impossible scenario, Julia had no idea, but the notion that he'd thought so highly of her and yet had no notion as to who she really was filled her with sadness and regret.

Julia's bicycle, once her favorite means of traveling to and from the bakery, now leaned against the wall in the back corner of Papa's workshop. The very sight of it disturbed her these days. Various dreams plagued her sleep, each one seeming to involve a bicycle or a train carrying Adam toward her.

Each day, a prayer rose up within and, whenever she found herself alone, she voiced it, asking God how long it would take for these feelings to fade away.

FRED SCHMIDT ADJUSTED his tie and his resolve. Leaving his wagon parked behind the bakery, he made his way through the next alley that took him to Main Street before heading north.

It had been several weeks since he'd walked through the back door of the bakery and gotten the jolt of a lifetime. The temporary shock had done him good. Seeing his mother, dabbing at her eyes with her apron, had taken him aback. He and his brother and partner, Rudy, had been busy at the grist mill. In the weeks prior, he'd only seen his parents at Sunday services at the little Lutheran congregation they attended.

Fred had rarely seen his mother cry. Her simple answer when he questioned her had been that Julia was gone. At the word, Fred had gone numb all over. *Gone. Gone away! Gone permanently?* His panic had subsided as he listened to his mother explain that she'd seen Julia and her mother off at the depot. They'd return in a month or so after visiting friends in Savannah.

Worried about their safety and already missing her little *Schnucki,* his mother hadn't seemed to notice Fred's emotional state. Glad of it, he'd fumbled around the bakery, muttering acceptance for the roll she handed him before making an excuse to walk to Finkle's for new bootlaces. Alone on Main Street with his thoughts, Fred had realized he'd taken Julia for granted. The thought, albeit momentary, of never seeing her again had shaken him. She'd been a permanent fixture at the bakery while he was growing up, hadn't she? She'd been the little blonde girl, eight years his junior, whom he had teased when he was bored and ignored when he had bigger and better things on his mind.

Julia had grown up. He'd noticed. Every fellow in Morgan's Landing who wasn't blind had noticed. Julia's mother kept her dressed in the finest, well-fitting clothes she could afford. She looked pretty, even covered with flour. Julia joked comfortably with him and Rudy whenever they stopped by. She had a good sense of humor. Always sweet and kind, Julia had been his friend. She'd become a beauty. How could he have been so stupid?

Gripped by the frightening thought that Julia might meet someone in Savannah and arrive home engaged or with some understanding, Fred had made himself a promise. He'd survive these weeks of torture until the Lansings returned somehow. Then, he'd set about courting Julia without delay. The decision, once he'd made it, had seemed a foolish one. Why would she want a big, overgrown miller with huge, clumsy hands and a head full of silly-looking, straw-colored curls? He was too old for her in the first place. After a few minutes of hesitation, Fred forced his doubts into submission. He may not be able to discount his other negative qualities, but he was definitely *not* too old.

Since Julia's return, the same doubts had caused him nothing but delay. A man such as he, in his prime, could provide a good living and, if Julia Lansing refused to marry him, it wasn't going to be because he hadn't given it a good try and he would try today!

After stopping at the barbershop to receive an additional splash of hair tonic to tame his unruly mane, Fred smiled at himself in the mirror. It failed to impress him. However, it was the only smile he had and the only one he could take with him when he knocked on the door of 324 Beech Tree Street.

JULIA PLACED a cloth over her basket of baked goods and told Mrs. Schmidt goodbye for the day. After a couple of quick errands, she'd hurry home to help Mother or Papa, whoever needed it most, before fixing supper. Stepping out onto the sunny street, she shifted the basket to her other arm and headed north, puzzling over the past week. Though the daily routine at the bakery had been pleasant, she'd had a troubled sense that something had been a bit odd.

Since the Schmidt boys had taken over the operation of the mill, Julia hadn't seen them as often. Still the same big teases she'd grown up with, they'd now stopped pulling her hair or throwing flour in it. She suspected, however, that they might still harbor the urge to slip a baby garter snake into her apron pocket. Though Rudy, younger by two years, stood an inch or two shorter than his brother, many people mistook the affable pair for twins. Once a week or so, when they came to town for supplies, they stopped at the bakery for a snack and a visit. This past week she'd seen Rudy once. Fred, however, had been in three times.

Julia came to the conclusion that there must be some sort of trouble at the mill in order for him to need supplies so frequently. He seemed preoccupied and ill-at-ease when she'd joked and teased him as she'd always done. Not wanting to alarm Mr. and Mrs. Schmidt, she promised herself that at her first opportunity, she'd speak to him alone and ask him what the trouble was.

At Mueller's Jewelry Store, Julia asked for Mother's brooch. She checked the clasp and paid for the repair, tucking the heirloom from her great-grandmother inside her jacket pocket. Mother entrusted many things to Papa for repairs, but this treasured item wasn't one of them. When she'd noticed the loose clasp while packing to leave for Savannah, it had been left behind in Mr. Mueller's expert hands.

As she exited Mueller's, Julia nearly collided with Bertina. They chatted for a few minutes before Julia noticed Bertina focusing her gaze over her shoulder.

"Oh, here comes that awful pest!"

Julia turned, sighing in disgust. "Archibald! He's the last thing I need right now."

"A couple of weeks ago, we left the front door of the drug store open—the weather was so nice—and he just strolled right in and made himself at home at the soda fountain as though he expected to be served! And, when I tried to get him to leave, he pawed at me and slobbered all over my face!"

"No!"

"Yes! He put his nasty paws on the counter and gawked around with his tongue hanging out."

Julia wrinkled her nose in disgust. "He pulled open our back screen door this summer and was in the kitchen eating what was left of Sunday's cake before Mother found him and threw him out. She was livid."

They had discussed Archibald's rude tendencies for too long. Having covered enough distance to bring his nose into range of Julia's basket of baked goods, he came at her at a canter. The huge mastiff was upon Julia before she could plan an escape.

"You can *not* have this basket, you filthy beast!" Julia seethed with anger at what seemed to her the thousandth time she'd dealt with Archibald's appalling manners. "Pull him off me, Bertina!"

Bertina fought to get a grip on the dog's leather collar, which his mistress had beautified with a blue ribbon she'd slipped through the buckle and tied in a bow. Archibald, the prized pet and watchdog of Dora Klein, kept his mistress in a perpetual state of worry for fear someone would do harm to the dear, sweet pup if they didn't recognize him as a proper member of society.

"I've got him, Julia. I'll hold him and give you a head start toward home."

"I wasn't going home just yet. Mother wanted some thread from Finkel's."

"I'll hold him here and you cross the street and get inside Finkel's. Then, I'm afraid I've got to get back to the drug store. What have you got in that basket, anyway? I have to say I don't blame him. It smells wonderful."

"Rolls, bread, and some bierocks. You've tasted them before. Mrs. Schmidt fills the pastry with beef, sausage, onions, cabbage, and such. I'm taking a big plate of them to Papa. They're his favorite."

"I always think of them as meat turnovers."

"That's more or less what they are. Hold onto that collar tight while I make my escape, or they'll likely get another turning over, and so will I!"

Julia dashed across Main Street and into Finkel's General Store. Safely inside, she waved to Bertina, who set Archibald free before continuing up the street.

Archibald charged across Main Street toward Finkel's. Julia had expected him to give up and wander off after the next temptation that wafted past his ever-expectant nostrils. However, he seemed to be taking a sudden interest in something on the sidewalk. As she leaned against the glass to see what had captured his interest, angry tears stung her eyes. Several of the bierocks lay scattered over the sidewalk as a variety of his canine friends joined Archibald to feast on Papa's supper.

Julia examined the basket's contents. The bread and rolls remained, along with seven bierocks—enough for supper even with the rest gone to the dogs. *I suppose I'll just buy thread and go home.* It couldn't be helped, and besides, no decent person in Morgan's Landing who knew Dora Klein would lodge a real complaint about Archibald. Dora took care of the whole town, it seemed, in times of sickness, loneliness, and grief. No one issued their complaints loud enough to reach the ears of his doting mistress. Since she'd been widowed, Dora depended on Archibald for protection. No one dared lift a hand against Dora or intrude upon her home with Archibald on duty.

Julia purchased the thread, tucked it into the basket, and returned to the door to find the pack of dogs still sniffing for missed tidbits. She glanced at the clock above the counter, debating on whether to face the mob on the sidewalk or wait them out. Crossing her arms with a frustrated sigh, Julia scowled at the dogs for a moment before she realized that the jacket pocket her arm now rested against seemed to be empty. She patted it and felt a wave of dread.

Mother's brooch! After feeling in her other pockets, Julia looked inside her basket before retracing the steps she'd taken to purchase the thread. She tried to reassure herself that she had, indeed, placed the brooch in the pocket and it had been there when she bumped into Bertina. *Was that when I lost it?* Perhaps it had slipped out when she raised the basket over her head to keep it from Archibald. She peered across the street, but saw nothing. Dogs or no dogs, she would have to go in search of it. She'd give Archibald and each of his friends a good, swift kick and chase the whole pack all the way to the river if necessary.

Dashing out the door, Julia raised her basket out of reach as the dogs rushed at her for second helpings. Relief flooded over her as she saw the brooch under Finkel's display window, appar-ently nuzzled there by the dogs while they'd been slurping up tastier morsels. As she bent to snatch it up, Archibald and his friends seized the advantage. With several pairs of paws on her back, Julia sank to her hands and knees. She put the packet with the brooch between her teeth, guarding the basket with both arms. As she tried to scramble to her feet, she heard the welcome voice of her rescuer.

"Hey! Off with you! Get out of here, you mangy bunch of... Julia? Is that you?"

Julia looked up, struggling to identify her knight in shining armor as he ran in all directions, kicking dogs and calling each one what sounded like as many names as he could think of applying in the presence of a lady. Focusing at last on his face, Julia felt surprised and somewhat embarrassed.

She removed the packet from her teeth. "Martin? Martin Baysinger? Is that you?"

"That's me," he said, helping her to her feet. "I'd ask you how you've been, but let me guess... as miserable as if you'd been attacked by a pack of dogs on Main Street in front of everybody in Morgan's Landing?"

"Oh, Martin, if I weren't so grateful for your help, I'd pinch you good for teasing me at a time like this. What are you doing here anyway?" she asked as she returned the brooch to her pocket and smoothed her skirts and hair. "I thought you were away at law school in St. Louis."

"I was. I'm only home for a few days. Somehow, I knew when I came home I'd find you surrounded by so many admirers that you'd need me to come along and run them all off for you."

Martin beamed at Julia, his blue eyes full of mischief. He'd been her self-appointed pest all his life. Now that they were no longer children, she'd begun to wonder if he'd come to rely on their long-standing friendship as a means to flirt with her. Surely there were plenty of girls in St. Louis to attract his attention—ones that weren't stumbling all over the street with their faces flushed and their hats askew. Yet, there he stood, smiling as though she were a welcome sight.

"You look a mess, you know. But even so, you still have someone intent on walking you home." Martin nodded toward Archibald, who sat nearby, waiting to have Julia to himself.

Julia tried not to smile.

"Oh, I think I can handle him as long as he's the only one. Thank you and good day, Martin. It was nice to see you again."

Julia started down the street with the basket held high as Martin and Archibald followed.

"My buggy is just ahead, if you'd like a ride home. Apparently, your other potential escort doesn't have any mode of transportation."

"I'll enjoy the exercise. Thank you, anyway."

It was difficult to refuse an offer to escape Archibald. If she had to run all the way down Main and Beech Tree Streets, Julia would hold her ground. She had her reasons for not riding in Martin's buggy.

Though at times she'd been tempted, Julia had already determined not to consider Martin as a suitor. He was what

Mother called a late bloomer. As school children, Julia had towered above Martin, who was two years older. A small, skinny boy with a keen intellect, he'd been far more interested in horseplay than schoolwork. If it hadn't been for the fact that he seemed to absorb information by sheer osmosis, he would likely have failed the lower grades. His existence seemed to depend on teasing, joking, and pulling pranks. His skill at imitating animals and humans made his audience laugh until they cried. Though Martin retained his fun-loving nature in the upper grades, he changed in more ways than one. Studying became a passion for him once he decided to become a lawyer like his father. This amazed everyone almost as much as the physical change in Martin. These days, those who only saw him infrequently were often heard to utter, "Is *that* the Baysinger boy?" By the time Martin entered law school, he stood six feet, two inches tall, displayed rippling muscles, and had become, by far, the handsomest man in Morgan's Landing.

Julia liked Martin. Her objections had to do with other matters. She hated to admit that there was anyone in Morgan's Landing toward whom she had such a strong aversion, but Julia couldn't bear the thought of being connected with Martin's sister, Amalda, much less spending ten minutes in the same room with her.

Amalda Baysinger could only be described as a horror. The only way Julia could have been treated worse during her school years would have been if she'd been Amalda's specially chosen target. However, the fact that the main target for her meanness happened to be Bertina Drexler had only served to make Julia dislike Amalda all the more. Seeing her dearest friend victimized infuriated her. A year older than her brother, Martin's perfect test scores had been a bitter gall to Amalda while she strove to succeed, sometimes to the point of cheating, yet barely passed. Bertina's intelligence seemed to rile her as well, and she took advantage of the younger girl's timid nature and taunted her without mercy. As Bertina grew in confidence and beauty, Amalda's jealousy had turned vicious. Imagining life as Amalda's sister-in-law, Julia saw only misery for herself as well as a slap in the face for her best friend. Besides, since returning home from Savannah, she found herself in no mood for a suitor, even if he was the handsomest man in town and had a special way of making her laugh.

Martin didn't seem ready to have his offer of a ride dismissed with such nonchalance. He followed Julia down the street.

"Whose dog is this anyway? Or, should I say horse?"

"He belongs to Dora Klein," Julia called over her shoulder. "He's an English mastiff. His name's Archibald and he's her dear, sweet pup."

"Oh, that's right. He must've doubled in size since I last saw him. That means he lives just up the street from you."

"Yes, Martin," Julia sighed wearily. "Archibald and I are neighbors."

"Then you know what that means."

Julia stopped and turned to face Martin. "What does it mean?" she smiled, waiting for a sample of Martin's wit.

"It means he's going to stick with you the whole way."

Martin removed his hat and gestured with a wide sweep of his arm. "Here's the buggy. Don't be so stubborn. Let me take you home. Say, by the way," he said, raking a hand through his dark hair and repositioning his hat, "I saw a nice rig when I passed the depot just now. When I get going in my law practice, I'm going to get one like that, unless I decide to go all out and get an automobile. What would you think of that? We can't let Mr. Adler and the Morgans have the only ones in Morgan's Landing. I asked the driver about it and he said he was hired out to pick up some Senator... Senator... what did he say his name was...?"

"*Thornhill!*" Julia shoved the basket into Martin's hands and scrambled into the buggy. "Hurry, Martin! Take me home!"

Chapter Twenty-Four

"Wait a second. Let me help you!" Martin set the basket behind the seat and tried to assist. "Thornhill. I think that's the name. I don't know when I've seen anyone, even a girl, change her mind so fast, but I'm glad you did. Get down, Archibald!" Martin stomped his foot and Archibald ceased his efforts to climb into the back of the buggy with the basket.

"I'm all set. May we go now?" Julia resisted the temptation to take the reins herself. How could anyone be so slow?

"Coming! Coming!" Martin circled to the other side of the buggy and climbed in. "What's the big hurry? How did you come to know this Senator Thornhill anyway?"

"Oh, well, when we first arrived in Savannah, I was... Never mind."

Martin turned off Main Street and, though he seemed willing to let the subject drop for the moment, a quick glance told Julia he was studying her out of the corner of his eye. As the buggy slowed in front of the house, she gathered her skirts for a speedy dash to the workshop. She hadn't seen a letter or telegram. Unless one had arrived today, Papa had no idea the senator had arrived. When Martin spoke, Julia looked up at him. Though his voice had its usual teasing tone, his eyes were serious.

"You know, Julia, I used to think what good manners you had when we were growing up. You were the most polite girl in school. Don't you think maybe you could wait till the buggy stops and I come around to help you out before you leap over the side?"

"I'm sorry, Martin. It's just that I've got to speak to Papa this instant."

"I'll get the basket and walk you to the door."

"Oh, don't bother. I'll be fine."

"Julia," Martin laid a hand on her arm. "I *will* get the basket and I *will* walk you to the door."

"Yes, Martin." Julia reseated herself, straining to be calm and polite. "Thank you. You've been so helpful to me today. I appreciate it, Martin. I really do. I'm not trying to be rude."

Martin lifted Julia to the ground and, taking the basket, walked her to the door in what felt like a crawl to Julia. As they stepped from the bright sunlight onto the shady porch, Martin reached for her arm again.

"I'd like it if I could come in and say 'hello' to your folks."

"I'm sure they'd love to see you, Martin, but right now, you see, we're... Oh!" As Julia's gesturing arm thudded against something large and solid, she turned to see what occupied the space that should have been thin air. "Fred!"

Julia's eyes adjusted to the dim light. It was Fred Schmidt, but a Fred Schmidt she'd rarely encountered. This Fred, attired in his Sunday clothes and scrubbed to gleaming perfection, had a fresh barber shop haircut.

Martin extended his hand. "Hello there, Fred! We didn't see you."

Fred gave Martin's hand a quick shake. "I just got here. Hello, Julia. Martin."

Julia studied him. He looked unusually sober. His eyes seemed focused on Martin's left hand, which still held her arm. She knew he must be making the very assumptions that had been her reasons for not wanting to ride home with Martin in the first place. It was understandable that Fred, like a protective big brother, might become riled and step in to intervene if he thought she'd received uninvited attentions.

"Martin brought me home. I had some trouble with Archibald."

Remembering her mission, Julia abandoned the idea of detailed explanations. Papa must be told about Senator Thornhill's arrival. *Why this profusion of callers just now?*

"Thank you again, Martin, and as I said, I'd be happy to ask you in if we didn't have..." Julia paused, searching for an explanation that wouldn't sound preposterous. "... well, circumstances... circumstances that require immediate attention. There's no real emergency. It's just that Papa needs me. I must say good day to both of you." She turned to Fred, softening. "You must have stopped by for a reason, Fred. Was there something in particular you needed?"

"No. I guess it's nothing in particular. I just thought I'd pay a visit and see how your family is getting along. I thought I'd offer to help your papa with some of his work since things are slow at the mill. I'll be getting along."

Fred brushed past Martin and Julia and headed down the steps.

Julia didn't believe it. Fred must have had a reason to come to town in his best clothes. *Has he come to see the doctor? A lawyer? Things are slow at the mill—the bank president?* She didn't like the grim look on his face. *Heaven forbid—the undertaker!* Dashing down the steps, she grabbed his elbow.

"Fred, is everything, I mean, *everyone*, all right? You came to town for some special reason, didn't you? What is it?"

"Nothing that won't keep."

Julia watched Fred walk away. She must get to the bottom of all this. *Oh, the senator!* She spun around and ran up the steps. Preoccupied with the Schmidts' troubles and Papa's looming meeting with the senator, she bumped into Martin. He caught her in his arms as she stumbled.

"Whoa! Watch where you're going, Julia! I think I'll be getting along myself. I can tell you're certainly not in the mood for visitors. If I hadn't known you all my life and understood you were half-addled in the head, I might take offense. As it is, I'll just try my luck on another day when you've got your manners, and your head, on straight."

"Oh, Martin! Don't be impossible! Sometimes you provoke me to no end."

"Me! Provoke *you*? Well, if that doesn't fix it! Don't be calling for my help if you're treed by a dozen Archibalds!"

Martin made an exaggerated gesture of tipping his hat before turning to go down the porch steps. Julia shook her head. It was all a game, one they'd played for as long as they could remember. Glancing over her shoulder as she opened the screen door, she saw what she expected—the flash of Martin's handsome smile as he looked back over his shoulder before climbing into his buggy.

As she turned again to go inside, something colorful caught her eye. She reached down and picked up a bouquet of flowers that lay on the porch swing. *Chrysanthemums? Where on earth did these come from?* Taking them into the house, she laid them on the kitchen table as she passed through on her way to the workshop.

Hurrying across the back yard, Julia burst into the workshop. Papa's eyes widened as she broke the news.

"Here? Now? You're sure?"

Julia could imagine the paralysis and panic that must be dancing in the pit of his stomach and wished that everything she had just heard from Martin would turn out to be a false alarm.

"Martin said he was a senator and when I mentioned the name Thornhill, he said he thought that sounded right."

"If it's true, he'll be staying at the Roth. I don't want him to show up until I'm ready."

"It's not ready, Papa?"

"Well, it is, but it isn't, you might say."

Julia and Papa jumped as the door to the workshop flew open. Mother entered.

"Julia, what's the matter? I looked out from the sewing room and the way you were running across the yard I thought we might have a fire!"

"We do have a crisis," Papa sighed. "He's here."

"Who's here?"

"Senator Thornhill," interjected Julia. "Martin Baysinger saw him at the depot."

"Oh, my!" Mother surveyed the workshop. "Roderick, what is all this? You can barely walk around in here. Never mind. Just tell me if it's ready."

"It is, but it isn't," Roderick and Julia answered in unison.

"What does that mean?" Mother circled the two boxed-in wagons which took up the majority of the floor space. She peered into the back of one. "This looks like an old peddler's wagon."

"It is. I bought it when Herman Zotz passed away and painted over all his advertising."

"This one has bars... Oh, Roderick! It's not for hauling *prisoners*?"

"It used to be, but now it's hauling the M.W.C.D."

"You mean it's big enough to take up this whole wagon?"

"Of course it is, by the time you get the steam engine in there, plus a load of wood and the electromotive force generator and all the pulleys..."

"Then, what's in the peddler wagon?"

"The other one."

"The other *what?*" Mother wriggled between the two wagons to have another look inside.

"The other M.W.C.D. If you're going to transmit, you've got to receive. Beatrice, you haven't been listening."

"And you questioned my need for two sewing machines! Well, at least when you saw them you knew what you were looking at. Why are there kites in here? Really, Roderick, I hate to cast doubt, but I simply can't picture the military putting much stock in something that sends messages by kite."

"Beatrice! I need your help!"

Julia disliked the sharpness she heard in Papa's voice. Mother meant well, of course, but sometimes they both puzzled as to her ability to focus her attention on something other than the critical issue at hand. In an instant, Julia saw on his face that he regretted being harsh and he seemed relieved to see a loving determination in his wife's eyes as she turned to face him.

"Of course, dear. Just tell me what to do."

"Get on over to the Roth Hotel. See if the senator has checked in. If he has, find out if he's brought his wife. I hope to blazes he has. They'll be likely to socialize more and give me a chance to finish."

After issuing a string of requests that would require Mother, Julia, and Hannah to keep the Thornhills rested, well-fed, and occupied, Roderick sat down on the tongue of the peddler wagon and buried his head in his hands.

"All this time I've kept this a secret. I made do without any outside help. Three or four more days and I could've gotten a couple of fellows I could trust and taken these outside of town to see how much distance I could achieve. Three or four more days—that's what I needed."

Julia blinked back a tear as she watched Mother begin stroking his head. "Everything will work out, dear. Just think how long you've worked and how we've prayed. God hasn't only heard, He's the one who gives you these ideas for witty inventions in the first place!"

Roderick took her hand and kissed it. "If He can cause a society woman to pay a king's ransom for a party dress, then why doubt that He'll convince a senator that the military needs a peddler wagon full of kites? Oh! I'll be needing some curtains. Could you sew some up for me? Nothing fancy—just some black material."

"Curtains?"

"I'll need to cover these little windows in the wagons."

"I'll find something for you, dear," Mother promised as she went out the door.

Roderick stood and stretched. He pulled his handkerchief from his pocket and wiped his brow.

"We'd better get going. I've got to go find three more horses."

Julia paused at the door. "Horses, Papa?"

"Hopefully, some less skittish than Molly. I brought that poor old mare in here the other day and lit a fire under this. When it got up a head of steam, she nearly had an apoplectic fit."

Julia jumped as her mother's head reappeared in the doorway.

"Oh, Roderick! What about the muse and tops? I won't know what to say if the senator asks about them."

"Muse and tops?" Roderick repeated, his face contorting.

Julia held her breath. Papa looked as though he might be on the verge of ordering Mother to stop speaking jibberish, especially when he needed to concentrate on more important matters.

"You said in your letter to stress the importance of the muse and to give absolutely no information on the tops. If Senator Thornhill asks about them, I won't know what I'm talking about."

"Beatrice, confound it! *I* don't know what you're talking about!"

"We'll if you don't, who does? It was *your* letter! M-U-S-E and T-O-P-S. That's exactly what it said. I remember it distinctly."

"Oh, that's short for 'military use' and 'technical operations'. Just an abbreviation. Everybody knows that."

"Ugh!"

Papa winced as the workshop door slammed. He looked up as Julia approached and heaved a sigh as she placed a kiss on his cheek.

"I'll go find Hannah and let her know what we need to do. We're all with you."

Entering through the back door, Julia found her mother in the kitchen, sniffing the bouquet of chrysanthemums.

"Oh, how nice. You should put them in a vase before they wilt, Julia."

"I was in such a hurry to get out to the workshop, Mother. I laid them there as I passed. I found them on the porch swing. I imagine they're Rebekah's, so I'll find her and have her take care of them. I'll be asking her where she got them as well. I want to be sure she didn't go flower-picking at one of the neighbors without permission. I can't imagine she did. She's such a sweet, mannerly girl."

"Oh, I wouldn't be too hasty, Lovely One. I don't think that bouquet is Rebekah's."

"Then who..."

"Doesn't Helga Schmidt have some mums this color blooming behind the store?"

"Yes. Several people in town have them."

"I know. But earlier, when I came downstairs to get a pitcher of water, it wasn't Rebekah I saw coming down our street all dressed up and carrying a bouquet of mums. It was Fred Schmidt."

Julia's jaw dropped. This *was* a bit of news! So, this was the reason Fred had been to town so often and had shown up in his Sunday best. He'd come to pay a call. Fred Schmidt had decided to start courting after all these years! A slow smile spread over her face.

"Mother, isn't it wonderful? I'm surprised, though. It's so sudden! I hope it all works out to a happy ending, don't you?"

"You do? Well! I must say I never thought you'd take it like this, especially after everything that's happened recently. You're happy about this?"

"I know there's a difference of religion, Mother, but the Lord can work all that out. I've prayed that Hannah would find a good husband and father for her children. She couldn't ask for anyone better than Fred! I wonder, though, how he's come to be sweet on her in such a short time. I didn't realize they'd been introduced."

"*Hannah*?"

"Didn't you just tell me you saw him bring the flowers...? Oh!" Julia gasped, putting a hand over her mouth. If Fred had come to call on Hannah, he wouldn't have left when she and Martin arrived. She reached for the abandoned bouquet, overwhelmed by a wave of emotion she couldn't quite identify. "Mother! *No!*"

RUDY SCHMIDT SAT at the counter, pondering the deliciousness of his doughnut and the whereabouts of Fred. The sight of his brother entering through the back door offered a new mystery to solve.

"Fred! Well now, what are you all gussied up for in the middle of the week? Did somebody die or are you going courtin'?"

Rudy's joke failed to provoke the round of pleasant banter he'd expected.

"I don't see how it's anything to you."

"Which one, the death or the courtin'?"

Their mother entered from the storeroom. "Someone has died? Who has died?"

Fred shook his head. "Nobody died, Mama."

Rudy, enjoying his quest for answers, persevered. "Well, then, I guess Fred's gone courtin', Mama!"

"What if I have?"

Rudy decided to keep quiet and let Fred simmer down. He'd let his mother do the questioning.

"You have a courtship, Friedrich? You haven't told us! Who is the girl?"

Rudy, studying his doughnut as though it were the first one he'd ever tasted, kept one eye on the proceedings. In all the years they'd worked together, neither he nor Fred had gone so far as to pay a formal call at a girl's home. While they'd shared their admiration of this pretty girl or that sensible one and marveled together over the utter silliness of others, they'd formed a mutual agreement to see that the mill provided a sizable income before they settled down to raise families. Up until now, life had revolved around their partnership. Now, his big brother had begun making calls on a girl without even telling him.

"I paid a call on Julia. She wasn't home... but... well, she *was,* but now she's... anyway, I paid a call on Julia."

"Ju..." Rudy rose from his stool and sank back down onto it, struck dumb by the shock. Julia couldn't be interested in Fred—or could she? No! His brother had gotten way above himself. Who did he think he was? It sickened him to hear his mother's voice quaver as she fawned over Fred.

"My *Schnucki*? Oh, Friedrich!"

"Mama, I only said I paid a call. I didn't even get to speak to her. She had... company."

"Oh, but she is like a daughter to me. She is a bit younger, but she knows you well. She will know whether or not this is a good match. Oh, I am so happy! So happy, Friedrich!"

Rudy stood, red-faced. Speech returned, bringing a sharpness to his tone that startled both his mother and brother and brought his father running from the storeroom. He pounded his fist on the counter. "She certainly *is*—too young for Fred, I mean. I mean, he's too old for her. Nobody said anything to *me* about any of this and *no*, it's *not* a good match! If anyone is going to court Julia, it's going to be *me*!"

Kansas City, Kansas

THE NEW GRAVE was easy to find. Adam sank to his knees near the mound of freshly turned earth, glad he'd come alone. He had much to say to God and to the man who could no longer hear him. Brushing a few leaves away, he picked up the remains of a bouquet, its stems now shrunken inside a loose ribbon. *Everything dies.* The simple truth still hurt. Tears rolled down Adam's cheeks. *You were always a wild one.* Visions of growing up alongside his best friend flooded his mind and Adam let them. The two fun-loving and ornery little boys had enjoyed great times together.

"Why did you have to change? You lie here because of your own..." Adam paused, remembering the futility of his words. The urge remained, however, to say what his friend refused to hear when he was alive. "It's all your fault! You had everything a man could want. You couldn't even die with dignity."

Adam tossed the bouquet aside. *Did you change, Malcolm, or was I blind to the fact that you were always headed this direction?* Over the years, it had become obvious to Adam that Malcolm's tendencies amounted to more than mere growing pains. Those who were taken in by his flashy, good looks enabled him to pursue his passion for drinking, fighting, and carousing even when his money ran short. Catastrophic gambling losses had prompted Adam to confront him.

Adam stood to go. "That was when you told me to take my God and my Bible and get out of your life." He brushed the leaves from his trouser legs and walked away, the knot in his chest tightening as he recalled the fury in the man's eyes the last time they'd spoken.

Adam had obeyed the request and stayed away until he'd gotten the telegram.

Devastation lay in the wake of this death. Adam accepted responsibility for much of it. His own actions, years ago, led to the aftermath. He must visit the family and do whatever was necessary, even if it meant he had to stay in Kansas City and postpone his studies again.

His sudden departure from Boston had been hard on Aunt Bethel. Adam could still hear her frantic voice calling from the bottom of the stairs. At first, he'd thought he'd merely overslept and would be late for class, but having scrambled into his clothes and grabbed his comb, he remembered it was Saturday and ran downstairs. The sight of his aunt standing there, her plump hands trembling as one of them twisted the side of her apron and the other extended an envelope toward him, told him that something dreadful must have happened.

Though he'd tried to calm her by reassuring her that sometimes telegrams carried good news, he soon discovered that her intuition had been right. Adam had sunk into a chair as the words on the paper pierced his heart.

"It's not what you think, Aunt Bethel," he reassured her. "The family is fine, but I have to go home. I have to go home right away."

Adam paused at the cemetery gate and looked back, knowing he would likely not return to this spot. Perhaps he had left Aunt Bethel and Boston behind for good as well. Responsibility loomed among the living on the other side of this gate and from that he could not turn away. He released the iron latch and stepped through.

Chapter Twenty-Five

MORGAN'S LANDING, MISSOURI

Senator Thornhill had, indeed, brought his wife with him to Morgan's Landing and, as a politician, seemed thrilled with Mother's ploys to delay an inspection of the invention by means of arranging speeches and handshaking opportunities for him. At times, Julia thought Mother might become hysterical and harbored similar opinions concerning herself. Each day's consuming schedule, designed to keep the Thornhills' social calendar filled, proved to be wearing. It succeeded, however, in giving Papa time to make final adjustments to the invention.

Julia felt grateful for Hannah, who did most of the sewing after Mother gave her instructions each morning. Florine Clark, the most talented of the basting girls, had been learning to use the new machines, freeing Mother to spend time with Senator and Mrs. Thornhill.

The challenge of sharing the kitchen with Hannah grew with the hectic schedule, bringing Julia near to tears. Hannah, too, seemed overwhelmed with her efforts to maintain a constant awareness of where and how each food was prepared. Julia hated to see her complete her cleaning rituals, knowing that her own life-long habits of working in the kitchen were apt to contaminate the space. Julia reported to the sewing room and the workshop each day as soon as she returned from the bakery and received instructions before taking a deep breath and entering the kitchen to commit another round of unintentional violations.

Julia now realized that even the busiest of mornings at Schmidt's Bakery hadn't left her as near her wits' end as she had previously assumed. At the bakery, the number of considerations were limited to following the recipe, keeping track of baking times, greeting the customers, and making change at the register. Now, she struggled to plan menus and keep several lists in order at home, only to be called away from concentrating on any one of them long enough to accomplish one or two of its tasks. The most frustrating were the lists containing dates the Lansings would be dining out with people who had issued invitations to the Thornhills and the lists of dates Julia needed to prepare dinner at home for those people they'd invited over to meet the Thornhills. It began to look as though most of Morgan's Landing could be found in the rotation.

It seemed that Julia heard her name called every ten minutes or so from the direction of the workshop. Papa's tone conveyed the intent that she appear instantly to hold, crank, or lift something. She'd given up asking what the "something" was. Mute cooperation left Papa to his scientific thoughts.

Former concerns that she might have disturbing dreams about Adam gave way to sleeplessness. No sooner would Julia drift off to sleep than she would be jolted awake by the thought of something she had omitted from the day's duties or must remember for the coming day. She resorted to keeping her lists at her bedside in hopes that, when morning came, she'd be able to decipher the scribbles she'd made in the middle of the night while tilting the paper toward the moonlight coming through the window.

On the nights when sleep came, Julia's dreams came in disturbing flashes, wakening her only to return again once she repositioned her pillow and drifted off. She knew the flashes reflected her fears, for each one transported her to the Wentworth Hotel in Savannah where, clad in her dressing gown, she entered the bath and encountered Senator Thornhill clad in nothing at all. The very thought that news of the scandal had somehow made its way to Morgan's Landing along with the senator made her wish Mother had never convinced him to come. Julia scolded herself daily for such selfishness. She must put her own concerns aside and stand in support of Papa's hopes and dreams.

Senator Thornhill's jolly disposition and willingness to shake hands and be fawned over by ninety percent of the populace stretched the visiting, dinners at home, dinners out, and tours of the town and surrounding area over several days. At times, it seemed he'd forgotten the purpose of his visit, for he had yet to call for an inspection of the invention.

After Sunday dinner, however, he seemed to have formed the opinion that ample time had passed. Though he'd been disturbing the peace in Morgan's Landing all the way from the river to the mill south of town ever since he'd arrived, Julia still jumped as he leaned back in his chair and boomed, "Well, Roderick, let's get down to brass tacks. I'll be needing to head back to Washington soon. I'll be here first thing in the morning and you can show me this invention of yours."

It seemed to take Papa a minute to resettle himself in his chair after the jolt.

"That'll be fine, Senator. That'll be just fine!"

Julia watched as her mother reached for a serving bowl and extended it toward the senator with a smile.

"More potatoes, Senator?"

MURMURING yet another prayer for Papa under her breath, Julia took her usual path to the bakery on Monday, knowing full well that there was no more help she could give Papa had she stayed home. There seemed nothing more to do except wait for a report and hope for good news.

Autumn had held on with beauty and warmth. The crisp air of mid-November seemed to make everyone in Morgan's Landing thankful. The fine year had brought an early harvest.

Savoring the perfect days, they prepared for winter. Pleasant weather would become a memory as the glorious fall days, rather than fading slowly into wintry chill, would likely abandon their revelers without warning. The collective residents would awaken one morning to discover that howling winds and blowing snow had laid siege to the town and would know to expect no favorable outlook until the following March came along and mercifully performed a miracle.

Julia needed only a light shawl on her walk. The scent of burning leaves made her feel a little sorry for anyone who couldn't be out on such a day. Hannah and Florine would miss it, being confined to the sewing room. Marcus and Rebekah would enjoy playing after school. Perhaps Mother and Mrs. Thornhill would take a walk. *Poor Papa!* The only thing before his eyes would be the Mobile Wireless Communication Device and the only sounds he'd hear above the awful din it made would be the approval or disapproval of the senator. Papa would, no doubt, stop by the bakery if he had the chance and let her know how things turned out.

Papa had enlisted Fred and Rudy to help out and give loan of their draft horses. Julia didn't understand all the details, but horses were bound to contribute to the mobility of the thing. The brothers had seemed happy to see her when they arrived, but appeared sullen and curt toward one another. She hoped they hadn't gotten into some sort of tiff on their way into town.

Beatrice slept well in spite of anticipation and dread of the coming morning, as was usually the case when she and Roderick prayed together before drifting off to sleep. Whatever the outcome, this great opportunity was a blessing. Now that the moment had arrived, however, she found herself returning again and again to the window. Though she tried her best to give Hannah and Florine their instructions for the day, the distraction going on below her window made her feel she must be talking in riddles. Resigning herself to the fact that she would never be able to tear her eyes away from Roderick at such a critical moment, she abandoned Hannah and Florine to their own instincts and hurried out onto the back lawn where Roderick stood, gesturing toward the rear of one of the wagons.

"You see, Senator, it's all inside. That is, except for the part that's on top. By a simple release of the lever which I have installed right here, next to the wagon brake, a series of pulleys lowers the Mobile Wireless Communication Device out of the containment area, where a fire can readily be built in order to get up a head of steam in the boiler."

Beatrice smiled with pride. Roderick's nervousness had vanished. The instant he'd begun to describe the invention to the senator, everything else had ceased to exist. His eyes glittered with the knowledge that he was about to change the world.

Rudy and Fred had arrived with the pair of draft horses they normally used for pulling wagonloads of grain and another, younger mare to be hitched alongside Molly. The brothers had named her Erma due to the resemblance she bore to a beloved aunt.

These two had reluctantly pulled the peddler wagon out of the workshop onto the east side of the lawn and the draft pair had brought the prison wagon out to the west side. Erma's usual partner had come up lame and been left behind at the last minute—a situation that left Erma and Molly eying one another in mutual distrust. Beatrice walked over to Molly and stroked her forehead. The poor horse seemed to share her case of nervous jitters.

She shook her head at the two oddities on the lawn. The short, black curtains she'd had Florine whip up hadn't improved the appearance of either of them to a measurable degree, especially the hideous prison wagon. *It would be ideal if the curtains were on the outside. If only there were a way to cover up those bars.* The thought of her husband driving around in such a thing embarrassed her.

Hurried paint jobs had altered their original appearance, but had done little to make the wagons presentable. The peddler wagon had been an array of gaudy colors in the days when it had advertised its wares. Roderick's decision to use the leftover red barn paint rendered an effect far from subtle, especially since the wheel spokes remained their original shade of bright yellow. The prison wagon had been a black and ominous-looking thing when performing its former duties. Beatrice blamed herself for the spectacle that marred the lawn. Roderick, in an attempt to please her, had attempted to change it as much as possible by applying what remained of the white porch paint. Having run out of time and paint when the senator arrived, it was now a sickly, milky gray. Mottled areas of black bled through in random areas, transforming the menacing into something mournfully repugnant.

Beatrice watched Fred and Rudy, hoping they understood more of what Roderick was saying than she did. Fred, as he stood with his arms crossed, seemed to be taking a keen interest in the proceedings as he watched Roderick and Senator Thornhill circle the mysterious, black-curtained conveyances. He stepped up onto the driver's seat of the nearest wagon and peered into the back. Beatrice followed Rudy as he stepped behind Roderick and the senator at the rear of the wagon and did likewise. The only identifiable part of the contraption appeared to be a small steam engine sitting on its side. Fred seemed to be concentrating on this thingamajig in case Roderick asked him to tinker with it.

Roderick stepped to the side of the prison wagon and released the lever next to the brake. A series of creakings, clangings, and knockings poured forth from the open doors at the rear of the wagon and Beatrice joined the men as they stepped aside to make way for whatever might occur next. By means of a pulley system, the hinged wooden platform that had filled the opening lowered to a position parallel to the ground.

Roderick ran to the rear of the wagon. "Rudy, grab the supports on your side and lock them into place."

"Sure, Mr. Lansing."

Studying Roderick's motions on the other side of the wagon, Rudy imitated his actions. Together they lowered legs on small wheels, inserting pins to hold them steady.

"The wheels," Roderick explained, "allow you to move the

device for better reception if needed. But, of course, it cannot be transported more than a few feet once there's a fire going."

"That makes sense." Rudy nodded.

Beatrice shook her head as she looked over the craziest looking mess of wires, tubes, and machinery she'd ever seen. She looked at Fred, whose eyes now met his brother's as if in search of some hint of confidence. She hoped it made sense to somebody, but Rudy's face betrayed the fact that he was likely as baffled as she was.

Roderick became animated as he watched Senator Thornhill study the invention with a knitted brow, a determined mouth, and a finger on the chin. He'd acknowledged Roderick's narrative with a series of mutterings. Though having to make do with a few 'So I see's, 'Is that so's, and 'My, my, my's, Roderick seemed to glory in his prize project, and Beatrice wondered if he were still aware of her presence or that of the brothers. His time had come. No more tweaking could be done. He swelled with pride, making his presentation with an air as though he'd been lecturing a university class on the topic for years.

He gestured toward his masterpiece. "What you see here, Senator, is a steam-driven, electromotive force generator of the most modern design. It is attached to a steam engine which is, of course, wood-fired. Each wagon contains identical equipment, except for minor differences in the types of steam engines I've been able to obtain and some slight differences in the two boilers. The military will naturally be able to manufacture something perfectly uniform in appearance, size, and function. Once the Mobile Wireless Communication Device is in place and the generator has reached a full head of steam, we've only to raise the antenna by means of this ratcheting device and begin sending signals. This appendage will extend approximately forty feet into the air if needed. When fully extended, it will, of course, need to be steadied by these ropes and anchored against the wind. If you'd care to go inside, Senator, you'll see an area especially equipped with a small chair and desk which is attached to the wagon and holds a railroad telegraph key."

Senator Thornhill, with some effort, climbed into the back of the wagon to have a closer look.

"Careful there, Senator!" Roderick warned. "Be sure not to step on those kites or balloons as you make your way over to the telegraph key."

This statement had an immediate effect on Fred and Rudy, who shoved their heads through the back door of the wagon.

Senator Thornhill looked puzzled. "Tell me, Lansing, what situation might call for the use of these kites? Or, on the other hand—balloons, did you say?"

"Oh, of course, Senator. Glad you asked me that. Yes... yes... yes. Here we have a series of twelve kites, or weather balloons, if need be, for use in receiving signals. Each M.W.C.D. is equipped with a spark-gap transmitter. The kites or balloons will receive the radio signals from the other M.W.C.D. The kites, of course, provide more gain and provide for a higher reception. The weather balloons—now that's another story. The hydrogen interferes with the reception, but they will, nevertheless, have to be used in the event that there is no wind. In this way, we naturally hope to provide for every possible circumstance."

"Naturally." The senator nodded.

Roderick paused. Beatrice could see by the way he fidgeted with his collar that his nervousness had returned. She hoped his passionate presentation proved effective. She knew he looked upon the M.W.C.D. affectionately, as something near to a first-born child. The time had come, however, to be silent. She held her breath, knowing that he waited to see if the senator might seize upon this technological miracle as something that would launch a revolutionary advance in military procedures.

Senator Thornhill stood scratching his side whiskers. "Does it work?"

"Work? Oh, definitely! Yes! Definitely. I've had it working many times."

"One of these, so you're saying, Lansing, transmits messages to the other one? And receives?"

"Yes, sir. Exactly."

"Interesting. Very Interesting." The senator, huffing and puffing, managed to stretch a foot to the ground and lower himself from the wagon box. He took another stroll around the wagon. "What kind of distance do you get?"

"Distance?" Roderick flushed, clearing his throat.

"Distance," the senator repeated. "Just how far apart can these two wagons be and still communicate?"

"Well..." Roderick hesitated as though searching for words. "The military will be able to use the latest materials in construction, which will undoubtedly increase reception and transmission. However, Senator, up to the present date, I've been working alone. In attempting to keep this a secret until the last minute, I've not had assistants to help me take these to separate remote locations in order to determine the range. I'm happy now to have Fred and Rudy. I know I can trust them. The device works exactly as it should within the confines of my workshop, I assure you. Beyond that, what they are capable of remains to be seen."

The senator scrutinized the M.W.C.D. for what seemed an eternity before placing a hand on Roderick's shoulder. He looked him in the eye.

"Well then, my boy, let's get going! Let's send one apparatus in one direction and one in the other and see what happens!"

Beatrice stifled a gasp. She saw in Roderick's eyes that, though he had the horses at the ready and Fred and Rudy to assist, he felt unprepared to perform the demonstration at a distance where the brothers would lose contact with him.

Beatrice gave Roderick a smile that she hoped carried encouragement. "Carry on, gentlemen. I'll leave you to it. I've promised to take Mrs. Thornhill to Dora Klein's for tea and muffins."

As she made her way to the house, Beatrice felt relieved to have an engagement this morning, for this was a thing she knew she couldn't bear to watch.

Chapter Twenty-Six

JULIA'S HANDS worked the dough. Her thoughts, however, had nothing to do with bread. She pondered the stuff of life and the multitude of uncontrollable occurrences it liked to throw at its participants. Ever since Mrs. Schmidt—who seemed to dote on her in excess lately—had left to run errands, Julia had let her mind go on this topic. Her thoughts flitted here and there like birds hopping from branch to branch, yet always returned to the subject of Papa and what might be happening at home with the demonstration. Would the machinery work or would it fall to pieces? Would Senator Thornhill be impressed or simply leave on the next train believing he had wasted his time? Had Papa's years of planning and hard work been all for nothing, or would there be a celebration at supper tonight? She concluded, more or less, that life was just one thing after another. A person could never tell what chain of events might unfold. *You just never know.*

She envisioned the day she'd arrived in Savannah, wondering if she would make any friends during her stay. The worst embarrassment of her life had brought friends who were willing to give Papa the opportunity of a lifetime. *And Abigail.* Who would have thought she'd become such a dear friend in so short a time? They'd already exchanged letters, Abigail's news being centered around her other correspondent, Robert Kensington. Perhaps she might visit the Hadleys in Atlanta one day —perhaps for a wedding.

Everything's different now. The financial pressure had eased for her parents. It was a pleasure to hear them converse about how to save and spend money rather than how to stretch it down to the last penny. Both their ventures, however, had turned the household upside down. Julia found it disorienting to have another family living in the house—one that had different beliefs and customs. She'd become attached to Hannah and her children. Still, she missed having her room to herself where she could be alone with her thoughts, for Rebekah and Marcus seemed to follow her there each time she sought to retreat. It seemed that, lately, the only time she had for this luxury came at these moments when the bakery quieted and she could get her hands into the dough and think. Her ponderings on Papa's future and Abigail's inevitably brought her mind back to thoughts concerning her own. Her recent trip and the events since she'd returned had been brimming with more male attention than she'd experienced in a lifetime.

Men! Julia reviewed her mental list. It looked cluttered and messy now. Prior to her time in Savannah, only the "No" and "Maybe" columns had ever had entries, and only in the lightest pencil, names having rested in one column before being demoted to another. One name in particular seemed determined to appear on the list, but Julia pushed it aside in hopes it would vanish if she forced herself to dwell on others.

Julia dropped the dough into the bread pan with a sigh. *Ah! The ball—what an experience! Paul Grayson—enough to sweep any girl off her feet!* Julia flushed, remembering how Paul had gone to extra lengths to secure the last dance with her when he could have had any girl in the room. Though she found it flattering, perhaps it hinted that Paul might have traits she wouldn't have found so attractive. None of the other men at the ball had mattered to her in a romantic way. Though she had detected a bit of interest on the part of Doctor Hancock, their paths had never crossed again. According to Abigail, he was to have been at the Graysons' but had been called out to deliver a baby. James Hadley had been sweet and attentive, but Julia had come to think of him merely as a good friend. She dropped the names, one by one, into the crowded "No" column. None of them had ever really mattered.

Only one name had mattered. It wasn't the stuff of life that interfered with the proper placement of Adam Cole's name on the list. Rather, it had been the stuff of her own stupid behavior and her futile attempts to set things straight. There was something special about Adam. Now it was over. Adam had gone home and so had she. The irredeemable situation left the "No" column as the only place for his name. *Then, why is it stuck in the "Maybes"?* Why did his name keep trying to leap over into that pure, white space under the word "Yes"? Julia felt a strange connection to Adam—a connection that needed to be severed. Her mental efforts would be better spent in figuring out what was to be done about the unexpected situations that faced her now.

Grabbing a second ball of dough, Julia pounded it down with a vengeance. Earlier, she'd applied a tender touch to the pastry. Now it felt good to take her frustrations out on something more sturdy. *Martin Baysinger—what am I supposed to think of these new attentions from Martin? Is he serious?* She'd known him all her life. She liked him. She had to admit that his name had hovered over her list once they'd both grown up enough to be interested in the opposite sex. However, each time Julia imagined Martin as a "Maybe", she saw herself writing "Martin and Amalda." *No! I could never do such a thing to insult Bertina!* Martin stood as a definite "No". This brought the Martin problem full circle. He'd made an attempt to call on her folks. She'd been seen riding in his buggy. How was she to avoid hurting his feelings? She didn't want to hurt Martin any more than she wanted to hurt Fred.

Fred! What am I supposed to do about Fred Schmidt? Fred and Rudy had always been loveable big brothers in Julia's eyes. She'd felt comfortable around both of them up until the incident on the porch a few days ago. Fred was a good man. Though eight years older—not that it mattered—Fred was a good man and a hard worker. Julia had no doubt that, as a husband, he would be good to her. They conversed easily, at least until he decided to take a romantic interest in her. There seemed no reason for her *not* to consider Fred, yet no particular reason to consider him either. She could just as easily consider Rudy as Fred, for she felt the same about both of them.

Catching herself at the instant she nearly pressed her flour-covered hands to her temples in frustration, Julia determined to chase the tangled mass of thoughts from her head and concentrate on the only thing that mattered today—Papa. Before leaving for the bakery this morning, she'd gone to the workshop to wish him well and found Fred and Rudy there with him receiving their instructions. Though they had both greeted her with smiles, they seemed somewhat out of sorts with one another. *I hope they're not having a spat.*

"*Schnucki!*"

Julia snapped out of her rumination. Mrs. Schmidt stood at the door, waving for her to come outside.

"*Schnucki*, what is your Papa doing?"

Julia ran outside. She stared at the spectacle coming toward her. The red peddler wagon, with her father and Senator Thornhill on the driver's seat, could be seen blocks away, having just turned onto Main Street from Beech Tree Street. Behind them, making the turn onto Main Street, Fred and Rudy followed, driving the hideous prison wagon. The sight of the unusual vehicles, identically topped with wires, coiled masses of ropes, and tower apparatuses drew a crowd. To Julia's horror, shopkeepers and shoppers alike scurried along the street, spreading the word to anyone who might not have been alerted that they needed to come out onto Main Street and witness the passing parade.

Papa and the senator passed by and turned left onto Oak Street, heading east. Fred and Rudy, who did not appear to be enjoying the adventure as much as the men in the first wagon, turned right once they reached Oak Street and headed west. Resolving to count her blessings, Julia uttered a quick prayer of thanks as the wagons turned off Main Street.

Julia peered into the bakery window at the clock. *Nearly noon.* Not only had they come right through the middle of town, but they'd chosen the busiest time of day as if they'd wanted an audience. Main Street began filling with clusters of people speculating on what they'd seen. In the distance, she could see guests pouring forth from the Roth Hotel to wait for hired carriages. A loud debate broke out over which wagon to follow.

Some of the onlookers, recognizing Julia, flocked to her. Thankful to be surrounded by a curious, rather than angry, mob, she tried to make sense of their questions. Julia caught sight of her mother and Dahlia Thornhill as they turned onto Main from Beech Tree Street. They strolled along unaccompanied, looking perplexed at the bustle of activity on the street. Julia pushed along toward them with some difficulty once the crowd spotted her, flustered by the barrage of questions that seemed to be coming from all sides .

"What's your father up to now, Julia?"

"Wasn't that Senator Thornhill?"

"Did your father build those contraptions?"

"Where are they headed?"

"What are the Schmidt boys doing with that old prison wagon?"

Julia hesitated to answer. The invention had remained a secret for years. She felt as though she'd be betraying Papa to speak of it. However, since it had just, for some reason unknown to her, paraded itself through the middle of town, Julia decided to stick to the truth—as little of it as possible.

"It's an invention Papa's been working on for quite some time. He's demonstrating it to Senator Thornhill."

The impact of these few words on the curious crowd was swift and thorough. They scattered in all directions, availing themselves of any mode of transportation they could access. Julia puzzled over this strange reaction for a moment before racing down the street to meet her mother and Mrs. Thornhill.

"Now what do you suppose has come over everyone?" Mrs. Thornhill mused as people rushed past her and Main Street began emptying of its occupants.

Julia reached her mother and grabbed her arm. As she gasped for air and tried to speak she saw Mother's eyes widen.

"Julia! What on earth are all these people talking about? We've been at Dora's all this time. I thought your father took the demonstration out into the countryside just after I left. Surely they didn't just bring it through town!"

Julia nodded. "They're all going, Mother! Everybody in Morgan's Landing is following those wagons out of town!"

ALL THEIR LIVES, the Schmidt brothers had been as happy with the rest of the world as two good-natured fellows could be. Now, forced to band together out of self-preservation, they determined to survive not only the curious crowd, but the fearsome task ahead. Neither intended to back down, but both feared what might unfold when the wagon came to a stop atop the highest hill west of Morgan's Landing.

The four hours they'd spent in the Lansings' back yard had held them in wonderment, but ended as a torturous episode. Listening as Roderick explained the machinery and its attached maze of gadgetry, they had tried to grasp what their eyes beheld. Forty-five minutes into the demonstration, Fred wished he'd seen fit to occupy himself with small repairs at the mill rather than having made the rash offer to help Julia's father. Rudy, who had thought it necessary to plaster himself to Fred like a medicinal poultice in order to remain between his brother and Julia, now questioned the wisdom of it. Personal rivalries fled like noonday shadows in the presence of the assignment that loomed before them.

The inventor's instructions had been clear as to the preliminaries. It would be necessary, he'd said, for the senator to accompany him in one wagon in order to hear the narrative and follow along with the demonstration. They would stop on high ground at the fairgrounds, near the hospital. Rudy and Fred would take the other wagon in the opposite direction and pull the clanking monstrosity as far up the hill as they could near the old Indian mounds west of town.

The brothers' initial wonder had undergone a metamorphosis. They'd fallen into momentary silence as they listened to what would happen once they arrived. Stunned by the revelation, they'd spent the following two and a half hours in a state of panic while their senses, flooded by a deluge of instructions, reeled. There was nothing to it, Mr. Lansing had said. Just watch him, he'd said.

While it seemed all well and fine to refer to the coiled contraption as a boiler for the sake of demonstration purposes, it looked far more like an old still for manufacturing corn liquor. Thus far, the brothers' experience with steam engines had been limited to agricultural purposes. Perplexed by the conglomeration of wires, they found themselves in agreement on one point. The M.W.C.D. looked like the perfect invention if one intended to become intoxicated, thresh wheat, and start sending telegrams.

Rudy, considering himself nobody's fool, knew when to panic. Seizing paper and pencil, he'd made a numbered list of the procedures. Fred followed Roderick's every move, adopting the policy that it was best to touch everything Roderick touched and repeat everything he said in hopes of committing it to memory.

The peddler wagon might have crossed Main Street on a direct route out of town, but Senator Thornhill had thought it best to have the other wagon follow along Main Street for a few blocks before they turned in opposite directions. The idea struck neither Roderick nor the Schmidt brothers as desirable, but the senator's desire for a grand demonstration prevailed, leaving the occupants of the peddler wagon full of nervous excitement and those of the prison wagon full of nervous indigestion.

Having reached the flattest area on Felder's Knoll, the brothers leaned around from their positions on the wagon seat, uttering simultaneous moans of disgust at the sight of the mass of onlookers who had followed them. It would be of little comfort to them when they later learned that a two-thirds majority had been more attracted to the senator's notoriety and the prospect of watching the inventor of this phenomenon. Fred and Rudy shared the prevailing opinion of most people—it would have been far better to make fools of themselves in front of total strangers. They had been followed, however, by those who knew them best.

BEATRICE GRABBED Julia and Dahlia by the elbows, pulling them down the street. "Hurry!"

"Where?" Julia stumbled along, trying to hold her balance.

"Where? To wherever your father's going! Succeed or fail—if he's going to do it in public, I'm going to be right by his side."

"Are we going to run the whole way? Molly's hitched to the peddler wagon."

"Oh, that's right." Beatrice stopped, gasping for air. "Bertina!"

Bertina ran toward them, disregarding the fact that she'd lifted her skirts almost to her knees. "What's happened? Where have they gone?"

Julia clutched her arm. "We don't know, but we've got to follow them."

"Come with me. There's no reason to keep the drug store open. All our customers have gone after the wagons. We'll take my rig."

They had little difficulty following the tracks of the crowd out of town. Julia feared they might fly out of the jostling buggy, but refrained from asking Bertina to slow down. Like Mother, she intended to be by Papa's side when he did whatever it was he was about to do. The crowd at the fairgrounds made it impossible to get close enough to watch from the buggy. Bertina parked at a distance and they made their way on foot through the crowd.

Julia clutched her mother's hand as it slipped into hers.

"Pray!" Mother mouthed as their eyes met.

Julia prayed. Papa was making a speech.

"WELL, FOLKS," Roderick paused, taking in the size of the crowd and becoming aware of how many of his fellow citizens had added themselves to the procession. "I'm sure you're a curious bunch. Of course you are." He gave a nervous laugh and, shuffling his feet, reminded himself that this was the accomplishment of a lifetime. He raised his chin. "What you are about to witness is a breakthrough in communication. You are all familiar with sending telegrams by wires connected to poles. This, however, is a *wireless* method in which two devices can send messages…" Roderick hesitated. The expressions on the faces of those in the crowd told him that this might take all day. He knew he'd best get started and leave the speech-making to someone well-practiced at it. He caught sight of Beatrice standing at the front of the crowd and took heart at the smile of encouragement she offered and saw that Julia, Bertina, and Mrs. Thornhill were watching as well. He took a deep breath. "I'm sure some of you have met the senator. For those who have not, allow me to introduce Senator and Mrs. Percival Thornhill."

Applause erupted. Dahlia stepped forward, joining her husband for a brief period of nodding, smiling, and waving. She wasted no time, however, in returning to Beatrice's side.

Roderick peered into the crowd. He pointed out a boy who appeared to be about fourteen years of age who looked as though he might have an ounce of sense.

"I've seen you before. Your name's Hauser?"

"Yes, sir. Billy Hauser."

"You know how to fly a kite?"

"Yes, sir?" The question seemed to perplex the boy.

Roderick reached into the back of the wagon and pulled out a kite, thrusting it toward the surprised youngster.

"Can you get this up in the air pretty quick?"

"Yes, sir. There's a good wind."

"Then get busy. As soon as you get it going, bring me the wire."

The day had, indeed, provided the wind. Roderick uttered a prayer under his breath. Much more wind and the antenna tower might not be stable.

"I will now position the apparatus. Senator Thornhill, would you be kind enough to enlighten the folks on any matters you consider appropriate to be made common knowledge? But first, if you wouldn't mind releasing that lever next to the wagon brake."

"Certainly. Certainly," muttered the senator as he fumbled about with the lever.

Senator Thornhill jumped back when the lever dropped out of his hand with a clank. He took a deep breath and roared at the crowd. He expounded on the government's interest in the latest technology in the area of advanced communication for the twentieth century, citing past accomplishments, including the telegraph and telephone. He apologized for the secrecy surrounding this particular device, citing high-level officials and closed-door meetings which bound him to silence concerning the reasons behind its importance. They must rest assured that these reasons were justified, lest technological advancements fall into the wrong hands and endanger the security of the country and the welfare of its citizens—men, women, and children alike.

Roderick became concerned as the senator expounded on the capability of two devices, each in a remote location, communicating without the need for poles and wires and heaved a sigh of relief when the senator concluded his remarks having omitted any mention of military use. However, he felt certain that he was the only person who heard a word the senator spoke, for from the moment he'd released the lever, the invention had sprung to life. Had the crowd wanted to hear what the senator had to say, it would have been impossible. The sounds of the M.W.C.D. were as impressive as the sights. He had no time to concern himself with the senator now. He knew Percival Thornhill understood politics and small towns and was aware that he hadn't been able to construct something like this without some degree of publicity already. Enlisting the Schmidt brothers as help had only served to let the M.W.C.D., if it had been a cat, further out of the bag. His arrival in town and visits with the Lansings had fueled speculation among the local residents. Capitalizing on it, the senator had insisted on taking the apparatus down Main Street. Now he could present it to his audience in a preferred light. Roderick had taken one comfort while making his unplanned appearance on Main Street. The senator must have high hopes for this demonstration. Though a politician through and through, he felt the senator liked him and didn't like the idea of a good man coming to shame before his neighbors. More importantly, he probably didn't much like the thought of it for himself either.

Taking a quick glance up from his invention, Roderick looked at Senator Thornhill. He seemed to have concluded his speech, for he stood smiling upon his audience with a satisfaction known only to himself. Checking on the horses, he saw that Molly and her unequally yoked partner, Erma, shifted their weight, nickering in response to the racket proceeding from their rear. Some of the human observers appeared to be reacting in similar fashion.

The platform holding the apparatus had lowered itself by means of its pulley system, clanking and rattling itself into a position parallel to the ground. Roderick lowered the supporting legs and inserted the pins. He climbed into the wagon and opened the curtains to let in some light. After hurling the firewood out onto the ground, he hopped down and threw some of it into place, firing up the steam engine. As it built up steam, Roderick busied himself with the electromotive force generator, checking to be sure that it hadn't been jostled into a state of disrepair.

Satisfied that the boiler on the old still hadn't also rattled itself to pieces, Roderick disappeared inside the wagon and began the process of raising the transmitting tower by means of the ratcheting system. He heard the crowd's murmur of amazement as it extended higher and higher into the sky. As the wagon began to sway, he suspected the tower had begun to weave and wobble in the wind. He peeked out the window. Fascination had bowed to self-preservation as people backed away. Small boys struggled against the strong grips of their mothers as they were dragged away to watch from a safe distance.

Roderick emerged from the wagon with a moan. The ropes dangled from the towers, whipping about in a way that unnerved him. Being one man with two hands, he couldn't be in a half dozen places at the same time. The steam engine had worked itself up to a deafening level, but not without effort. Roderick ran to it, giving it a few well-placed kicks. It chugged on in a smoother fashion, but louder. Satisfied to see it running as well as it ever would, he switched on the generator only to regret it instantly. He'd forgotten to drive the stakes into the ground to secure the ropes.

Running to the horses, Roderick tried to reassure them that the key to the mission at hand lay in their ability to stand their ground.

"Whoa, Molly. Easy there, Erma."

JULIA COULD TAKE it no longer. "Mother, we have to grab the ropes before this thing topples over!"

Running to opposite sides of the wagon, they each grabbed a rope, pulling them to steady the weaving tower. Julia saw Bertina following suit, but before running to the far side of the wagon, she picked up a dangling rope on the near side and shoved it toward Senator Thornhill, shouting at him. He took the rope and began to pull, apparently interpreting her actions as an order to make himself useful.

The tower continued to sway in the wind and the wagon jerked in response to the nervous dancing of Molly and Erma. Despite their valiant effort, the women lost control. Three male onlookers rushed in, taking the ropes. Mother, Julia, and Bertina stumbled back to their places in the audience looking worse for wear, but far too upset to attend to such trivial matters as hats, hair, smudged faces, and exposed petticoats.

Julia turned her head as a darting figure lunged forward. She saw her mother take a firm grip on Dahlia Thornhill's arm and restrain her. Julia grasped Mrs. Thornhill's right arm and helped keep her from running to the wagon.

"Percy! Percy, let go!" Dahlia screamed.

The poor woman, staring in horror, had likely forgotten that this fruitless instruction, had it been able to reach his ears through the din, would likely have gone unheard anyway.

Billy, having managed to get the kite aloft, handed the antenna wire to Papa, who jumped on the wagon and attached it to the antenna. The generator sounded as though it now had a full head of steam. Sparks began generating from the antenna. The crowd moved back another thirty feet, but seemed to show a determination to see the thing to the finish. As the sparks from the generator intensified, a strange glow surrounded the wagon.

Julia heard a girl behind her speaking with awe. "It's a dream come true, Mama!"

"It's like nothing I've ever seen, Nancy," observed the mother.

"It's just like that book we read about the Arctic region. We may never see the aurora borealis, but this is the next best thing. Isn't it beautiful?"

"Just imagine watching this at night!"

Julia may have found some beauty in the display if she hadn't been frozen with the fear of watching Papa being electrocuted or blown to bits at any moment. She resisted the urge to turn around and slap mother and daughter alike. Trembling from head to toe, she felt as jumpy as poor Molly. She wanted to scream out loud, plead with Papa to stop this madness.

How could Papa have spent his life in the workshop and produced something this extreme right under our noses? As she watched the faces in the crowd and listened to their comments,

Julia's heart ached with embarrassment, not for herself, but for him. Earlier murmurs of doubt and whispers of ridicule now gave way to apprehension. Folks yelled at one another above the din, sharing their concerns as to whether there would be any survivors. She heard several words she didn't care to hear applied to Papa, including dreamer, half-cocked, and insane. *Please, Lord, let it end!* Oh, to rush home with Mother and Papa, close the doors to the outside world, and pretend this day had never happened. She glanced at Bertina, whose smile of lifelong devotion and loyalty warmed her soul like a soothing medicine.

The wind shifted a bit and Julia could make out Papa's voice as he yelled at the rope-holders. "All right, men! Let's stake these ropes. We should have had that done a long time ago!" Turning back to the wagon, he groped under the seat and peered into the back of the wagon, his head disappearing though the curtained window. When he emerged, Julia saw his face transformed with ecstasy and he ran forward, screaming at Senator Thornhill at the top of his lungs.

"Senator! We're getting something! We're getting a transmission!"

Chapter Twenty-Seven

ATOP FELDER'S KNOLL, the experienced draft horses, having seen a thing or two in their time, performed their task reluctantly, but without rearing in panic. Much time had been saved in speech-making. Fred started off by informing the crowd that nothing would make him happier than to demonstrate his ability to inflict physical injury on the first person to cause trouble. Rudy offered to assist him, demanding absolute quiet in order to concentrate on his written instructions. Following these to the letter, they managed to set up the device.

The main problem presenting itself to the brothers was the prospect of being unwilling participants in suicide. Having been around steam engines all their lives and witnessing, more than once, the operation of Ollie Beltz's still for making corn liquor, they succeeded in getting the fire started and the boiler working. Ratcheting the antenna tower to its full height, they staked the ropes—a feat they hoped never to repeat. Once things appeared to be stable, Fred occupied himself with the kites, feeling a fool all the while, but grateful that Rudy had paid attention to their brief lesson in radio wave transmission that morning and might be able to follow the instructions on the sheet of paper he now studied.

After reading each instruction out loud and repeating it, they shrugged their shoulders and did their best, pausing at intervals to distribute a round of kicks to the steam engine or to adjust parts on the old still which seemed determined to fall off due to the vibrations.

"Kick it again, Fred!"

"I am!"

"Not there—kick it on the left side. *Ouch!* That's the fourth time I've burned myself on these blasted coils. This thing is nothing but junk."

"Do you think we're ready to turn on the generator?"

"May as well. How do we know when to send the Morse code?"

"We don't know Morse code, Rudy."

"We don't have to *know* it. Mr. Lansing has all the dots and dashes written in there by the telegraph key. He says even if we get it all wrong, that's fine. He just wants to hear some noise on the other end."

Fred drew in a deep breath, bracing himself for unknown perils. "Then let's get it over with before we blow ourselves to kingdom come and back again!"

ONCE RODERICK HAD GOTTEN his attention, Senator Thornhill yelled for assistance and handed his rope to the first brave volunteer. Once again displaying an amazing amount of speed in ratio to his girth, he climbed into the back of the wagon. Roderick knelt on the wagon seat and inserted his head through the small window, his eyes welling with joyous tears.

"You hear that, Senator? It's *working*! We're getting a message from the remote location! The boys got set up before we did! *They're sending us a message!*"

Percival Thornhill stared at the apparatus and exhaled a sigh of relief. "Excellent, my boy! What are they saying?"

"Nothing whatsoever, as near as I can tell!" Roderick began to laugh.

"I thought you said we were getting a message."

"I left some simple code beside the telegraph key, but I didn't think Fred or Rudy would make much out of it. I told them to use the key—to send something, *anything*—just make noise! And it's *working*! As soon as it stops, start tapping on the key and they'll let us know if they hear anything."

ONCE RUDY RELEASED the telegraph key, he looked up at Fred. Fred returned his look of nervous expectation. Together, they waited. Lifting the curtain, Rudy peered through the small gap at the crowd. Likely, they'd begun to wonder whether they should have gone east rather than west. Ever since he and Fred had disappeared inside the wagon, they'd been waiting in a strained hush, unable to hear anything over the deafening sound of the steam engine. Unaware of the miracle inside the wagon, most of them probably lamented that they'd missed out on the noon meal for nothing.

"Fred! They're answering!"

"Well, I'll be... *they sure are!*"

"We did it, Fred! We're *communicating!*"

"What are we saying?"

"Like I said before—it doesn't matter! If they can hear our clicks and we can hear theirs, then it's working! People who know the code can use it to send messages without wires!"

Fred's jaw dropped. "Rudy! Julia's papa is a real inventor, isn't he? He did it, didn't he? And *we* helped him!"

"You bet we did! This is the stuff history books are full of!" Rudy laughed uncontrollably. "We're *part* of it, Fred! *We're part of it all!*"

The grievances of recent days forgotten, the brothers embraced. Grasping arms and jumping up and down, they spun each other in circles, an activity cut short when Fred tore his shirt on a nail and Rudy stumbled into the pulley system.

"Say something else, Rudy! Answer them again."

Rudy stuck his head out the side window, grinning at the crowd. "It's working! Ha! Ha! It's working!"

RODERICK LOOKED AT HIS WATCH. After five minutes of suspense, the telegraph had begun to click again.

"Hear that, Senator? They *did* hear our reply! They're sending another message!"

"My boy," the senator bellowed, "I do believe you've done it!" He thrust a congratulatory hand toward Roderick.

Roderick wriggled an arm through the small window opening, giving the senator's hand a vigorous shake. Then, jerking his head out of the window, he searched the sea of faces.

"Beatrice! Beatrice!"

"Here I am!" Beatrice stood on tiptoe, waving her handkerchief.

"I've done it, Beatrice! It's working! They've answered! We're communicating!"

"Oh, that's wonderful, dear!"

Roderick looked over the crowd. The whole assembly erupted in a chorus of questions and commentary. He wished he had time to explain to them what they had just witnessed, but speeches would have to wait. The horses were getting the jitters and something seemed to be going awry with the device.

A loud hum, unearthly and eerie, came from the wagon, bringing the conversation amongst the onlookers to a stop. Several babies began to wail.

Roderick stuck his head through the small window again.

"You hear that, Senator?"

The senator, of course, had not.

"I think we must be receiving some radio waves that are

causing... Ouch! Don't touch anything metal, Senator. I think we've accumulated a static charge!"

"My boy, my skin's starting to feel prickly. Do you think that's cause for alarm?"

Roderick glanced over his shoulder at the horses. Their backs flinched and their ears twitched as they reared and jerked. All the careful training they'd received at the hands of human masters was of little concern to them in their desire for a speedy escape.

"Maybe we'd better shut it down," Roderick yelled.

"Roderick!"

Feeling a tug at his trouser leg, Roderick pulled his head back out of the window. "Beatrice..." He'd been about to tell his wife to step away while he shut down the device, but he paused, taken aback at the sight of her. "You... You... You're *blue!*"

"We're *all* blue! Roderick, what is happening?"

Roderick stared into her panicked eyes, which were also blue instead of their usual lively green. He took in his surroundings. Everything had a strong tinge of blue—the wagon, the horses, the air. A mass of blue humanity watched in confusion, curiosity, and fear. They seemed to be debating whether to stay and observe the phenomenon or flee for their lives. He felt sorry for them and for Molly and Erma, who strained with every fiber of their beings in their efforts to execute the latter strategy.

The senator's head emerged from the small window. "Lansing! Shut this confounded... Why... Everybody's *blue!*"

"I believe it's an ionic haze, Senator, due to the buildup of static charge from the receiver. I'm going around back to shut down the device."

"Well, hurry!"

The instruction may as well have been given directly to Molly and Erma. Whinnying, they reared and jerked all the more violently. The wagon brake, a loose-fitting mechanism due to decades of daily use, gave up the effort and released itself. At their first inkling of possible escape, the horses ran for freedom.

Roderick clung to the back of the wagon seat, his mind racing. He needed a strategy that would enable him to turn around and grab the reigns without getting himself killed. Having seen Senator Thornhill's head disappear through the window, he assumed he must be sprawled on the floor amongst the pulleys and equipment. Nothing could be done about that now. From what he could hear, the senator was still alive. His injuries, if any, were not so severe as to keep him from expressing opinions and giving orders at the top of his lungs.

JULIA SCREAMED as the wagon lurched away. Bertina and Dahlia ran with her to where Mother lay on the ground, moaning.

"Mother! Are you all right? *Mother!*"

She looked around for help. The men who had been holding the ropes had realized the futility of their efforts within seconds and let go. They were now picking themselves up off the ground and checking for broken bones. Her heart gave a leap as she watched the runaway wagon cut a swath through the screaming crowd and clatter down the hill toward town with the Mobile Wireless Communication Device and all its paraphernalia bouncing along behind on its two-wheeled platform. It seemed that the whole crowd, having considered the health benefits of being behind the apparatus rather than in front of it, followed. Buggies and wagons stuffed with passengers made their way down the hill as soon as their horses recovered from the fright.

Julia patted her mother's cheeks. "Help me, Bertina!" Mother, blinking and disoriented, allowed them to help her sit up. The noise of the wagon could still be heard. Papa hadn't crashed—yet. *Who's going to help Papa?*

Mother tottered as they helped her to her feet. Her eyes widened in surprise.

"I'm just fine, my Lovely One. Now don't you worry. Why, Dahlia Thornhill! How nice of you to come! And what a blessing you're not blue! Won't you stay for lunch?"

Julia patted her cheeks again, hoping to bring her back to reality. Mother's far-away peaceful expression frightened her.

"Mother, we've got to get you home. You've had quite an ordeal."

"That's just what I was saying, Julia—We'll have quite a nice meal. Oh, we're at the fairgrounds, aren't we? It's a lovely day. Let's make it a picnic!" She waggled a finger at Bertina, whispering, "What are you doing here in the middle of the day, Bertina? You and Julia had better be getting back to school. The teacher will be upset with you. You can't be playing hooky and going on picnics!"

Julia looked around. The three exhausted and disillusioned rope-holders were the only other people left on the fairgrounds. Dahlia Thornhill ran to them, begging for help. Julia climbed into the buggy and, when the men had lifted her mother onto the seat, she settled next to her. Mother's head dropped onto her shoulder. Tears stung Julia's eyes as she cautioned Bertina to avoid bumpy ground and tried to answer Mother's questions as to Papa's whereabouts. *Please, Lord, don't let Doctor Schwartz be out on a call.* The thought of the emergency call he may be handling at the moment frightened her too much to think about. *Where are Papa and Senator Thornhill by now?*

WHEN NO MORE REPLIES CAME, Fred and Rudy abandoned further attempts at Morse code. They'd found the blue haze, a nameless and unheard of scientific phenomenon, disturbing. Following the crowd's example, they'd backed away. After several minutes, they deemed it best to shut down the device and extinguish the fire in the boiler. Once it cooled, it could be loaded back into the wagon. After a small speech stating that the experiment had been a success and the show was over, they began pulling up the stakes and lowering the antenna tower. They hurried, excited at the thought of sharing congratulations all around with the inventor and promoter of the miracle they had just experienced.

The crowd dispersed. Everyone made their way back to town believing that, if there had been anything out of the ordinary happening in Morgan's Landing that day, it had happened on Felder's Knoll and they had witnessed it.

BY THE TIME the apparatus reached the bottom of the hill, Roderick had managed to turn around on the wagon seat and take hold of the reigns. Molly, though having had some experience in her youth at pulling alongside another horse, hadn't done it in years and seemed eager to break up this new-found partnership. Erma, full of the rebelliousness of youth, struggled to go her own way. Roderick's pulling and *"whoa"*-ing had little effect on their mutual will to rid themselves of the M.W.C.D. Despite the intense concentration it took to stay alive, Roderick clung to the fact that his invention had, if only for a moment, been a success. Various pieces had flown off the old still as it bounced down the hill, making him keenly aware that he jostled a fire along behind him. Near the bottom of the hill, a group of trees lightened the load by snatching the carefree ropes and removing the tower assembly altogether.

The dream that had inspired him for years had, in a matter of seconds, become his worst nightmare. The demonstration's success at communicating had been erased from the minds of everyone as the disaster unfolded before their eyes. What would have been his triumphal return to town had become a fear-filled fight for his life and the life of Senator Thornhill.

Help me, Lord! Help me not to kill anyone! Roderick prayed between each "Whoa!" The faces of his loved ones flashed through his mind. What shame he might bring Beatrice and Julia! His own reputation meant nothing to him now. He'd much rather end up on the front page of the Roth County Clarion for the failure of his invention than for the slaying of a United States senator.

The peddler wagon reached the intersection of Hickory Street and Main at a frightening rate of speed. Roderick had hoped to make a right turn, but gave up the notion of a sharp turn in favor of crossing over Main Street. His fear of crossing traffic lessened as he considered the likelihood that the whole town was behind him. Mumbling a quick prayer for whoever might be the only individual who either didn't get the news or had been devoid of curiosity, he braced himself for impact.

Molly favored the right turn. She knew the way home. Erma opposed this. At the intersection, they struggled against one another, jolting and rearing until younger and stronger muscles prevailed and Erma had her way. Swinging a wide left turn, they headed south with the two-wheeled platform swaying like a fish's tail. It smashed against a watering trough, discarding most of the remaining parts of the old still. Roderick, once again hearing constructive criticism from the rear, gave thanks that the senator was alive and able to speak.

The horses slowed with exhaustion at the edge of town. Residents of the elegant homes along the south end of Main Street, who had been tending to their own business and missed the downtown exodus, ventured out to see what the clattering and yelling was all about. Roderick pulled the wagon to a stop and set the brake before running to the back to help Senator Thornhill. He hesitated, then ran back. Reaching under the wagon seat for a rope, he tied the brake in place.

Having dreadful expectations of Senator Thornhill's injuries, Roderick prepared himself to offer cowering apologies in response to his wrath. Peering into the back of the wagon, he was surprised to see that the senator's spirits seemed to be in far better condition than his outward appearance.

"Well, there you are, my boy! I saw your head bobbing around through that little window so I knew somebody had to be driving this confounded thing. I don't know why in tarnation you didn't do what I told you, but I guess we both made it out alive. Say, I'm bleeding from somewhere," he said, wiping his forehead.

Percival Thornhill had the appearance of someone who had been pulled a mile through thorn bushes by the ankles. There had been nothing substantial to grab hold of in the back of the wagon during his ride over rough terrain. His clothes and skin, having been snagged by pulleys, nails, and other protruding parts of the device, revealed that he had bounced from one wall of the wagon box to another as he'd tried to keep himself from being tossed out the door and run over by the steam engine platform. He appeared to be aware of the bruises and swelling that covered his body from the top of his head to the soles of his feet.

"Senator, you're bleeding from everywhere. I'll drop you off at Doctor Schwartz's office on the way home and come back for you in the buggy when I get this contraption home and unhitched."

Senator Thornhill climbed out of the wagon with a moan. "If you don't mind, Roderick, I've had my fill of traveling Main Street today. I suggest we go home by some secluded side streets."

Roderick nodded. "Just my thought, Senator, but I'm afraid we've left a trail of parts and pieces along Main and we'll have to backtrack in order to pick them up. I think it's best if you climb up on the seat and I walk. That'll give me a chance to calm the horses while I pick up the pieces."

Senator Thornhill retrieved his hat from the back of the wagon and sighed as he pronounced it beyond all hope.

"I guess even the finest hat can't be expected to be stepped on and sat upon repeatedly by a fellow my size and still look like a hat." Placing the wreckage on his head, he climbed onto the wagon seat with a series of groans.

"Senator, I apologize. If I'd only been more prepared before you arrived..."

"Apologize?" The senator looked at Roderick through the eye that hadn't swollen shut. "My boy, you've done it! I wish you'd done it in some manner of sturdy conveyance and I wish you'd done it with a team of horses that hadn't lost what little minds God gave them, but still, *you've done it*! We sent the code and we received the code, didn't we?" He nodded, slapping Roderick's shoulder.

Roderick stared at Senator Thornhill, a slow smile creeping across his face as the words took effect. Untying the brake and leading the horses in a wide turn, he headed north, whispering to himself.

"We sent the code. They *answered* the code. It works. *It really works!* I did it. I really *did it!*"

Roderick knew that, for the most part, the decent folks in Morgan's Landing took no delight in the misfortunes of their neighbors. These saints, happy to see him and Senator Thornhill alive and reasonably sound in limb, assumed the demonstration to have utterly failed. Taking no joy at the thought, they made as little appearance of noticing the procession as they could. One or two called out, asking about the senator's condition. Others approached, sorrowfully helping Roderick gather far-flung pieces of the invention and tossing them in the back of the wagon. A few small children spoke with honesty, making comments they couldn't be expected to be held accountable for, while some older ones cast observations that made it plain to one and all that they would have been wiser if they had kept them to themselves.

Roderick, though touched by the dignity that most people tried to extend toward what must have looked like a circus stunt, stifled a desire to dance about and scream at the top of his lungs. He wanted them to know that he had achieved success, not failure. Not understanding the technicalities of the invention, they would have considered it ludicrous and demeaning. At any rate, they couldn't deny that the show turned out to be worth the price of admission.

He'd had enough of being in the limelight for one day. Roderick longed for the peace awaiting him at 324 Beech Tree

Street. He'd stop at Doctor Schwartz's office, just ahead on the right, and put the senator into capable hands. Then, he'd go home to the one person who would understand.

As he looked ahead to the spot where he would need to have Senator Thornhill pull the wagon to a stop, Roderick's heart leaped.

"Beatrice!"

A group of people fluttered around Bertina Drexler's buggy. Doctor Schwartz, grasping Beatrice's wrist, walked beside her as Bertina, Dahlia Thornhill, and Julia assisted her into his office.

Chapter Twenty-Eight

Julia changed into her shabbiest dress and descended the stairs with all the resolve she could muster. *Today is the day.* She'd give the kitchen stove the cleaning and polishing it deserved. She hoped to finish before Rebekah and Marcus got home from school and became enthralled with the novelty of having sooty rags, grates and a bucket of ash strewn about. Their eager assistance might result in black stove polish covering rugs, walls, and everyone in the house. She'd not ask Hannah to do such a dirty job. She could have had Delia do it, of course. Delia O'Sullivan was always glad to have a little extra money in addition to what she made by taking in washing, but today Julia felt that working out her frustrations on something like the sooty cast-iron stove might offer her some much needed therapy. She found her mother in the room they referred to as the rose parlor because of its wallpaper.

"Mother, do you need anything before I get messy? I'll be busy for a while cleaning the stove."

No answer came. Julia stepped closer, laying a hand on her mother's arm. "You're not having another headache?" Over a week had passed since the incident with the wagon at the fairgrounds and Julia had been concerned about Mother ever since.

"Hmmm? Oh, Julia! No... no... no! No more headaches. I haven't had one in three or four days now. I think that's all behind us. I've been absorbed in this letter from Sarah Cohen."

Julia took the letter from Mother's outstretched hand. It touched her heart. The Cohens expressed gratitude once again for Mother's kindness. They asked that she write soon with her thoughts concerning the most recent book they had decided to read together. Their closing comments showered lavish blessings on the whole Lansing family.

"And their questions... Oh dear!" Mother sighed. "I don't know if I can address them properly."

"It sounds to me like you've addressed the Cohens properly by loving them, Mother."

Mother nodded. "I can only share what I gleaned from George MacDonald's writings myself and what I've come to believe in my own heart. The point isn't that one of us should change the opinions of the other, but to simply share our thoughts."

"Perhaps you should send them *Paul Faber, Surgeon*, Mother. Isn't that the next book in the series?"

"That's a wonderful idea!" Mother exclaimed, brightening. "I'll send them my copy and then I'll replace it when I get the chance." Opening the drawer of the writing desk, she pulled out a piece of stationery, "I'm not sure I'm up to addressing some of the things they ask in letters, but I'll write to Ruby. Perhaps she knows someone scholarly in Savannah who can help if they have theological and prophetic questions." Mother paused, then placed the paper back in the drawer. "No, maybe I should send a telegram so I won't keep the Cohens waiting."

"While you're doing that, I'll start on the stove."

"Stove?" Mother wrinkled her brow.

Julia smiled. "Yes, Mother. The stove. You were so engrossed in the letter you didn't hear me. I'm going to clean and polish the stove." Julia crossed through the hall, surprised to encounter Hannah at the bottom of the stairs. "Oh! Hannah! You startled me!"

"I'm sorry, Miss Julia. I'm going out for a package of needles."

"Are you? Mother's going out, too, when she finishes her telegram. Maybe she could get them for you. Or, maybe you could send Mother's telegram for her. There's no sense in you both going. I'm going to clean the stove. If I wait any longer, it'll be in constant use for heat and I won't get it done till spring."

"I suppose it needs it."

Julia paused, surprised by Hannah's clipped remark.

"Hannah, is something wrong?"

"No. Everything is fine. I'll be in the sewing room. Tell Mrs. Lansing to call me when she finishes her telegram and I'll send it for her."

Julia stepped back into the rose parlor. "Mother…"

"I heard."

"Did I say something I shouldn't have?"

"No, I think she overheard us discussing Sarah's letter."

"You mean you think she was offended somehow?"

"No, I don't see how she could have taken offense at anything we've said. Perhaps it was just a sad reminder of all the Jewish friends she's left behind. Since she's been living with us, I don't think we've given her any cause to believe we have anything but love for her and respect for her beliefs. I suppose everything seems wrong to you when you're in new surroundings and you're homesick."

"I suppose she must be."

"She's been telling me how the Jews celebrate Hanukkah in December. I'll let her take the children when she goes with me to Savannah for the fittings. It will do them good to celebrate with friends. We'll celebrate Thanksgiving this week and leave the first of next week. I want to be home for Christmas. You and your father will just have to take care of each other."

Julia nodded in agreement and went into the kitchen. She rolled up her sleeves before getting down on her hands and knees.

"Lovely One…"

"Mmmm…?" Julia didn't look up. She yanked the lever on the ash grate back and forth with one hand, holding her apron over her face with the other.

"Would you mind turning around so that I don't have to converse with your opposite end?"

Julia turned around and sat on the floor. "I'm sorry, Mother. What is it?"

"Are you disappointed? Were you wanting to go to Savannah with us?"

Julia sighed. "Not really. Savannah is lovely, but I've really enjoyed being home again. Besides, Abigail won't be there. I suppose I did come home with a few regrets, but it's not as though I'd have an opportunity to repair my mistakes if I went back. It'll be nice to be home between Thanksgiving and Christmas. Papa needs me and so does Mrs. Schmidt." She paused, noticing her mother's playful smile. "What is it?"

"Oh, I was thinking that perhaps one of the reasons you might want to stay close to home is so that you can attend to this new flock of suitors that seems to be hovering so near at all times."

Julia moaned. She'd rather clean all the stoves in Morgan's Landing than deal with the attentions of her new admirers.

"As a matter of fact," Mother continued, "I saw Martin Baysinger on the street yesterday when I went for my check-up with Doctor Schwartz. He said he'd like to pay us a visit in the next few days. I've always liked Martin. I didn't know what to do except to tell him to stop by Saturday evening."

With another moan, Julia went to work on the stove as though it had done something to offend her.

"You know, Julia, I think he gets handsomer every day. If I weren't already spoken for, I might be... well, I just might *be*!"

"Mother! Sometimes you're terrible!" Julia laughed.

"I may be older than you are, but I've still got my eyesight!"

Julia shook her head as she heard her mother's footsteps fading through the hall. She turned back to the stove, scraping the ashes forward with the shovel.

"Flock of suitors," she mumbled. "Why now? Why now, when I'd just as soon forget men even exist?"

Kansas City, Kansas

MOONLIGHT ILLUMINATED THE BEDROOM. Adam climbed out of bed and drew the curtains over both windows, hoping the blackness that enveloped the room would help him fall asleep. His mind had rehearsed scenarios for the past two hours. Only one had brought him any peace. He crawled back into bed, grabbed his pillow, and tortured it with his fists.

When he'd rushed home to Kansas City, he hadn't expected to face this choice. Now, because of his decision, he would wake up tomorrow to a whole new world. *But haven't I already— and more than once? Julia is gone. Malcolm is gone.* At least he had his parents, for the time being anyway. Their support meant a lot to him and he'd found it comforting to be spending Thanksgiving in his childhood home before stepping into the unknown.

Adam stared into the blankness of the room. He could make out faint outlines of the furniture—a far easier task than envisioning the twists and turns of the life that stretched out before him. This dread made no sense. He wouldn't be the first man to have to choose to act on principles rather than passions.

I don't know why I still feel this way, Lord. I've already decided to do what's right. "Help me!" The words of a familiar song came back to him. *Trust and obey, for there's no other way.*

I'm walking away, Lord! I'm giving up everything—school and the other thing I wanted most—but I trust You.

As he lay in the darkness, peace washed over him. God wouldn't walk away. God wouldn't give up. God would go with him. Christmas would be here soon and a new year lay ahead. Adam's decision settled in his mind and, as it took root, sleep came.

Morgan's Landing, Missouri

JULIA LOOKED out the kitchen window. The workshop had been silent lately. Further repairs to the M.W.C.D. had to wait until Senator Thornhill introduced the idea to the proper authorities in Washington and received funding to build a model that would be fit for use in the military. Papa instead had busied himself with research and paperwork much of the time, aware of the importance of having a patent in place. He'd been a bundle of nerves. *Poor Papa!* She knew patience to be a virtue that he had to practice purposefully and Julia thought he resembled a caged animal lately. She tried to think of something she could do to help.

Julia could identify with his feelings. Weariness hung over her like a wet shawl. Exhaustion and restlessness had both seemed to pull at her in the two weeks since Mother had been gone. Though glad she hadn't left Papa to himself, she longed for a means of escape. At times, she regretted not making the trip with Mother and the Levitts.

Pulling her apron from the hook on the wall, Julia tied the strings with a sigh. It made her tired to think, but she opened the pantry door, determined to fix something that might put a smile on Papa's face. The pantry needed sorting. Like life's events, it seemed full of strange and unexpected things piled one on top of the other. It frustrated her to think that this glorious time of year might be stolen away. Christmas would come in spite of it all, but Julia wanted to revel in the season rather than be preoccupied with things that hadn't even existed in previous years. If they must exist, why couldn't they do so in a less complicated manner?

In the days following what the family referred to in an overly simplistic way as "the demonstration", Julia had suffered a mixture of embarrassment, pity, and defensiveness to a degree that may have caused her to become a recluse if she'd been the offspring of any other parents. She'd learned from them both that no one, having done their best, need feel shame. Papa had done his best. No amount of ridicule could provide an excuse for her to leave Mrs. Schmidt without help at the bakery. Keeping her chin up, Julia served the customers with an outward appearance of assurance. Every day, however, she counted the minutes until she could arrive at home, close the door to the world, and avoid the public eye. When some mindless chore allowed her to daydream, Julia's mind rehearsed her newest fantasy in which she opened a letter of invitation from Abigail and rushed to buy three train tickets to Atlanta. If only her family could stay with the Hadleys until the whole thing blew over!

Julia picked up a quart jar of green beans and closed the pantry door. With the biscuits she'd brought home from the bakery and the leftover ham from breakfast, she could offer Papa something nice. She looked around the kitchen and sighed. This certainly wasn't Atlanta and she had no means of escaping Morgan's Landing just now. Julia leaned back against the door frame, staring at the jar of beans absentmindedly as she pondered her reasons to flee.

It would have been an understatement to say that no one understood. Julia, her parents, and to some degree the Levitts, by virtue of living in the same house, were bombarded with questions from the nosy ignorant, sympathy from the well-meaning ignorant, jokes from the insensitive ignorant, and flagrant taunting from the cruelly ignorant. The Levitts had made their escape and Julia was happy for them.

Julia looked at the jar of beans in her hand, realizing that half the amount would do. She and Papa couldn't possibly eat a whole quart. She returned it to the pantry shelf, picked up a pint jar, and carried them to the stove where she opened the seal, poured them into a small saucepan, and set them on the burner.

The talk around town that disturbed Julia most were the

complaints that came from the folks who felt justified in expressing their views that the M.W.C.D. was a menace to man and beast. Dora Klein, in her distress, no longer considered Papa nearly capable of walking on water. Archibald had been making his daily rounds, no doubt spreading sunshine on all sides, when the demonstration went awry. Due to his sensitive nature, her poor, precious pup hadn't been to town since. While the population of Morgan's Landing gloried in their respite from his unannounced displays of affection and sudden acts of thievery, Dora despaired. Each morning after Archibald breakfasted, he either refused to leave the house or circled the yard before returning to the doormat to rest for the remainder of the day. It had been a psychological shock, Dora claimed, and what if her precious pup never recovered? The whole town would have Roderick Lansing to blame, she'd prophesied with a quiver in her voice, if Archibald never graced their presence again.

Gretel Hunt had been sweet when she apologized for being unable to supply eggs for two weeks following the event. It seemed that hers were not the only chickens within a five-mile radius of the fairgrounds or Felder's Knoll that had stopped laying. Taking the positive view, Gretel expressed her happiness for the country folk who had benefited from the temporary price increase when they brought their eggs into town to sell.

Gretel's husband, John, in his capacity as sheriff, hadn't paid an official visit, but had asked Papa to stop by his office for a chat. Having witnessed the demonstration and dealt with all the ensuing rumors and reports, he assured Papa that people were making mountains out of molehills and generally trying to outdo one another with tales of the aftereffects.

Livestock owners in the vicinity of the fairgrounds had complained that it took several days to round up horses, cattle, and sheep that had scattered over the countryside as they fled in sheer terror from the sights, sounds, and electrical charge given off by the demonstration. Julia suspected that if some of them had reacted in any way similar to Molly, this rumor might hold some truth.

Mother had been only the first to need Doctor Schwartz's attention. He'd assisted the hospital with the chaos that erupted amongst patients and staff who, in the confusion, reported symptoms they imagined had been brought on by the electrically charged air and the blue ionic haze.

Bertina had been the one to break the news that the invention was rumored to have had lethal effects. The apparatus, even before its wild ride through town, had been dribbling some odorous substance. By the time it came to its stop, the dribble had become a stream. A teary-eyed child and her mother had come into the drug store in a state of grief. After the demonstration, when they called their beloved kitty home, it had run across the street, stepping in the spill. A day or two after the kitty's fastidious cleaning of its little paws, the poor thing had been discovered dead. Though no one knew what actually occurred, Papa tried to make amends. After paying a visit to apologize and offering to find the little girl another kitten, he'd come away feeling as though he'd never received a pair of icier stares.

Julia opened the stove door and added two more sticks of wood to the fire before placing the pan of biscuits near the beans to warm. Returning to the pantry, she retrieved the ham and carried it to the table. After a few minutes of trying to determine where Hannah or Mother had left the carving knife, Julia found it and began slicing the ham carefully, just the right thickness to suit Papa. After arranging the slices on a plate, she placed it near the stove and sat the cutting board and knife aside to be washed. In the absence of the Levitts, there was no need to take extra precautions to keep utensils and foods separated.

Julia smiled at the thought that Hannah might likely be experiencing this same relief from miles away as she shared meals with her Jewish friends. Hanukkah would have been a lonely celebration if the Levitts had stayed in Morgan's Landing. The only other Jewish family in town, the Ziegels, owned the Marvel Emporium and they had left town as well, taking the train to Saint Louis to celebrate with the Jewish community there, which seemed to be their habit during each Jewish feast or holiday. Poor Hannah! She must truly feel like a fish out of water in this town. *I wouldn't blame her if she never came back.* For Mother's sake, Julia hoped that wouldn't be the case. She hadn't found a single person in Morgan's Landing who had Hannah's talent. It would bring her business to a crawl and she'd likely have to turn away over half the amount of orders she was getting now. Such a setback would cause quite a hardship considering Papa had yet to make a single penny off his invention and it now lay on the workshop floor in a pile of wreckage.

No one understood the invention's purpose and design.

Many speculated as to whether claims of its success had been fabricated in order to save face. Marcus, however, held Papa in high esteem as not only an inventor who had shown his invention to a United States senator, but as a hero in the runaway wagon episode. He'd been in school during the demonstration, but stories abounded. In the days before he'd left for Savannah, he talked of little other than the noise, speed, and success of the invention. The only others who took a supportive interest were Fred and Rudy, who now seemed eager to learn as much as possible about the M.W.C.D. They appeared often and unannounced these days, asking if Papa needed their help.

Julia wiped her hands and began gathering things to be washed. *Fred and Rudy.* She wouldn't have minded if their interest in the invention hadn't been equaled by their sudden interest in courting her. Though she'd known about Fred ever since finding the flowers on the porch, she'd been appalled at Papa's announcement one evening after supper. With an air of amusement, he'd told the family that, earlier in the day, he'd been visited in the workshop by first one Schmidt brother and then the other, each asking permission to call on her. The news of Rudy's romantic interest came as a shock. Papa had voiced no objections to Fred, who had providentially arrived first, as long as Julia was favorable to the idea. Papa had admitted to being stunned when Rudy arrived, reciting the same monologue nearly word for word. Papa, after considering that ignorance would not likely induce bliss, had told Rudy that, although he had no objections providing Julia had none, he would probably receive an abundance of them from Fred. Rudy hadn't seemed surprised that Fred had been there, but had displayed a great deal of peevishness that he'd gotten there first.

Ever since, under a deluge of Schmidts, Julia had had no time to call her own. Apparently, the brothers shared the attitude that it was every man for himself with the prize awarded for endurance. While she didn't mind visiting with either of them, she felt uncomfortable with their constant habit of appearing as a set. It seemed that if one brother saw the other head for town with a clean shave and a fresh shirt, the other made a mad dash to follow suit. Julia couldn't get more than two minutes' conversation in with Fred before Rudy appeared, or with Rudy before a knock at the door revealed Fred. It would never do to let them down in front of one another, so Julia tried to tolerate their visits with a smile. *Why couldn't it have been one or the other?* The slightest thing might be interpreted as a positive response on her part, turning brother against brother. Such a rivalry had the potential to devastate not only the Schmidt family, but the long-standing relations between the Schmidts and Lansings. *Those boys wear me to a frazzle!*

Julia had enjoyed Fred's and Rudy's company all her life, but now she felt trapped—a helpless witness to a never-ending contest as they seemed determined to sit each other out. The flow of conversation during their visits slowed to a crawl. Soon, she would have to speak to each of them alone, letting them know that she considered them brothers, not suitors. Something had to be done before one or both of them did something silly, such as ask to escort her to the annual Christmas Eve party given by the Morgans.

Julia jumped, jarred back to the present by the sizzling noise behind her. The beans were boiling over. Grabbing a towel, she wrapped it around the handle of the pan and moved the beans to a cooler spot on the stove and placed the biscuits in the warming cupboard above. The stove would have to be cleaned after it cooled. She greased the cast iron skillet, placed it where the beans had been, and filled it with ham slices. Standing ready with the meat fork, Julia watched over the ham, flipping the slices often to avoid another mishap and ensure the browning came out just right.

Fred and Rudy had only reinforced her feelings that she was not ready for a romantic suitor, and since she'd returned from Savannah, she sometimes wondered if she ever would be. *Martin.* Things with Martin didn't seem to have much of a chance of turning out just right. Julia had mixed feelings about him. He was not a wish or a regret or a fantasy—he was a reality. She had fun with Martin. Julia had to admit that his handsome looks would cause any girl, including herself, to make every effort to overlook his shortcomings. People referred to his family as "well set". If he did as he said and joined his father's law practice, he would be able to provide for a family. If she were to consider Martin in a romantic light, she'd need to discover his interests—his deeper thoughts and beliefs. Julia hadn't heard about or seen his sister, Amalda, in quite some time. *Perhaps she isn't as vindictive and horrible as she used to be. Then again, perhaps she's worse!* Each time Julia entertained favorable thoughts toward spending a lifetime with Martin, she envisioned the look of betrayal on Bertina's face if she were to tell her that she'd allowed Amalda's brother to come courting.

Don't dwell on it! Don't let it ruin everything! Julia set the ham aside and put a lid over it. Now she had only to go set the table and call Papa. She must put on a happy face first. Julia pulled her Christmas list out of her pocket in an effort to shake away the gloom. *I'm going to enjoy everything about Christmas this year.* The extra money in the household would enable her to purchase a few things she wanted in order to make gifts. Concentrating on creating something to bless others always helped to keep her mind from being occupied with her past and present troubles.

Chapter Twenty-Nine

THE MISSOURI WINTER began in its usual style. Crisp, sunny days abandoned everyone without forewarning, leaving them shivering and throwing extra logs on the fire in hopes of driving away the bone-chilling cold and its gloomy companion —skies so gray that one could barely read without a lamp at noonday. The hardy Missourians braced themselves with an attitude that although it was a depressing way to live, things could be worse. Then, as if the weather had determined to prove them wrong, things got worse. Freezing rain fell. Tree limbs cracked, giving way under the strain. For two days, the cheery hustle and bustle of Christmas preparations all along Main Street quieted, replaced by a disheartening hush.

Julia stayed home on Thursday morning, nursing feelings of guilt for leaving Mrs. Schmidt to do the Christmas baking alone. After a futile attempt at walking to work, she'd decided to confine her embarrassment to her own front lawn. Despite holding onto the porch railing with an iron grip, she had sailed off the second step. The thick ice that covered what remained of the grass had increased her momentum, sending Julia down the gentle slope toward the street with arms and legs flailing in a useless effort to gain traction. Grabbing onto the rose trellis as she flew past, she'd managed to avoid paying an unintended visit to the house across the street. Her ungraceful crawl back to the porch on hands and knees had convinced her that she needed to use Papa's ice cleats or stay home until conditions improved.

She heard Papa rustling into his coat. Julia found him at the back door, staring through the glass with a hard, set look on his face.

"I'm back, Papa." She waited for an answer. "Papa."

When Julia touched his sleeve, he turned to look at her in surprise.

"Julia! You came back?"

She nodded. "I fell and nearly slid into the street! Be careful when you feed Molly. When you get back, I'll try again with your cleats if you won't be needing them."

"Why don't you just stay home, Julia? You may fall again. I'd be worried about you all morning. Surely Mrs. Schmidt can handle the few customers who could manage to get out in weather like this."

"I suppose that's true. I just hate for Mrs. Schmidt to wonder why I didn't come."

"She won't wonder. She'll take one look out the window and know why you didn't come. She's probably praying you won't try it. Here it comes. I was hoping it wouldn't, but there it is."

Julia followed his gaze. Huge snowflakes had begun to fall. As they watched, the air grew thick with snow. The weather appeared determined to prove that it was by no means limited to ice in its methods of calling civilization to a halt.

Responding to Papa's sigh, Julia moved closer. They slipped their arms around each other's backs and watched the thing happen.

"It would be beautiful if it weren't happening *now*, wouldn't it, Papa?"

"After I feed Molly, I'll walk up and check to see if there's been any news of weather toward the east or if we've had a telegram. I want your mother home."

Julia watched him stomp across the back yard, digging the cleats into the ice. She knew he felt helpless. Her heart ached for him. He wanted to rescue Mother and so did she. Enough snow on the tracks could cause delays. If it stayed on schedule, Mother and the Levitts would arrive tomorrow morning—two days before Christmas—unless they had to wait for the tracks to be cleared. Severe snowstorms sometimes caused deep drifts, stranding passengers for such a long period that they ran out of food and a means of keeping warm. Though glad she'd stayed home to keep Papa company, Julia felt a pang of guilt as she stood in the warm kitchen with its full pantry, knowing that Mother and the Levitts may be in danger.

Julia fell victim to the great paralyzer. Fear of the unknown stampeded through her mind like a heard of wild horses before she could slam shut the gates of hope and trust. Thoughts crowded in, one after the other, questioning whether Mother and the Levitts might not make it home for Christmas or—even worse—not make it home at all. If the weather worsened to the east, the snow might become so deep that it would take days to clear the tracks. Mother and Hannah and the children would be cold and hungry. The temperatures might drop even further. Julia remembered hearing stories through the years of times when the railroad crews couldn't reach a stranded train for days and days. Visions of huddled passengers waiting for help that might not come drove her to her knees. Even while praying, she felt the guilt of being able to do so in the comfort of the warm kitchen. As she cast her cares before God, the still, small voice spoke. *Everything's going to be all right.* Julia released a long sigh as her head lifted and a sense of comfort enveloped her. Still, the thought of making final Christmas preparations without Mother seemed a lonely prospect.

The door opened a few inches and Papa's head came through.

"I'm on my way to see about the weather. You doing all right?"

Julia brightened and rose to her feet. "Yes, I'm fine—just praying. If you can stay upright long enough to do so, could you stop in at the bakery? Tell Mrs. Schmidt I'll be there tomorrow."

"I will. And don't worry, my girl. Everything's going to be just fine."

RODERICK WALKED HOME in a world of white, trying to convince himself that no news was good news. There had been no telegram and no reports on snowfall to the east. Morgan's Landing lay blanketed in the silent beauty of a deep, fresh snow, marred only by the tracks of a few animals and the fact that Beatrice wasn't home. He felt as though he'd been divided in two, his other half lost somewhere in this great, whispering force of nature. How could anything be so delicate and transient, yet so powerful to control the lives of the human race? He must keep his thoughts on the lighter side. No need to alarm Julia. He tried to focus his mind on the conversations he'd had with the few people he had seen out and about who'd had anything on their minds other than snow.

Smells of yeast, sugar, ginger, and cinnamon came to his nostrils as he paused on the back porch to remove his cleats and dust off the snow. He entered the kitchen to find two loaves of bread rising and Julia cutting out Christmas cookies.

"Mmm. Ginger cookies! Do I get a sample?"

Julia smiled. "You only get the ones that come really ugly. All the pretty ones are for Christmas. Marcus and Rebekah will enjoy helping me decorate the little people."

Roderick reached for a piece of dough, knowing he'd receive an affectionate smack on his hand. He gave her the plain truth that there had been no news pertaining to the weather or the train before attempting to lighten the mood.

"I saw someone in Finkel's who asked about you."

"Who? Oh, never mind... You don't have to tell me. I'll take two guesses." Julia placed one handle of the rolling pin on the table, steadying it with the other. "My first guess is Fred Schmidt and, should I be incorrect, my next guess is... Oh, my... Oh, dear... I think I shall have to guess... Rudy Schmidt."

"Neither. You're forgetting about someone else who's been hovering around lately."

"Oh, you mean Martin."

"I do mean Martin. I know where you stand about Fred and Rudy. The bigger pests they make of themselves, the more I can tell you're getting fed up with them. Martin's a different story. I can't really tell what you think of him."

"Papa! Martin didn't ask you right there in Finkel's if he could court me, did he?"

"Not in so many words. According to Martin, he got himself out on this nasty day because he'd planned to stop by the bakery today and have a little talk with you. When I told him you'd stayed home, he asked me if I'd give you a message. I understand him not wanting to come all the way over here in this ice and snow."

Roderick watched his daughter press the rolling pin onto a ball of dough, keeping her eyes on her hands as she rolled out the ginger cookies. She seemed a little flushed.

"What was the message?"

"He said he knew it was short notice, but he'd be pleased if you would attend the Christmas Eve party at the Morgans' with him. Weather permitting, he'll be by the bakery tomorrow morning to get your answer. I guess it's his way of asking you and finding out what I think of him at the same time."

"It certainly is short notice! What *do* you think of him, Papa?"

"Oh, I've got nothing against Martin, or Fred, or Rudy, for that matter. Martin's turned out to be a nice young fellow. He knows how to do a day's work. From the way he talks, he'll be going into business here with Walter. His father's a good man. So is Martin. I don't think he's going to take my girl and move half way across the country so that I'd never get to see her or my grandchildren. Agatha's always been a nice person. Amalda is sweet as molasses to my face, but she's nothing but trouble. I still remember you coming home from school, mad as a hornet about the way she treated people, especially Bertina. The question is, Julia, what do *you* think of Martin? If you like him, I wouldn't dawdle. I can tell every girl in town has taken a shine to him. He's not the awkward little sack of bones he used to be. I think he's what you girls call 'dashing'. Is this a new recipe or are you trying to set a record for making the thinnest cookies in town?"

Julia gasped at the circle of paper-thin dough and laid the rolling pin aside. "No, but now they'll be the toughest cookies in town from being rolled out twice. You put it in a nutshell, Papa. I like Martin a lot. But, Amalda! How would you feel if you were Bertina and your best friend started up a courtship with the brother of that wicked... well, I don't even know what I'd call her! She's wicked, Papa, just wicked!"

Roderick studied her face. "What do you mean by 'I like Martin a lot'?"

"I do. He's kind and funny and, even though we're grown, we still laugh and tease a lot when we're together. He *has* turned out to be handsome. I'm flattered that Martin's interested. I just don't know if I should consider him because of Amalda. Can you imagine having a sister-in-law like that?"

"Seems you have more to say about his sister than you do about him. You're up to your ears in suitors these days. Can you think of a fellow you'd prefer over all the others?" *She blushed! Who is she thinking of? Is she going to speak, or keep staring at the flour can?*

He lowered his voice, speaking to the treasure of his heart. "Julia, when your mother makes you a new dress, you'll describe it to me and show it to me. Sometimes you look in the mirror like you're studying it hard, like you're asking yourself if it suits its purpose and if it fits just right. But sometimes, when a dress is special, I see a look in your eye that makes me happy. You're happy with everything about it. I know you'll be pleased to walk down the street in it. That's what I want to see when you talk about some fellow. I haven't seen it yet—not even with Martin." Pausing, Roderick swallowed hard. Though he wanted nothing more than her future happiness, the thought that the time may have come to give her over to another man brought a stab of pain to his heart. "It's all right to enjoy the attention. Have some fun and test the waters. Go with Martin to the party if you like. Just don't string any of these fellows along and make them think you're serious if you're not. You're the best-looking girl in town besides your mother. You're smart and conscientious and you know how to work hard at something. There's not a man in this town who deserves you. You just be sure you don't settle for somebody who isn't the right one."

"I won't, Papa," Julia whispered.

Roderick pinched some dough off the cutting board and went upstairs to change his snowy trousers. Things had changed. Over the last several years, his little girl had turned into a beauty. He'd known that young men would come calling eventually. He'd become familiar with the fatherly struggle within that made him want to beat them all off with a stick and yet see his daughter happy, raising a family of her own. He had noticed the boys watching Julia from the time she was twelve or fourteen, but they'd done it from a distance, sharing their school lunch or sitting near her at a church program. He'd observed fellows on the street develop a sudden urge for a doughnut when they looked through the window and saw Julia at the bakery counter. She had a steady stream of dance partners at social events, but this new rash of serious callers took him into unknown territory.

I hope I said the right thing. If only Beatrice would come home—she'd have some womanly advice.

JULIA BRUSHED the flour away from the edge of the table. Pulling out a chair, she sat down, propping her elbows on the table. She sat for a while, chin in hands, feeling much loved— and thoroughly confused.

Chapter Thirty

Returning to the window, Julia glanced up and down Main Street. *Nervous wreck. That's what I am—a nervous wreck!* She had arrived at the bakery with a waterlogged skirt and petticoats after battling the deep, soggy mush. As she wiped the front counter and arranged the day-old items, Julia debated whether to be glad, or angry, or fearful. Her thoughts had played this game of leapfrog all morning, vying for position at the forefront of her mind. *Today is the day—in more ways than one.* She felt as though she'd heard a voice from inside a closet. Opening the door might suddenly make her a heroine or a victim. The outcome lay beyond her control, waiting to be faced head-on.

The weather, like a quick-change artist who had put on quite a show in its fluffy, frozen costume of white, had transformed itself overnight into a different character. A warm front had arrived and Missouri, once again, displayed her versatility. Without the wind, the sun's bright warmth could be felt through coats and shawls. Temperatures had been above freezing since the wee hours of the morning. The citizens of Morgan's Landing, while buoyed in spirit by the sunshine and warmth, floundered as they mushed through the rapidly melting snow, picking themselves up at far too frequent intervals as they sank through the slosh and came in contact with the layer of ice that remained beneath.

The nine o'clock train hadn't arrived. There had been no news except that it had been delayed by the snow somewhere on the other side of St. Louis. Papa had gone to meet it anyway before stopping by the bakery to inform Julia that it hadn't come. Julia knew he'd keep wandering Main Street, waiting for the whistle. Papa wouldn't want to go home to an empty house.

Julia knew that he'd stopped in just for moral support. Everyone in town could hear the train's whistle. The sound was as commonplace as the sound of barking dogs or passing traffic, unless it was almost Christmas and you were waiting for someone special.

Fred and Rudy passed by. They seemed to be having yet another spat. Julia waited a moment before going to the door and sticking her head out. It appeared they'd called enough of a truce that they were able to enter the barber shop together. *Fresh haircuts again—a bad sign.* They might surprise her by slipping in the back door and installing themselves on the stools at the counter for another tense stand-off. *I must put a stop to this today!* One or both of them might do something silly, such as get her a Christmas present. Through the years, they'd given her little things—hair ribbons, candy—but she couldn't accept anything that might encourage them. *But what's the method? How? Where? In front of their mother at the bakery? Absolutely not! Invite them to dinner? No! If Mother were here, she'd know what to do.* Julia crossed her arms, fuming at Fred and Rudy for starting this whole thing. *Bertina! She's always so sensible!*

They hadn't spoken much since the onset of bad weather. Julia hated to go out in the sloppy streets again, but since the drug store was on the same side of Main Street as Schmidt's, there would be no need to cross the street. Someone had attempted to shovel a path in front of the stores and the rest appeared to be melting. Promising Mrs. Schmidt she'd return in a few minutes, Julia hurried up the street.

A few yards from the drug store she heard her name called out in chorus. *I'd rather have Archibald, muddy paws and all.* Julia hurried toward Drexler's, but the brothers arrived at her elbow before she could navigate the icy patch in front of it.

"Julia!" Rudy seemed cheerful.

"Hello, Julia!" Fred was a step behind his brother as they surrounded the object of their affections.

Julia forced a smile. *You look like twin pups waiting for a bone.* "Hello, Rudy. Hello, Fred."

Rudy inclined his chin toward her. "I was hoping I'd see you, Julia. If I hadn't, I would have stopped by the house. I have something to ask you."

"So do I," Fred nodded.

"I'm in a terrible hurry, boys. I was just on my way to the drug store."

"What do you mean *you* had something to ask her?" Fred glared at Rudy. "*I* had something to ask her myself."

"Boys, you're starting to embarrass me!" Julia looked up and down the street to see if anyone took notice.

"Would it be all right if I stopped by later?" Rudy nodded his head as though doing so would produce a positive response.

Fred scowled at Rudy as though he were a squatter who had taken up residence near his gold mine. "Listen, Rudy, if you'll just shut your mouth for half a second, I'll go ahead and ask my question and there won't be any need for you to stop by!"

"Oh, there won't? Listen Fred, I've put up with you long enough. Every time I turn around, there you are again! Why don't you just go home?"

Julia had never seen Fred and Rudy like this before. Had she somehow caused two loving and friendly brothers to treat one another like this? Tears came to her eyes. *If they come to blows, it'll be all my fault! Wait! I'm not the one who started this!* She'd been going about her own life as usual when they started this feud. She gave Fred and Rudy a look which may have frozen them to their very bones if they had stopped arguing with one another long enough to notice.

Fred cleared his throat, as though he were about to make a public address.

"Julia, I would be honored to escort you to the Christmas Eve party at the Morgans'."

Rudy nearly tied himself in knots. "Honored, *my foot*! Julia, that was exactly what I was going to ask you! You're not going with Fred. You're going with me! Fred, you'd better mind your own business!"

Julia couldn't remember the last time she'd been so angry. Yet, these two, who would have her believe that they wanted to impress her, failed to notice that she couldn't have built up a more impressive head of steam if she'd been a mobile wireless communication device. Her last ounce of patience departed with a hiss as though it had been released through a high-pressure valve.

"*Well!*"

Both brothers jumped to silent attention.

"Let me tell you two something! Do I look like the last piece of pie on the dinner table? I will *not* be the prize in this... this... *contest!* I have said that I'm going into the drug store and *so I shall*! Neither of you listen! I've known you all my life and you've been like big brothers to me, but I'm *not* going to the party with either one of you and *that's final*. If you're still here when I come out, I'll tell you what I *really* think of you!"

Julia took a step backward, grabbing the brass door handle. Turning, she gave them each another glare, hoping to drive home her point.

"Maybe you need a little while to think it over," Rudy suggested.

"I'll respect your choice, whatever you decide," Fred offered magnanimously.

"*Ugh!*" Julia tightened her grip on the door handle and stamped her feet in fury, an act that may have succeeded in sending the Schmidt brothers running for their lives had she remained upright. The ice beneath her feet sent Julia's lower half sliding toward the street just as the door of Drexler's was pulled open from the inside. She sprawled across the threshold with a shriek.

Still angry, Julia sputtered at Fred and Rudy, demanding that they stop fussing over her and allow her to get up on her own. A third set of arms endeavored to lift her to her feet. She looked over her shoulder, expecting to see Bertina.

"Martin!"

He grinned at her. "Do you just go out looking for trouble? First dogs and now this!"

"I slipped on the ice."

"So I noticed. I could see through the window that you looked a little... worked up."

"I'm fine, I was just chatting with Fred and Rudy and they were about to be *running along*."

Rudy seemed to have an endless supply of nods. "I'm happy to walk with you so that you don't slip again."

"That won't be necessary..." Fred began.

"It certainly *won't* be necessary! I'm sure Martin would be happy to walk with me, wouldn't you, Martin?"

Martin seemed a little surprised, but pleased. "Of course!" He put out his arm and Julia grasped his elbow.

"And as far as the Christmas Eve party is concerned, Martin, I was just about to tell Fred and Rudy that you've offered to escort me and that I am happy to accept."

"Wonderful!" Martin flashed a handsome smile at Julia and

then at Fred and Rudy, who glared at him as though only their strict upbringing prevented them from wiping it off his face with their fists.

Julia gestured northward. "Shall we go, Martin?"

Rudy seemed determined to display his powers of recollection. "I thought you were going to Drexler's."

"*I've changed my mind!*"

Stepping over the icy patch with Martin's assistance, Julia brushed past the brothers with her chin in the air.

DRAWN to the window by the commotion, Bertina watched as Martin Baysinger made his way north on Main Street with Julia on his arm. She smiled and greeted Fred and Rudy as they entered, settling themselves on stools at the counter and mumbling to one another. In no mood for idle chatter, Bertina nodded at the soda clerk, who stepped up to help them. She paused at the office door when Rudy asked if she'd witnessed the scene on the sidewalk.

"It was a little difficult to miss, seeing as how it fell through my front door."

"You're her best friend, Bertina." Fred leaned toward her, whispering, "What's wrong with Julia?"

"I don't suppose there's anything wrong with her, except for a few bruises."

"No," said Rudy. "What we mean is, what made her take a shine to Martin Baysinger all of a sudden?"

"I don't think you need to make a whole lot out of a girl taking someone's arm when it's *this* icy and slick outside. I'm sure that's all it is."

"It's more than that," said Fred. "She's going with him to the Christmas Eve party!"

"Are you sure?" Bertina looked from Fred to Rudy and back again.

Both brothers nodded.

"We heard her accept him plain as day, just now," Rudy marveled.

"Well, if that's the case, it's nobody's business but their own."

Bertina slipped through the office door and closed it behind her. It had been a busy morning. She felt tired. Sinking into the chair at the desk, she lowered her head onto her crossed arms and closed her eyes.

RUDY AND FRED looked at one another, each finding his own feelings mirrored in the face of his brother.

"Maybe it's the shopping and all the other extra things they have to do to get ready for Christmas that makes women so fractious," observed Rudy.

Fred sighed in agreement. "Must be."

Julia and Martin picked their way along, making arrangements for him to call on her the next night for the party. As her feet slipped again, he passed his arm around her. With his handsome face so near, Julia toyed with the urge to test the waters as far as Martin was concerned. Thoughts of Amalda rose to the surface and pushed the idea aside. There seemed no harm, however, in accepting this one invitation if it solved the problem with Fred and Rudy. Since Martin would only be in town for Christmas, things could go back to normal next week when he returned to school.

"Say, Julia, I hear your father tested his invention while I was gone. It must have really been something—"

Though she usually took Martin's teasing in stride, she was in no mood for banter concerning the M.W.C.D. Thankfully, Papa offered a diversion by appearing just down the street.

"There's Papa!" Julia waved in the direction of Finkel's General Store.

As he approached, Julia could see the look of curiosity and surprise in his eyes.

"I slipped on the ice. Martin was kind enough to help me along."

At the sudden sound of the train whistle, she watched Papa's face light with anticipation. "There she is!"

"Mother's home! Papa and I have to meet the train. Thank you, Martin. I'll see you tomorrow evening. Goodbye!"

Martin watched them go, pondering the subject of Julia Lansing. He'd known her all his life and she'd always been a level-headed sort. *She's beautiful now. And fun.* The one thing he'd have to come to terms with was whether or not he could spend the rest of his life with someone who habitually came and went with such shocking abruptness.

Chapter Thirty-One

As she dressed and arranged her hair, Beatrice pondered recent events and offered up a prayer of thanks. It meant the world to have everyone home, safe and sound, for Christmas. The Levitts, to her extreme joy and relief, had come home with her.

Picking up another hairpin, Beatrice leaned toward the mirror, coercing a stray curl into place. Her reflection smiled back at her as she recalled the greeting that had been lavished on her at the train station by a husband half-crazed with worry.

Wrapped in his long embrace, she'd felt his shoulders tremble as he whispered her name into her ear. After hearing her account of being stranded in the cold train car awaiting the railroad crew, he'd made it plain to one and all that even the most talented designers ought to have enough sense to avoid unnecessary peril. He'd insisted that, in the future, she needn't promise any orders that required trips in winter. Beatrice admitted to her pouting reflection that he might be right. Perhaps a timetable chart for the sewing room wall was in order.

She looked at the list on her dressing table. *How on earth will I ever get all of this finished in time? I haven't even finished unpacking. Bake treats for neighbors and friends. Finish sewing projects for gifts. Get ready for the Christmas Eve party. Buy groceries. Prepare Christmas dinner.* She pushed the list to the back of her mind as she heard Julia call to her through the door.

She tried to focus on Julia's story. After a few minutes, she grasped the general idea that Julia, not having found a kind way to rebuff either of the Schmidt brothers, had sent them packing with a bold and public acceptance of Martin's invitation to the party. Now, a stream of regrets gushed from the poor girl. In attempting to dissuade Fred or Rudy from their wrong ideas, she'd given Martin the wrong idea!

"Or was it the wrong idea, Mother? What about Amalda? What about Bertina? What about the party? What about life?"

Beatrice leaned over the bed, where Julia had thrown herself in frustration, and stroked her forehead.

"Julia! Did you or did you not accept an invitation to this party from Martin Baysinger, a perfectly nice, young gentleman?"

"Yes," Julia whined.

"Do we break our engagements, especially at the last minute, unless it is a dire emergency, which, by the way, sounds like something Amalda Baysinger would do?"

"No," Julia whispered.

"Then you're going because you said you would. Martin leaves again for school after the first of the year. If nothing comes of this, so be it. If he asks to correspond, you can always decline, even though it will be difficult. We can't discuss this any longer or we'll both be mad as hatters by the time of the party!"

"I know."

"Sigh," ordered Beatrice. "Take several deep breaths. It'll make you feel better."

Julia obeyed and pulled in a deep sigh.

EASING the door closed until she heard the latch click, Julia wriggled and side-stepped among the parts and pieces cluttering the workshop floor. She peeked out the window, hoping that her trip across the back yard had gone unnoticed. Taking two wrapped gifts from under her shawl, she straightened the bows and checked to be sure she hadn't torn the paper. Pausing, she turned in a circle, searching for a new route. Papa had blocked the path to her usual hiding place with a pile of heavy parts. Julia took the long way around to the ladder in the corner which led to the loft.

She hoped Rebekah would be pleased with the doll she'd made for her. Mr. Finkle had let her have a doll with a broken leg from his store. Julia had taken it and, with Papa's help, removed the lower extremities. After inserting the half-lady into a cardboard cone, she'd kept it at the bakery where, each day, she glued the seashells she'd collected on her trip to Savannah. A doll such as this would never replace Dinah, the rag doll Rebekah always clutched to her bosom. This fine lady, dressed in her ball gown of multi-colored shells, would smile down from a shelf as a remembrance of home.

Mother had made Rebekah a warm hat and, while in Savannah, purchased a copy of *Uncle Ben's Cobblestones* for Marcus. The little wagon that Papa had made and painted red had already been taken up to the loft. He'd banished the children from the workshop, telling them that his invention now left no room for them to play. They hadn't argued, for a look around the workshop validated the excuse.

Julia, happy that Hannah had granted them permission to include the children in their circle of gift-giving, looked forward to seeing their faces as they opened their gifts. They'd come to occupy a special place in her heart these last few months.

Making her way along the west wall, Julia stopped, staring at the bicycle that leaned against the wall. Shifting the gifts into one arm, she reached out, swiping a path through the thick dust on the seat. It hadn't been ridden since before she'd gone to Savannah. Turning away at the rush of memories, Julia took off her shawl. Wrapping it around the packages and tying a double knot, she slipped her arm through the opening and grasped the ladder.

"No!" she whispered, turning back to the bicycle. "We will not be parted like this. You and I have traveled many miles together and have many miles to go. I'll not let Adam Cole or anybody else dictate my actions. Come spring... I promise."

NO ONE BLESSED with an invitation to the annual Christmas Eve party at the Morgans' would dream of missing it. Morgan's Landing's patriarch, Rance Morgan, had brought river trade to the area. His son, Captain Rance Morgan, Jr., had made his fortune in river trade after his father before him. He'd built the biggest house in town on the east end of Morgan Street—another namesake—and had echoed his love for his work by commissioning the architect to design it as nearly like a river-boat as possible. From time to time, Roderick remarked that it lacked only a paddle wheel, which he suspected may be added any time.

Though the wealthiest people in town, the Morgans were not unkind. Neither were they overly friendly. They under-stood their social standing, visiting mainly with other families of impressive means and traveling extensively around the coun-try. Rance's wife, Genevieve, and the children made their over-seas trips without him, for he boarded no vessel that he himself did not captain.

The Morgans stayed in town each December, inviting most of the town to the Christmas Eve party by word of mouth. Roderick, exiting Lehman's Hardware with a sack of bolts, had received a handshake and an invitation from Captain Rance Morgan himself. Genevieve, while purchasing croissants, had invited the Schmidts. Martin and his father had received a visit from Rance III at their law office. Ida, Lottie, and Rosa Morgan had stopped in at Drexler's, issuing an invitation to the family through Bertina.

Beatrice often commented that the Morgans invited everyone but the town drunk and those who just didn't clean up well. The enormous crowd understood, just as their hosts did, that the Morgans could afford it and considered it a Christmas gift to the community from the founding family.

The party, beginning in the afternoon as a less formal open house, included food, poetry readings, music, and games for children. Later, when the Morgan family changed into evening clothes, the atmosphere took on a more festive tone.

Having made certain that her family was well-turned-out, Beatrice looked forward to staying for the evening. After seeing Julia out the door on Martin's arm, she turned to Roderick, raising her eyebrows. They stood for a moment in silent agreement. Life was, indeed, strange and unpredictable.

THE CROWDED FOYER, glittering in candlelight, smelled of fragrant greenery. Through the massive pocket doors, Beatrice could see Lottie Morgan seated at the grand piano, accompanying her cousin Lizzie who led a group of enthusiastic carolers. Scanning the crowd in search of Julia and Martin, Beatrice checked the dining hall first, where the grand buffet, spread out in all its glory, lured the guests. Across the room, Bertina stood with her parents, Miles and Leah. Beatrice made her way to join them, leaving Roderick to discuss equipment repairs with a couple of local farmers. Bertina's calm beauty seemed clouded tonight. After chatting for a moment, Beatrice asked if she'd seen Julia.

Beatrice followed the soulful eyes as they moved, attributing Bertina's lack of enthusiasm to the fact that Julia and Martin stood conversing with Amalda. *Hmmm... Seeing your best friend consorting with the enemy is bound to hurt.*

Fred and Rudy appeared to be handling their rebuff pretty well. Considering they'd both been told a thing or two just a day prior, they displayed keen appetites. Posting themselves in a corner with mounded plates and gloomy faces, they chomped away, watching Julia and Martin.

Beatrice made her way to where Julia stood and pulled her aside for quiet word, only to discover that she'd lacked the time, and the nerve, to give Bertina advance notice that she had accepted Martin's invitation. Beatrice determined to keep a watchful eye. It saddened her to see best friends keeping to opposite sides of the room on what should have been the happiest night of the year.

Bound by her upbringing, Beatrice repressed an urge to take the two biggest pests in the room and toss them into the street. The first, Amalda Baysinger, appeared to be in top form as she moved from one small cluster of people to another, making her presence known and her whispers audible. In feigned inno-cence, as though mystified, Amalda professed to be amazed at the momentary lapse of good judgment on the part of her usually intelligent brother. Men sometimes fell under the wiles of some shopgirl, she supposed, due to being innocent of their conniving ways. Martin, she speculated, had been too well-bred to back out of it.

Seizing an opportune moment when Martin had stepped away for punch, Beatrice slipped up beside Julia, giving her elbow a squeeze.

"How are you holding up?"

"I wanted to pinch her, Mother! At the crowded buffet, with everyone listening—Ugh, that sticky-sweet voice! Telling me that she was sure that I could have prepared any one of these dishes just as well as the help, being a worker in a bake shop, after all. She said she didn't know why on earth the Morgans hadn't thought of hiring me to cook for the party. How condescending! She let everyone within earshot know how much more at home I'd feel if I were cooking and serving, rather than being a guest. Then, she asked if I wanted her to ask the Morgans to consider me for next year!"

Beatrice gasped. "What did Martin say?"

"He'd stepped away. She plans her attacks carefully, Mother. I told her she needn't bother, as I knew her to be far too busy with her social engagements to take time out to help someone with such a silly pastime as catering to their hungry fellow human beings. It was wicked of me. I shouldn't have said it, but you know as well as I do that she only gets invited on occasions when her parents have been invited and people can't avoid it. She does her best to get into the good graces of the Morgan girls, but only because they're rich."

"It's a shame—she's a nice-looking girl. I'm glad, though, that most of the men in Morgan's Landing have sense enough to steer clear of her once they've spent a little time with her. The only exception lately seems to be young Rance."

Beatrice gave a subtle nod toward the other pest she desperately wished she could toss out onto the street, Rance Morgan III.

The suave heir to the Morgan fortune stood in the center of the room, announcing the formation of a dancing area through the middle of the parlor and drawing room. He encouraged those who didn't consider themselves young or young at heart to seat themselves around the perimeter.

Beatrice went in search of Roderick. He'd be good for one dance just to make her happy. He seemed especially attentive as he led her about the floor and when the music stopped, he kept her hand in his, smiling as he offered a second dance. She suspected this to be a result of his knowing that she'd danced the night away at the Graysons' ball and had enjoyed every minute of it. Afterward, she found a seat near Leah Drexler where she could enjoy watching the others as they continued dancing.

Martin and Julia do make a nice couple. Rance is a handsome devil, but devil is the word! He suggested the dancing and now look at him—holding himself aloof, as if he alone is master of their movements!

Rance's superior attitude seemed more pronounced since he'd been away to college. He seemed determined to prove to Morgan's Landing that he was *the* Rance Morgan, whose inheritance entitled him to be looked upon as a benefactor. Before acquiring this extra dose of conceit, he'd been paying particular attention to Amalda. Beatrice observed him as he appeared to be watching her now. *Her father's position in the community makes her acceptable to the Morgans, I suppose.*

Rance made his way across the room. Beatrice followed his gaze to where Amalda stood with Martin and Julia. Amalda's hazel eyes flickered toward him, then darted away.

She's noticed him. Smile, Amalda. Try to act casual. Appear indifferent. Beatrice would have thought Amalda attractive if she hadn't known her. Amalda's light brown, fluffy hair and dainty figure created a false air of delicacy. Her close-set eyes and perky nose didn't detract from her beauty, but when considered alongside her cruelties, reminded Beatrice of a small, vicious dog who, while it might make a pretense of napping, waited to snap with razor-like teeth. *If she were a dog, she'd have a severe case of the wags!* Beatrice stifled a chuckle as she observed Amalda's ill-concealed excitement at Rance's approach.

Rance offered the two girls a pretentious bow and nodded at Martin. "May I have the honor of this dance, Julia?"

It seemed to pass in a blur. Julia declined on account of Martin. Martin excused her as he had been about to ask his sister to dance. As the couples twirled about the floor, Beatrice watched daggers fly from Amalda's eyes each time Rance turned Julia to face her.

When Roderick appeared, offering her a cup of punch, Beatrice whispered in his ear. "A vicious, little dog. That's what she reminds me of, Roderick."

"Amalda?" he murmured behind his punch cup. "I hadn't noticed."

"Oh, *please*, dear. I know you better than to believe that!"

"Right now, I'm concentrating on the weasel who's dancing with our daughter."

Beatrice put her handkerchief over her mouth, choking. "You're getting better at this than I am. We should be ashamed of ourselves."

"I will be. But for right now, I think I'll do some cutting in. I don't see any need for him to be holding her that close."

Knowing Roderick would rather not be out on the dance floor, Beatrice's heart swelled as she watched him rescue Julia. *I love you, Roderick Lansing.*

Pondering his description of Rance, Beatrice had to agree. Though a handsome fellow, his swarthy, dark complexion did make him look a bit wild. His black eyes and black hair, combed straight back from his low hairline with a little too much hair oil, combined with the way he inclined his head toward Julia while dancing, completed the vision. *Yes—a weasel.*

Rance hadn't been so bad in his growing-up years—no worse than any boy born to privilege who had the opportunity to hold it over others' heads every once in a while. As a man, however, his arrogance and pride had become extreme, especially where young ladies were concerned. Watching Martin and the other young men in the room who were offering attention to Julia didn't cause Beatrice any apprehension, but she couldn't shake the feeling that when it came to Rance, Julia had better be careful.

∼

JULIA GLANCED at the grandfather clock in the dining room. *Just after eleven. Where's Martin?* Though she'd danced often with Martin, Rance had managed to cut in three times since their first dance. Though his actions had been too subtle to give her cause to chastise her host, he'd held her a bit too close and his hand, when pressed against her dress, had persisted in giving her back a massage.

Martin passed by, dancing with his mother. Julia smiled at them. She liked the polite, yet easy manner he seemed to have with his parents. After this dance, she hoped he'd be ready to take her home. Mother and Papa had already gone, and so had the Drexlers.

Shrinking back as she saw Rance excusing himself from a conversation and beginning to cross the room, Julia looked around for a means of escape. Refusing to dance with one's host would be unthinkable. Though a tall potted plant and a pair of heavy drapes offered themselves as concealment, Julia discarded the notion as ridiculous. Reaching behind her back, she groped for the door handle. It seemed to obey her unspoken plea that it might be silent and she slipped out, gasping as she stepped onto the cold porch.

The temperature had dropped considerably. Clutching her shoulders, Julia scurried along the west side of the house. The wraparound porch would lead her back to the front door. She hoped to enter unnoticed and keep away from Rance until Martin finished dancing.

Hurrying past the glow of the front windows, Julia stopped

short as she heard the click of a latch. Rance stood between her and the front door, eying her with curiosity.

"My, my, my. What have we here? I stepped out for a smoke, but I'm a little curious. Do you smoke, too, or are you running away from the party?"

"The dancing made me a bit warm. I came out for a little fresh air."

"Well, you're certainly getting lots of it—if you like it frozen."

"I hadn't quite expected it to be this cold."

Rance moved toward her. "If you insist on being out here, at least take my coat."

Julia stepped back, but the coat and Rance's arms had already enveloped her.

"No," Julia insisted, "it was silly of me. I'd best be going in."

Grasping her shoulders and turning her toward the railing, Rance wrapped his arms around her from behind, tightening them around her as Julia gave a twist she hoped would signal him to release her.

"Not until we take a peek at the last of the stars." He pointed a finger at the sky. "Look! To the east, you can still make them out by the millions, but to the west, all clouds. They're bringing this cold air, and snow, if I'm not mistaken."

Julia lifted her head, but lowered it again, turning her face away from the smell of liquor. Despite the cold, she warmed with the desire to flee as Rance's hands roamed over her arms. She turned to face him.

"You're right. It is too cold out here, and I don't want the others to wonder where I've gone."

"No one will miss us. Let's slip away and get inside. The library is nice and warm."

Julia braced her feet as Rance pulled at her. She stumbled a few steps forward as he tugged her toward the far end of the porch to where it wrapped around to the dimly lit part of the house. Julia knew there to be a door there—a door that would lead her into rooms far from the music and dancing.

"No, Rance! I..."

"Julia."

Julia spun around at the sound of her name.

"Martin! You startled me. How did you know where to find me?"

"I missed you, and Mother said she'd seen you leave through the dining room doors. I came out that way, hoping you hadn't taken ill."

"No, I stepped out for some air, but it's turned out to be far too cold. Rance was kind enough to offer me his coat." Removing the coat from her shoulders and returning it to Rance, Julia stepped toward Martin and slipped her hand into the crook of his elbow. "I'd like to go back inside now."

"I enjoyed our time counting the stars," Rance called out as Martin opened the front door.

Offering a weak smile and a nod, Julia stepped inside, forcing her eyes to meet Martin's after he'd closed the door. Finding his impossible to read, she waited for him to speak.

"How far did you get?"

"I beg your pardon?" Julia bristled.

"Counting the stars. How many?"

"Martin Baysinger! I didn't... He said he came out for a smoke... You're... Oh, don't be silly. I really think I'd like for you to take me home."

"One more dance?"

Julia felt the corners of her mouth twitch as she watched Martin's do the same.

"One more."

Chapter Thirty-Two

FOLDING the cape a little closer around her, Julia waited in the buggy while Martin climbed in and spread the wool blanket over her. To have him tuck it in around her seemed a natural thing. Why, then, this flutter inside her chest at having him so near and attentive? Mother was right. Martin had grown up. How strange that everything had changed—that a lifelong friendship could develop into this unexplainable, yet not unpleasant, tension. It felt nothing like the rush to flight that had overwhelmed her when she'd found herself alone with Rance.

Picking up the reigns, Martin spoke to the horse. They rode along Morgan Street in and out of the darkness between lampposts.

"I hope you're warm enough."

"Yes, thanks. But, Martin, wouldn't you like to have part of this blanket over your knees?"

Julia lifted the edge of it and Martin took it, pulling it over his lap.

"Thank you. I didn't like to assume. I think I'll cross Main and go down and around. Then we'll come up Beech Tree Street right in front of your door."

"That sounds fine. Thank you for taking me tonight. I had a wonderful time."

"The Morgans always go all out, don't they?"

"Yes, they certainly do."

After crossing Main Street, Martin pulled at the reigns, pausing in the circle of light beneath the lamppost on the corner. He turned to Julia.

"I hope you weren't unhappy that I came outside tonight to look for you. I didn't mean to interrupt anything."

"Nonsense. I'm glad you came."

"I hear all the girls think Rance is handsome. He's got a lot to offer, if you go by what's in the bank. I'm sure he must be pretty fascinating."

"Well, he isn't fascinating to *me*, if that's what you're thinking."

Julia let his eyes hold hers. *Oh, Martin, don't you know you're ten times handsomer than Rance Morgan?* As her pulse quickened, she looked away, fearful of the message she may have sent.

Martin pulled out his watch, tilting it toward the light. Returning it to his pocket, he flicked the reigns.

"I'd best get you home before the clock strikes. It's almost Christmas!"

They continued on, chatting of family, feasting, and gift-giving. As she listened to Martin, Julia felt guilt and wariness return. Being escorted by Martin and socializing with the Baysingers all evening had already put a strain on her friendship with Bertina, who had failed to conceal that she considered her actions a slap in the face. And Amalda! Perhaps tonight indicated what may lie ahead should her friendship with Martin deepen. Julia shuddered at the thought.

Martin stopped the buggy in front of the house.

Julia turned to him. "I suppose you'll go back to school soon."

"Yes, after the first of the year. I'm not sure when I'm leaving just yet. Perhaps we'll see one another New Year's Eve?"

"Perhaps," Julia smiled.

"I have a feeling that this year will be full of changes."

"Oh?"

"Don't you always feel that way? I do." Martin stared into the darkness. "I feel that way about this year especially. If nothing else, I'll be finishing school and coming home to work with my father. Then, you'll have me around all the time, just like when we were kids. Think you can put up with me?"

"I'll try," Julia laughed, "but you've proven to be a pest more times than I can count."

Martin climbed down from the buggy. Circling it, he held out his arms.

"It's muddy along the edges here. Let me lift you over."

"Thank you."

As her feet reached the ground, Julia felt Martin's hands slip from around her waist. The simple act, in contrast to how Rance may have behaved, brought a new wave of affection for Martin. As he walked her to the door, her mental list unfolded in her mind, his name hovering over the "Maybe" column. Other names flitted by—*Bertina—Amalda—Adam?* She shook herself back to reality as she became aware that Martin had spoken again.

"I'm sorry, Martin. What were you saying?"

"I was saying that I'll look forward to coming home. I'm going to miss the way you laugh at my jokes—or don't laugh at them. Sometimes I think you're pretending when you don't laugh, just to aggravate me."

"You're not *always* funny, you know. Someone has to keep your pride in check."

Martin flashed a boyish grin before placing a hand on her elbow as they walked up the porch steps. "Anyhow, we always get a break in order to be home over Good Friday and Resurrection Sunday. Perhaps, if the weather's nice, we could get some friends together and ride our bicycles."

Julia started. "Bicycles?"

"Yes, bicycles. You haven't become one of those girls who pretend they're too refined for it, have you? I know you can do it," Martin teased. "I've seen it with my own eyes."

"Yes, of course, I can. It's just that... well, I just haven't ridden my bicycle in a long time."

As they stopped in front of the door, Martin turned to face

her. He looked as though he were about to speak, then gestured over her shoulder. "Look! It's starting to snow!"

Julia watched the large flakes drift to the ground.

"How perfect! I didn't enjoy this last round of snow one bit, but a fresh snowfall for Christmas Day is just what we need."

Julia put her gloved hand into Martin's outstretched one, allowing him to lead her to the railing.

"I think I've just thought of a New Year's resolution," he said.

"Oh?"

"I might need your help in keeping it, however."

"Oh?"

"I can't study every minute, you know. How does this sound? I'll do my best to come up with better jokes to impress you. I could send them to you, in the form of letters, if you don't mind. Then, you can write back, giving an honest review. Does that sound agreeable?"

Julia allowed her eyes to meet his questioning ones.

"Yes. I think that sounds agreeable."

"Try not to crush me."

"I'll try," she giggled.

They stood for a moment, watching the night sky thicken with snowflakes.

"Julia."

Turning toward his tender whisper, Julia caught her breath as their eyes met.

"Yes?"

"I'm sorry I've kept you out here on the porch. You must be freezing." Martin squeezed her hand. "Merry Christmas!"

"Merry Christmas, Martin!"

Julia went inside. Hurrying to the window, she returned his wave as he flicked the reins and drove away.

RODERICK LAY ON HIS BACK, smiling in the dark as Beatrice wriggled closer, kissed his cheek, and nestled her head on his shoulder. He swatted away the hand that flew up to ruffle his mustache, retaliating by tickling her.

"Stop that," she giggled.

"You stop that."

"Merry Christmas, dear."

"Christmas is tomorrow."

"Merry Christmas Eve, if you insist, but I suspect I'm right. I'm sure it's past midnight."

"You were the prettiest girl at the party tonight."

"You think so? I thought Julia was."

"I'm sure Martin thought so. I'm pretty sure the weasel thought so."

"Hmm... He makes me cringe."

"He makes me want to forbid her to leave the house without the Pocket Protector!"

"Oh, Roderick! I don't think he'd ever... Surely not."

"I hear the buggy again. That must be Martin driving away. It's about time Julia got home so I can get some sleep."

"I trust Martin."

"So do I, but I'm still not sleeping till she's home. I have to get up early. I have sneaky things to do in the morning before everybody gets up."

"She's here. I heard the front door close."

"Christmas tomorrow," Roderick sighed. "Then, we get ready for a whole new year."

"Have any resolutions?"

"Just one. I'm going to become the money-maker in this household if I have to hog-tie Senator Thornhill and tote him into the offices of every bigshot in Washington myself. The M.W.C.D. works, and waiting on these politicians and military masterminds is getting on my nerves. What about you?"

"Hmm?"

"Any resolutions?"

"Not really. I'd just like to have a calm, normal household and see Julia happy again."

Roderick pulled Beatrice closer, but then released her and raised himself to rest on one elbow. Turning an ear toward the door, he lowered his voice. "What's that? Do you hear something?"

Beatrice slipped from under the covers and tiptoed to the door. Placing her ear against it, she listened to the sound that accompanied the footsteps on the stairs.

"Oh, Roderick! She's singing!"

The End

From the Author

The *Morgan's Landing* series marks my debut in novel writing. You might be wondering whether seeing it come to publication has been a dream come true for me. It is—in the most literal sense. I've written for a long time—mostly short stories, journals, or perhaps a poem for a special occasion. Now and then I would be inspired by an idea, a true story, or another author's work to tackle a novel, but each time I would counsel myself to abandon this silly notion due to the colossal amount of research and work involved and the fact that I wouldn't have known what to do with it once I finished it. The idea of my loved ones cleaning out my house upon my demise and pulling dusty manuscripts from under my bed didn't seem very appealing somehow.

One night several years ago, however, I had one of my Technicolor dreams and awoke to not only remember every bit of it, but also realize that it contained not a single oddity such as someone like me (or Alice on her trip through Wonderland) might tend to have. I spent hours recording every detail and, upon finishing my notes, I knew I had received a download—a gift. It no longer mattered how much research and work it required. It no longer mattered that I didn't have a thimble-full of knowledge concerning the publishing world or a single connection within it.

What I did *not* dream was that this would become a series. Along the way, it made me laugh and it made me cry. I think it might do the same for you.

With *Hear My Whisper* you'll begin your own journey to Morgan's Landing, and my hope is that you return again and again.

Acknowledgments

There are so many people and events that contributed to bringing *Morgan's Landing* to fruition and I feel I am bound to come up short in expressing my gratitude.

Of course, if I had not dreamed the story in the first place, it wouldn't exist, so I want to offer the first fruits of my thanks to my Heavenly Father for giving it to me. A sure way to know that something is "not me" is for me to receive it when I'm not even conscious.

Without my beautiful daughter, Jillian, there would be no main character, for she appeared in my dream and is the basis for Julia in this series. My wonderful husband, affectionately known as "Smuffy", encouraged me all the way and tolerated my prolonged writing sessions with amazing grace. My unending appreciation goes to my sister, Ruby, and my niece, Amy, who both spent countless hours reading and editing the entire series and making sure it was ready for the eyes of publishers. I thank my dear friend, Margaret, for reading the manuscript in its roughest form and being my constant, listening ear. There's a special lady, Tiffany, who agreed to read three manuscripts in the *Morgan's Landing* series, though we barely knew each other, and give me her input. Becki, I needed your eagle eyes and expertise in the home stretch and you were there for me. I truly appreciate you both.

This book would never be in your hands without the constant help and encouragement from my dear friend and fellow author, Diane Yates. We met by divine appointment just when I needed her! I am eternally grateful, Diane, for all your handholding and expert advice. As I told you once, I intended to hitch my wagon to a star and I am so blessed that God sent you to be that guiding star.

Book Two Sneak Peek

Liked *Hear My Whisper* and want to know what's next for Julia Lansing? Check out these snippets from book two, *Answer My Call*, coming soon!

Speechless, Beatrice fought to organize her thoughts. It had been several months, but unless time had altered her memories, she now found herself face-to-face with the same young man over whom Julia had shed many a tear.

Julia tried to keep up the pretense, but a sidelong glance at the handsome profile next to her revealed the slightest twitching at the corner of his mouth. Dropping her eyes, she saw an expectant elbow extended toward her. Julia slipped her hand through, letting it rest on Martin's sleeve. Hearing his sigh in unison with her own, she felt safe.

"Oh, Julia! Oh, Lovely One! Oh! I may as well say it."
Julia placed both perspiring palms over her heart,
hoping to slow its pounding. "What do you mean,
Mother? How do you know?"

Tears burned her cheeks. "I suppose it would serve me
right if it were true. I never told him the truth. Oh, I
know you can't compare your own lies to someone
else's, but I still feel he's misled me far worse than I've
misled him."